A Son of the Middle Border

A Son of the Middle Border

Hamlin Garland

With an introduction by

KEITH NEWLIN

Borealis Books is an imprint of the
Minnesota Historical Society Press.

www.borealisbooks.org

The Minnesota Historical Society Press is a member of the Association of American University Presses.

Manufactured in the
United States of America

10 9 8 7 6 5 4 3 2 1

∞ The paper used in this publication meets the minimum requirements of the American National Standard for Information Sciences—Permanence for Printed Library Materials, ANSI Z39.48-1984.

International Standard Book Number
ISBN 13: 978-0-87351-565-8
ISBN 10: 0-87351-565-X

Library of Congress
Cataloging-in-Publication Data

Garland, Hamlin, 1860–1940.
A son of the middle border /
Hamlin Garland ; with an introduction
by Keith Newlin.
p. cm.
ISBN-13: 978-0-87351-565-8
(pbk. : alk. paper)
ISBN-10: 0-87351-565-X
(pbk. : alk. paper)
1. Garland, Hamlin, 1860–1940.
2. Authors, American—19th century—Biography.
3. Authors, American—20th century—Biography.
4. Frontier and pioneer life—Middle West.
I. Title.

PS1733.A47 2007
813′.52—dc22
[B]
2006029435

Cover photos:
Courtesy of the Wisconsin Historical Society and iStockphoto

Cover design:
Jamison Cockerham

A Son of the Middle Border

Introduction

HAMLIN GARLAND (1860–1940) is remembered today chiefly for two books: *Main-Travelled Roads* (1891), an innovative collection of stories that sought to depict the actual working life of midwestern farmers, and his autobiography *A Son of the Middle Border* (1917), a remarkably honest and moving account of his rise from life on a frontier farm to international celebrity. During the 1890s Garland achieved considerable prominence as a literary radical who agitated for realistic fiction and drama that celebrated the commonplace even as it underscored the discrepancies between the haves and have-nots. His vitality and commitment led him to an astonishingly productive career, which he inaugurated by flooding the nation's magazines with stories, poems, and a number of controversial essays arguing for progress of all sorts—in literature, in women's rights, and especially in the Single Tax, a proposal to alter a tax system that favored wealthy landowners at the expense of small farmers. Garland was the author of more than forty books, and his early years were especially prolific: in 1892 alone he published four novels, *Jason Edwards, A Member of the Third House, A Little Norsk,* and *A Spoil of Office.* The publication in 1894 of his literary manifesto, *Crumbling Idols,* crowned his reputation as a literary radical, for in it he argued that writers needed to shrug off their reliance upon eastern and British masters to realize their identity as American writers with an intimate connection to the land.

When *Rose of Dutcher's Coolly* appeared in 1895, reviewers promptly pounced on his, for the time, graphic portrayal of a girl's emerging sexuality. Tiring of the personal assaults the novel occasioned and equally weary of the attacks caused by *Crumbling Idols,* Garland cast about for new literary material. In 1898 he published a well-regarded biography, *Ulysses S. Grant: His Life and Character,* before turning to western romances, of which readers and reviewers largely approved. By the 1910s Garland had grown weary of writing fiction, and in 1917, after a long, painful, and complicated process, he completed *A Son of the Middle Border*, discovering a fulfillment in autobiography that was to occupy him for the next twenty-three years. The success of *Son,* in which he told the story of his life until 1893, led to two additional sequences of installments. The first continues his personal story in the middle border books: *A Daughter of the Middle Border* (1921), which carries his autobiography until 1914 and the death of his father; *Trail-Makers of the Middle Border* (1926), a semifictional prequel to *Son* that relates his father's life until his return from the Civil War; and *Back-Trailers from the Middle Border* (1928), which carries the family saga to the year 1927 and the marriage of his second daughter. The second sequence comprises his literary logbooks, based on the daily diary he had begun in 1898. The logbooks largely recount his meetings with authors and other celebrities, interspersed with the daily events of a busy author and lecturer. They include *Roadside Meetings* (1930), *Companions on the Trail* (1931), *My Friendly Contemporaries* (1932), and *Afternoon Neighbors* (1934).

Garland actively involved himself in American literary life both as a writer and as a member of America's literary elite. He was an inveterate traveler, crisscrossing the continent innumerable times as he lectured throughout the country. In 1898, for instance, he made an arduous overland trek to the Klondike Gold Rush to gather literary material. He befriended and interviewed Indians, as well, preserving their traditions in stories later gathered in *The Book of the American Indian* (1923), and acted to alter government policies that sought to deprive them of their lands. Garland was also privileged to have known many of America's most important writers and statesmen, among them Stephen Crane, Walt Whitman, Mark Twain, William Dean Howells, James Whitcomb Riley, John Burroughs, Edith Wharton, Henry James, Theodore Roosevelt, Will Rogers, and Zane Grey; as his celebrity spread he also came to know George Bernard Shaw, James M. Barrie, Arthur Conan Doyle, Joseph Conrad, and Rudyard Kipling, among many others. He founded or helped establish a number of cultural organizations devoted to encouraging and rewarding literary achievement, among them the American Academy of Arts and Letters, the Authors' League of America, the Midland Authors Society, the Cliff Dwellers, and the MacDowell Colony.

Born at a time when gas lamps illuminated the night and the railroad was a transportation marvel, in his autobiographies he faithfully recorded his encounters with the new technologies of the typewriter, electricity, the automobile, the radio, motion pictures, and the airplane. By the time he died on March 4, 1940, in Hollywood, California, he had witnessed the nation rebuild itself from the ashes of the Civil War, enjoyed the economic prosperity of the 1920s, survived the economic collapse of the Depression, and listened to the ranting of Adolph Hitler.

Born in a squatter's cabin in the village of West Salem, Wisconsin, on September 14, 1860, Garland was raised in impoverished surroundings as his father struggled to wrest a living from a series of frontier farms. By the time he was ten, young Hamlin had moved four times, eventually settling on a 160-acre farm of unplowed prairie in Mitchell County, Iowa, near the town of Osage, where he would set many of his most effective stories. As the oldest of four children, Hamlin took his first turn driving a heavy, sod-breaking plow at the age of ten, turning some seventy acres of prairie during his first season in the field—hard, brutal labor that would mark him forever. When he was sixteen, he entered the Cedar Valley Seminary in Osage, a combination high school and junior college, returning to the farm for the planting and harvesting seasons. When he graduated in 1881 at age twenty-one, he was determined to leave farm life forever, and in 1884, after a brief stint at homesteading in Dakota Territory, he made his way to Boston. Like many youths of twenty-four, he didn't know what he wanted to do with his life. For a time he dreamed of becoming a great orator and, later, a playwright and an actor. After he had drifted into what was effectively an adjunct position as a lecturer at the Boston School of Oratory, he tried his hand at fiction writing and discovered his calling.

Garland was a remarkably industrious and studious youth, and soon he began flooding the newspapers and magazines with submissions and corresponding with the leading writers of the day, testing his judgments while preparing his lectures. A naturally gregarious man with a gift for friendship, he soon made the acquaintance of many of Boston's writers and intellectuals. His years on the farm had made him deeply sympathetic to the often arduous life of the working farmer, and his involvement with the artists of Boston underscored the comparative cultural deprivation of the Midwest. He therefore seized upon Henry George's Single Tax as a remedy, for he believed that a more equitable system of taxation would lead to economic prosperity and a more rewarding cultural life. He became an enthusiastic and vocal Single Tax lecturer and wrote a number of stories combining George's economic theories with realistic depictions of farm life. When the best of these stories appeared as *Main-Travelled Roads* in 1891, reviewers praised his method but were disturbed by the bleak subject. "I have never before felt the desperate unspeakable pathos of the prairie farmer's struggle with life," the reviewer for the *Boston Herald* observed before confessing that the book "was far too minutely and baldly real to please my own taste." While admitting the stories "are singularly vivid and very true," a reviewer for *America* regretted that "the seamy side of the Western farmer's life is the only one revealed." While he wished Garland had described the "thousands of farmers" who "have homes of comfort and even elegance" that better suited the prevailing myth of the western farm as a place of nourishing sustenance, he reluctantly admitted that "for power, truth and pathos it would be difficult to find six stories by another American author which would bear comparison to these."[1]

A number of other novels and story collections followed, all receiving similar criticism and lackluster sales. Tiring of controversy and the accompanying personal attacks and desiring to improve his financial resources, Garland eventually shifted to the more lucrative western romance with such novels as *The Captain of the Gray Horse-Troop* (1902) and *Hesper* (1903), which sold well, improving his reputation and leading to financial prosperity. By 1910, however, Garland had grown tired of cranking out an average of one novel per year. Worse, he had become bored with the romance genre, for at fifty the passions of youth seemed increasingly distant. After the publication of *Cavanagh, Forest Ranger* in 1910, his friend William Dean Howells wrote to warn Garland about a decline in his style and to urge him to return to the subject matter of *Main-Travelled Roads*. Garland replied:

> I'm running low on motives. I don't care to write love-stories or stories of adventure and I can not revert to the prairie life without falling into the reminiscent sadness of the man of fifty.
>
> My own belief is that my work is pretty well done but as I remember the cordial endorsement of men like yourself and [*Century* editor Richard Watson Gilder] I have no reason to complain. I have had in way of honor (and pay) all I deserve—probably. I am dissatisfied only on the artistic side. Why does not our literature tally with the big things we do as a people? I had hopes of doing it once but that was only the foolish egotism of youth.[2]

Twelve years before, in 1898, as he was preparing to set out for the Klondike—mindful that he might not return from the dangerous journey—Garland had dictated the semiautobiographical narrative "The Story of Grant McLane." When he returned, he mined it for parts of *Boy Life on the Prairie* (1899), a fictionalization of his childhood and early adolescence in Iowa based on six descriptive sketches, published in 1888, that chronicled one year of a boy's life on the Iowa prairie. In 1911 he dusted off "The Story of Grant McLane" and began to revise what he had written, hoping that a change to nonfiction would reengage his creative energy. Soon, he became absorbed as he slipped into the past and relived former triumphs.

By March a chapter had come back from the typist. "It reads very well, plain and direct as it should be," he recorded in his diary about this early version of *A Son of the Middle Border*. "It is a difficult job this writing an egotistic story in a way that shall seem frank and yet not prove offensive."[3] By June 1912 he had completed a manuscript of 100,000 words and approached his publisher, Harper and Brothers. But Frederick Leigh, Harper's vice president, worried about the effect of a Garland autobiography on the sale of future Garland novels and feared that it would spell the end of a book-a-year property. Garland wrote to Howells, his old counselor, for advice. "I think it highly probable that I shall never write another novel," he told Howells, "for the reason that love stories no longer seem to me worth while." He asked for Howells's opinion and concluded, "I don't think it is an egotistical book, because I have gone beyond that stage. It is rather an attempt to catch for my children some part of the beauty and significance of the life of the border during the forty years of my remembrance." Howells replied that he thought the book "would be important and delightful, and would add to the interest of your other books."[4] Encouraged, Garland returned to the manuscript.

Unlike fiction, autobiography did not come easily to Garland, for he was baffled about how to tell his story and escape being charged with egotism. That it was published at all is a testament to both his belief in the value of his story and his dogged determination to find a form that would resonate with readers. He was convinced the story itself was worthwhile, for he had led an exceedingly fortunate life. From his inauspicious beginnings he had, by age fifty-two, attained considerable celebrity both in the United States and abroad. He had authored twenty-nine books and hundreds of magazine articles, knew virtually every significant writer of his day, and was well known throughout the country as a popular lecturer. More important than his celebrity, he had gained perspective on the development and closing of the prairie and sought to combine the story of his life with the story of U.S. westward expansion, though the events themselves were now filtered through a nostalgic haze.

Hoping for a lucrative serial, he sent the manuscript to the editors of the *Century*, the *Ladies' Home Journal*, and the *Saturday Evening Post*, all long-standing friends. But even they were put off by Garland's detailed description of family events. As Edward Bok, the editor of the *Ladies' Home Journal*, told him, "I think that your belief in realism has led you to go too much into details. . . . I cannot get away from the intimate quality of it all, and on that ground I shouldn't like to see it published."[5] In an effort to ameliorate the egotism of first-person narration, Garland decided to present the story as an "abandoned autobiography" left by one Lincoln Stewart that he, Garland, had edited. In his guise as a "conscientious historian," Garland alternated quotations from this manuscript with his own third-person commentary. The result was a tale still largely in first person interspersed with occasional passages in third person. He sent it to Edward Wheeler, the editor of *Current Literature*, who found the narrative "very interesting" but was also jarred by the alternating point of view.[6] In April he tried Harper's again, hoping that the new form might persuade his publisher to accept it. But his editor, Frederick Duneka, offered to publish the book only if Garland would forego the customary advance on royalties. Garland was partly to blame, however, because he had grown so depressed over the book's prospects that, as Duneka reminded him, "In all our talks . . . you voiced your belief (and ours) that the book would never sell in paying quantities, and that we might even be out of pocket on the venture." Now thoroughly discouraged, Garland decided to forego publication, for "it is sure to expose me to unfriendly criticism and I do not feel like opening myself to the scoffer."[7]

In 1914, after a number of revisions in which he experimented with point of view, refined his style, and deepened his story, he finally succeeded in placing it with *Collier's Magazine*, which offered him $2,500 for a six-part serial. Garland still worried about the presumption that his life was significant enough to warrant an autobiography. To forestall criticism, he prefaced the first installment with an elaborate explanation in the guise of Lincoln Stewart:

> It is now a quarter of a century since I began to write of the West, and here (midway on the trail) I am minded to pause and look back on the long, hard road over which I have trudged, eager to make a final record of my joys before they escape me, and in order that I may preserve for my children some few of the intimate details of a life which is already passing if not completely vanished.

After warning his readers that the story would not contain the "whole truth" about an author or a man, Garland noted that the chronicle should be read as "the study of a family and an epoch."[8] Following this awkward device, the first installment opens, "In beginning this story of Lincoln Stewart, I am almost wholly dependent upon the man's own words in order to account for his boyhood. He says: 'All of this universe known to me in 1865 was bounded by the wooded hills of a little Wisconsin coulee. . . .'" The narrative then proceeds in blocks of first-person quotation introduced rather clumsily by brief introductory phrases.[9] Five installments of "Son" appeared from March to August, carrying the story to "Lincoln Enters Hostile Territory"—an account of his fifteenth year in Osage, Iowa—when publication was interrupted by the outbreak of World War I. Garland's story could not compete with the news from Europe, and *Collier's* filled the September and October issues with features on the conflict, assuring the disappointed author that publication would resume at a later date. So Garland put off searching for a publisher for the book version.

The serial resumed publication in March 1917 with three more installments. To make room for articles on the war, Mark Sullivan, *Collier's* editor, encouraged Garland to condense the story and to put the narrative back in first person. "No one will criticize it on the score of egotism," he reassured him. "Most readers will want to know that Hamlin Garland is telling the story of his pioneer relations and friends."[10] When the installments concluded in May, Garland had carried his story from his Cedar Valley Seminary days to the close of his Dakota homesteading experience.

Garland had also succeeded in interesting the Macmillan Company in the book version. When the proofs arrived in July 1917, Garland was in a panic, apprehensive about how his life story would be perceived, all too aware that reviews calling him "egotistic" could knock sales to the floor. As he recorded in his diary, "At times I have a feeling that the book is of no value whatsoever. Then I think of certain passages and find them good. Probably it is good in spots and bad in spots. My brain is pretty clear now—too clear I am afraid—enabling me to see the faults in the book."[11]

He need not have worried, for when *A Son of the Middle Border* was published in October 1917, reviews were nearly unanimous in their praise, and none was more gratifying than that by his old friend Howells. Appearing on the front page of the *New York Times Review of Books* and accompanied by a distinguished portrait of Garland, Howells's review began, "In all the region of autobiography, so far as I know it, I do not know quite the like of Mr. Garland's story of his life, and I should rank it with the very greatest of its kind in literature." Because of its "grasp of the great serious, elemental things, the endeavor and the endurance which have constituted us as a people," Howells went so far as to rank *Son* as better than autobiographies by Goethe, Rousseau, and Franklin. He described Garland's method of making his personal story stand for a nation's westward movement as "a psychological synthesis of personal and general conditions in a new country, such as has not got into our literature before. That in itself, if it were nothing else, is a precious contribution to human knowledge." After noting the minor "fault" of Garland's lack of accounting for his father's "iron persistence ready, if not willing, to sacrifice the youth of wife and children to the realization" of his westering dream, he concluded that the story is both "the memorial of a generation, of a whole order of American experience" and "an epic of such mood and make as has not been imagined before."[12]

As a novelist Garland knew that every good story needed a conflict, and in telling his story, he structured *Son* around two related conflicts: The first is the story of a boy rebelling against a strict father, his "commander-in-chief," whose outlook on child raising has been shaped by his military service and whose incessant drive to improve the family economic condition has led him to move his family ever westward, with the consequence of prematurely aging the boy's beloved and work-worn mother. The second is the story of a young man who hates farm life but loves the land and who eventually discovers in that love-hate relationship the material for his art.[13] In developing the first conflict, which dominates the early sections of the narrative, Garland casts his father as a representative of America's pioneer spirit whose unwavering determination to succeed repeatedly uproots his family, reflecting America's own resolve to conquer a hostile land. The effects of his father's drive to succeed on young Hamlin are predictable but nonetheless evocative, as he rebels by becoming emotionally distant from his demanding father and being drawn to his more supportive mother. Much of the power of *A Son of the Middle Border* stems from the author's ability to shift between sympathy with the adolescent Garland's perception of his family and his adult perspective that relates his family's constant movement to the nation's development of the West. That Garland is able to combine these two perspectives effectively illustrates the "psychological synthesis of personal and general conditions" that Howells alludes to in his review.

When Garland left the Midwest for Boston in 1884, he gradually became overwhelmed by guilt at leaving his mother behind, especially as his involvement in the cultural life of the city magnified the disparity between the comparative richness and ease of city life and the often brutal conditions on the farm. Much of the power of the second half of *Son* comes from Garland's determination to rescue his mother and thus supplant his father as leader of the Garland family. But to do so, he first had to earn a living, and the latter portions of the narrative are dominated by his learning to make his ambivalence about the Midwest the subject of his art. The autobiography appropriately ends when Garland, having achieved literary success while his father has failed at his Dakota farm, moves his parents to the village of his birth and takes his father's place at the head of the table to carve the Thanksgiving turkey. "The pen had proved mightier than the plow," Garland observed. "Going east had proved more profitable than going west!" Grumbling, his father could only mutter, "I don't know how I'm going to come down from operating a six-horse header to scraping with a hoe in a garden patch,"[14] thus acknowledging his son's triumph. The year is 1893, ironically and appropriately the same year Frederick Jackson Turner announced to the World's Columbian Exposition in Chicago that the frontier had closed.

NOTES TO THE INTRODUCTION

1. "A Drama of the West," *Boston Herald,* May 31, 1891, 22; "Pictures of Western Farm Life," *America* 6 (June 18, 1891), 332, 333.

2. Garland to Howells, March 29, 1910, *Selected Letters of Hamlin Garland,* Keith Newlin and Joseph B. McCullough, eds. (Lincoln: University of Nebraska Press, 1998), 199–200.

3. Diary, March 6, 1912 (Huntington Library, San Marino, CA, item GD 1–43; further quotations to Garland's diaries are by permission of the Huntington Library).

4. Garland to Howells, June 29, 1912, *Selected Letters,* 212–13.

5. Bok to Garland, December 12, 1912 (Hamlin Garland Papers, University of Southern California).

6. *Companions on the Trail* (New York: Macmillan, 1931), 519.

7. Duneka to Garland, April 4, 1913 (Hamlin Garland Papers, University of Southern California); Diary, April 7, 1913.

8. Garland, "A Son of the Middle Border. I. Half Lights," *Collier's* 53 (March 28, 1914), 5.

9. Ibid.

10. Hamlin Garland, *Back-Trailers from the Middle Border* (New York: Macmillan, 1928), 18.

11. Diary, July 7, 1917.

12. "*A Son of the Middle Border,* by Hamlin Garland: An Appreciation," *New York Times Review of Books,* August 26, 1917, 309, 317.

13. Donald Pizer has thoroughly and convincingly developed this point in "Hamlin Garland's *A Son of the Middle Border:* An Appreciation," *South Atlantic Quarterly* 65 (1966): 448–59.

14. *A Son of the Middle Border* (New York: Macmillan, 1917), 464.

A Son of the Middle Border

1

Home from the War

All of this universe known to me in the year 1864 was bounded by the wooded hills of a little Wisconsin coulee, and its center was the cottage in which my mother was living alone—my father was in the war. As I project myself back into that mystical age, half lights cover most of the valley. The road before our doorstone begins and ends in vague obscurity—and Granma Green's house at the fork of the trail stands on the very edge of the world in a sinister region peopled with bears and other menacing creatures. Beyond this point all is darkness and terror.

It is Sunday afternoon and my mother and her three children, Frank, Harriet and I (all in our best dresses) are visiting the Widow Green, our nearest neighbor, a plump, jolly woman whom we greatly love. The house swarms with stalwart men and buxom women and we are all sitting around the table heaped with the remains of a harvest feast. The women are "telling fortunes" by means of tea-grounds. Mrs. Green is the seeress. After shaking the cup with the grounds at the bottom, she turns it bottom side up in a saucer. Then whirling it three times to the right and three times to the left, she lifts it and silently studies the position of the leaves which cling to the sides of the cup, what time we all wait in breathless suspense for her first word.

"A soldier is coming to you!" she says to my mother. "See," and she points into the cup. We all crowd near, and I perceive a leaf with a stem sticking up from its body like a bayonet over a man's shoulder. "He is almost home," the widow goes on. Then with sudden dramatic turn she waves her hand toward the road, "Heavens and earth!" she cries. "There's Richard now!"

We all turn and look toward the road, and there, indeed, is a soldier with a musket on his back, wearily plodding his way up the low hill just north of the gate. He is too far away for mother to call, and besides I think she must have been a little uncertain, for he did not so much as turn his head toward the house. Trembling with excitement she hurries little Frank into his wagon and telling Hattie to bring me, sets off up the road as fast as she can draw the baby's cart. It all seems a dream to me and I move dumbly, almost stupidly like one in a mist. . . .

We did not overtake the soldier, that is evident, for my next vision is that of a blue-coated figure leaning upon the fence, studying with intent gaze our empty cottage. I cannot, even now, precisely divine why he stood thus, sadly contemplating his silent home,—but so it was. His knapsack lay at his feet, his musket was propped against a post on whose top a cat was dreaming, unmindful of the warrior and his folded hands.

He did not hear us until we were close upon him, and even after he turned, my mother hesitated, so thin, so hollow-eyed, so changed was he. "Richard, is that you?" she quaveringly asked.

His worn face lighted up. His arms rose. "Yes, Belle! Here I am," he answered.

Nevertheless though he took my mother in his arms, I could not relate him to the father I had heard so much about. To me he was only a strange man with big eyes and care-worn face. I did not recognize in him anything I had ever known, but my sister, who was two years older than I, went to his bosom of her own motion. She knew him, whilst I submitted to his caresses rather for the reason that my mother urged me forward than because of any affection I felt for him. Frank, however, would not even permit a kiss. The gaunt and grizzled stranger terrified him.

"Come here, my little man," my father said.—*"My little man!"* Across the space of half-a-century I can still hear the sad reproach in his voice. "Won't you come and see your poor old father when he comes home from the war?"

"My little man!" How significant that phrase seems to me now! The war had in very truth come between this patriot and his sons. I had forgotten him—the baby had never known him.

Frank crept beneath the rail fence and stood there, well out of reach, like a cautious kitten warily surveying an alien dog. At last the soldier stooped and drawing from his knapsack a big red apple, held it toward the staring babe, confidently calling, "Now, I guess he'll come to his poor old pap home from the war."

The mother apologized. "He doesn't know you, Dick. How could he? He was only nine months old when you went away. He'll go to you by and by."

The babe crept slowly toward the shining lure. My father caught him despite his kicking, and hugged him close. "Now I've got you," he exulted.

Then we all went into the little front room and the soldier laid off his heavy army shoes. My mother brought a pillow to put under his head, and so at last he stretched out on the floor the better to rest his tired, aching bones, and there I joined him.

"Oh, Belle!" he said, in tones of utter content. "This is what I've dreamed about a million times."

Frank and I grew each moment more friendly and soon began to tumble over him while mother hastened to cook something for him to eat. He asked for "hot biscuits and honey and plenty of coffee."

That was a mystic hour—and yet how little I can recover of it! The afternoon glides into evening while the soldier talks, and at last we all go out to the barn to watch mother milk the cow. I hear him ask about the crops, the neighbors.—The sunlight passes. Mother leads the way back to the house. My father follows carrying little Frank in his arms.

He is a "strange man" no longer. Each moment his voice sinks deeper into my remembrance. He is my father—that I feel ringing through the dim halls of my consciousness. Harriet clings to his hand in perfect knowledge and confidence. We eat our bread and milk, the trundle-bed is pulled out, we children clamber in, and I go to sleep to the music of his resonant voice recounting the story of the battles he had seen, and the marches he had made.

The emergence of an individual consciousness from the void is, after all, the most amazing fact of human life and I should like to spend much of this first chapter in groping about in the luminous shadow of my infant world because, deeply considered, childish impressions are the fundamentals upon which an author's fictional out-put is based; but to linger might weary my reader at the outset, although I count myself most fortunate in the fact that my boyhood was spent in the midst of a charming landscape and during a certain heroic era of western settlement.

The men and women of that far time loom large in my thinking for they possessed not only the spirit of adventurers but the courage of warriors. Aside from the natural distortion of a boy's imagination I am quite sure that the pioneers of 1860 still retained something broad and fine in their action, something a boy might honorably imitate.

The earliest dim scene in my memory is that of a soft warm evening. I am cradled in the lap of my sister Harriet who is sitting on the doorstep beneath a low roof. It is mid-summer and at our feet lies a mat of dark-green grass from which a frog is croaking. The stars are out, and above the high hills to the east a mysterious glow is glorifying the sky. The cry of the small animal at last conveys to my sister's mind a notion of distress, and rising she peers closely along the path. Starting back with a cry of alarm, she calls and my mother hurries out. She, too, examines the ground, and at last points out to me a long striped snake with a poor, shrieking little tree-toad in its mouth. The horror of this scene fixes it in my mind. My mother beats the serpent with a stick. The mangled victim hastens away, and the curtain falls.

I must have been about four years old at this time, although there is nothing to determine the precise date. Our house, a small frame cabin, stood on the eastern slope of a long ridge and faced across a valley which seemed very wide to me then, and in the middle of it lay a marsh filled with monsters, from which the Water People sang night by night. Beyond was a wooded mountain.

This doorstone must have been a favorite evening seat for my sister, for I remember many other delicious gloamings. Bats whirl and squeak in the odorous dusk. Night hawks whiz and boom, and over the dark forest wall a prodigious moon miraculously rolls. Fire-flies dart through the grass, and in a lone tree just outside the fence, a whippoorwill sounds his plaintive note. Sweet, very sweet, and wonderful are all these!

The marsh across the lane was a sinister menacing place even by day for there (so my sister Harriet warned me) serpents swarmed, eager to bite runaway boys. "And if you step in the mud between the tufts of grass," she said, "you will surely sink out of sight."—At night this teeming bog became a place of dank and horrid mystery. Bears and wolves and wildcats were reported as ruling the dark woods just beyond—only the door yard and the road seemed safe for little men—and even there I wished my mother to be within immediate call.

My father who had bought his farm "on time," just before the war, could not enlist among the first volunteers, though he was deeply moved to do so, till his land was paid for—but at last in 1863 on the very day that he made the last payment on the mortgage, he put his name down on the roll and went back to his wife, a soldier.

I have heard my mother say that this was one of the darkest moments of her life and if you think about it you will understand the reason why. My sister was only five years old, I was three and Frank was a babe in the cradle. Broken hearted at the thought of the long separation, and scared by visions of battle my mother begged the soldier not to go; but he was of the stern stuff which makes patriots—and besides his name was already on the roll, therefore he went away to join Grant's army at Vicksburg. "What sacrifice! What folly!" said his pacifist neighbors—"to leave your wife and children for an idea, a mere sentiment; to put your life in peril for a striped silken rag." But he went. For thirteen dollars a month he marched and fought while his plow rusted in the shed and his cattle called to him from their stalls.

My conscious memory holds nothing of my mother's agony of waiting, nothing of the dark days when the baby was ill and the doctor far away—but into my sub-conscious ear her voice sank, and the words *Grant, Lincoln, Sherman, "furlough," "mustered out,"* ring like bells, deep-toned and vibrant. I shared dimly in every emotional utterance of the neighbors who came to call and a large part of what I am is due to the impressions of these deeply passionate and poetic years.

Dim pictures come to me. I see my mother at the spinning wheel, I help her fill the candle molds. I hold in my hands the queer carding combs with their crinkly teeth, but my first definite connected recollection is the scene of my father's return at the close of the war.

I was not quite five years old, and the events of that day are so commingled with later impressions,—experiences which came long after—that I cannot be quite sure which are true and which imagined, but the picture as a whole is very vivid and very complete.

Thus it happened that my first impressions of life were martial, and my training military, for my father brought back from his two years' campaigning under Sherman and Thomas the temper and the habit of a soldier.

He became naturally the dominant figure in my horizon, and his scheme of discipline impressed itself almost at once upon his children.

I suspect that we had fallen into rather free and easy habits under mother's government, for she was too jolly, too tender-hearted, to engender fear in us even when she threatened us with a switch or a shingle. We soon learned, however, that the soldier's promise of punishment was swift and precise in its fulfillment. We seldom presumed a second time on his forgetfulness or tolerance. We knew he loved us, for he often took us to his knees of an evening and told us stories of marches and battles, or chanted war-songs for us, but the moments of his tenderness were few and his fondling did not prevent him from almost instant use of the rod if he thought either of us needed it.

His own boyhood had been both hard and short. Born of farmer folk in Oxford County, Maine, his early life had been spent on the soil in and about Lock's Mills with small chance of schooling. Later, as a teamster, and finally as shipping clerk for Amos Lawrence, he had enjoyed three mightily improving years in Boston. He loved to tell of his life there, and it is indicative of his character to say that he dwelt with special joy and pride on the actors and orators he had heard. He could describe some of the great scenes and repeat a few of the heroic lines of Shakespeare, and the roll of his deep voice as he declaimed, "Now is the winter of our discontent made glorious summer by this son of York," thrilled us—filled us with desire of something far off and wonderful. But best of all we loved to hear him tell of "Logan at Peach Tree Creek," and "Kilpatrick on the Granny White Turnpike."

He was a vivid and concise story-teller and his words brought to us (sometimes all too clearly), the tragic happenings of the battlefields of Atlanta and Nashville. To him Grant, Lincoln, Sherman and Sheridan were among the noblest men of the world, and he would not tolerate any criticism of them.

Next to his stories of the war I think we loved best to have him picture "the pineries" of Wisconsin, for during his first years in the

State he had been both lumberman and raftsman, and his memory held delightful tales of wolves and bears and Indians.

He often imitated the howls and growls and actions of the wild animals with startling realism, and his river narratives were full of unforgettable phrases like "the Jinny Bull Falls," "Old Moosinee" and "running the rapids."

He also told us how his father and mother came west by way of the Erie Canal, and in a steamer on the Great Lakes, of how they landed in Milwaukee with Susan, their twelve-year-old daughter, sick with the smallpox; of how a farmer from Monticello carried them in his big farm wagon over the long road to their future home in Green county and it was with deep emotion that he described the bitter reception they encountered in the village.

It appears that some of the citizens in a panic of dread were all for driving the Garlands out of town—then uprose old Hugh McClintock, big and gray as a grizzly bear, and put himself between the leader of the mob and its victims, and said, "You shall not lay hands upon them. Shame on ye!" And such was the power of his mighty arm and such the menace of his flashing eyes that no one went further with the plan of casting the new comers into the wilderness.

Old Hugh established them in a lonely cabin on the edge of the village, and thereafter took care of them, nursing grandfather with his own hands until he was well. "And that's the way the McClintocks and the Garlands first joined forces," my father often said in ending the tale. "But the name of the man who carried your Aunt Susan in his wagon from Milwaukee to Monticello I never knew."

I cannot understand why that sick girl did not die on that long journey over the rough roads of Wisconsin, and what it all must have seemed to my gentle New England grandmother I grieve to think about. Beautiful as the land undoubtedly was, such an experience should have shaken her faith in western men and western hospitality. But apparently it did not, for I never heard her allude to this experience with bitterness.

In addition to his military character, Dick Garland also carried with him the odor of the pine forest and exhibited the skill and training of a forester, for in those early days even at the time when

I began to remember the neighborhood talk, nearly every young man who could get away from the farm or the village went north, in November, into the pine woods which covered the entire upper part of the State, and my father, who had been a raftsman and timber cruiser and pilot ever since his coming west, was deeply skilled with axe and steering oars. The lumberman's life at that time was rough but not vicious, for the men were nearly all of native American stock, and my father was none the worse for his winters in camp.

His field of action as lumberman was for several years, in and around Big Bull Falls (as it was then called), near the present town of Wausau, and during that time he had charge of a crew of loggers in winter and in summer piloted rafts of lumber down to Dubuque and other points where saw mills were located. He was called at this time, "Yankee Dick, the Pilot."

As a result of all these experiences in the woods, he was almost as much woodsman as soldier in his talk, and the heroic life he had led made him very wonderful in my eyes. According to his account (and I have no reason to doubt it) he had been exceedingly expert in running a raft and could ride a canoe like a Chippewa. I remember hearing him very forcefully remark, "God forgot to make the man I could not follow."

He was deft with an axe, keen of perception, sure of hand and foot, and entirely capable of holding his own with any man of his weight. Amid much drinking he remained temperate, and strange to say never used tobacco in any form. While not a large man he was nearly six feet in height, deep-chested and sinewy, and of dauntless courage. The quality which defended him from attack was the spirit which flamed from his eagle-gray eyes. Terrifying eyes they were, at times, as I had many occasions to note.

As he gathered us all around his knee at night before the fire, he loved to tell us of riding the whirlpools of Big Bull Falls, or of how he lived for weeks on a raft with the water up to his knees (sleeping at night in his wet working clothes), sustained by the blood of youth and the spirit of adventure. His endurance even after his return from the war, was marvellous, although he walked a little bent and with a peculiar measured swinging stride—the stride of Sherman's veterans.

As I was born in the first smoke of the great conflict, so all of my early memories of Green's coulee are permeated with the haze of the passing war-cloud. My soldier dad taught me the manual of arms, and for a year Harriet and I carried broomsticks, flourished lath sabers, and hammered on dishpans in imitation of officers and drummers. Canteens made excellent water-bottles for the men in the harvest fields, and the long blue overcoats which the soldiers brought back with them from the south lent many a vivid spot of color to that far-off landscape.

All the children of our valley inhaled with every breath this mingled air of romance and sorrow, history and song, and through those epic days runs a deep-laid consciousness of maternal pain. My mother's side of those long months of waiting was never fully delineated, for she was natively reticent and shy of expression. But piece by piece in later years I drew from her the tale of her long vigil, and obtained some hint of the bitter anguish of her suspense after each great battle.

It is very strange, but I cannot define her face as I peer back into those childish times, though I can feel her strong arms about me. She seemed large and quite middle-aged to me, although she was in fact a handsome girl of twenty-three. Only by reference to a rare daguerreotype of the time am I able to correct this childish impression.

Our farm lay well up in what is called Green's coulee, in a little valley just over the road which runs along the LaCrosse river in western Wisconsin. It contained one hundred and sixty acres of land which crumpled against the wooded hills on the east and lay well upon a ridge to the west. Only two families lived above us, and over the height to the north was the land of the red people, and small bands of their hunters used occasionally to come trailing down across our meadow on their way to and from LaCrosse, which was their immemorial trading point.

Sometimes they walked into our house, always without knocking—but then we understood their ways. No one knocks at the wigwam of a red neighbor, and we were not afraid of them, for they were friendly, and our mother often gave them bread and meat which they took (always without thanks) and ate with much relish while sitting beside our fire. All this seemed very curious to us, but as they were accustomed to share their food and lodging with one another so they accepted my mother's bounty in the same matter-of-fact fashion.

Once two old fellows, while sitting by the fire, watched Frank and me bringing in wood for the kitchen stove, and smiled and muttered between themselves thereat. At last one of them patted my brother on the head and called out admiringly, "Small pappoose, heap work—good!" and we were very proud of the old man's praise.

2

The McClintocks

The members of my mother's family must have been often at our home during my father's military service in the south, but I have no mental pictures of them till after my father's home-coming in '65. Their names were familiar—were, indeed, like bits of old-fashioned song. "Richard" was a fine and tender word in my ear, but "David" and "Luke," "Deborah" and "Samantha," and especially "Hugh," suggested something alien as well as poetic.

They all lived somewhere beyond the hills which walled our coulee on the east, in a place called Salem, and I was eager to visit them, for in that direction my universe died away in a luminous mist of unexplored distance. I had some notion of its near-by loveliness for I had once viewed it from the top of the tall bluff which stood like a warder at the gate of our valley, and when one bright morning my father said, "Belle, get ready, and we'll drive over to Grandad's," we all became greatly excited.

In those days people did not "call," they went "visitin'." The women took their knitting and stayed all the afternoon and sometimes all night. No one owned a carriage. Each family journeyed in a heavy farm wagon with the father and mother riding high on the wooden spring seat while the children jounced up and down on the hay in the bottom of the box or clung desperately to the side-boards to keep from being jolted out. In such wise we started on our trip to the McClintocks'.

The road ran to the south and east around the base of Sugar Loaf Bluff, thence across a lovely valley and over a high wooded ridge which was so steep that at times we rode above the tree tops. As father stopped the horses to let them rest, we children gazed about us with wondering eyes. Far behind us lay the LaCrosse valley through which a slender river ran, while before us towered wind-worn cliffs of stone. It was an exploring expedition for us.

The top of the divide gave a grand view of wooded hills to the northeast, but father did not wait for us to enjoy that. He started the team on the perilous downward road without regard to our wishes, and so we bumped and clattered to the bottom, all joy of the scenery swallowed up in fear of being thrown from the wagon.

The roar of a rapid, the gleam of a long curving stream, a sharp turn through a pair of bars, and we found ourselves approaching a low unpainted house which stood on a level bench overlooking a river and its meadows.

"There it is. That's Grandad's house," said mother, and peering over her shoulder I perceived a group of people standing about the open door, and heard their shouts of welcome.

My father laughed. "Looks as if the whole McClintock clan was on parade," he said.

It was Sunday and all my aunts and uncles were in holiday dress and a merry, hearty, handsome group they were. One of the men helped my mother out and another, a roguish young fellow with a pock-marked face, snatched me from the wagon and carried me under his arm to the threshold where a short, gray-haired smiling woman was standing. "Mother, here's another grandson for you," he said as he put me at her feet.

She greeted me kindly and led me into the house, in which a huge old man with a shock of perfectly white hair was sitting with a Bible on his knee. He had a rugged face framed in a circle of gray beard and his glance was absent-minded and remote. "Father," said my grandmother, "Belle has come. Here is one of her boys."

Closing his book on his glasses to mark the place of his reading he turned to greet my mother who entered at this moment. His way of speech was as strange as his look and for a few moments I studied him with childish intentness. His face was rough-hewn as a rock but it was kindly, and though he soon turned from his guests and resumed his reading no one seemed to resent it.

Young as I was I vaguely understood his mood. He was glad to see us but he was absorbed in something else, something of more importance, at the moment, than the chatter of the family. My uncles who came in a few moments later drew my attention and the white-haired dreamer fades from this scene.

The room swarmed with McClintocks. There was William, a black-bearded, genial, quick-stepping giant who seized me by the collar with one hand and lifted me off the floor as if I were a puppy just to see how much I weighed; and David, a tall young man with handsome dark eyes and a droop at the outer corner of his eyelids which gave him in repose a look of melancholy distinction. He called me and I went to him readily for I loved him at once. His voice pleased me and I could see that my mother loved him too.

From his knee I became acquainted with the girls of the family. Rachel, a demure and sweet-faced young woman, and Samantha, the beauty of the family, won my instant admiration, but Deb, as everybody called her, repelled me by her teasing ways. They were all gay as larks and their hearty clamor, so far removed from the quiet gravity of my grandmother Garland's house, pleased me. I had an immediate sense of being perfectly at home.

There was an especial reason why this meeting should have been, as it was, a joyous hour. It was, in fact, a family reunion after the war. The dark days of sixty-five were over. The Nation was at peace and its warriors mustered out. True, some of those who had gone "down South" had not returned. Luke and Walter and Hugh were sleeping in The Wilderness, but Frank and Richard were safely at home and father was once more the clarion-voiced and tireless young man he had been when he went away to fight. So they all rejoiced, with only a passing tender word for those whose bodies filled a soldier's nameless grave.

There were some boys of about my own age, William's sons, and as they at once led me away down into the grove, I can say little of what went on in the house after that. It must have been still in the warm September weather for we climbed the slender leafy trees and swayed and swung on their tip-tops like bobolinks. Perhaps I did not go so very high after all but I had the feeling of being very close to the sky.

The blast of a bugle called us to dinner and we all went scrambling up the bank and into the "front room" like a swarm of hungry shotes responding to the call of the feeder. Aunt Deb, however shooed us out into the kitchen. "You can't stay here," she said. "Mother'll feed you in the kitchen."

Grandmother was waiting for us and our places were ready, so what did it matter? We had chicken and mashed potato and nice hot biscuit and honey—just as good as the grown people had and could eat all we wanted without our mothers to bother us. I am quite certain about the honey for I found a bee in one of the cells of my piece of comb, and when I pushed my plate away in dismay grandmother laughed and said, "That is only a little baby bee. You see this is wild honey. William got it out of a tree and didn't have time to pick all the bees out of it."

At this point my memories of this day fuse and flow into another visit to the McClintock homestead which must have taken place the next year, for it is my final record of my grandmother. I do not recall a single word that she said, but she again waited on us in the kitchen, beaming upon us with love and understanding. I see her also smiling in the midst of the joyous tumult which her children and grandchildren always produced when they met. She seemed content to listen and to serve.

She was the mother of seven sons, each a splendid type of sturdy manhood, and six daughters almost equally gifted in physical beauty. Four of the sons stood over six feet in height and were of unusual strength. All of them—men and women alike—were musicians by inheritance, and I never think of them without hearing the sound of singing or the voice of the violin. Each of them could play some instrument and some of them could play any instrument. David, as you shall learn, was the finest fiddler of them all. Grandad himself was able to play the violin but he no longer did so. "'Tis the Devil's instrument," he said, but I noticed that he always kept time to it.

Grandmother had very little learning. She could read and write of course, and she made frequent pathetic attempts to open her Bible or glance at a newspaper—all to little purpose, for her days were filled from dawn to dark with household duties.

I know little of her family history. Beyond the fact that she was born in Maryland and had been always on the border, I have little to record. She was in truth overshadowed by the picturesque figure of her husband who was of Scotch-Irish descent and a most singular and interesting character.

He was a mystic as well as a minstrel. He was an "Adventist"—that is to say a believer in the Second Coming of Christ, and a constant student of the Bible, especially of those parts which predicted the heavens rolling together as a scroll, and the destruction of the earth. Notwithstanding his lack of education and his rude exterior, he was a man of marked dignity and sobriety of manner.

Indeed he was both grave and remote in his intercourse with his neighbors.

He was like Ezekiel, a dreamer of dreams. He loved the Old Testament, particularly those books which consisted of thunderous prophecies and passionate lamentations. The poetry of *Isaiah,* The visions of *The Apocalypse,* formed his emotional outlet, his escape into the world of imaginative literature. The songs he loved best were those which described chariots of flaming clouds, the sound of the resurrection trump—or the fields of amaranth blooming "on the other side of Jordan."

As I close my eyes and peer back into my obscure childish world I can see him sitting in his straight-backed cane-bottomed chair, drumming on the rungs with his fingers, keeping time to some inaudible tune—or chanting with faintly-moving lips the wondrous words of *John* or *Daniel.* He must have been at this time about seventy years of age, but he seemed to me as old as a snow-covered mountain.

My belief is that Grandmother did not fully share her husband's faith in The Second Coming but upon her fell the larger share of the burden of entertainment when Grandad made "the travelling brother" welcome. His was an open house to all who came along the road, and the fervid chantings, the impassioned prayers of these meetings lent a singular air of unreality to the business of cooking or plowing in the fields.

I think he loved his wife and children, and yet I never heard him speak an affectionate word to them. He was kind, he was just, but he was not tender. With eyes turned inward, with a mind filled with visions of angel messengers with trumpets at their lips announcing "The Day of Wrath," how could he concern himself with the ordinary affairs of human life?

Too old to bind grain in the harvest field, he was occasionally intrusted with the task of driving the reaper or the mower—and generally forgot to oil the bearings. His absent-mindedness was a source of laughter among his sons and sons-in-law. I've heard Frank say: "Dad would stop in the midst of a swath to announce the end of the world." He seldom remembered to put on a hat even in the blazing sun of July and his daughters had to keep an eye on him to be sure he had his vest on right-side out.

Grandmother was cheerful in the midst of her toil and discomfort, for what other mother had such a family of noble boys and handsome girls? They all loved her, that she knew, and she was perfectly willing to sacrifice her comfort to promote theirs. Occasionally Samantha or Rachel remonstrated with her for working so hard, but she only put their protests aside and sent them back to their callers, for when the McClintock girls were at home, the horses of their suitors tied before the gate would have mounted a small troop of cavalry.

It was well that this pioneer wife was rich in children, for she had little else. I do not suppose she ever knew what it was to have a comfortable well-aired bed-room, even in child-birth. She was practical and a good manager, and she needed to be, for her husband was as weirdly unworldly as a farmer could be. He was indeed a sad husbandman. Only the splendid abundance of the soil and the manual skill of his sons, united to the good management of his wife, kept his family fed and clothed. "What is the use of laying up a store of goods against the early destruction of the world?" he argued.

He was bitterly opposed to secret societies, for some reason which I never fully understood, and the only fury I ever knew him to express was directed against these "dens of iniquity."

Nearly all his neighbors, like those in our coulee, were native American as their names indicated. The Dudleys, Elwells, and Griswolds came from Connecticut, the McEldowneys and McKinleys from New York and Ohio, the Baileys and Garlands from Maine. Buoyant, vital, confident, these sons of the border bent to the work of breaking sod and building fence quite in the spirit of sportsmen.

They were always racing in those days, rejoicing in their abounding vigor. With them reaping was a game, husking corn a test of endurance and skill, threshing a "bee." It was a Dudley against a McClintock, a Gilfillan against a Garland, and my father's laughing descriptions of the barn-raisings, harvestings and rail-splittings of the valley filled my mind with vivid pictures of manly deeds. Every phase of farm work was carried on by hand. Strength and skill counted high and I had good reason for my idolatry of David and William. With the hearts of woodsmen and fists of sailors they were precisely the type to appeal to the imagination of a boy. Hunters, athletes, skilled horsemen—everything they did was to me heroic.

Frank, smallest of all these sons of Hugh, was not what an observer would call puny. He weighed nearly one hundred and eighty pounds and never met his match except in his brothers. William could outlift him, David could out-run him and outleap him, but he was more agile than either—was indeed a skilled acrobat.

His muscles were prodigious. The calves of his legs would not go into his top boots, and I have heard my father say that once when the "tumbling" in the little country "show" seemed not to his liking, Frank sprang over the ropes into the arena and went around the ring in a series of professional flip-flaps, to the unrestrained delight of the spectators. I did not witness this performance, I am sorry to say, but I have seen him do somersaults and turn cart-wheels in the dooryard just from the pure joy of living. He could have been a professional acrobat—and he came near to being a professional ball-player.

He was always smiling, but his temper was fickle. Anybody could get a fight out of Frank McClintock at any time, simply by expressing a desire for it. To call him a liar was equivalent to contracting a doctor's bill. He loved hunting, as did all his brothers, but was too excitable to be a highly successful shot—whereas William and David were veritable Leather-stockings in their mastery of the heavy, old-fashioned rifle. David was especially dreaded at the turkey shoots of the county.

William was over six feet in height, weighed two hundred and forty pounds, and stood "straight as an Injun." He was one of the most formidable men of the valley—even at fifty as I first recollect him, he walked with a quick lift of his foot like that of a young Chippewa. To me he was a huge gentle black bear, but I firmly believed he could whip any man in the world—even Uncle David—if he wanted to. I never expected to see him fight, for I could not imagine anybody foolish enough to invite his wrath.

Such a man did develop, but not until William was over sixty, gray-haired and ill, and even then it took two strong men to engage him fully, and when it was all over (the contest filled but a few seconds), one assailant could not be found, and the other had to call in a doctor to piece him together again.

William did not have a mark—his troubles began when he went home to his quaint little old wife. In some strange way she divined that he had been fighting, and soon drew the story from him. "William McClintock," said she severely, "hain't you old enough to keep your temper and not go brawling around like that and at a school meeting too!"

William hung his head. "Well, I dunno!—I suppose my dyspepsy has made me kind o' irritable," he said by way of apology.

My father was the historian of most of these exploits on the part of his brothers-in-law, for he loved to exalt their physical prowess at the same time that he deplored their lack of enterprise and system. Certain of their traits he understood well. Others he was never able to comprehend, and I am not sure that they ever quite understood themselves.

A deep vein of poetry, of sub-conscious Celtic sadness, ran through them all. It was associated with their love of music and was wordless. Only hints of this endowment came out now and again, and to the day of his death my father continued to express perplexity, and a kind of irritation at the curious combination of bitterness and sweetness, sloth and tremendous energy, slovenliness and exaltation which made Hugh McClintock and his sons the jest and the admiration of those who knew them best.

Undoubtedly to the Elwells and Dudleys, as to most of their definite, practical, orderly and successful New England neighbors, my uncles were merely a good-natured, easy-going lot of "fiddlers," but to me as I grew old enough to understand them, they became a group of potential poets, bards and dreamers, inarticulate and moody. They fell easily into somber silence. Even Frank, the most boisterous and outspoken of them all, could be thrown into sudden melancholy by a melody, a line of poetry or a beautiful landscape.

The reason for this praise of their quality, if the reason needs to be stated, lies in my feeling of definite indebtedness to them. They furnished much of the charm and poetic suggestion of my childhood. Most of what I have in the way of feeling for music, for rhythm, I derive from my mother's side of the house, for it was almost entirely Celt in every characteristic. She herself was a wordless poet, a sensitive singer of sad romantic songs.

Father was by nature an orator and a lover of the drama. So far as I am aware, he never read a poem if he could help it, and yet he responded instantly to music, and was instinctively courtly in manner. His mind was clear, positive and definite, and his utterances fluent. Orderly, resolute and thorough in all that he did, he despised William McClintock's easy-going habits of husbandry, and found David's lack of "push," of business enterprise, deeply irritating. And yet he loved them both and respected my mother for defending them.

To me, in those days, the shortcomings of the McClintocks did not appear particularly heinous. All our neighbors were living in log houses and frame shanties built beside the brooks, or set close against the hillsides, and William's small unpainted dwelling seemed a natural feature of the landscape, but as the years passed and other and more enterprising settlers built big barns, and shining white houses, the gray and leaning stables, sagging gates and roofs of my uncle's farm, became a reproach even in my eyes, so that when I visited it for the last time just before our removal to Iowa, I, too, was a little ashamed of it. Its disorder did not diminish my regard for the owner, but I wished he would clean out the stable and prop up the wagon-shed.

My grandmother's death came soon after our second visit to the homestead. I have no personal memory of the event, but I heard Uncle David describe it. The setting of the final scene in the drama was humble. The girls were washing clothes in the yard and the silent old mother was getting the mid-day meal. David, as he came in from the field, stopped for a moment with his sisters and in their talk Samantha said: "Mother isn't at all well today."

David, looking toward the kitchen, said, "Isn't there some way to keep her from working?"

"You know how she is," explained Deborah. "She's worked so long she don't know how to rest. We tried to get her to lie down for an hour but she wouldn't."

David was troubled. "She'll have to stop sometime," he said, and then they passed to other things, hearing meanwhile the tread of their mother's busy feet.

Suddenly she appeared at the door, a frightened look on her face.

"Why, mother!—what is the matter?" asked her daughter.

She pointed to her mouth and shook her head, to indicate that she could not speak. David leaped toward her, but she dropped before he could reach her.

Lifting her in his strong arms he laid her on her bed and hastened for the doctor. All in vain! She sank into unconsciousness and died without a word of farewell.

She fell like a soldier in the ranks. Having served uncomplainingly up to the very edge of her evening bivouac, she passed to her final sleep in silent dignity.

3

The Home in the Coulee

Our postoffice was in the village of Onalaska, situated at the mouth of the Black River, which came down out of the wide forest lands of the north. It was called a "boom town" for the reason that "booms" or yards for holding pine logs laced the quiet bayou and supplied several large mills with timber. Busy saws clamored from the islands and great rafts of planks and lath and shingles were made up and floated down into the Mississippi and on to southern markets.

It was a rude, rough little camp filled with raftsmen, loggers, mill-hands and boomsmen. Saloons abounded and deeds of violence were common, but to me it was a poem. From its position on a high plateau it commanded a lovely southern expanse of shimmering water bounded by purple bluffs. The spires of LaCrosse rose from the smoky distance, and steamships' hoarsely giving voice suggested illimitable reaches of travel. Some day I hoped my father would take me to that shining market-place whereto he carried all our grain.

In this village of Onalaska, lived my grandfather and grandmother Garland, and their daughter Susan, whose husband, Richard Bailey, a quiet, kind man, was held in deep affection by us all. Of course he could not quite measure up to the high standards of David and William, even though he kept a store and sold candy, for he could neither kill a bear, nor play the fiddle, nor shoot a gun—much less turn hand-springs or tame a wild horse, but we liked him notwithstanding his limitations and were always glad when he came to visit us.

Even at this time I recognized the wide differences which separated the McClintocks from the Garlands. The fact that my father's people lived to the west and in a town, helped to emphasize the divergence.

All the McClintocks were farmers, but grandfather Garland was a carpenter by trade, and a leader in his church which was to him a club, a forum and a commercial exchange. He was a native of Maine and proud of the fact. His eyes were keen and gray, his teeth fine and white, and his expression stern. His speech was neat and nipping. As a workman he was exact and his tools were always in perfect order. In brief he was a Yankee, as concentrated a bit of New England as was ever transplanted to the border. Hopelessly "sot" in all his eastern ways, he remained the doubter, the critic, all his life.

We always spoke of him with formal precision as Grandfather Garland, never as "Grandad" or "Granpap" as we did in alluding to Hugh McClintock, and his long prayers (pieces of elaborate oratory) wearied us, while those of Grandad, which had the extravagance, the lyrical abandon of poetry, profoundly pleased us. Grandfather's church was a small white building in the edge of the village, Grandad's place of worship was a vision, a cloudbuilt temple, a house not made with hands.

The contrast between my grandmothers was equally wide. Harriet Garland was tall and thin, with a dark and serious face. She was an invalid, and confined to a chair, which stood in the corner of her room. On the walls within reach of her hand hung many small pockets, so ordered that she could obtain her sewing materials without rising. She was always at work when I called, but it was her habit to pause and discover in some one of her receptacles a piece of candy or a stick of "lickerish root" which she gave to me "as a reward for being a good boy."

She was always making needle rolls and thimble boxes and no doubt her skill helped to keep the family fed and clothed.

Notwithstanding all divergence in the characters of Grandmother Garland and Grandmother McClintock, we held them both in almost equal affection. Serene, patient, bookish, Grandmother Garland brought to us, as to her neighbors in this rude river port, some of the best qualities of intellectual Boston, and from her lips we acquired many of the precepts and proverbs of our Pilgrim forbears.

Her influence upon us was distinctly literary. She gloried in New England traditions, and taught us to love the poems of Whittier and Longfellow. It was she who called us to her knee and told us sadly yet benignly of the death of Lincoln, expressing only pity for the misguided assassin. She was a constant advocate of charity, piety, and learning. Always poor, and for many years a cripple, I never heard her complain, and no one, I think, ever saw her face clouded with a frown.

Our neighbors in Green's Coulee were all native American. The first and nearest, Al Randal and his wife and son, we saw often and on the whole liked, but the Whitwells who lived on the farm above us were a constant source of comedy to my father. Old Port, as he was called, was a mild-mannered man who would have made very little impression on the community, but for his wife, a large and rather unkempt person, who assumed such man-like freedom of speech that my father was never without an amusing story of her doings.

She swore in vigorous pioneer fashion, and dominated her husband by force of lung power as well as by a certain painful candor. "Port, you're an old fool," she often said to him in our presence. It was her habit to apologize to her guests, as they took their seats at her abundant table, "Wal, now, folks, I'm sorry, but there ain't a blank thing in this house fit for a dawg to eat—" expecting of course to have everyone cry out, "Oh, Mrs. Whitwell, this is a splendid dinner!" which they generally did. But once my father took her completely aback by rising resignedly from the table—"Come, Belle," said he to my mother, "let's go home. I'm not going to eat food not fit for a dog."

The rough old woman staggered under this blow, but quickly recovered. "Dick Garland, you blank fool. Sit down, or I'll fetch you a swipe with the broom."

In spite of her profanity and ignorance she was a good neighbor and in time of trouble no one was readier to relieve any distress in the coulee. However, it was upon Mrs. Randal and the widow Green that my mother called for aid, and I do not think Mrs. Whitwell was ever quite welcome even at our quilting bees, for her loud voice silenced every other, and my mother did not enjoy her vulgar stories.—Yes, I can remember several quilting bees, and I recall molding candles, and that our "company light" was a large kerosene lamp, in the glass globe of which a strip of red flannel was coiled. Probably this was merely a device to lengthen out the wick, but it made a memorable spot of color in the room just as the watch-spring gong in the clock gave off a sound of fairy music to my ear. I don't know why the ring of that coil had such a wondrous appeal, but I often climbed upon a chair to rake its spirals with a nail in order that I might float away on its "dying fall."

Life was primitive in all the homes of the coulee. Money was hard to get. We always had plenty to eat, but little in the way of luxuries. We had few toys except those we fashioned for ourselves, and our garments were mostly homemade. I have heard my father say, "Belle could go to town with me, buy the calico for a dress and be wearing it for supper"—but I fear that even this did not happen very often. Her "dress up" gowns, according to certain precious old tintypes, indicate that clothing was for her only a sort of uniform,—and yet I will not say this made her unhappy. Her face was always smiling. She knit all our socks, made all our shirts and suits. She even carded and spun wool, in addition to her housekeeping, and found time to help on our kites and bows and arrows.

Month by month the universe in which I lived lightened and widened. In my visits to Onalaska, I discovered the great Mississippi River, and the Minnesota Bluffs. The light of knowledge grew stronger. I began to perceive forms and faces which had been hidden in the dusk of babyhood. I heard more and more of LaCrosse, and out of the mist filled lower valley the booming roar of steamboats suggested to me distant countries and the sea.

My father believed in service. At seven years of age, I had regular duties. I brought firewood to the kitchen and broke nubbins for the calves and shelled corn for the chickens. I have a dim memory of helping him (and grandfather) split oak blocks into rafting pins in the kitchen. This seems incredible to me now, and yet it must have been so. In summer Harriet and I drove the cows to pasture, and carried "switchel" to the men in the hay-fields by means of a jug hung in the middle of a long stick.

Haying was a delightful season to us, for the scythes of the men occasionally tossed up clusters of beautiful strawberries, which we joyfully gathered. I remember with especial pleasure the delicious shortcakes which my mother made of the wild fruit which we picked in the warm odorous grass along the edge of the meadow.

Harvest time also brought a pleasing excitement (something

unwonted, something like entertaining visitors) which compensated for the extra work demanded of us. The neighbors usually came in to help and life was a feast.

There was, however, an ever-present menace in our lives, the snake! During mid-summer months blue racers and rattlesnakes swarmed and the terror of them often chilled our childish hearts. Once Harriet and I, with little Frank in his cart, came suddenly upon a monster diamond-back rattler sleeping by the roadside. In our mad efforts to escape, the car was overturned and the baby scattered in the dust almost within reach of the snake. As soon as she realized what had happened, Harriet ran back bravely, caught up the child and brought him safely away.

Another day, as I was riding on the load of wheat sheaves, one of the men, in pitching the grain to the wagon lifted a rattlesnake with his fork. I saw it writhing in the bottom of the sheaf, and screamed out, "A snake, a snake!" It fell across the man's arm but slid harmlessly to the ground, and he put a tine through it.

As it chanced to be just dinner time he took it with him to the house and fastened it down near the door of a coop in which an old hen and her brood of chickens were confined. I don't know why he did this but it threw the mother hen into such paroxysms of fear that she dashed herself again and again upon the slats of her house. It appeared that she comprehended to the full the terrible power of the writhing monster.

Perhaps it was this same year that one of the men discovered another enormous yellow-back in the barnyard, one of the largest ever seen on the farm—and killed it just as it was moving across an old barrel. I cannot now understand why it tried to cross the barrel, but I distinctly visualize the brown and yellow band it made as it lay for an instant just before the bludgeon fell upon it, crushing it and the barrel together. He was thicker than my leg and glistened in the sun with sinister splendor. As he hung limp over the fence, a warning to his fellows, it was hard for me to realize that death still lay in his square jaws and poisonous fangs.

Innumerable garter-snakes infested the marsh, and black snakes inhabited the edges of the woodlands, but we were not so much afraid of them. We accepted them as unavoidable companions in the wild. They would run from us. Bears and wildcats we held in real terror, though they were considered denizens of the darkness and hence not likely to be met with if one kept to the daylight.

The "hoop snake" was quite as authentic to us as the blue racer, although no one had actually seen one. Den Green's cousin's uncle had killed one in Michigan, and a man over the ridge had once been stung by one that came rolling down the hill with his tail in his mouth. But Den's cousin's uncle, when he saw the one coming toward him, had stepped aside quick as lightning, and the serpent's sharp fangs had buried themselves so deep in the bark of a tree, that he could not escape.

Various other of the myths common to American boyhood, were held in perfect faith by Den and Ellis and Ed, myths which made every woodland path an ambush and every marshy spot a place of evil. Horsehairs would turn to snakes if left in the spring, and a serpent's tail would not die till sundown.

Once on the high hillside, I started a stone rolling, which as it went plunging into a hazel thicket, thrust out a deer, whose flight seemed fairly miraculous to me. He appeared to drift along the hillside like a bunch of thistle-down, and I took a singular delight in watching him disappear.

Once my little brother and I, belated in our search for the cows, were far away on the hills when night suddenly came upon us. I could not have been more than eight years old and Frank was five. This incident reveals the fearless use our father made of us. True, we were hardly a mile from the house, but there were many serpents on the hillsides and wildcats in the cliffs, and eight is pretty young for such a task.

We were following the cows through the tall grass and bushes, in the dark, when father came to our rescue, and I do not recall being sent on a similar expedition thereafter. I think mother protested against the danger of it. Her notions of our training were less rigorous.

I never hear a cow-bell of a certain timbre that I do not relive in some degree the terror and despair of that hour on the mountain, when it seemed that my world had suddenly slipped away from me.

Winter succeeds summer abruptly in my memory. Behind our house rose a sharp ridge down which we used to coast. Over this hill, fierce winds blew the snow, and wonderful, diamonded drifts covered the yard, and sometimes father was obliged to dig deep trenches in order to reach the barn.

On winter evenings he shelled corn by drawing the ears across a spade resting on a wash tub, and we children built houses of the cobs, while mother sewed carpet rags or knit our mittens. Quilting bees of an afternoon were still recognized social functions and the spread quilt on its frame made a gorgeous tent under which my brother and I camped on our way to "Colorado." Lath swords and tin-pan drums remained a part of our equipment for a year or two.

One stormy winter day, Edwin Randal, riding home in a sleigh behind his uncle, saw me in the yard and, picking an apple from an open barrel beside which he was standing, threw it at me. It was a very large apple, and as it struck the drift it disappeared leaving a round deep hole. Delving there I recovered it, and as I brushed the rime from its scarlet skin it seemed the most beautiful thing in this world. From this vividly remembered delight, I deduce the fact that apples were not very plentiful in our home.

My favorite place in winter time was directly under the kitchen stove. It was one of the old-fashioned high-stepping breed, with long hind legs and an arching belly, and as the oven was on top, the space beneath the arch offered a delightful den for a cat, a dog or small boy, and I was usually to be found there, lying on my stomach, spelling out the "continued" stories which came to us in the county paper, for I was born with a hunger for print.

We had few books in our house. Aside from the Bible I remember only one other, a thick, black volume filled with gaudy pictures of cherries and plums, and portraits of ideally fat and prosperous sheep, pigs and cows. It must have been a *Farmer's Annual* or State agricultural report, but it contained in the midst of its dry prose, occasional poems like *I remember, I remember, The Old Armchair* and other pieces of a domestic or rural nature. I was especially moved by *The Old Armchair,* and although some of the words and expressions were beyond my comprehension, I fully understood the defiant tenderness of the lines:

> I love it, I love it, and who shall dare
> To chide me for loving the old armchair?

I fear the horticultural side of this volume did not interest me, but this sweetly-sad poem tinged even the gaudy pictures of prodigious plums and shining apples with a literary glamor. The preposterously plump cattle probably affected me as only another form of romantic fiction. The volume also had a pleasant smell, not so fine an odor as the Bible, but so delectable that I loved to bury my nose in its opened pages. What caused this odor I cannot tell—perhaps it had been used to press flowers or sprigs of sweet fern.

Harriet's devotion to literature, like my own, was a nuisance. If my mother wanted a pan of chips she had to wrench one of us from a book, or tear us from a paper. If she pasted up a section of *Harper's Weekly* behind the washstand in the kitchen, I immediately discovered a special interest in that number, and likely enough forgot to wash myself. When mother saw this (as of course she very soon did), she turned the paper upside down, and thereafter accused me, with some justice, of standing on my head in order to continue my tale. "In fact," she often said, "it is easier for me to do my errands myself than to get either of you young ones to move."

The first school which we attended was held in a neighboring farmhouse, and there is very little to tell concerning it, but at seven I began to go to the public school in Onalaska and memory becomes definite, for the wide river which came silently out of the unknown north, carrying endless millions of pine logs, and the clamor of saws in the island mills, and especially the men walking the rolling logs with pike-poles in their hands filled me with a wordless joy. To be one of these brave and graceful "drivers" seemed almost as great an honor as to be a Captain in the army. Some of the boys of my acquaintance were sons of these hardy boomsmen, and related wonderful stories of their fathers' exploits—stories which we gladly believed. We all intended to be rivermen when we grew up.

The quiet water below the booms harbored enormous fish at that time, and some of the male citizens who were too lazy to work in the mills got an easy living by capturing cat-fish, and when in liquor joined the rivermen in their drunken frays. My father's tales of the exploits of some of these redoubtable villains filled my mind with mingled admiration and terror. No one used the pistol, however, and very few the knife. Physical strength counted. Foot and fist were the weapons which ended each contest and no one was actually slain in these meetings of rival crews.

In the midst of this tumult, surrounded by this coarse, unthinking life, my Grandmother Garland's home stood, a serene small sanctuary of lofty womanhood, a temple of New England virtue. From her and from my great aunt Bridges who lived in St. Louis, I received my first literary instruction, a partial off-set to the vulgar yet heroic influence of the raftsmen and mill hands.

The school-house, a wooden two story building, occupied an unkempt lot some distance back from the river and near a group of high sand dunes which possessed a sinister allurement to me. They had a mysterious desert quality, a flavor as of camels and Arabs. Once you got over behind them it seemed as if you were in another world, a far-off arid land where no water ran and only sear, sharp-edged grasses grew. Some of these mounds were miniature peaks of clear sand, so steep and dry that you could slide all the way down from top to bottom, and do no harm to your Sunday-go-to-meeting clothes. On rainy days you could dig caves in their sides.

But the mills and the log booms were after all much more dramatic and we never failed to hurry away to the river if we had half an hour to spare. The "drivers," so brave and skilled, so graceful, held us in breathless admiration as they leaped from one rolling log to another, or walked the narrow wooden bridges above the deep and silently sweeping waters. The piles of slabs, the mounds of saw-dust, the intermittent, ferocious snarl of the saws, the slap of falling lumber, the never ending fires eating up the refuse—all these sights and sounds made a return to school difficult. Even the life around the threshing machine seemed a little tame in comparison with the life of the booms.

We were much at the Greens', our second-door neighbors to the south, and the doings of the men-folks fill large space in my memory. Ed, the oldest of the boys, a man of twenty-three or four, was as prodigious in his way as my Uncle David. He was mighty with the axe. His deeds as a railsplitter rivaled those of Lincoln. The number of cords of wood he could split in a single day was beyond belief. It was either seven or eleven, I forget which—I am perfectly certain of the number of buckwheat pancakes he could eat for I kept count on several occasions. Once he ate nine the size of a dinner plate together with a suitable number of sausages—but what would you expect of a man who could whirl a six pound axe all day in a desperate attack on the forest, without once looking at the sun or pausing for breath?

However, he fell short of my hero in other ways. He looked like a fat man and his fiddling was only middling, therefore, notwithstanding his prowess with the axe and the maul, he remained subordinate to David, and though they never came to a test of strength we were perfectly sure that David was the finer man. His supple grace and his unconquerable pride made him altogether admirable.

Den, the youngest of the Greens, was a boy about three years my senior, and a most attractive lad. I met him some years ago in California, a successful doctor, and we talked of the days when I was his slave and humbly carried his powder horn and game bag. Ellis Usher, who lived in Sand Lake and often hunted with Den, is an editor in Milwaukee and one of the political leaders of his state. In those days he had a small opinion of me. No doubt I *was* a nuisance.

The road which led from our farm to the village school crossed a sandy ridge and often in June our path became so hot that it burned the soles of our feet. If we went out of the road there were sand-burrs and we lost a great deal of time picking needles from our toes. How we hated those sand-burrs!—However, on these sand barrens many luscious strawberries grew. They were not large, but they gave off a delicious odor, and it sometimes took us a long time to reach home.

There was a recognized element of danger in this road. Wildcats were plentiful around the limestone cliffs, and bears had been seen under the oak trees. In fact a place on the hillside was often pointed out with awe as "the place where Al Randal killed the bear." Our way led past the village cemetery also, and there was to me something vaguely awesome in that silent bivouac of the dead.

Among the other village boys in the school were two lads named Gallagher, one of whom, whose name was Matt, became my daily terror. He was two years older than I and had all of a city gamin's cunning and self-command. At every intermission he sidled close to me, walking round me, feeling my arms, and making much of my muscle. Sometimes he came behind and lifted me to see how heavy I was, or called attention to my strong hands and wrists, insisting with the most terrifying candor of conviction, "I'm sure you can lick me." We never quite came to combat, and finally he gave up this baiting for a still more exquisite method of torment.

My sister and I possessed a dog named Rover, a meek little yellow, bow-legged cur of mongrel character, but with the frankest, gentlest and sweetest face, it seemed to us, in all the world. He was not allowed to accompany us to school and scarcely ever left the yard, but Matt Gallagher in some way discovered my deep affection for this pet and thereafter played upon my fears with a malevolence which knew no mercy. One day he said, "Me and brother Dan are going over to your place to get a calf that's in your pasture. We're going to get excused fifteen minutes early. We'll get there before you do and we'll fix that dog of yours!—There won't be nothin' left of him but a grease spot when we are done with him."

These words, spoken probably in jest, instantly filled my heart with an agony of fear. I saw in imagination just how my little playmate would come running out to meet his cruel foes, his brown eyes beaming with love and trust,—I saw them hiding sharp stones behind their backs while snapping their left-hand fingers to lure him within reach, and then I saw them drive their murdering weapons at his head.

I could think of nothing else. I could not study, I could only sit and stare out of the window with tears running down my cheeks, until at last, the teacher observing my distress, inquired, "What is the matter?" And I, not knowing how to enter upon so terrible a tale, whined out, "I'm sick, I want to go home."

"You may go," said the teacher kindly.

Snatching my cap from beneath the desk where I had concealed it at recess, I hurried out and away over the sand-lot on the shortest way home. No stopping now for burrs!—I ran like one pursued. I shall never forget as long as I live, the pain, the panic, the frenzy of that race against time. The hot sand burned my feet, my side ached, my mouth was dry, and yet I ran on and on and on, looking back from moment to moment, seeing pursuers in every moving object.

At last I came in sight of home, and Rover frisked out to meet me just as I had expected him to do, his tail wagging, his gentle eyes smiling up at me. Gasping, unable to utter a word, I frantically dragged the dog into the house and shut the door.

"What is the matter?" asked my mother.

I could not at the moment explain even to her what had threatened me, but her calm sweet words at last gave my story vent. Out it came in torrential flow.

"Why, you poor child!" she said. "They were only fooling—they wouldn't dare to hurt your dog!"

This was probably true. Matt had spoken without any clear idea of the torture he was inflicting.

It is often said, "How little is required to give a child joy," but men—and women too—sometimes forget how little it takes to give a child pain.

4

Father Sells the Farm

Green's Coulee was a delightful place for boys. It offered hunting and coasting and many other engrossing sports, but my father, as the seasons went by, became thoroughly dissatisfied with its disadvantages. More and more he resented the stumps and ridges which interrupted his plow. Much of his quarter-section remained unbroken. There were ditches to be dug in the marsh and young oaks to be uprooted from the forest, and he was obliged to toil with unremitting severity. There were times, of course, when field duties did not press, but never a day came when the necessity for twelve hours' labor did not exist.

Furthermore, as he grubbed or reaped he remembered the glorious prairies he had crossed on his exploring trip into Minnesota before the war, and the oftener he thought of them the more bitterly he resented his up-tilted, horse-killing fields, and his complaining words sank so deep into the minds of his sons that for years thereafter they were unable to look upon any rise of ground as an object to be admired.

It irked him beyond measure to force his reaper along a steep slope, and he loathed the irregular little patches running up the ravines behind the timbered knolls, and so at last like many another of his neighbors he began to look away to the west as a fairer field for conquest. He no more thought of going east than a liberated eagle dreams of returning to its narrow cage. He loved to talk of Boston, to boast of its splendor, but to live there, to earn his bread there, was unthinkable. Beneath the sunset lay the enchanted land of opportunity and his liberation came unexpectedly.

Sometime in the spring of 1868, a merchant from LaCrosse, a plump man who brought us candy and was very cordial and condescending, began negotiations for our farm, and in the discussion of plans which followed, my conception of the universe expanded. I began to understand that "Minnesota" was not a bluff but a wide land of romance, a prairie, peopled with red men, which lay far beyond the big river. And then, one day, I heard my father read to my mother a paragraph from the county paper which ran like this, "It is reported that Richard Garland has sold his farm in Green's Coulee to our popular grocer, Mr. Speer. Mr. Speer intends to make of it a model dairy farm."

This intention seemed somehow to reflect a ray of glory upon us, though I fear it did not solace my mother, as she contemplated the loss of home and kindred. She was not by nature an emigrant, —few women are. She was content with the pleasant slopes, the kindly neighbors of Green's Coulee. Furthermore, most of her brothers and sisters still lived just across the ridge in the valley of the Neshonoc, and the thought of leaving them for a wild and unknown region was not pleasant.

To my father, on the contrary, change was alluring. Iowa was now the place of the rainbow, and the pot of gold. He was eager to push on toward it, confident of the outcome. His spirit was reflected in one of the songs which we children particularly enjoyed hearing our mother sing, a ballad which consisted of a dialogue between a husband and wife on this very subject of emigration. The words as well as its wailing melody still stir me deeply, for they lay hold of my sub-conscious memory—embodying admirably the debate which went on in our home as well as in the homes of other farmers in the valley—only, alas! our mothers did not prevail.

It begins with a statement of unrest on the part of the husband who confesses that he is about to give up his plow and his cart—

> Away to Colorado a journey I'll go,
> For to double my fortune as other men do,
> *While here I must labor each day in the field*
> *And the winter consumes all the summer doth yield.*

To this the wife replies:

> Dear husband, I've noticed with a sorrowful heart
> That you long have neglected your plow and your cart,
> Your horses, sheep, cattle at random do run,
> And your new Sunday jacket goes every day on.
> *Oh, stay on your farm and you'll suffer no loss,*
> *For the stone that keeps rolling will gather no moss.*

But the husband insists:

> Oh, wife, let us go; Oh, don't let us wait;
> I long to be there, and I long to be great,
> While you some fair lady and who knows but I
> May be some rich governor long 'fore I die,
> *Whilst here I must labor each day in the field,*
> *And the winter consumes all the summer doth yield.*

But wife shrewdly retorts:

> Dear husband, remember those lands are so dear
> They will cost you the labor of many a year.
> Your horses, sheep, cattle will all be to buy,
> You will hardly get settled before you must die.
> Oh, stay on the farm,—etc.

The husband then argues that as in that country the lands are all cleared to the plow, and horses and cattle not very dear, they would soon be rich. Indeed, "we will feast on fat venison one-half of the year." Thereupon the wife brings in her final argument:

> Oh, husband, remember those lands of delight
> Are surrounded by Indians who murder by night.
> Your house will be plundered and burnt to the ground
> While your wife and your children lie mangled around.

This fetches the husband up with a round turn:

> Oh, wife, you've convinced me, I'll argue no more,
> I never once thought of your dying before.
> love my dear children although they are small
> And you, my dear wife, I love greatest of all.
> REFRAIN (both together)
> We'll stay on the farm and we'll suffer no loss
> For the stone that keeps rolling will gather no moss.

This song was not an especial favorite of my father. Its minor strains and its expressions of womanly doubts and fears were antipathetic to his sanguine, buoyant, self-confident nature. He was inclined to ridicule the conclusions of its last verse and to say that the man was a molly-coddle—or whatever the word of contempt was in those days. As an antidote he usually called for "O'er the hills in legions, boys," which exactly expressed his love of exploration and adventure.

This ballad which dates back to the conquest of the Allegheny mountains opens with a fine uplifting note,

> Cheer up, brothers, as we go
> O'er the mountains, westward ho,
> Where herds of deer and buffalo
> Furnish the fare.

and the refrain is at once a bugle call and a vision:

> Then o'er the hills in legions, boys,
> Fair freedom's star
> Points to the sunset regions, boys,
> Ha, ha, ha-ha!

and when my mother's clear voice rose on the notes of that exultant chorus, our hearts responded with a surge of emotion akin to that which sent the followers of Daniel Boone across the Blue Ridge, and lined the trails of Kentucky and Ohio with the canvas-covered wagons of the pioneers.

A little farther on in the song came these words,

> When we've wood and prairie land,
> Won by our toil,
> We'll reign like kings in fairy land,
> Lords of the soil!

which always produced in my mind the picture of a noble farmhouse in a park-like valley, just as the line, "We'll have our rifles ready, boys," expressed the boldness and self-reliance of an armed horseman.

The significance of this song in the lives of the McClintocks and the Garlands cannot be measured. It was the marching song of my Grandfather's generation and undoubtedly profoundly influenced my father and my uncles in all that they did. It suggested shining mountains, and grassy vales, swarming with bear and elk. It called to green savannahs and endless flowery glades. It voiced as no other song did, the pioneer impulse throbbing deep in my father's blood. That its words will not bear close inspection today takes little from its power. Unquestionably it was a directing force in the lives of at least three generations of my pioneering race. Its strains will be found running through this book from first to last, for its pictures continued to allure my father on and on toward "the sunset regions," and its splendid faith carried him through many a dark vale of discontent.

Our home was a place of song, notwithstanding the severe toil which was demanded of every hand, for often of an evening, especially in winter time, father took his seat beside the fire, invited us to his knees, and called on mother to sing. These moods were very sweet to us and we usually insisted upon his singing for us. True, he hardly knew one tune from another, but he had a hearty resounding chant which delighted us, and one of the ballads which we especially like to hear him repeat was called *Down the Ohio.* Only one verse survives in my memory:

> The river is up, the channel is deep,
> The winds blow high and strong.
> The flash of the oars, the stroke we keep,
> As we row the old boat along,
> Down the O-h-i-o.

Mother, on the contrary, was gifted with a voice of great range and sweetness, and from her we always demanded *Nellie Wildwood, Lily Dale, Lorena* or some of Root's stirring war songs. We loved her noble, musical tone, and yet we always enjoyed our father's tuneless roar. There was something dramatic and moving in each of his ballads. He made the words mean so much.

It is a curious fact that nearly all of the ballads which the McClintocks and other of these powerful young sons of the border loved to sing were sad. *Nellie Wildwood, Minnie Minturn, Belle Mahone, Lily Dale* were all concerned with dead or dying maidens or with mocking birds still singing o'er their graves. Weeping willows and funeral urns ornamented the cover of each mournful ballad. Not one smiling face peered forth from the pages of *The Home Diadem.*

> Lonely like a withered tree,
> What is all the world to me?
> Light and life were all in thee,
> Sweet Belle Mahone,

wailed stalwart David and buxom Deborah, and ready tears moistened my tanned plump cheeks.

Perhaps it was partly by way of contrast that the jocund song of *Freedom's Star* always meant so much to me, but however it came about, I am perfectly certain that it was an immense subconscious force in the life of my father as it had been in the westward marching of the McClintocks. In my own thinking it became at once a vision and a lure.

The only humorous songs which my uncles knew were negro ditties, like *Camp Town Racetrack* and *Jordan am a Hard Road to Trabbel* but in addition to the sad ballads I have quoted, they joined my mother in *The Pirate's Serenade, Erin's Green Shore, Bird of the Wilderness,* and the memory of their mellow voices creates a golden dusk between me and that far-off cottage.

During the summer of my eighth year, I took a part in haying and harvest, and I have a painful recollection of raking hay after the wagons, for I wore no shoes and the stubble was very sharp. I used to slip my feet along close to the ground, thus bending the stubble away from me before throwing my weight on it, otherwise walking was painful. If I were sent across the field on an errand I always sought out the path left by the broad wheels of the mowing machine and walked therein with a most delicious sense of safety.

It cannot be that I was required to work very hard or very steadily, but it seemed to me then, and afterward, as if I had been made one of the regular hands and that I toiled the whole day through. I rode old Josh for the hired man to plow corn, and also guided the lead horse on the old McCormick reaper, my short legs sticking out at right angles from my body, and I carried water to the field.

It appears that the blackbirds were very thick that year and threatened, in August, to destroy the corn. They came in gleeful clouds, settling with multitudinous clamor upon the stalks so that it became the duty of Den Green to scare them away by shooting at them, and I was permitted to follow and pick up the dead birds and carry them as "game."

There was joy and keen excitement in this warfare. Sometimes when Den fired into a flock, a dozen or more came fluttering down. At other times vast swarms rose at the sound of the gun with a rush of wings which sounded like a distant storm. Once Den let me fire the gun, and I took great pride in this until I came upon several of the shining little creatures bleeding, dying in the grass. Then my heart was troubled and I repented of my cruelty.

Mrs. Green put the birds into potpies but my mother would not do so. "I don't believe in such game," she said. "It's bad enough to shoot the poor things without eating them."

Once we came upon a huge mountain rattlesnake and Den killed it with a shot of his gun. How we escaped being bitten is a mystery, for we explored every path of the hills and meadows in our bare feet, our trousers rolled to the knee. We hunted plums and picked blackberries and hazel nuts with very little fear of snakes, and yet we must have always been on guard. We loved our valley, and while occasionally we yielded to the lure of "Freedom's star," we were really content with Green's Coulee and its surrounding hills.

5

The Last Threshing in the Coulee

Life on a Wisconsin farm, even for the women, had its compensations. There were times when the daily routine of lonely and monotonous housework gave place to an agreeable bustle, and human intercourse lightened the toil. In the midst of the slow progress of the fall's plowing, the gathering of the threshing crew was a most dramatic event to my mother, as to us, for it not only brought unwonted clamor, it fetched her brothers William and David and Frank, who owned and ran a threshing machine, and their coming gave the house an air of festivity which offset the burden of extra work which fell upon us all.

In those days the grain, after being brought in and stacked around the barn, was allowed to remain until October or November when all the other work was finished.

Of course some men got the machine earlier, for all could not thresh at the same time, and a good part of every man's fall activities consisted in "changing works" with his neighbors, thus laying up a stock of unpaid labor against the home job. Day after day, therefore, father or the hired man shouldered a fork and went to help thresh, and all through the autumn months, the ceaseless ringing hum and the *bow-ouw, ouw-woo, boo-oo-oom* of the great balance wheels on the separator and the deep bass purr of its cylinder could be heard in every valley like the droning song of some sullen and gigantic autumnal insect.

I recall with especial dearness the events of that last threshing in the coulee.—I was eight, my brother was six. For days we had looked forward to the coming of "the threshers," listening with the greatest eagerness to father's report of the crew. At last he said, "Well, Belle, get ready. The machine will be here tomorrow."

All day we hung on the gate, gazing down the road, watching, waiting for the crew, and even after supper, we stood at the windows still hoping to hear the rattle of the ponderous separator.

Father explained that the men usually worked all day at one farm and moved after dark, and we were just starting to "climb the wooden hill" when we heard a far-off faint halloo.

"There they are," shouted father, catching up his old square tin lantern and hurriedly lighting the candle within it. "That's Frank's voice."

The night air was sharp, and as we had taken off our boots we could only stand at the window and watch father as he piloted the teamsters through the gate. The light threw fantastic shadows here and there, now lighting up a face, now bringing out the separator which seemed a weary and sullen monster awaiting its den. The men's voices sounded loud in the still night, causing the roused turkeys in the oaks to peer about on their perches, uneasy silhouettes against the sky.

We would gladly have stayed awake to greet our beloved uncles, but mother said, "You must go to sleep in order to be up early in the morning," and reluctantly we turned away.

Lying thus in our cot under the sloping raftered roof we could hear the squawk of the hens as father wrung their innocent necks, and the crash of the "sweeps" being unloaded sounded loud and clear and strange. We longed to be out there, but at last the dance of lights and shadows on the plastered wall died away, and we fell into childish dreamless sleep.

We were awakened at dawn by the ringing beat of the iron mauls as Frank and David drove the stakes to hold the "power" to the ground. The rattle of trace chains, the clash of iron rods, the clang of steel bars, intermixed with the laughter of the men, came sharply through the frosty air, and the smell of sizzling sausage from the kitchen warned us that our busy mother was hurrying the breakfast forward. Knowing that it was time to get up, although it was not yet light, I had a sense of being awakened into a romantic new world, a world of heroic action.

As we stumbled down the stairs, we found the lamp-lit kitchen empty of the men. They had finished their coffee and were out in the stack-yard oiling the machine and hitching the horses to the power. Shivering yet entranced by the beauty of the frosty dawn we crept out to stand and watch the play. The frost lay white on every surface, the frozen ground rang like iron under the steel-shod feet of the horses, and the breath of the men rose up in little white puffs of steam.

Uncle David on the feeder's stand was impatiently awaiting the coming of the fifth team. The pitchers were climbing the stacks like blackbirds, and the straw-stackers were scuffling about the stable door.—Finally, just as the east began to bloom, and long streamers of red began to unroll along the vast gray dome of sky Uncle Frank, the driver, lifted his voice in a "Chippewa war-whoop."

On a still morning like this his signal could be heard for miles. Long drawn and musical, it sped away over the fields, announcing to all the world that the McClintocks were ready for the day's race. Answers came back faintly from the frosty fields where dim figures of laggard hands could be seen hurrying over the plowed ground, the last team came clattering in and was hooked into its place, David called "All right!" and the cylinder began to hum.

In those days the machine was either a "J. I. Case" or a "Buffalo Pitts," and was moved by five pairs of horses attached to a "power" staked to the ground, round which they travelled pulling at the ends of long levers or sweeps, and to me the force seemed tremendous. "Tumbling rods" with "knuckle joints" carried the motion to the cylinder, and the driver who stood upon a square platform above the huge, greasy cog-wheels (round which the horses moved) was a grand figure in my eyes.

Driving, to us, looked like a pleasant job, but Uncle Frank thought it very tiresome, and I can now see that it was. To stand on that small platform all through the long hours of a cold November day, when the cutting wind roared down the valley sweeping the dust and leaves along the road, was work. Even I perceived that it was far pleasanter to sit on the south side of the stack and watch the horses go round.

It was necessary that the "driver" should be a man of judgment, for the horses had to be kept at just the right speed, and to do this he must gauge the motion of the cylinder by the pitch of its deep bass song.

The three men in command of the machine, were set apart as "the threshers."—William and David alternately "fed" or "tended," that is, one of them "fed" the grain into the howling cylinder while the other, oilcan in hand, watched the sieves, felt of the pinions and so kept the machine in good order. The feeder's position was the high place to which all boys aspired, and on this day I stood in silent admiration of Uncle David's easy powerful attitudes as he caught each bundle in the crook of his arm and spread it out into a broad, smooth band of yellow straw on which the whirling teeth caught and tore with monstrous fury. He was the ideal man in my eyes, grander in some ways than my father, and to be able to stand where he stood was the highest honor in the world.

It was all poetry for us and we wished every day were threshing day. The wind blew cold, the clouds went flying across the bright blue sky, and the straw glistened in the sun. With jarring snarl the circling zone of cogs dipped into the sturdy greasy wheels, and the single-trees and pulley-chains chirped clear and sweet as crickets. The dust flew, the whip cracked, and the men working swiftly to get the sheaves to the feeder or to take the straw away from the tail-end of the machine, were like warriors, urged to desperate action by battle cries. The stackers wallowing to their waists in the fluffy straw-pile seemed gnomes acting for our amusement.

The straw-pile! What delight we had in that! What joy it was to go up to the top where the men were stationed, one behind the other, and to have them toss huge forkfuls of the light fragrant stalks upon us, laughing to see us emerge from our golden cover. We were especially impressed by the bravery of Ed Green who stood in the midst of the thick dust and flying chaff close to the tail of the stacker. His teeth shone like a negro's out of his dust-blackened face and his shirt was wet with sweat, but he motioned for "more straw" and David, accepting the challenge, signalled for more speed. Frank swung his lash and yelled at the straining horses, the sleepy growl of the cylinder rose to a howl and the wheat came pulsing out at the spout in such a stream that the carriers were forced to trot on their path to and from the granary in order to keep the grain from piling up around the measurer.— There was a kind of splendid rivalry in this back-breaking toil— for each sack weighed ninety pounds.

We got tired of wallowing in the straw at last, and went down to help Rover catch the rats which were being uncovered by the pitchers as they reached the stack bottom.—The horses, with their straining, outstretched necks, the loud and cheery shouts, the whistling of the driver, the roar and hum of the great wheel, the flourishing of the forks, the supple movement of brawny arms, the shouts of the men, all blended with the wild sound of the wind in the creaking branches of the oaks, forming a glorious poem in our unforgetting minds.

At last the call for dinner sounded. The driver began to call, "Whoa there, boys! Steady, Tom," and to hold his long whip before the eyes of the more spirited of the teams in order to convince them that he really meant "stop." The pitchers stuck their forks upright in the stack and leaped to the ground. Randal, the band-cutter, drew from his wrist the looped string of his big knife, the stackers slid down from the straw-pile, and a race began among the teamsters to see whose span would be first unhitched and at the watering trough. What joyous rivalry it seemed to us!—

Mother and Mrs. Randal, wife of our neighbor, who was "changing works," stood ready to serve the food as soon as the men were seated.—The table had been lengthened to its utmost and pieced out with boards, and planks had been laid on stout wooden chairs at either side.

The men came in with a rush, and took seats wherever they could find them, and their attack on the boiled potatoes and chicken should have been appalling to the women, but it was not. They enjoyed seeing them eat. Ed Green was prodigious. One cut at a big potato, followed by two stabbing motions, and it was gone.—Two bites laid a leg of chicken as bare as a slate pencil. To us standing in the corner waiting our turn, it seemed that every "smitch" of the dinner was in danger, for the others were not far behind Ed and Dan.

At last even the gauntest of them filled up and left the room and we were free to sit at "the second table" and eat, while the men rested outside. David and William, however, generally had a belt to sew or a bent tooth to take out of the "concave." This seemed of grave dignity to us and we respected their self-sacrificing labor.

Nooning was brief. As soon as the horses had finished their oats, the roar and hum of the machine began again and continued steadily all the afternoon, till by and by the sun grew big and red, the night began to fall, and the wind died out.

This was the most impressive hour of a marvellous day. Through the falling dusk, the machine boomed steadily with a new sound, a solemn roar, rising at intervals to a rattling impatient yell as the cylinder ran momentarily empty. The men moved now in silence, looming dim and gigantic in the half-light. The straw-pile mountain high, the pitchers in the chaff, the feeder on his platform, and especially the driver on his power, seemed almost super-human to my childish eyes. Gray dust covered the handsome face of David, changing it into something both sad and stern, but Frank's cheery voice rang out musically as he called to the weary horses, "Come on, Tom! Hup there, Dan!"

The track in which they walked had been worn into two deep circles and they all moved mechanically round and round, like parts of a machine, dull-eyed and covered with sweat.

At last William raised the welcome cry, "All done!"—the men threw down their forks. Uncle Frank began to call in a gentle, soothing voice, "*Whoa,* lads! *Steady,* boys! Whoa, there!"

But the horses had been going so long and so steadily that they could not at once check their speed. They kept moving, though slowly, on and on till their owners slid from the stacks and seizing the ends of the sweeps, held them. Even then, after the power was still, the cylinder kept its hum, till David throwing a last sheaf into its open maw, choked it into silence.

Now came the sound of dropping chains, the clang of iron rods, and the thud of hoofs as the horses walked with laggard gait and weary down-falling heads to the barn. The men, more subdued than at dinner, washed with greater care, and combed the chaff from their beards. The air was still and cool, and the sky a deep cloudless blue starred with faint fire.

Supper though quiet was more dramatic than dinner had been. The table lighted with kerosene lamps, the clean white linen, the fragrant dishes, the women flying about with steaming platters, all seemed very cheery and very beautiful, and the men who came into the light and warmth of the kitchen with aching muscles and empty stomachs, seemed gentler and finer than at noon. They were nearly all from neighboring farms, and my mother treated even the few hired men like visitors, and the talk was all hearty and good tempered though a little subdued.

One by one the men rose and slipped away, and father withdrew to milk the cows and bed down the horses, leaving the women and the youngsters to eat what was left and "do up the dishes."

After we had eaten our fill Frank and I also went out to the barn (all wonderfully changed now to our minds by the great stack of straw), there to listen to David and father chatting as they rubbed their tired horses.—The lantern threw a dim red light on the harness and on the rumps of the cattle, but left mysterious shadows in the corners. I could hear the mice rustling in the straw of the roof, and from the farther end of the dimly-lighted shed came the regular *strim-stram* of the streams of milk falling into the bottom of a tin pail as the hired hand milked the big roan cow.

All this was very momentous to me as I sat on the oat box, shivering in the cold air, listening with all my ears, and when we finally went toward the house, the stars were big and sparkling. The frost had already begun to glisten on the fences and well-curb, and high in the air, dark against the sky, the turkeys were roosting uneasily, as if disturbed by premonitions of approaching Thanksgiving. Rover pattered along by my side on the crisp grass and my brother clung to my hand.

How bright and warm it was in the kitchen with mother putting things to rights while father and my uncles leaned their chairs against the wall and talked of the west and of moving. "I can't get away till after New Year's," father said. "But I'm going. I'll never put in another crop on these hills."

With speechless content I listened to Uncle William's stories of bears and Indians, and other episodes of frontier life, until at last we were ordered to bed and the glorious day was done.

Oh, those blessed days, those entrancing nights! How fine they were then, and how mellow they are now, for the slow-paced years have dropped nearly fifty other golden mists upon that far-off valley. From this distance I cannot understand how my father brought himself to leave that lovely farm and those good and noble friends.

6

David and His Violin

Most of the events of our last autumn in Green's Coulee have slipped into the fathomless gulf, but the experiences of Thanksgiving day, which followed closely on our threshing day, are in my treasure house. Like a canvas by Rembrandt only one side of the figures therein is defined, the other side melts away into shadow—a luminous shadow, through which faint light pulses, luring my wistful gaze on and on, back into the vanished world where the springs of my life lie hidden.

It is a raw November evening. Frank and Harriet and I are riding into a strange land in a clattering farm wagon. Father and mother are seated before us on the spring seat. The ground is frozen and the floor of the carriage pounds and jars. We cling to the iron-lined sides of the box to soften the blows. It is growing dark. Before us (in a similar vehicle) my Uncle David is leading the way. I catch momentary glimpses of him outlined against the pale yellow sky. He stands erect, holding the reins of his swiftly-moving horses in his powerful left hand. Occasionally he shouts back to my father, whose chin is buried in a thick buffalo-skin coat. Mother is only a vague mass, a figure wrapped in shawls. The wind is keen, the world gray and cheerless.

My sister is close beside me in the straw. Frank is asleep. I am on my knees looking ahead. Suddenly with rush of wind and clatter of hoofs, we enter the gloom of a forest and the road begins to climb. I see the hills on the right. I catch the sound of wheels on a bridge. I am cold. I snuggle down under the robes and the gurgle of ice-bound water is fused with my dreams.

I am roused at last by Uncle David's pleasant voice, "Wake up, boys, and pay y'r lodging!" I look out and perceive him standing beside the wheel. I see a house and I hear the sound of Deborah's voice from the warmly-lighted open door.

I climb down, heavy with cold and sleep. As I stand there my uncle reaches up his arms to take my mother down. Not knowing that she has a rheumatic elbow, he squeezes her playfully. She gives a sharp scream, and his team starts away on a swift run around the curve of the road toward the gate. Dropping my mother, he dashes across the yard to intercept the runaways. We all stand in silence, watching the flying horses and the wonderful race he is making toward the gate. He runs with magnificent action, his head thrown high. As the team dashes through the gate his outflung left hand catches the end-board of the wagon,—he leaps into the box, and so passes from our sight.

We go into the cottage. It is a small building with four rooms and a kitchen on the ground floor, but in the sitting room we come upon an open fireplace—the first I had ever seen, and in the light of it sits Grandfather McClintock, the glory of the flaming logs gilding the edges of his cloud of bushy white hair. He does not rise to greet us, but smiles and calls out, "Come in! Come in! Draw a cheer. Sit ye down."

A clamor of welcome fills the place. Harriet and I are put to warm before the blaze. Grandad takes Frank upon his knee and the cutting wind of the gray outside world is forgotten.

This house in which the McClintocks were living at this time, belonged to a rented farm. Grandad had sold the original homestead on the LaCrosse River, and David who had lately married a charming young Canadian girl, was the head of the family. Deborah, it seems, was also living with him and Frank was there—as a visitor probably.

The room in which we sat was small and bare but to me it was very beautiful, because of the fire, and by reason of the merry voices which filled my ears with music. Aunt Rebecca brought to us a handful of crackers and told us that we were to have oyster soup for supper. This gave us great pleasure even in anticipation, for oysters were a delicious treat in those days.

"Well, Dick," Grandad began, "so ye're plannin' to go west, air ye?"

"Yes, as soon as I get all my grain and hogs marketed I'm going to pull out for my new farm over in Iowa."

"Ye'd better stick to the old coulee," warned my grandfather, a touch of sadness in his voice. "Ye'll find none better."

My father was disposed to resent this. "That's all very well for the few who have the level land in the middle of the valley," he retorted, "but how about those of us who are crowded against the hills? You should see the farm I have in Winneshiek! Not a hill on it big enough for a boy to coast on. It's right on the edge of Looking Glass Prairie, and I have a spring of water, and a fine grove of trees just where I want them, not where they have to be grubbed out."

"But ye belong here," repeated Grandfather. "You were married here, your children were born here. Ye'll find no such friends in the west as you have here in Neshonoc. And Belle will miss the family."

My father laughed. "Oh, you'll all come along. Dave has the fever already. Even William is likely to catch it."

Old Hugh sighed deeply. "I hope ye're wrong," he said. "I'd like to spend me last days here with me sons and daughters around me, sich as are left to me," here his voice became sterner. "It's the curse of our country,—this constant moving, moving. I'd have been better off had I stayed in Ohio, though this valley seemed very beautiful to me the first time I saw it."

At this point David came in, and everybody shouted, "Did you stop them?" referring of course to the runaway team.

"I did," he replied with a smile. "But how about the oysters. I'm holler as a beech log."

The fragrance of the soup thoroughly awakened even little Frank, and when we drew around the table, each face shone with the light of peace and plenty, and all our elders tried to forget that this was the last Thanksgiving festival which the McClintocks and Garlands would be able to enjoy in the old valley. How good those oysters were! They made up the entire meal,—excepting mince pie which came as a closing sweet.

Slowly, one by one, the men drew back and returned to the sitting room, leaving the women to wash up the dishes and put the kitchen to rights. David seized the opportunity to ask my father to tell once again of the trip he had made, of the lands he had seen, and the farm he had purchased, for his young heart was also fired with desire of exploration. The level lands toward the sunset allured him. In his visions the wild meadows were filled with game, and the free lands needed only to be tickled with a hoe to laugh into harvest.

He said, "As soon as Dad and Frank are settled on a farm here,

I'm going west also. I'm as tired of climbing these kills as you are. I want a place of my own—and besides, from all you say of that wheat country out there, a threshing machine would pay wonderfully well."

As the women came in, my father called out, "Come, Belle, sing 'O'er the Hills in Legions Boys!'—Dave get out your fiddle—and tune us all up."

David tuned up his fiddle and while he twanged on the strings mother lifted her voice in our fine old marching song.

> Cheer up, brothers, as we go,
> O'er the mountains, westward ho—

and we all joined in the jubilant chorus—

> Then o'er the hills in legions, boys,
> Fair freedom's star
> Points to the sunset regions, boys,
> Ha, ha, ha-ha!—

My father's face shone with the light of the explorer, the pioneer. The words of this song appealed to him as the finest poetry. It meant all that was fine and hopeful and buoyant in American life, to him—but on my mother's sweet face a wistful expression deepened and in her fine eyes a reflective shadow lay. To her this song meant not so much the acquisition of a new home as the loss of all her friends and relatives. She sang it submissively, not exultantly, and I think the other women were of the same mood though their faces were less expressive to me. To all of the pioneer wives of the past that song had meant deprivation, suffering, loneliness, heartache.

From this they passed to other of my father's favorite songs, and it is highly significant to note that even in this choice of songs he generally had his way. He was the dominating force. "Sing 'Nellie Wildwood,'" he said, and they sang it.—This power of getting his will respected was due partly to his military training but more to a distinctive trait in him. He was a man of power, of decision, a natural commander of men.

They sang "Minnie Minturn" to his request, and the refrain,—

> I have heard the angels warning,
> I have seen the golden shore—

meant much to me. So did the line,

But I only hear the drummers
As the armies march away.

Aunt Deb was also a soul of decision. She called out, "No more of these sad tones," and struck up "The Year of Jubilo," and we all shouted till the walls shook with the exultant words:

Ol' massa run—ha-ha!
De darkies stay—ho-ho!
It must be now is the kingdom a-comin'
In the year of Jubilo.

At this point the fire suggested an old English ballad which I loved, and so I piped up, "Mother, sing, 'Pile the Wood on Higher!' " and she complied with pleasure, for this was a song of home, of the unbroken fire-side circle.

Oh, the winds howl mad outdoors
  The snow clouds hurry past,
The giant trees sway to and fro
  Beneath the sweeping blast.

and we children joined in the chorus:

Then we'll gather round the fire
  And we'll pile the wood on higher,
Let the song and jest go round;
  What care we for the storm,
  When the fireside is so warm,
  And pleasure here is found?

Never before did this song mean so much to me as at this moment when the winds were actually howling outdoors, and Uncle Frank was in very truth piling the logs higher. It seemed as though my stuffed bosom could not receive anything deeper and finer, but it did, for father was saying, "Well, Dave, now for some *tunes*."

This was the best part of David to me. He could make any room mystical with the magic of his bow. True, his pieces were mainly venerable dance tunes, cotillions, hornpipes,—melodies which had passed from fiddler to fiddler until they had become veritable folksongs—pieces like "Money Musk," "Honest John," "Haste to the Wedding," and many others whose names I have forgotten, but with a gift of putting into even the simplest song an emotion which subdued us and silenced us, he played on, absorbed and intent. From these familiar pieces he passed to others for which he had no names; melodies strangely sweet and sad, full of longing cries, voicing something which I dimly felt but could not understand.

At the moment he was the somber Scotch Highlander, the true Celt, and as he bent above his instrument his black eyes glowing, his fine head drooping low, my heart bowed down in worship of his skill. He was my hero, the handsomest, most romantic figure in all my world.

He played, "Maggie, Air Ye Sleepin," and the wind outside went to my soul. Voices wailed to me out of the illimitable hill-land forests, voices that pleaded:

> Oh, let me in, for loud the linn
> Goes roarin' o'er the moorland craggy.

He appeared to forget us, even his young wife. His eyes looked away into gray storms. Vague longing ached in his throat. Life was a struggle, love a torment.

He stopped abruptly, and put the violin into its box, fumbling with the catch to hide his emotion and my father broke the tense silence with a prosaic word. "Well, well! Look here, it's time you youngsters were asleep. Beckie, where are you going to put these children?"

Aunt Rebecca, a trim little woman with brown eyes, looked at us reflectively, "Well, now, I don't know. I guess we'll have to make a bed for them on the floor."

This was done, and for the first time in my life, I slept before an open fire. As I snuggled into my blankets with my face turned to the blaze, the darkness of the night and the denizens of the pineland wilderness to the north had no terrors for me.

I was awakened in the early light by Uncle David building the fire, and then came my father's call, and the hurly burly of jovial greeting from old and young. The tumult lasted till breakfast was called, and everybody who could find place sat around the table and attacked the venison and potatoes which formed the meal. I do not remember our leave-taking or the ride homeward. I bring to mind only the desolate cold of our own kitchen into which we tramped late in the afternoon, sitting in our wraps until the fire began to roar within its iron cage.

Oh, winds of the winter night! Oh, firelight and the shine of tender eyes! How far away you seem tonight!

> So faint and far,
> Each dear face shineth as a star.

Oh, you by the western sea, and you of the south beyond the reach of Christmas snow, do not your hearts hunger, like mine tonight for that Thanksgiving Day among the trees? For the glance of eyes undimmed of tears, for the hair untouched with gray?

It all lies in the unchanging realm of the past—this land of my childhood. Its charm, its strange dominion cannot return save in the poet's reminiscent dream. No money, no railway train can take us back to it. It did not in truth exist—it was a magical world, born of the vibrant union of youth and firelight, of music and the voice of moaning winds—a union which can never come again to you or me, father, uncle, brother, till the coulee meadows bloom again unscarred of spade or plow.

7

Winnesheik "Woods and Prairie Lands"

Our last winter in the Coulee was given over to preparations for our removal but it made very little impression on my mind which was deeply engaged on my school work. As it was out of the question for us to attend the village school the elders arranged for a neighborhood school at the home of John Roche, who had an unusually large living room. John is but a shadowy figure in this chronicle but his daughter Indiana, whom we called "Ingie," stands out as the big girl of my class.

Books were scarce in this house as well as in our own. I remember piles of newspapers but no bound volumes other than the Bible and certain small Sunday school books. All the homes of the valley were equally barren. My sister and I jointly possessed a very limp and soiled cloth edition of "Mother Goose." Our stories all came to us by way of the conversation of our elders. No one but grandmother Garland ever deliberately told us a tale except the hired girls, and their romances were of such dark and gruesome texture that we often went to bed shivering with fear of the dark.

Suddenly, unexpectedly, miraculously, I came into possession of two books, one called *Beauty and The Beast,* and the other *Aladdin and His Wonderful Lamp*. These volumes mark a distinct epoch in my life. The grace of the lovely Lady as she stood above the cringing Beast gave me my first clear notion of feminine dignity and charm. On the magic Flying Carpet I rose into the wide air of Oriental romance. I attended the building of towered cities and the laying of gorgeous feasts. I carried in my hand the shell from which, at the word of command, the cool clear water gushed. My feet were shod with winged boots, and on my head was the Cap of Invisibility. My body was captive in our snow-bound little cabin but my mind ranged the golden palaces of Persia—so much I know. Where the wonder-working romances came from I cannot now tell but I think they were Christmas presents, for Christmas came this year with unusual splendor.

The sale of the farm had put into my father's hands a considerable sum of money and I assume that some small part of this went to make our holiday glorious. In one of my stockings was a noble red and blue tin horse with a flowing mane and tail, and in the other was a monkey who could be made to climb a stick. Harriet had a new china doll and Frank a horn and china dog, and all the corners of our stockings were stuffed with nuts and candies. I hope mother got something beside the potatoes and onions which I remember seeing her pull out and unwrap with delightful humor—an old and rather pathetic joke but new to us.

The snow fell deep in January and I have many glorious pictures of the whirling flakes outlined against the darkly wooded hills across the marsh. Father was busy with his team drawing off wheat and hogs and hay, and often came into the house at night, white with the storms through which he had passed. My trips to school were often interrupted by the cold, and the path which my sister and I trod was along the ever-deepening furrows made by the bob-sleighs of the farmers. Often when we met a team or were overtaken by one, we were forced out of the road into the drifts, and I can feel to this moment, the wedge of snow which caught in the tops of my tall boots and slowly melted into my gray socks.

We were not afraid of the drifts, however. On the contrary mother had to fight to keep us from wallowing beyond our depth. I had now a sled which was my inseparable companion. I could not feed the hens or bring in a pan of chips without taking it with me. My heart swelled with pride and joy whenever I regarded it, and yet it was but a sober-colored thing, a frame of hickory built by the village blacksmith in exchange for a cord of wood—delivered. I took it to school one day, but Ed Roche abused it, took it up and threw it into the deep snow among the weeds.—Had I been large enough, I would have killed that boy with pleasure, but being small and fat and numb with cold I merely rescued my treasure as quickly as I could and hurried home to pour my indignant story into my mother's sympathetic ears.

I seldom spoke of my defeats to my father for he had once said, "Fight your own battles, my son. If I hear of your being licked by a boy of anything like your own size, I'll give you another when you get home." He didn't believe in molly-coddling, you will perceive. His was a stern school, the school of self-reliance and resolution.

Neighbors came in now and again to talk of our migration, and yet in spite of all that, in spite of our song, in spite of my father's preparation I had no definite premonition of coming change, and when the day of departure actually dawned, I was as surprised, as unprepared as though it had all happened without the slightest warning.

So long as the kettle sang on the hearth and the clock ticked on its shelf, the idea of "moving" was pleasantly diverting, but when one raw winter day I saw the faithful clock stuffed with rags and laid on its back in a box, and the chairs and dishes being loaded into a big sleigh, I began to experience something very disturbing and very uncomfortable. "O'er the hills in legions, boys," did not sound so inspiring to me then. "The woods and prairie lands" of Iowa became of less account to me than the little cabin in which I had lived all my short life.

Harriet and I wandered around, whining and shivering, our own misery augmented by the worried look on mother's face. It was February, and she very properly resented leaving her home for a long, cold ride into an unknown world, but as a dutiful wife she worked hard and silently in packing away her treasures, and clothing her children for the journey.

At last the great sleigh-load of bedding and furniture stood ready at the door, the stove, still warm with cheerful service, was lifted in, and the time for saying good-bye to our coulee home had come.

"Forward march!" shouted father and led the way with the big bob-sled, followed by cousin Jim and our little herd of kine, while mother and the children brought up the rear in a "pung" drawn by old Josh, a flea-bit gray.—It is probable that at the moment the master himself was slightly regretful.

A couple of hours' march brought us to LaCrosse, the great city whose wonders I had longed to confront. It stood on the bank of a wide river and had all the value of a sea-port to me for in summer-time great hoarsely bellowing steamboats came and went from its quay, and all about it rose high wooded hills. Halting there, we overlooked a wide expanse of snow-covered ice in the midst of which a dark, swift, threatening current of open water ran. Across this chasm stretching from one ice-field to another lay a flexible narrow bridge over which my father led the way toward hills of the western shore. There was something especially terrifying in the boiling heave of that black flood, and I shivered with terror as I passed it, having vividly in my mind certain grim stories of men whose teams had broken through and been swept beneath the ice never to reappear.

It was a long ride to my mother, for she too was in terror of the ice, but at last the Minnesota bank was reached, La Crescent was passed, and our guide entering a narrow valley began to climb the snowy hills. All that was familiar was put behind; all that was strange and dark, all that was wonderful and unknown, spread out before us, and as we crawled along that slippery, slanting road, it seemed that we were entering on a new and marvellous world.

We lodged that night in Hokah, a little town in a deep valley. The tavern stood near a river which flowed over its dam with resounding roar and to its sound I slept. Next day at noon we reached Caledonia, a town high on the snowy prairie. Caledonia! For years that word was a poem in my ear, part of a marvellous and epic march. Actually it consisted of a few frame houses and a grocery store. But no matter. Its name shall ring like a peal of bells in this book.

It grew colder as we rose, and that night, the night of the second day, we reached Hesper and entered a long stretch of woods, and at last turned in towards a friendly light shining from a low house beneath a splendid oak.

As we drew near my father raised a signal shout, "Hallo-o-o the House!" and a man in a long gray coat came out. "Is that thee, friend Richard?" he called, and my father replied, "Yea, neighbor Barley, here we are!"

I do not know how this stranger whose manner of speech was so peculiar, came to be there, but he was and in answer to my question, father replied, "Barley is a Quaker," an answer which explained nothing at that time. Being too sleepy to pursue the matter, or to remark upon anything connected with the exterior, I dumbly followed Harriet into the kitchen which was still in possession of good Mrs. Barley.

Having filled our stomachs with warm food mother put us to bed, and when we awoke late the next day the Barleys were gone, our own stove was in its place, and our faithful dock was ticking calmly on the shelf. So far as we knew, mother was again at home and entirely content.

This farm, which was situated two miles west of the village of Hesper, immediately won our love. It was a glorious place for boys. Broad-armed white oaks stood about the yard, and to the east and north a deep forest invited to exploration. The house was of logs and for that reason was much more attractive to us than to our mother. It was, I suspect, both dark and cold. I know the roof was poor, for one morning I awoke to find a miniature peak of snow on the floor at my bedside. It was only a rude little frontier cabin, but it was perfectly satisfactory to me.

Harriet and I learned much in the way of woodcraft during the months which followed. Night by night the rabbits, in countless numbers printed their tell-tale records in the snow, and quail and partridges nested beneath the down-drooping branches of the red oaks. Squirrels ran from tree to tree and we were soon able to distinguish and name most of the tracks made by the birds and small animals, and we took a never-failing delight in this study of the wild. In most of my excursions my sister was my companion. My brother was too small.

All my memories of this farm are of the fiber of poetry. The silence of the snowy aisles of the forest, the whirring flight of partridges, the impudent bark of squirrels, the quavering voices of owls and coons, the music of the winds in the high trees,—all these impressions unite in my mind like parts of a woodland symphony. I soon learned to distinguish the raccoon's mournful call from the quavering cry of the owl, and I joined the hired man in hunting rabbits from under the piles of brush in the clearing. Once or twice some ferocious, larger animal, possibly a panther, hungrily yowled in the impenetrable thickets to the north, but this only lent a still more enthralling interest to the forest.

To the east, an hour's walk through the timber, stood the village, built and named by the "Friends" who had a meeting house not far away, and though I saw much of them, I never attended their services.

Our closest neighbor was a gruff loud-voiced old Norwegian

and from his children (our playmates) we learned many curious facts. All Norwegians, it appeared, ate from wooden plates or wooden bowls. Their food was soup which they called "bean swaagen" and they were all yellow haired and blue-eyed.

Harriet and I and one Lars Peterson gave a great deal of time to an attempt to train a yoke of yearling calves to draw our handsled. I call it an attempt, for we hardly got beyond a struggle to overcome the stubborn resentment of the stupid beasts, who very naturally objected to being forced into service before their time. Harriet was ten, I was not quite nine, and Lars was only twelve, hence we spent long hours in yoking and unyoking our unruly span. I believe we did actually haul several loads of firewood to the kitchen door, but at last Buck and Brin "turned the yoke" and broke it, and that ended our teaming.

The man from whom we acquired our farm had in some way domesticated a flock of wild geese, and though they must have been a part of the farm-yard during the winter, they made no deep impression on my mind till in the spring when as the migratory instinct stirred in their blood they all rose on the surface of the water in a little pool near the barn and with beating wings lifted their voices in brazen clamor calling to their fellows driving by high overhead. At times their cries halted the flocks in their arrowy flight and brought them down to mix indistinguishably with the captive birds.

The wings of these had been clipped but as the weeks went on their pinions grew again and one morning when I went out to see what had happened to them, I found the pool empty and silent. We all missed their fine voices and yet we could not blame them for a reassertion of their freeborn nature. They had gone back to their summer camping grounds on the lakes of the far north.

Early in April my father hired a couple of raw Norwegians to assist in clearing the land, and although neither of these immigrants could speak a word of English, I was greatly interested in them. They slept in the granary but this did not prevent them from communicating to our house-maid a virulent case of smallpox. Several days passed before my mother realized what ailed the girl. The discovery must have horrified her, for she had been through an epidemic of this dread disease in Wisconsin, and knew its danger.

It was a fearsome plague in those days, much more fatal than now, and my mother with three unvaccinated children, a helpless handmaid to be nursed, was in despair when father developed the disease and took to his bed. Surely it must have seemed to her as though the Lord had visited upon her more punishment than belonged to her, for to add the final touch, in the midst of all her other afflictions she was expecting the birth of another child.

I do not know what we would have done had not a noble woman of the neighborhood volunteered to come in and help us. She was not a friend, hardly an acquaintance, and yet she served us like an angel of mercy. Whether she still lives or not I cannot say, but I wish to acknowledge here the splendid heroism which brought Mary Briggs, a stranger, into our stricken home at a time when all our other neighbors beat their horses into a mad gallop whenever forced to pass our gate.

Young as I was I realized something of the burden which had fallen upon my mother, and when one night I was awakened from deep sleep by hearing her calling out in pain, begging piteously for help, I shuddered in my bed, realizing with childish, intuitive knowledge that she was passing through a cruel convulsion which could not be softened or put aside. I went to sleep again at last, and when I woke, I had a little sister.

Harriet and I having been vaccinated, escaped with what was called the "verylide" but father was ill for several weeks. Fortunately he was spared, as we all were, the "pitting" which usually follows this dreaded disease, and in a week or two we children had forgotten all about it. Spring was upon us and the world was waiting to be explored.

One of the noblest features of this farm was a large spring which boiled forth from the limestone rock about eighty rods north of the house, and this was a wonder-spot to us. There was something magical in this never-failing fountain, and we loved to play beside its waters. One of our delightful tasks was riding the horses to water at this spring, and I took many lessons in horsemanship on these trips.

As the seeding time came on, enormous flocks of pigeons, in clouds which almost filled the sky, made it necessary for some one to sentinel the new-sown grain, and although I was but nine years of age, my father put a double-barrelled shotgun into my hands, and sent me out to defend the fields.

This commission filled me with the spirit of the soldier. Proudly walking my rounds I menaced the flocks as they circled warily over my head, taking shot at them now and again as they came near enough, feeling as duty bound and as martial as any Roman sentry standing guard over a city. Up to this time I had not been allowed to carry arms, although I had been the companion of Den Green and Ellis Usher on their hunting expeditions in the coulee—now with entire discretion over my weapon, I loaded it, capped it and fired it, marching with sedate and manly tread, while little Frank at my heels, served as subordinate in his turn.

The pigeons passed after a few days, but my warlike duties continued, for the ground-squirrels, called "gophers" by the settlers, were almost as destructive of the seed corn as the pigeons had been of the wheat. Day after day I patrolled the edge of the field listening to the saucy whistle of the striped little rascals, tracking them to their burrows and shooting them as they lifted their heads above the ground. I had moments of being sorry for them, but the sight of one digging up the seed, silenced my complaining conscience and I continued to slay.

The school-house of this district stood out upon the prairie to the west a mile distant, and during May we trudged our way over a pleasant road, each carrying a small tin pail filled with luncheon. Here I came in contact with the Norwegian boys from the colony to the north, and a bitter feud arose (or existed) between the "Yankees," as they called us, and "the Norskies,"as we called them. Often when we met on the road, showers of sticks and stones filled the air, and our hearts burned with the heat of savage conflict. War usually broke out at the moment of parting. Often after a fairly amicable half-mile together we suddenly split into hostile ranks, and warred with true tribal frenzy as long as we could find a stone or a clod to serve as missile. I had no personal animosity in this, I was merely a Pict willing to destroy my Angle enemies.

As I look back upon my life on that woodland farm, it all seems very colorful and sweet. I am re-living days when the warm sun, falling on radiant slopes of grass, lit the meadow phlox and tall tiger lilies into flaming torches of color. I think of blackberry thickets and odorous grapevines and cherry trees and the delicious nuts which grew in profusion throughout the forest to the north. This forest which seemed endless and was of enchanted solemnity served as our wilderness. We explored it at every opportunity. We loved every day for the color it brought, each season for the wealth of its experience, and we welcomed the thought of spending all our years in this beautiful home where the wood and the prairie of our song did actually meet and mingle.

8

We Move Again

One day there came into our home a strange man who spoke in a fashion new to me. He was a middle-aged rather formal individual, dressed in a rough gray suit, and father alluded to him privately as "that English duke." I didn't know exactly what he meant by this, but our visitor's talk gave me a vague notion of "the old country."

"My home," he said, "is near Manchester. I have come to try farming in the American wilderness."

He was kindly, and did his best to be democratic, but we children stood away from him, wondering what he was doing in our house. My mother disliked him from the start for as he took his seat at our dinner table, he drew from his pocket a case in which he carried a silver fork and spoon and a silver-handled knife. Our cutlery was not good enough for him!

Every family that we knew at that time used three-tined steel forks and my mother naturally resented the implied criticism of her table ware. I heard her say to my father, "If our ways don't suit your English friend he'd better go somewhere else for his meals."

This fastidious pioneer also carried a revolver, for he believed that having penetrated far into a dangerous country, he was in danger, and I am not at all sure but that he was right, for the Minnesota woods at this time were filled with horse-thieves and counterfeiters, and it was known that many of these landhunting Englishmen carried large sums of gold on their persons.

We resented our guest still more when we found that he was trying to buy our lovely farm and that father was already half-persuaded. We loved this farm. We loved the log house, and the oaks which sheltered it, and we especially valued the glorious spring and the plum trees which stood near it, but father was still dreaming of the free lands of the farther west, and early in March he sold to the Englishman and moved us all to a rented place some six miles directly west, in the township of Burr Oak.

This was but a temporary lodging, a kind of camping place, for no sooner were his fields seeded than he set forth once again with a covered wagon, eager to explore the open country to the north and west of us. The wood and prairie land of Winnishiek County did not satisfy him, although it seemed to me then, as it does now, the fulfillment of his vision, the realization of our song.

For several weeks he travelled through southern Minnesota and northern Iowa, always in search of the perfect farm, and when he returned, just before harvest, he was able to report that he had purchased a quarter section of "the best land in Mitchell County" and that after harvest we would all move again.

If my mother resented this third removal she made no comment which I can now recall. I suspect that she went rather willingly this time, for her brother David wrote that he had also located in Mitchell County, not two miles from the place my father had decided upon for our future home, and Samantha, her younger sister, had settled in Minnesota. The circle in Neshonoc seemed about to break up. A mighty spreading and shifting was going on all over the west, and no doubt my mother accepted her part in it without especial protest.

Our life in Burr Oak township that summer was joyous for us children. It seems to have been almost all sunshine and play. As I reflect upon it I relive many delightful excursions into the northern woods. It appears that Harriet and I were in continual harvest of nuts and berries. Our walks to school were explorations and we spent nearly every Saturday and Sunday in minute study of the country-side, devouring everything which was remotely edible. We gorged upon May-apples until we were ill, and munched black cherries until we were dizzy with their fumes. We clambered high trees to collect baskets of wild grapes which our mother could not use, and we garnered nuts with the insatiable greed of squirrels. We ate oak-shoots, fern-roots, leaves, bark, seed-balls,—everything!—not because we were hungry but because we loved to experiment and we came home, only when hungry or worn out or in awe of the darkness.

It was a delightful season, full of the most satisfying companionship and yet of the names of my playmates I can seize upon only two—the others have faded from the tablets of my memory. I remember Ned who permitted me to hold his plow, and Perry who taught me how to tame the half-wild colts that filled his father's pasture. Together we spent long days lassoing—or rather snaring—the feet of these horses and subduing them to the halter. We had many fierce struggles but came out of them all without a serious injury.

Late in August my father again loaded our household goods into wagons, and with our small herd of cattle following, set out toward the west, bound once again to overtake the actual line of the middle border.

This journey has an unforgettable epic charm as I look back upon it. Each mile took us farther and farther into the unsettled prairie until in the afternoon of the second day, we came to a meadow so wide that its western rim touched the sky without revealing a sign of man's habitation other than the road in which we travelled.

The plain was covered with grass tall as ripe wheat and when my father stopped his team and came back to us and said, "Well, children, here we are on The Big Prairie," we looked about us with awe, so endless seemed this spread of wild oats and waving blue-joint.

Far away dim clumps of trees showed, but no chimney was in sight, and no living thing moved save our own cattle and the hawks lazily wheeling in the air. My heart filled with awe as well as wonder. The majesty of this primeval world exalted me. I felt for the first time the poetry of the unplowed spaces. It seemed that the "herds of deer and buffalo" of our song might, at any moment, present themselves,—but they did not, and my father took no account even of the marsh fowl.

"Forward march!" he shouted, and on we went.

Hour after hour he pushed into the west, the heads of his tired horses hanging ever lower, and on my mother's face the shadow deepened, but her chieftain's voice cheerily urging his team lost nothing of its clarion resolution. He was in his element. He loved this shelterless sweep of prairie. This westward march entranced him, I think he would have gladly kept on until the snowy wall of the Rocky Mountains met his eyes, for he was a natural explorer.

Sunset came at last, but still he drove steadily on through the sparse settlements. Just at nightfall we came to a beautiful little stream, and stopped to let the horses drink. I heard its rippling, reassuring song on the pebbles. Thereafter all is dim and vague to me until my mother called out sharply, "Wake up, children! Here we are!"

Struggling to my feet I looked about me. Nothing could be seen but the dim form of a small house.—On every side the land melted into blackness, silent and without boundary.

Driving into the yard, father hastily unloaded one of the wagons and taking mother and Harriet and Jessie drove away to spend the night with Uncle David who had preceded us, as I now learned, and was living on a farm not far away. My brother and I were left to camp as best we could with the hired man.

Spreading a rude bed on the floor, he told us to "hop in" and in ten minutes we were all fast asleep.

The sound of a clattering poker awakened me next morning and when I opened my sleepy eyes and looked out a new world displayed itself before me.

The cabin faced a level plain with no tree in sight. A mile away to the west stood a low stone house and immediately in front of us opened a half-section of unfenced sod. To the north, as far as I could see, the land billowed like a russet ocean, with scarcely a roof to fleck its lonely spread.—I cannot say that I liked or disliked it. I merely marvelled at it, and while I wandered about the yard, the hired man scorched some cornmeal mush in a skillet and this with some butter and gingerbread, made up my first breakfast in Mitchell County.

An hour or two later father and mother and the girls returned and the work of setting up the stove and getting the furniture in place began. In a very short time the experienced clock was voicing its contentment on a new shelf, and the kettle was singing busily on its familiar stove. Once more and for the sixth time since her marriage, Belle Garland adjusted herself to a pioneer environment, comforted no doubt by the knowledge that David and Deborah were near and that her father was coming soon. No doubt she also congratulated herself on the fact that she had not been carried beyond the Missouri River—and that her house was not "surrounded by Indians who murder by night."

A few hours later, while my brother and I were on the roof of the house with intent to peer "over the edge of the prairie" something grandly significant happened. Upon a low hill to the west a herd of horses suddenly appeared running swiftly, led by a beautiful sorrel pony with shining white mane. On they came, like a platoon of cavalry rushing down across the open sod which lay before our door. The leader moved with lofty and graceful action, easily out-stretching all his fellows. Forward they swept, their long tails floating in the wind like banners,—on in a great curve as if scenting danger in the smoke of our fire. The thunder of their feet filled me with delight. Surely, next to a herd of buffalo this squadron of wild horses was the most satisfactory evidence of the wilderness into which we had been thrust.

Riding as if to intercept the leader, a solitary herder now appeared, mounted upon a horse which very evidently was the mate of the leader. He rode magnificently, and under him the lithe mare strove resolutely to overtake and head off the leader.—All to no purpose! The halterless steeds of the prairie snorted derisively at their former companion, bridled and saddled, and carrying the weight of a master. Swiftly they thundered across the sod, dropped into a ravine, and disappeared in a cloud of dust.

Silently we watched the rider turn and ride slowly homeward. The plain had become our new domain, the horseman our ideal.

9

Our First Winter on the Prairie

For a few days my brother and I had little to do other than to keep the cattle from straying, and we used our leisure in becoming acquainted with the region round about.

It burned deep into our memories, this wide, sunny, windy country. The sky so big, and the horizon line so low and so far away, made this new world of the plain more majestic than the world of the Coulee.—The grasses and many of the flowers were also new to us. On the uplands the herbage was short and dry and the plants stiff and woody, but in the swales the wild oat shook its quivers of barbed and twisted arrows, and the crow's foot, tall and sere, bowed softly under the feet of the wind, while everywhere, in the lowlands as well as on the ridges, the bleaching white antlers of by-gone herbivora lay scattered, testifying to "the herds of deer and buffalo" which once fed there. We were just a few years too late to see them.

To the south the sections were nearly all settled upon, for in that direction lay the county town, but to the north and on into Minnesota rolled the unplowed sod, the feeding ground of the cattle, the home of foxes and wolves, and to the west, just beyond the highest ridges, we loved to think the bison might still be seen.

The cabin on this rented farm was a mere shanty, a shell of pine boards, which needed re-enforcing to make it habitable and one day my father said, "Well, Hamlin, I guess you'll have to run the plow-team this fall. I must help neighbor Button wall up the house and I can't afford to hire another man."

This seemed a fine commission for a lad of ten, and I drove my horses into the field that first morning with a manly pride which added an inch to my stature. I took my initial "round" at a "land" which stretched from one side of the quarter section to the other, in confident mood. I was grown up!

But alas! my sense of elation did not last long. To guide a team for a few minutes as an experiment was one thing—to plow all day like a hired hand was another. It was not a chore, it was a job. It meant moving to and fro hour after hour, day after day, with no one to talk to but the horses. It meant trudging eight or nine miles in the forenoon and as many more in the afternoon, with less than an hour off at noon. It meant dragging the heavy implement around the corners, and it meant also many ship-wrecks, for the thick, wet stubble matted with wild buckwheat often rolled up between the coulter and the standard and threw the share completely out of the ground, making it necessary for me to halt the team and jerk the heavy plow backward for a new start.

Although strong and active I was rather short, even for a ten-year-old, and to reach the plow handles I was obliged to lift my hands above my shoulders; and so with the guiding lines crossed over my back and my worn straw hat bobbing just above the cross-brace I must have made a comical figure. At any rate nothing like it had been seen in the neighborhood and the people on the road to town looking across the field, laughed and called to me, and neighbor Button said to my father in my hearing, "That chap's too young to run a plow," a judgment which pleased and flattered me greatly.

Harriet cheered me by running out occasionally to meet me as I turned the nearest corner, and sometimes Frank consented to go all the way around, chatting breathlessly as he trotted along behind. At other times he was prevailed upon to bring to me a cookie and a glass of milk, a deed which helped to shorten the forenoon. And yet, notwithstanding all these ameliorations, plowing became tedious.

The flies were savage, especially in the middle of the day, and the horses, tortured by their lances, drove badly, twisting and turning in their despairing rage. Their tails were continually getting over the lines, and in stopping to kick their tormentors from their bellies they often got astride the traces, and in other ways made trouble for me. Only in the early morning or when the sun sank low at night were they able to move quietly along their ways.

The soil was the kind my father had been seeking, a smooth dark sandy loam, which made it possible for a lad to do the work of a man. Often the share would go the entire "round" without striking a root or a pebble as big as a walnut, the steel running steadily with a crisp craunching ripping sound which I rather liked to hear. In truth work would have been quite tolerable had it not been so long drawn out. Ten hours of it even on a fine day made about twice too many for a boy.

Meanwhile I cheered myself in every imaginable way. I whistled. I sang. I studied the clouds. I gnawed the beautiful red skin from the seed vessels which hung upon the wild rose bushes, and I counted the prairie chickens as they began to come together in winter flocks running through the stubble in search of food. I stopped now and again to examine the lizards unhoused by the share, tormenting them to make them sweat their milky drops (they were curiously repulsive to me), and I measured the little granaries of wheat which the mice and gophers had deposited deep under the ground, storehouses which the plow had violated. My eyes dwelt enviously upon the sailing hawk, and on the passing of ducks. The occasional shadowy figure of a prairie wolf made me wish for Uncle David and his rifle.

On certain days nothing could cheer me. When the bitter wind blew from the north, and the sky was filled with wild geese racing southward, with swiftly-hurrying clouds, winter seemed about to spring upon me. The horses' tails streamed in the wind. Flurries of snow covered me with clinging flakes, and the mud "gummed" my boots and trouser legs, clogging my steps. At such times I suffered from cold and loneliness—all sense of being a man evaporated. I was just a little boy, longing for the leisure of boyhood.

Day after day, through the month of October and deep into November, I followed that team, turning over two acres of stubble each day. I would not believe this without proof, but it is true! At last it grew so cold that in the early morning everything was white with frost and I was obliged to put one hand in my pocket to keep it warm, while holding the plow with the other, but I didn't mind this so much, for it hinted at the close of autumn. I've no doubt facing the wind in this way was excellent discipline, but I didn't think it necessary then and my heart was sometimes bitter and rebellious.

The soldier did not intend to be severe. As he had always been an early riser and a busy toiler it seemed perfectly natural and good discipline, that his sons should also plow and husk corn at ten years of age. He often told of beginning life as a "bound boy" at nine, and these stories helped me to perform my own tasks without whining. I feared to voice my weakness.

At last there came a morning when by striking my heel upon the ground I convinced my boss that the soil was frozen too deep for the mold-board to break. "All right," he said, "you may lay off this forenoon."

Oh, those beautiful hours of respite! With time to play or read I usually read, devouring anything I could lay my hands upon. Newspapers, whether old or new, or pasted on the wall or piled up in the attic,—anything in print was wonderful to me. One enthralling book, borrowed from Neighbor Button, was *The Female Spy,* a Tale of the Rebellion. Another treasure was a story called *Cast Ashore,* but this volume unfortunately was badly torn and fifty pages were missing so that I never knew, and do not know to this day, how those indomitable shipwrecked seamen reached their English homes. I dimly recall that one man carried a pet monkey on his back and that they all lived on "Bustards."

Finally the day came when the ground rang like iron under the feet of the horses, and a bitter wind, raw and gusty, swept out of the northwest, bearing gray veils of sleet. Winter had come! Work in the furrow had ended. The plow was brought in, cleaned and greased to prevent its rusting, and while the horses munched their hay in well-earned holiday, father and I helped farmer Button husk the last of his corn.

Osman Button, a quaint and interesting man of middle age, was a native of York State and retained many of the traditions of his old home strangely blent with a store of vivid memories of Colorado, Utah and California, for he had been one of the gold-seekers of the early fifties. He loved to spin yarns of "When I was in gold camps," and he spun them well. He was short and bent and spoke in a low voice with a curious nervous sniff, but his diction was notably precise and clear. He was a man of judgment, and a citizen of weight and influence. From O. Button I got my first definite notion of Bret Harte's country, and of the long journey which they of the ox team had made in search of Eldorado.

His family "mostly boys and girls" was large, yet they all lived in a low limestone house which he had built (he said) to serve as a granary till he should find time to erect a suitable dwelling. In order to make the point dramatic, I will say that he was still living in the "granary" when last I called on him thirty years later!

A warm friendship sprang up between him and my father, and he was often at our house but his gaunt and silent wife seldom accompanied him. She was kindly and hospitable, but a great sufferer. She never laughed, and seldom smiled, and so remains a pathetic figure in all my memories of the household.

The younger Button children, Eva and Cyrus, became our companions in certain of our activities, but as they were both very sedate and slow of motion, they seldom joined us in our livelier sports. They were both much older than their years. Cyrus at this time was almost as venerable as his father, although his years were, I suppose, about seventeen. Albert and Lavinia, we heard, were much given to dancing and parties.

One night as we were all seated around the kerosene lamp my father said, "Well, Belle, I suppose we'll have to take these young ones down to town and fit 'em out for school." These words so calmly uttered filled our minds with visions of new boots, new caps and new books, and though we went obediently to bed we hardly slept, so excited were we, and at breakfast next morning not one of us could think of food. All our desires converged upon the wondrous expedition—our first visit to town.

Our only carriage was still the lumber wagon but it had now two spring seats, one for father, mother and Jessie, and one for Harriet, Frank and myself. No one else had anything better, hence we had no sense of being poorly out-fitted. We drove away across the frosty prairie toward Osage—moderately comfortable and perfectly happy.

Osage was only a little town, a village of perhaps twelve hundred inhabitants, but to me as we drove down its Main Street, it was almost as impressive as LaCrosse had been. Frank clung close to father, and mother led Jessie, leaving Harriet and me to stumble over nail-kegs and dodge whiffle trees what time our eyes absorbed jars of pink and white candy, and sought out boots and buckskin mittens. Whenever Harriet spoke she whispered, and we pointed at each shining object with cautious care.—Oh! the marvellous exotic smells! Odors of salt codfish and spices, calico and kerosene, apples and ginger-snaps mingle in my mind as I write.

Each of us soon carried a candy marble in his or her cheek (as a chipmunk carries a nut) and Frank and I stood like sturdy hitching posts whilst the storekeeper with heavy hands screwed cotton-plush caps upon our heads,—but the most exciting moment, the crowning joy of the day, came with the buying of our new boots.—If only father had not insisted on our taking those which were a size too large for us!

They were real boots. No one but a Congressman wore "gaiters" in those days. War fashions still dominated the shoe-shops, and high-topped cavalry boots were all but universal. They were kept in boxes under the counter or ranged in rows on a shelf and were of all weights and degrees of fineness. The ones I selected had red tops with a golden moon in the center but my brother's taste ran to blue tops decorated with a golden flag. Oh! that deliciously oily *new* smell! My heart glowed every time I looked at mine. I was especially pleased because they did *not* have copper toes. Copper toes belonged to little boys. A youth who had plowed seventy acres of land could not reasonably be expected to dress like a child.—How smooth and delightfully stiff they felt on my feet.

Then came our new books, a McGuffey reader, a Mitchell geography, a Ray's arithmetic, and a slate. The books had a delightful new smell also, and there was singular charm in the smooth surface of the unmarked slates. I was eager to carve my name in the frame. At last with our treasures under the seat (so near that we could feel them), with our slates and books in our laps we jolted home, dreaming of school and snow. To wade in the drifts with our fine high-topped boots was now our desire.

It is strange but I cannot recall how my mother looked on this trip. Even my father's image is faint and vague (I remember only his keen eagle-gray terrifying eyes), but I can see every acre of that rented farm. I can tell you exactly how the house looked. It was an unpainted square cottage and stood bare on the sod at the edge of Dry Run ravine. It had a small lean-to on the eastern side and a sitting room and bedroom below. Overhead was a low unplastered chamber in which we children slept. As it grew too cold to use the summer kitchen we cooked, ate and lived in the square room which occupied the entire front of the two story upright, and which was, I suppose, sixteen feet square. As our attic was warmed only by the stove-pipe, we older children of a frosty morning made extremely simple and hurried toilets. On very cold days we hurried down stairs to dress beside the kitchen fire.

Our furniture was of the rudest sort. I cannot recall a single piece in our house or in our neighbors' houses that had either beauty or distinction. It was all cheap and worn, for this was the middle border, and nearly all our neighbors had moved as we had done in covered wagons. Farms were new, houses were mere shanties, and money was scarce. "War times" and "war prices" were only just beginning to change. Our clothing was all cheap and ill fitting. The women and children wore home-made "cotton flannel" underclothing for the most part, and the men wore rough, ready-made suits over which they drew brown denim blouses or overalls to keep them clean.

Father owned a fine buffalo overcoat (so much of his song's promise was redeemed) and we possessed two buffalo robes for use in our winter sleigh, but mother had only a sad coat and a woolen shawl. How she kept warm I cannot now understand—I think she stayed at home on cold days.

All of the boys wore long trousers, and even my eight year old brother looked like a miniature man with his full-length overalls, high-topped boots and real suspenders. As for me I carried a bandanna in my hip pocket and walked with determined masculine stride.

My mother, like all her brothers and sisters, was musical and played the violin—or fiddle, as we called it,—and I have many dear remembrances of her playing. *Napoleon's March, Money Musk, The Devil's Dream* and half-a-dozen other simple tunes made up her repertoire. It was very crude music of course but it added to the love and admiration in which her children always held her. Also in some way we had fallen heir to a Prince melodeon—one that had belonged to the McClintocks, but only my sister played on that.

Once at a dance in neighbor Button's house, mother took the "dare" of the fiddler and with shy smile played *The Fisher's Hornpipe* or some other simple melody and was mightily cheered at the close of it, a brief performance which she refused to repeat. Afterward she and my father danced and this seemed a very wonderful performance, for to us they were "old"—far past such frolicking, although he was but forty and she thirty-one!

At this dance I heard, for the first time, the local professional fiddler, old Daddy Fairbanks, as quaint a character as ever entered fiction, for he was not only butcher and horse doctor but a renowned musician as well. Tall, gaunt and sandy, with enormous nose and sparse projecting teeth, he was to me the most enthralling figure at this dance and his queer "Calls" and his "York State" accent filled us all with delight. "*Ally* man left," "Chassay *by* your pardners," "*Dozy-do*" were some of the phrases he used as he played *Honest John* and *Haste to the Wedding.* At times he sang his calls in high nasal chant, "First lady lead to the *right,* deedle, deedle dum-dum—*gent* foller after—dally-deedle-do-do—*three* hands round"—and everybody laughed with frank enjoyment of his words and action.

It was a joy to watch him "start the set." With fiddle under his chin he took his seat in a big chair on the kitchen table in order to command the floor. "Farm on, farm on!" he called disgustedly. "Lively now!" and then, when all the couples were in position, with one mighty No. 14 boot uplifted, with bow laid to strings he snarled, "Already—GELANG!" and with a thundering crash his foot came down, "Honors TEW your pardners—right and left FOUR!" And the dance was on!

I suspect his fiddlin' was not even "middlin'," but he beat time fairly well and kept the dancers somewhere near to rhythm, and so when his ragged old cap went round he often got a handful of quarters for his toil. He always ate two suppers, one at the beginning of the party and another at the end. He had a high respect for the skill of my Uncle David and was grateful to him and other better musicians for their noninterference with his professional engagements.

The school-house which was to be the center of our social life stood on the bare prairie about a mile to the southwest and like thousands of other similar buildings in the west, had not a leaf to shade it in summer nor a branch to break the winds of savage winter. "There's been a good deal of talk about setting out a windbreak," neighbor Button explained to us, "but nothing has as yet been done." It was merely a square pine box painted a glaring white on the outside and a desolate drab within; at least drab was the original color, but the benches were mainly so greasy and hacked that original intentions were obscured. It had two doors on the eastern end and three windows on each side.

A long square stove (standing on slender legs in a puddle of bricks), a wooden chair, and a rude table in one corner, for the use of the teacher, completed the movable furniture. The walls were roughly plastered and the windows had no curtains.

It was a barren temple of the arts even to the residents of Dry Run, and Harriet and I, stealing across the prairie one Sunday morning to look in, came away vaguely depressed. We were fond of school and never missed a day if we could help it, but this neighborhood center seemed small and bleak and poor.

With what fear, what excitement we approached the door on that first day, I can only faintly indicate. All the scholars were strange to me except Albert and Cyrus Button, and I was prepared for rough treatment. However, the experience was not so harsh as I had feared. True, Rangely Field did throw me down and wash my face in snow, and Jack Sweet tripped me up once or twice, but I bore these indignities with such grace as I could command, and soon made a place for myself among the boys.

Burton Babcock was my seat-mate, and at once became my chum. You will hear much of him in this chronicle. He was two years older than I and though pale and slim was unusually swift and strong for his age. He was a silent lad, curiously timid in his classes and not at ease with his teachers.

I cannot recover much of that first winter of school. It was not an experience to remember for its charm. Not one line of grace, not one touch of color relieved the room's bare walls or softened its harsh windows. Perhaps this very barrenness gave to the poetry in our readers an appeal that seems magical, certainly it threw over the faces of Frances Babcock and Mary Abbie Gammons a lovelier halo.—They were "the big girls" of the school, that is to say, they were seventeen or eighteen years old,—and Frances was the special terror of the teacher, a pale and studious pigeon-toed young man who was preparing for college.

In spite of the cold, the boys played open air games all winter. "Dog and Deer," "Dare Gool" and "Fox and Geese" were our favorite diversions, and the wonder is that we did not all die of pneumonia, for we battled so furiously during each recess that we often came in wet with perspiration and coughing so hard that for several minutes recitations were quite impossible.—But we were a hardy lot and none of us seemed the worse for our colds.

There was not much chivalry in the school—quite the contrary, for it was dominated by two or three big rough boys and the rest of us took our tone from them. To protect a girl, to shield her from remark or indignity required a good deal of bravery and few of us were strong enough to do it. Girls were foolish, ridiculous creatures, set apart to be laughed at or preyed upon at will. To shame them was a great joke.—How far I shared in these barbarities I cannot say but that I did share in them I know, for I had very little to do with my sister Harriet after crossing the school-house yard. She kept to her tribe as I to mine.

This winter was made memorable also by a "revival" which came over the district with sudden fury. It began late in the winter—fortunately, for it ended all dancing and merry-making for the time. It silenced Daddy Fairbanks' fiddle and subdued my moth-er's glorious voice to a wail. A cloud of puritanical gloom settled upon almost every household. Youth and love became furtive and hypocritic.

The evangelist, one of the old-fashioned shouting, hysterical, ungrammatical, gasping sort, took charge of the services, and in his exhortations phrases descriptive of lakes of burning brimstone and ages of endless torment abounded. Some of the figures of speech and violent gestures of the man still linger in my mind, but I will not set them down on paper. They are too dreadful to perpetuate. At times he roared with such power that he could have been heard for half a mile.

And yet we went, night by night, mother, father, Jessie, all of us. It was our theater. Some of the roughest characters in the neighborhood rose and professed repentance, for a season, even old Barton, the profanest man in the township, experienced a "change of heart."

We all enjoyed the singing, and joined most lustily in the tunes. Even little Jessie learned to sing *Heavenly Wings, There is a Fountain filled with Blood,* and *Old Hundred.*

As I peer back into that crowded little school-room, smothering hot and reeking with lamp smoke, and recall the half-lit, familiar faces of the congregation, it all has the quality of a vision, something experienced in another world. The preacher, leaping, sweating, roaring till the windows rattle, the mothers with sleeping babes in their arms, the sweet, strained faces of the girls, the immobile wondering men, are spectral shadows, figures encountered in the phantasmagoria of disordered sleep.

10

The Homestead on the Knoll

Spring came to us that year with such sudden beauty, such sweet significance after our long and depressing winter, that it seemed a release from prison, and when at the close of a warm day in March we heard, pulsing down through the golden haze of sunset, the mellow *boom, boom, boom* of the prairie cock our hearts quickened, for this, we were told, was the certain sign of spring.

Day by day the call of this gay herald of spring was taken up by others until at last the whole horizon was ringing with a sunrise symphony of exultant song. "*Boom, boom, boom!*" called the roosters; "*cutta, cutta, wha-whoop-squaw, squawk!*" answered the hens as they fluttered and danced on the ridges—and mingled with their jocund hymn we heard at last the slender, wistful piping of the prairie lark.

With the coming of spring my duties as a teamster returned. My father put me in charge of a harrow, and with old Doll and Queen—quiet and faithful span—I drove upon the field which I had plowed the previous October, there to plod to and fro behind my drag, while in the sky above my head and around me on the mellowing soil the life of the season thickened.

Aided by my team I was able to study at close range the prairie roosters as they assembled for their parade. They had regular "stamping grounds" on certain ridges, where the soil was beaten smooth by the pressure of their restless feet. I often passed within a few yards of them.—I can see them now, the cocks leaping and strutting, with trailing wings and down-thrust heads, displaying their bulbous orange-colored neck ornaments while the hens flutter and squawk in silly delight. All the charm and mystery of that prairie world comes back to me, and I ache with an illogical desire to recover it and hold it, and preserve it in some form for my children.—It seems an injustice that they should miss it, and yet it is probable that they are getting an equal joy of life, an equal exaltation from the opening flowers of the single lilac bush in our city back-yard or from an occasional visit to the lake in Central Park.

Dragging is even more wearisome than plowing, in some respects, for you have no handles to assist you and your heels sinking deep into the soft loam bring such unwonted strain upon the tendons of your legs that you can scarcely limp home to supper, and it seems that you cannot possibly go on another day,—but you do—at least I did.

There was something relentless as the weather in the way my soldier father ruled his sons, and yet he was neither hardhearted nor unsympathetic. The fact is easily explained. His own boyhood had been task-filled and he saw nothing unnatural in the regular employment of his children. Having had little play-time himself, he considered that we were having a very comfortable boyhood. Furthermore the country was new and labor scarce. Every hand and foot must count under such conditions.

There are certain ameliorations to child-labor on a farm. Air and sunshine and food are plentiful. I never lacked for meat or clothing, and mingled with my records of toil are exquisite memories of the joy I took in following the changes in the landscape, in the notes of birds, and in the play of small animals on the sunny soil.

There were no pigeons on the prairie but enormous flocks of ducks came sweeping northward, alighting at sunset to feed in the fields of stubble. They came in countless myriads and often when they settled to earth they covered acres of meadow like some prodigious cataract from the sky. When alarmed they rose with a sound like the rumbling of thunder.

At times the lines of their cloud-like flocks were so unending that those in the front rank were lost in the northern sky, while those in the rear were but dim bands beneath the southern sun.—I tried many times to shoot some of them, but never succeeded, so wary were they. Brant and geese in formal flocks followed and to watch these noble birds pushing their arrowy lines straight into the north always gave me special joy. On fine days they flew high—so high they were but faint lines against the shining clouds.

I learned to imitate their cries, and often caused the leaders to turn, to waver in their course as I uttered my resounding call.

The sand-hill crane came last of all, loitering north in lonely easeful flight. Often of a warm day, I heard his sovereign cry falling from the azure dome, so high, so far his form could not be seen, so close to the sun that my eyes could not detect his solitary, majestic circling sweep. He came after the geese. He was the herald of summer. His brazen, reverberating call will forever remain associated in my mind with mellow, pulsating earth, springing grass and cloudless glorious May-time skies.

As my team moved to and fro over the field, ground sparrows rose in countless thousands, flinging themselves against the sky like grains of wheat from out a sower's hand, and their chatter fell upon me like the voices of fairy sprites, invisible and multitudinous. Long swift narrow flocks of a bird we called "the prairie-pigeon" swooped over the swells on sounding wing, winding so close to the ground, they seemed at times like slender air-borne serpents,—and always the brown lark whistled as if to cheer my lonely task.

Back and forth across the wide field I drove, while the sun crawled slowly up the sky. It was tedious work and I was always hungry by nine, and famished at ten. Thereafter the sun appeared to stand still. My chest caved in and my knees trembled with weakness, but when at last the white flag fluttering from a chamber window summoned to the mid-day meal, I started with strength miraculously renewed and called, *"Dinner!"* to the hired hand. Unhitching my team, with eager haste I climbed upon old Queen, and rode at ease toward the barn.

Oh, it was good to enter the kitchen, odorous with fresh biscuit and hot coffee! We all ate like dragons, devouring potatoes and salt pork without end, till mother mildly remarked, "Boys, boys! Don't 'founder' yourselves!"

From such a meal I withdrew torpid as a gorged snake, but luckily I had half an hour in which to get my courage back,—and besides, there was always the stirring power of father's clarion call. His energy appeared superhuman to me. I was in awe of him. He kept track of everything, seemed hardly to sleep and never complained of weariness. Long before the nooning was up, (or so it seemed to me) he began to shout: "Time's up, boys. Grab a root!"

And so, lame, stiff and sore, with the sinews of my legs shortened, so that my knees were bent like an old man's, I hobbled away to the barn and took charge of my team. Once in the field, I felt better. A subtle change, a mellower charm came over the afternoon earth. The ground was warmer, the sky more genial, the wind more amiable, and before I had finished my second "round" my joints were moderately pliable and my sinews relaxed.

Nevertheless the temptation to sit on the corner of the harrow and dream the moments away was very great, and sometimes as I laid my tired body down on the tawny, sunlit grass at the edge of the field, and gazed up at the beautiful clouds sailing by, I wished for leisure to explore their purple valleys.—The wind whispered in the tall weeds, and sighed in the hazel bushes. The dried blades touching one another in the passing winds, spoke to me, and the gophers, glad of escape from their dark, underground prisons, chirped a cheery greeting. Such respites were strangely sweet.

So day by day, as I walked my monotonous round upon the ever mellowing soil, the prairie spring unrolled its beauties before me. I saw the last goose pass on to the north, and watched the green grass creeping up the sunny slopes. I answered the splendid challenge of the loitering crane, and studied the ground sparrow building her grassy nest. The prairie hens began to seek seclusion in the swales, and the pocket gopher, busily mining the sod, threw up his purple-brown mounds of cool fresh earth. Larks, blue-birds and king-birds followed the robins, and at last the full tide of May covered the world with luscious green.

Harriet and Frank returned to school but I was too valuable to be spared. The unbroken land of our new farm demanded the plow and no sooner was the planting on our rented place finished than my father began the work of fencing and breaking the sod of the homestead which lay a mile to the south, glowing like a garden under the summer sun. One day late in May my uncle David (who had taken a farm not far away), drove over with four horses hitched to a big breaking plow and together with my father set to work overturning the primeval sward whereon we were to be "lords of the soil."

I confess that as I saw the tender plants and shining flowers bow beneath the remorseless beam, civilization seemed a sad business, and yet there was something epic, something large-gestured and splendid in the "breaking" season. Smooth, glossy, almost unwrinkled the thick ribbon of jet-black sod rose upon the share and rolled away from the mold-board's glistening curve to tuck itself upside down into the furrow behind the horse's heels, and the picture which my uncle made, gave me pleasure in spite of the sad changes he was making.

The land was not all clear prairie and every ounce of David's great strength was required to guide that eighteen-inch plow as it went ripping and snarling through the matted roots of the hazel thickets, and sometimes my father came and sat on the beam in order to hold the coulter to its work, while the giant driver braced himself to the shock and the four horses strained desperately at their traces. These contests had the quality of a wrestling match but the men always won. My own job was to rake and burn the brush which my father mowed with a heavy scythe.—Later we dug postholes and built fences but each day was spent on the new land.

Around us, on the swells, gray gophers whistled, and the nesting plover quaveringly called. Blackbirds clucked in the furrow and squat badgers watched with jealous eye the plow's inexorable progress toward their dens. The weather was perfect June. Fleecy clouds sailed like snowy galleons from west to east, the wind was strong but kind, and we worked in a glow of satisfied ownership.

Many rattlesnakes ("massasaugas" Mr. Button called them), inhabited the moist spots and father and I killed several as we cleared the ground. Prairie wolves lurked in the groves and swales, but as foot by foot and rod by rod, the steady steel rolled the grass and the hazel brush under, all of these wild things died or hurried away, never to return. Some part of this tragedy I was able even then to understand and regret.

At last the wide "quarter section" lay upturned, black to the sun and the garden that had bloomed and fruited for millions of years, waiting for man, lay torn and ravaged. The tender plants, the sweet flowers, the fragrant fruits, the busy insects, all the swarming lives which had been native here for untold centuries were utterly destroyed. It was sad and yet it was not all loss, even to my thinking, for I realized that over this desolation the green wheat would wave and the corn silks shed their pollen. It was not precisely the romantic valley of our song, but it was a rich and promiseful plot and my father seemed entirely content.

Meanwhile, on a little rise of ground near the road, neighbor Gammons and John Bowers were building our next home. It did not in the least resemble the foundation of an everlasting family seat, but it deeply excited us all. It was of pine and had the usual three rooms below and a long garret above and as it stood on a plain, bare to the winds, my father took the precaution of lining it with brick to hold it down. It was as good as most of the dwellings round about us but it stood naked on the sod, devoid of grace as a dry goods box. Its walls were rough plaster, its door of white pine, its furniture poor, scanty and worn. There was a little picture on the face of the clock, a chromo on the wall, and a printed portrait of General Grant—nothing more. It was home by reason of my mother's brave and cheery presence, and the prattle of Jessie's clear voice filled it with music. Dear child,—with her it was always spring!

11

School Life

Our new house was completed during July but we did not move into it till in September. There was much to be done in way of building sheds, granaries and corn-cribs and in this work father was both carpenter and stone-mason. An amusing incident comes to my mind in connection with the digging of our well.

Uncle David and I were "tending mason," and father was down in the well laying or trying to lay the curbing. It was a tedious and difficult job and he was about to give it up in despair when one of our neighbors, a quaint old Englishman named Barker, came driving along. He was one of these men who take a minute inquisitive interest in the affairs of others; therefore he pulled his team to a halt and came in.

Peering into the well he drawled out, "Hello, Garland. W'at ye doin' down there?"

"Tryin' to lay a curb," replied my father lifting a gloomy face, "and I guess it's too complicated for me."

"Nothin' easier," retorted the old man with a wink at my uncle, "jest putt two a-top o' one and one a-toppo two—and the big eend out,"—and with a broad grin on his red face he went back to his team and drove away.

My father afterwards said, "I saw the whole process in a flash of light. He had given me all the rule I needed. I laid the rest of that wall without a particle of trouble."

Many times after this Barker stopped to offer advice but he never quite equalled the startling success of his rule for masonry.

The events of this harvest, even the process of moving into the new house, are obscured in my mind by the clouds of smoke which rose from calamitous fires all over the west. It was an unprecedentedly dry season so that not merely the prairie, but many weedy cornfields burned. I had a good deal of time to meditate upon this for I was again the plow-boy. Every day I drove away from the rented farm to the new land where I was cross-cutting the breaking, and the thickening haze through which the sun shone with a hellish red glare, produced in me a growing uneasiness which became terror when the news came to us that Chicago was on fire. It seemed to me then that the earth was about to go up in a flaming cloud just as my grandad had so often prophesied.

This general sense of impending disaster was made keenly personal by the destruction of uncle David's stable with all his horses. This building like most of the barns of the region was not only roofed with straw but banked with straw, and it burned so swiftly that David was trapped in a stall while trying to save one of his teams. He saved himself by burrowing like a gigantic mole through the side of the shed, and so, hatless, covered with dust and chaff, emerged as if from a fiery burial after he had been given up for dead.

This incident combined with others so filled my childish mind that I lived in apprehension of similar disaster. I feared the hot wind which roared up from the south, and I never entered our own stable in the middle of the day without a sense of danger. Then came the rains—the blessed rains—and put an end to my fears.

In a week we had forgotten all the "conflagrations" except that in Chicago. There was something grandiose and unforgettable in the tales which told of the madly fleeing crowds in the narrow streets. These accounts pushed back the walls of my universe till its far edge included the ruined metropolis whose rebuilding was of the highest importance to us, for it was not only the source of all our supplies, but the great central market to which we sent our corn and hogs and wheat.

My world was splendidly romantic. It was bounded on the west by THE PLAINS with their Indians and buffalo; on the north by THE GREAT WOODS, filled with thieves and counterfeiters; on the south by OSAGE AND CHICAGO; and on the east by HESPER, ONALASKA and BOSTON. A luminous trail ran from Dry Run Prairie to Neshonoc—all else was "chaos and black night."

For seventy days I walked behind my plow on the new farm while my father finished the harvest on the rented farm and moved to the house on the knoll. It was lonely work for a boy of eleven but there were frequent breaks in the monotony and I did not greatly suffer. I disliked cross-cutting for the reason that the unrotted sods would often pile up in front of the coulter and make me a great deal of trouble. There is a certain pathos in the sight of that small boy tugging and kicking at the stubborn turf in the effort to free his plow. Such misfortunes loom large in a lad's horizon.

One of the interludes, and a lovely one, was given over to gathering the hay from one of the wild meadows to the north of us. Another was the threshing from the shock on the rented farm. This was the first time we had seen this done and it interested us keenly. A great many teams were necessary and the crew of men was correspondingly large. Uncle David was again the thresher with a fine new separator, and I would have enjoyed the season with almost perfect contentment had it not been for the fact that I was detailed to hold sacks for Daddy Fairbanks who was the measurer.

Our first winter had been without much wind but our second taught us the meaning of the word "blizzard" which we had just begun to hear about. The winds of Wisconsin were "gentle zephyrs" compared to the blasts which now swept down over the plain to hammer upon our desolate little cabin and pile the drifts around our sheds and granaries, and even my pioneer father was forced to admit that the hills of Green's Coulee had their uses after all.

One such storm which leaped upon us at the close of a warm and beautiful day in February lasted for two days and three nights, making life on the open prairie impossible even to the strongest man. The thermometer fell to thirty degrees below zero and the snow-laden air moving at a rate of eighty miles an hour pressed upon the walls of our house with giant power. The sky of noon was darkened, so that we moved in a pallid half-light, and the windows thick with frost shut us in as if with gray shrouds.

Hour after hour those winds and snows in furious battle, howled and roared and whistled around our frail shelter, slashing at the windows and piping on the chimney, till it seemed as if the Lord Sun had been wholly blotted out and that the world would never again be warm. Twice each day my father made a desperate sally toward the stable to feed the imprisoned cows and horses or to replenish our fuel—for the remainder of the long pallid day he sat beside the fire with gloomy face. Even his indomitable spirit was awed by the fury of that storm.

So long and so continuously did those immitigable winds howl in our ears that their tumult persisted, in imagination, when on the third morning, we thawed holes in the thickened rime of the window panes and looked forth on a world silent as a marble sea and flaming with sunlight. My own relief was mingled with surprise—surprise to find the landscape so unchanged. True, the yard was piled high with drifts and the barns were almost lost to view but the far fields and the dark lines of Burr Oak Grove remained unchanged.

We met our school-mates that day, like survivors of shipwreck, and for many days we listened to gruesome stories of disaster, tales of stages frozen deep in snow with all their passengers sitting in their seats, and of herders with their silent flocks around them, lying stark as granite among the hazel bushes in which they had sought shelter. It was long before we shook off the awe with which this tempest filled our hearts.

The school-house which stood at the corner of our new farm was less than half a mile away, and yet on many of the winter days which followed, we found it quite far enough. Hattie was now thirteen, Frank nine and I a little past eleven but nothing, except a blizzard such as I have described, could keep us away from school. Facing the cutting wind, wallowing through the drifts, battling like small intrepid animals, we often arrived at the door moaning with pain yet unsubdued, our ears frosted, our toes numb in our boots, to meet others in similar case around the roaring hot stove.

Often after we reached the school-house another form of suffering overtook us in the "thawing out" process. Our fingers and toes, swollen with blood, ached and itched, and our ears burned. Nearly all of us carried sloughing ears and scaling noses. Some of the pupils came two miles against these winds.

The natural result of all this exposure was of course, chilblains! Every foot in the school was more or less touched with this disease to which our elders alluded as if it were an amusing trifle, but to us it was no joke.

After getting thoroughly warmed up, along about the middle of the forenoon, there came into our feet a most intense itching and burning and aching, a sensation so acute that keeping still was impossible, and all over the room an uneasy shuffling and drumming arose as we pounded our throbbing heels against the floor or scraped our itching toes against the edge of our benches. The teacher understood and was kind enough to overlook this disorder.

The wonder is that any of us lived through that winter, for at recess, no matter what the weather might be we flung ourselves out of doors to play "fox and geese" or "dare goal," until, damp with perspiration, we responded to the teacher's bell, and came pouring back into the entry ways to lay aside our wraps for another hour's study.

Our readers were almost the only counterchecks to the current of vulgarity and baseness which ran through the talk of the older boys, and I wish to acknowledge my deep obligation to Professor McGuffey, whoever he may have been, for the dignity and literary grace of his selections. From the pages of his readers I learned to know and love the poems of Scott, Byron, Southey, Wordsworth and a long line of the English masters. I got my first taste of Shakespeare from the selected scenes which I read in these books.

With terror as well as delight I rose to read *Lochiel's Warning, The Battle of Waterloo* or *The Roman* Captive. Marco Bozzaris and William Tell were alike glorious to me. I soon knew not only my own reader, the fourth, but all the selections in the fifth and sixth as well. I could follow almost word for word the recitations of the older pupils and at such times I forgot my squat little body and my mop of hair, and became imaginatively a page in the train of Ivanhoe, or a bowman in the army of Richard the Lion Heart battling the Saracen in the Holy Land.

With a high ideal of the way in which these grand selections should be read, I was scared almost voiceless when it came my turn to read them before the class. "STRIKE FOR YOUR ALTARS AND YOUR FIRES. STRIKE FOR THE GREEN GRAVES OF YOUR SIRES—GOD AND YOUR NATIVE LAND," always reduced me to a trembling breathlessness. The sight of the emphatic print was a call to the best that was in me and yet I could not meet the test. Excess of desire to do it just right often brought a ludicrous gasp and I often fell back into my seat in disgrace, the titter of the girls adding to my pain.

Then there was the famous passage, "Did ye not hear it?" and the careless answer, "No, it was but the wind or the car rattling o'er the stony street."—I knew exactly how those opposing emotions should be expressed but to do it after I rose to my feet was impossible. Burton was even more terrified than I. Stricken blind as well as dumb he usually ended by helplessly staring at the words which, I conceive, had suddenly become a blur to him.

No matter, we were taught to feel the force of these poems and to reverence the genius that produced them, and that was worth while. Falstaff and Prince Hal, Henry and his wooing of Kate, Wolsey and his downfall, Shylock and his pound of flesh all became a part of our thinking and helped us to measure the large figures of our own literature, for Whittier, Bryant and Longfellow also had place in these volumes. It is probable that Professor McGuffey, being a Southern man, did not value New England writers as highly as my grandmother did, nevertheless *Thanatopsis* was there and *The Village Blacksmith,* and extracts from *The Deer Slayer* and *The Pilot* gave us a notion that in Cooper we had a novelist of weight and importance, one to put beside Scott and Dickens.

A by-product of my acquaintance with one of the older boys was a stack of copies of the *New York Weekly,* a paper filled with stories of noble life in England and hair-breadth escapes on the plain, a shrewd mixture, designed to meet the needs of the entire membership of a prairie household. The pleasure I took in these tales should fill me with shame, but it doesn't—I rejoice in the memory of it.

I soon began, also, to purchase and trade "Beadle's Dime Novels" and, to tell the truth, I took an exquisite delight in *Old Sleuth* and *Jack Harkaway.* My taste was catholic. I ranged from *Lady Gwendolin* to *Buckskin Bill* and so far as I can now distinguish one was quite as enthralling as the other. It is impossible for any print to be as magical to any boy these days as those weeklies were to me in 1871.

One day a singular test was made of us all. Through some agency now lost to me my father was brought to subscribe for *The Hearth and Home* or some such paper for the farmer, and in this I read my first chronicle of everyday life.

In the midst of my dreams of lords and ladies, queens and dukes, I found myself deeply concerned with backwoods farming, spelling schools, protracted meetings and the like familiar homely scenes. This serial (which involved my sister and myself in many a spat as to who should read it first) was *The Hoosier Schoolmaster,* by Edward Eggleston, and a perfectly successful attempt to interest western readers in a story of the middle border.

To us "Mandy" and "Bud Means," "Ralph Hartsook," the teacher, "Little Shocky" and sweet patient "Hannah," were as real as Cyrus Button and Daddy Fairbanks. We could hardly wait for the next number of the paper, so concerned were we about "Hannah" and "Ralph." We quoted old lady Means and we made bets on "Bud" in his fight with the villainous drover. I hardly knew where Indiana was in those days, but Eggleston's characters were near neighbors.

The illustrations were dreadful, even in my eyes, but the artist contrived to give a slight virginal charm to Hannah and a certain childish sweetness to Shocky, so that we accepted the more than mortal ugliness of old man Means and his daughter Mirandy (who simpered over her book at us as she did at Ralph), as a just interpretation of their worthlessness.

This book is a milestone in my literary progress as it is in the development of distinctive western fiction, and years afterward I was glad to say so to the aged author who lived a long and honored life as a teacher and writer of fiction.

It was always too hot or too cold in our schoolroom and on certain days when a savage wind beat and clamored at the loose windows, the girls, humped and shivering, sat upon their feet to keep them warm, and the younger children with shawls over their shoulders sought permission to gather close about the stove.

Our dinner pails (stored in the entry way) were often frozen solid and it was necessary to thaw out our mince pie as well as our bread and butter by putting it on the stove. I recall, vividly, gnawing, dog-like, at the mollified outside of a doughnut while still its frosty heart made my teeth ache.

Happily all days were not like this. There were afternoons when the sun streamed warmly into the room, when long icicles formed on the eaves, adding a touch of grace to the desolate building, moments when the jingling bells of passing wood-sleighs expressed the natural cheer and buoyancy of our youthful hearts.

12

Chores and Almanacs

Our farmyard would have been uninhabitable during this winter had it not been for the long ricks of straw which we had piled up as a shield against the prairie winds. Our horse-barn, roofed with hay and banked with chaff, formed the west wall of the cowpen, and a long low shed gave shelter to the north.

In this triangular space, in the lee of shed and straw-rick, the cattle passed a dolorous winter. Mostly they burrowed in the chaff, or stood about humped and shivering—only on sunny days did their arching backs subside. Naturally each animal grew a thick coat of long hair, and succeeded in coming through to grass again, but the cows of some of our neighbors were less fortunate. Some of them got so weak that they had to be "tailed" up as it was called. This meant that they were dying of hunger and the sight of them crawling about filled me with indignant wrath. I could not understand how a man, otherwise kind, could let his stock suffer for lack of hay when wild grass was plentiful.

One of my duties, and one that I dreaded, was pumping water for our herd. This was no light job, especially on a stinging windy morning, for the cows, having only dry fodder, required an enormous amount of liquid, and as they could only drink while the water was fresh from the well, some one must work the handle till the last calf had absorbed his fill—and this had to be done when the thermometer was thirty below, just the same as at any other time.

And this brings up an almost forgotten phase of bovine psychology. The order in which the cows drank as well as that in which they entered the stable was carefully determined and rigidly observed. There was always one old dowager who took precedence, all the others gave way before her. Then came the second in rank who feared the leader but insisted on ruling all the others, and so on down to the heifer. This order, once established, was seldom broken (at least by the females of the herd, the males were more unstable) even when the leader grew old and almost helpless.

We took advantage of this loyalty when putting them into the barn. The stall furthest from the door belonged to "old Spot," the second to "Daisy" and so on, hence all I had to do was to open the door and let them in—for if any rash young thing got out of her proper place she was set right, very quickly, by her superiors.

Some farms had ponds or streams to which their flocks were driven for water but this to me was a melancholy winter function, and sometimes as I joined Burt or Cyrus in driving the poor humped and shivering beasts down over the snowy plain to a hole chopped in the ice, and watched them lay their aching teeth to the frigid draught, trying a dozen times to temper their mouths to the chill I suffered with them. As they streamed along homeward, heavy with their sloshing load, they seemed the personification of a desolate and abused race.

Winter mornings were a time of trial for us all. It required stern military command to get us out of bed before daylight, in a chamber warmed only by the stovepipe, to draw on icy socks and frosty boots and go to the milking of cows and the currying of horses. Other boys did not rise by candle-light but I did, not because I was eager to make a record but for the very good reason that my commander believed in early rising. I groaned and whined but I rose—and always I found mother in the kitchen before me, putting the kettle on.

It ought not to surprise the reader when I say that my morning toilet was hasty—something less than "a lick and a promise." I couldn't (or didn't) stop to wash my face or comb my hair; such refinements seem useless in an attic bed-chamber at five in the morning of a December day—I put them off till breakfast time. Getting up at five A.M. even in June was a hardship, in winter it was a punishment.

Our discomforts had their compensations! As we came back to the house at six, the kitchen was always cheery with the smell of browning flapjacks, sizzling sausages and steaming coffee, and mother had plenty of hot water on the stove so that in "half a jiffy," with shining faces and sleek hair we sat down to a noble feast. By this time also the eastern sky was gorgeous with light, and two misty "sun dogs" dimly loomed, watching at the gate of the new day.

Now that I think of it, father was the one who took the brunt of our "revellee." He always built the fire in the kitchen stove before calling the family. Mother, silent, sleepy, came second. Sometimes she was just combing her hair as I passed through the kitchen, at other times she would be at the biscuit dough or stirring the pancake batter—but she was always there!

"What did you gain by this disagreeable habit of early rising?"—This is a question I have often asked myself since. Was it only a useless obsession on the part of my pioneer dad? Why couldn't we have slept till six, or even seven? Why rise before the sun?

I cannot answer this, I only know such was our habit summer and winter, and that most of our neighbors conformed to the same rigorous tradition. None of us got rich, and as I look back on the situation, I cannot recall that those "sluggards" who rose an hour or two later were any poorer than we. I am inclined to think it was all a convention of the border, a custom which might very well have been broken by us all.

My mother would have found these winter days very long had it not been for baby Jessie, for father was busily hauling wood from the Cedar River some six or seven miles away, and the almost incessant, mournful piping of the wind in the chimney was dispiriting. Occasionally Mrs. Button, Mrs. Gammons or some other of the neighbors would drop in for a visit, but generally mother and Jessie were alone till Harriet and Frank and I came home from school at half-past four.

Our evenings were more cheerful. My sister Hattie was able to play a few simple tunes on the melodeon and Cyrus and Eva or Mary Abbie and John occasionally came in to sing. In this my mother often took part. In church her clear soprano rose above all the others like the voice of some serene great bird. Of this gift my father often expressed his open admiration.

There was very little dancing during our second winter but Fred Jewett started a singing school which brought the young folks together once a week. We boys amused ourselves with "Dare Gool" and "Dog and Deer." Cold had little terror for us, provided the air was still. Often we played "Hi Spy" around the barn with the thermometer twenty below zero, and not infrequently we took long walks to visit Burton and other of our boy friends or to borrow something to read. I was always on the trail of a book.

Harriet joined me in my search for stories and nothing in the neighborhood homes escaped us. Anything in print received our most respectful consideration. Jane Porter's *Scottish Chiefs* brought to us both anguish and delight. *Tempest and Sunshine* was another discovery. I cannot tell to whom I was indebted for *Ivanhoe* but I read and reread it with the most intense pleasure. At the same time or near it I borrowed a huge bundle of *The New York Saturday Night* and *The New York Ledger* and from them I derived an almost equal enjoyment. "Old Sleuth" and "Buckskin Bill" were as admirable in their way as "Cedric the Saxon."

At this time *Godey's Ladies Book* and *Peterson's Magazine* were the only high-class periodicals known to us. *The Toledo Blade* and *The New York Tribune* were still my father's political advisers and Horace Greeley and "Petroleum V. Nasby" were equally corporeal in my mind.

Almanacs figured largely in my reading at this time, and were a source of frequent quotation by my father. They were nothing but small, badly-printed, patent medicine pamphlets, each with a loop of string at the corner so that they might be hung on a nail behind the stove, and of a crude green or yellow or blue. Each of them made much of a calm-featured man who seemed unaware of the fact that his internal organs were opened to the light of day. Lines radiated from his middle to the signs of the zodiac. I never knew what all this meant, but it gave me a sense of something esoteric and remote. Just what "Aries" and "Pisces" had to do with healing or the weather is still a mystery.

These advertising bulletins could be seen in heaps on the counter at the drug store especially in the spring months when "Healey's Bitters" and "Allen's Cherry Pectoral" were most needed to "purify the blood." They were given out freely, but the price of the marvellous mixtures they celebrated was always one dollar a bottle and many a broad coin went for a "bitter" which should have gone to buy a new dress for an overworked wife.

These little books contained, also, concise aphorisms and weighty words of advice like "After dinner rest awhile; after supper run a mile," and "Be vigilant, be truthful and your life will never be ruthful." "Take care of the pennies and the pounds will take care of themselves" (which needed a little translating to us) probably came down a long line of English copy books. No doubt they were all stolen from *Poor Richard.*

Incidentally they called attention to the aches and pains of humankind, and each page presented the face, signature and address of some far-off person who had been miraculously relieved by the particular "balsam" or "bitter" which that pamphlet presented. Hollow-cheeked folk were shown "before taking," and the same individuals plump and hearty "after taking," followed by very realistic accounts of the diseases from which they had been relieved gave encouragement to others suffering from the same "complaints."

Generally the almanac which presented the claims of a "pectoral" also had a "salve" that was "sovereign for burns" and some of them humanely took into account the ills of farm animals and presented a cure for bots or a liniment for spavins. I spent a great deal of time with these publications and to them a large part of my education is due.

It is impossible that printed matter of any kind should possess for any child of today the enchantment which came to me, from a grimy, half-dismembered copy of Scott or Cooper. *The Life of P. T. Barnum,* and Franklin's *Autobiography* we owned and they were also wellsprings of joy to me. Sometimes I hold with the Lacedemonians that "hunger is the best sauce" for the mind as well as for the palate. Certainly we made the most of all that came our way.

Naturally the school-house continued to be the center of our interest by day and the scene of our occasional neighborhood recreation by night. In its small way it was our Forum as well as our Academy and my memories of it are mostly pleasant.

Early one bright winter day Charles Babcock and Albert Button, two of our big boys, suddenly appeared at the school-house door with their best teams hitched to great bob-sleds, and amid much shouting and laughter, the entire school (including the teacher) piled in on the straw which softened the bottom of the box, and away we raced with jangling bells, along the bright winter roads with intent to "surprise" the Burr Oak teacher and his flock.

I particularly enjoyed this expedition for the Burr Oak School was larger than ours and stood on the edge of a forest and was protected by noble trees. A deep ravine near it furnished a mild form of coasting. The schoolroom had fine new desks with iron legs and the teacher's desk occupied a deep recess at the front. Altogether it possessed something of the dignity of a church. To go there was almost like going to town, for at the corners where the three roads met, four or five houses stood and in one of these was a postoffice.

That day is memorable to me for the reason that I first saw Bettie and Hattie and Agnes, the prettiest girls in the township. Hattie and Bettie were both fair-haired and blue-eyed but Agnes was dark with great velvety black eyes. Neither of them was over sixteen, but they had all taken on the airs of young ladies and looked with amused contempt on lads of my age. Nevertheless, I had the right to admire them in secret for they added the final touch of poetry to this visit to "the Grove School House."

Often, thereafter, on a clear night when the thermometer stood twenty below zero, Burton and I would trot away toward the Grove to join in some meeting or to coast with the boys on the banks of the creek. I feel again the iron clutch of my frozen boots. The tippet around my neck is solid ice before my lips. My ears sting. Low-hung, blazing, the stars light the sky, and over the diamond-dusted snow-crust the moonbeams splinter.

Though sensing the glory of such nights as these I was careful about referring to it. Restraint in such matters was the rule. If you said, "It is a fine day," or "The night is as clear as a bell," you had gone quite as far as the proprieties permitted. Love was also a forbidden word. You might say, "I love pie," but to say "I love Bettie," was mawkish if not actually improper.

Caresses or terms of endearment even between parents and their children were very seldom used. People who said "Daddy dear," or "Jim dear," were under suspicion. "They fight like cats and dogs when no one else is around" was the universal comment on a family whose members were very free of their terms of affection. We were a Spartan lot. We did not believe in letting our wives and children know that they were an important part of our contentment.

Social changes were in progress. We held no more quilting bees or barn-raisings. Women visited less than in Wisconsin. The work on the new farms was never ending, and all teams were in constant use during week days. The young people got together on one excuse or another, but their elders met only at public meetings.

Singing, even among the young people was almost entirely confined to hymn-tunes. The new Moody and Sankey Song Book was in every home. *Tell Me the Old Old Story* did not refer to courtship but to salvation, and *Hold the Fort for I am Coming* was no longer a signal from Sherman, but a Message from Jesus. We often spent a joyous evening singing *O, Bear Me Away on Your Snowy Wings,* although we had no real desire to be taken "to our immortal home." Father no longer asked for *Minnie Minturn* and *Nellie Wildwood,*— but his love for Smith's *Grand March* persisted and my sister Harriet was often called upon to play it for him while he explained its meaning. The war was passing into the mellow, reminiscent haze of memory and he loved the splendid pictures which this descriptive piece of martial music recalled to mind. So far as we then knew his pursuit of the Sunset was at an end.

13

Boy Life on the Prairie

The snows fell deep in February and when at last the warm March winds began to blow, lakes developed with magical swiftness in the fields, and streams filled every swale, transforming the landscape into something unexpected and enchanting. At night these waters froze, bringing fields of ice almost to our door. We forgot all our other interests in the joy of the games which we played thereon at every respite from school, or from the wood-pile, for splitting fire-wood was our first spring task.

From time to time as the weather permitted, father had been cutting and hauling maple and hickory logs from the forests of the Cedar River, and these logs must now be made into stove-wood and piled for summer use. Even before the school term ended we began to take a hand at this work, after four o'clock and on Saturdays. While the hired man and father ran the cross-cut saw, whose pleasant song had much of the seed-time suggestion which vibrated in the *caw-caw* of the hens as they burrowed in the dust of the chip-yard, I split the easy blocks and my brother helped to pile the finished product.

The place where the wood-pile lay was slightly higher than the barnyard and was the first dry ground to appear in the almost universal slush and mud. Delightful memories are associated with this sunny spot and with a pond which appeared as if by some conjury, on the very field where I had husked the down-row so painfully in November. From the wood-pile I was often permitted to go skating and Burton was my constant companion in these excursions. However, my joy in his companionship was not unmixed with bitterness, for I deeply envied him the skates which he wore. They were trimmed with brass and their runners came up over his toes in beautiful curves and ended in brass acorns which transfigured their wearer. To own a pair of such skates seemed to me the summit of all earthly glory.

My own wooden "contraptions" went on with straps and I could not make the runners stay in the middle of my soles where they belonged, hence my ankles not only tipped in awkwardly but the stiff outer edges of my boot counters dug holes in my skin so that my outing was a kind of torture after all. Nevertheless, I persisted and, while Burton circled and swooped like a hawk, I sprawled with flapping arms in a mist of ignoble rage. That I learned to skate fairly well even under these disadvantages argues a high degree of enthusiasm.

Father was always willing to release us from labor at times when the ice was fine, and at night we were free to explore the whole country round about, finding new places for our games. Sometimes the girls joined us, and we built fires on the edges of the swales and played "gool" and a kind of "shinny" till hunger drove us home.

We held to this sport to the last—till the ice with prodigious booming and cracking fell away in the swales and broke through the icy drifts (which lay like dams along the fences) and vanished, leaving the corn-rows littered with huge blocks of ice. Often we came in from the pond, wet to the middle, our boots completely soaked with water. They often grew hard as iron during the night, and we experienced the greatest trouble in getting them on again. Greasing them with hot tallow was a regular morning job.

Then came the fanning mill. The seed grain had to be fanned up, and that was a dark and dusty "trick" which we did not like anything near as well as we did skating or even piling wood. The hired man turned the mill, I dipped the wheat into the hopper, Franklin held sacks and father scooped the grain in. I don't suppose we gave up many hours to this work, but it seems to me that we spent weeks at it. Probably we took spells at the mill in the midst of the work on the chip pile.

Meanwhile, above our heads the wild ducks again pursued their northward flight, and the far honking of the geese fell to our ears from the solemn deeps of the windless night. On the first dry warm ridges the prairie cocks began to boom, and then at last came the day when father's imperious voice rang high in familiar command. "Out with the drags, boys! We start seeding tomorrow."

Again we went forth on the land. this time to wrestle with the tough, unrotted sod of the new breaking, while all around us the larks and plover called and the gray badgers stared with disapproving bitterness from their ravaged hills.

Maledictions on that tough northwest forty! How many times I harrowed and cross-harrowed it I cannot say, but I well remember the maddening persistency with which the masses of hazel roots clogged the teeth of the drag, making it necessary for me to raise the corner of it—a million times a day! This had to be done while the team was in motion, and you can see I did not lack for exercise. It was necessary also to "lap-half" and this requirement made careful driving needful for father could not be fooled. He saw every "balk."

As the ground dried off the dust: arose from under the teeth of the harrow and flew so thickly that my face was not only coated with it but tears of rebellious rage stained my cheeks with comic lines. At such times it seemed unprofitable to be the twelve-year-old son of a western farmer.

One day, just as the early sown wheat was beginning to throw a tinge of green over the brown earth, a tremendous wind arose from the southwest and blew with such devastating fury that the soil, caught up from the field, formed a cloud, hundreds of feet high,—a cloud which darkened the sky, turning noon into dusk and sending us all to shelter. All the forenoon this blizzard of loam raged, filling the house with dust, almost smothering the cattle in the stable. Work was impossible, even for the men. The growing grain, its roots exposed to the air, withered and died. Many of the smaller plants were carried bodily away.

As the day wore on father fell into dumb, despairing rage. His rigid face and smoldering eyes, his grim lips, terrified us all. It seemed to him (as to us), that the entire farm was about to take flight and the bitterest part of the tragic circumstance lay in the reflection that our loss (which was much greater than any of our neighbors) was due to the extra care with which we had pulverized the ground.

"If only I hadn't gone over it that last time," I heard him groan in reference to the "smooch" with which I had crushed all the lumps making every acre friable as a garden. "Look at Woodring's!"

Sure enough. The cloud was thinner over on Woodring's side of the line fence. His rough clods were hardly touched. My father's bitter revolt, his impotent fury appalled me, for it seemed to me (as to him), that nature was, at the moment, an enemy. More than seventy acres of this land had to be resown.

Most authors in writing of "the merry merry farmer" leave out experiences like this—they omit the mud and the dust and the grime, they forget the army worm, the flies, the heat, as well as the smells and drudgery of the barns. Milking the cows is spoken of in the traditional fashion as a lovely pastoral recreation, when as a matter of fact it is a tedious job. We all hated it. We saw no poetry in it. We hated it in summer when the mosquitoes bit and the cows slashed us with their tails, and we hated it still more in the winter time when they stood in crowded malodorous stalls.

In summer when the flies were particularly savage we had a way of jamming our heads into the cows' flanks to prevent them from kicking into the pail, and sometimes we tied their tails to their legs so that they could not lash our ears. Humboldt Bunn tied a heifer's tail to his boot straps once—and regretted it almost instantly.—No, no, it won't do to talk to me of "the sweet breath of kine." I know them too well—and calves are not "the lovely, fawn-like creatures" they are supposed to be. To the boy who is teaching them to drink out of a pail they are nasty brutes quite unlike fawns. They have a way of filling their nostrils with milk and blowing it all over their nurse. They are greedy, noisy, ill-smelling and stupid. They look well when running with their mothers in the pasture, but as soon as they are weaned they lose all their charm—for me.

Attendance on swine was less humiliating for the reason that we could keep them at arm's length, but we didn't enjoy that. We liked teaming and pitching hay and harvesting and making fence, and we did not greatly resent plowing or husking corn but we did hate the smell, the filth of the cow-yard. Even hostling had its "outs," especially in spring when the horses were shedding their hair. I never fully enjoyed the taste of equine dandruff, and the eternal smell of manure irked me, especially at the table.

Clearing out from behind the animals was one of our never ending jobs, and hauling the compost out on the fields was one of the tasks which, as my father grimly said, "We always put off till it rains so hard we can't work out doors." This was no joke to us, for not only did we work out doors, we worked while standing ankle deep in the slime of the yard, getting full benefit of the drizzle. Our new land did not need the fertilizer, but we were forced to haul it away or move the barn. Some folks moved the barn. But then my father was an idealist.

Life was not all currying or muck-raking for Burt or for me. Herding the cows came in to relieve the monotony of farm-work. Wide tracts of unbroken sod still lay open to the north and west, and these were the common grazing grounds for the community. Every farmer kept from twenty-five to a hundred head of cattle and half as many colts, and no sooner did the green begin to show on the fire-blackened sod in April than the winter-worn beasts left the straw-piles under whose lee they had fed during the cold months, and crawled out to nip the first tender spears of grass in the sheltered swales. They were still "free commoners" in the eyes of the law.

The colts were a fuzzy, ungraceful lot at this season. Even the best of them had big bellies and carried dirty and tangled manes, but as the grazing improved, as the warmth and plenty of May filled their veins with new blood, they sloughed off their mangy coats and lifted their wide-blown nostrils to the western wind in exultant return to freedom. Many of them had never felt the weight of a man's hand, and even those that had wintered in and around the barn-yard soon lost all trace of domesticity. It was not unusual to find that the wildest and wariest of all the leaders bore a collar mark or some other ineffaceable badge of previous servitude.

They were for the most part Morgan grades or "Canuck," with a strain of broncho to give them fire. It was curious, it was glorious to see how deeply-buried instincts broke out in these halterless herds. In a few days, after many trials of speed and power the bands of all the region united into one drove, and a leader, the swiftest and most tireless of them all, appeared from the ranks and led them at will.

Often without apparent cause, merely for the joy of it, they left their feeding grounds to wheel and charge and race for hours over the swells, across the creeks and through the hazel thickets. Sometimes their movements arose from the stinging of gadflies, sometimes from a battle between two jealous leaders, sometimes from the passing of a wolf—often from no cause at all other than that of abounding vitality.

In much the same fashion, but less rapidly, the cattle went forth upon the plain and as each herd not only contained the growing steers, but the family cows, it became the duty of one boy from each farm to mount a horse at five o'clock every afternoon and "hunt the cattle," a task seldom shirked. My brother and I took turn and turn about at this delightful task, and soon learned to ride like Comanches. In fact we lived in the saddle, when freed from duty in the field. Burton often met us on the feeding grounds, and at such times the prairie seemed an excellent place for boys. As we galloped along together it was easy to imagine ourselves Wild Bill and Buckskin Joe in pursuit of Indians or buffalo.

We became, by force of unconscious observation, deeply learned in the language and the psychology of kine as well as colts. We watched the big bull-necked stags as they challenged one another, pawing the dust or kneeling to tear the sod with their horns. We possessed perfect understanding of their battle signs. Their boastful, defiant cries were as intelligible to us as those of men. Every note, every motion had a perfectly definite meaning. The foolish, inquisitive young heifers, the staid self-absorbed dowagers wearing their bells with dignity, the frisky two-year-olds and the lithe-bodied wide-horned truculent three-year-olds all came in for interpretation.

Sometimes a lone steer ranging the sod came suddenly upon a trace of blood. Like a hound he paused, snuffling the earth. Then with wide mouth and outthrust, curling tongue, uttered voice. Wild as the tiger's food-sick cry, his warning roar burst forth, ending in a strange, upward explosive whine. Instantly every head in the herd was lifted, even the old cows heavy with milk stood as if suddenly renewing their youth, alert and watchful.

Again it came, that prehistoric bawling cry, and with one mind the herd began to center, rushing with menacing swiftness, like warriors answering their chieftain's call for aid. With awkward lope or jolting trot, snorting with fury they hastened to the rescue, only to meet in blind bewildered mass, swirling to and fro in search of an imaginary cause of some ancestral danger.

At such moments we were glad of our swift ponies. From our saddles we could study these outbreaks of atavistic rage with serene enjoyment.

In herding the cattle we came to know all the open country

round about and found it very beautiful. On the uplands a short, light-green, hair-like grass grew, intermixed with various resinous weeds, while in the lowland feeding grounds luxuriant patches of blue-joint, wild oats, and other tall forage plants waved in the wind. Along the streams and in the "sloos" cat-tails and tiger-lilies nodded above thick mats of wide-bladed marsh grass.—Almost without realizing it, I came to know the character of every weed, every flower, every living thing big enough to be seen from the back of a horse.

Nothing could be more generous, more joyous, than these natural meadows in summer. The flash and ripple and glimmer of the tall sunflowers, the myriad voices of gleeful bobolinks, the chirp and gurgle of red-winged blackbirds swaying on the willows, the meadow-larks piping from grassy bogs, the peep of the prairie chick and the wailing call of plover on the flowery green slopes of the uplands made it all an ecstatic world to me. It was a wide world with a big, big sky which gave alluring hint of the still more glorious unknown wilderness beyond.

Sometimes of a Sunday afternoon, Harriet and I wandered away to the meadows along Dry Run, gathering bouquets of pinks, sweet-williams, tiger-lilies and lady-slippers, thus attaining a vague perception of another and sweeter side of life. The sun flamed across the splendid serial waves of the grasses and the perfumes of a hundred spicy plants rose in the shimmering mid-day air. At such times the mere joy of living filled our young hearts with wordless satisfaction.

Nor were the upland ridges less interesting, for huge antlers lying bleached and bare in countless numbers on the slopes told of the herds of elk and bison that had once fed in these splendid savannahs, living and dying in the days when the tall Sioux were the only hunters.

The gray hermit, the badger, still clung to his deep den on the rocky unplowed ridges, and on sunny April days the mother fox lay out with her young, on southward-sloping swells. Often we met the prairie wolf or startled him from his sleep in hazel copse, finding in him the spirit of the wilderness. To us it seemed that just over the next long swell toward the sunset the shaggy brown bulls still fed in myriads, and in our hearts was a longing to ride away into the "sunset regions" of our song.

All the boys I knew talked of Colorado, never of New England. We dreamed of the plains, of the Black Hills, discussing cattle raising and mining and hunting. "We'll have our rifles ready, boys, ha, ha, ha-ha!" was still our favorite chorus, "Newbrasky" and Wyoming our far-off wonderlands, Buffalo Bill our hero.

David, my hunter uncle who lived near us, still retained his long old-fashioned, muzzle-loading rifle, and one day offered it to me, but as I could not hold it at arm's length, I sorrowfully returned it. We owned a shotgun, however, and this I used with all the confidence of a man. I was able to kill a few ducks with it and I also hunted gophers during May when the sprouting corn was in most danger. Later I became quite expert in catching chickens on the wing.

On a long ridge to the north and west, the soil, too wet and cold to cultivate easily, remained unplowed for several years and scattered over these clay lands stood small groves of popple trees which we called "tow-heads." They were usually only two or three hundred feet in diameter, but they stood out like islands in the waving seas of grasses. Against these dark-green masses, breakers of blue-joint radiantly rolled.—To the east some four miles ran the Little Cedar River, and plum trees and crabapples and haws bloomed along its banks. In June immense crops of strawberries offered from many meadows. Their delicious odor rose to us as we rode our way, tempting us to dismount and gather and eat.

Over these uplands, through these thickets of hazel brush, and around these coverts of popple, Burton and I careered, hunting the cows, chasing rabbits, killing rattlesnakes, watching the battles of bulls, racing the half-wild colts and pursuing the prowling wolves. It was an alluring life, and Harriet, who rode with us occasionally, seemed to enjoy it quite as much as any boy. She could ride almost as well as Burton, and we were all expert horse-tamers.

We all rode like cavalrymen,—that is to say, while holding the reins in our left hands we guided our horses by the pressure of the strap across the neck, rather than by pulling at the bit. Our ponies were never allowed to trot. We taught them a peculiar gait which we called "the lope," which was an easy canter in front and a trot behind (a very good gait for long distances), and we drilled them to keep this pace steadily and to fall at command into a swift walk without any jolting intervening trot.—We learned to ride like circus performers standing on our saddles, and practised other of the tricks we had seen, and through it all my mother remained unalarmed. To her a boy on a horse was as natural as a babe in the cradle. The chances we took of getting killed were so numerous that she could not afford to worry.

Burton continued to be my almost inseparable companion at school and whenever we could get together, and while to others he seemed only a shy, dull boy, to me he was something more. His strength and skill were remarkable and his self-command amazing. Although a lad of instant, white-hot, dangerous temper, he suddenly, at fifteen years of age, took himself in hand in a fashion miraculous to me. He decided (I never knew just why or how)—that he would never again use an obscene or profane word. He kept his vow. I knew him for over thirty years and I never heard him raise his voice in anger or utter a word a woman would have shrunk from,—and yet he became one of the most fearless and indomitable mountaineers I ever knew.

This change in him profoundly influenced me and though I said nothing about it, I resolved to do as well. I never quite succeeded, although I discouraged as well as I could the stories which some of the men and boys were so fond of telling, but alas! when the old cow kicked over my pail of milk, I fell from grace and told her just what I thought of her in phrases that Burton would have repressed. Still, I manfully tried to follow his good trail.

Cornplanting, which followed wheat-seeding, was done by hand, for a year or two, and this was a joyous task.—We "changed works" with neighbor Button, and in return Cyrus and Eva came to help us. Harriet and Eva and I worked side by side, "dropping" the corn, while Cyrus and the hired man followed with the hoes to cover it. Little Frank skittered about, planting with desultory action such pumpkin seeds as he did not eat. The presence of our young friends gave the job something of the nature of a party and we were sorry when it was over.

After the planting a fortnight of less strenuous labor came on, a period which had almost the character of a holiday. The wheat needed no cultivation and the corn was not high enough to plow.

This was a time for building fence and fixing up things generally. This, too, was the season of the circus. Each year one came along from the east, trailing clouds of glorified dust and filling our minds with the color of romance.

From the time the "advance man" flung his highly colored posters over the fence till the coming of the glorious day we thought of little else. It was India and Arabia and the jungle to us. History and the magic and pomp of chivalry mingled in the parade of the morning, and the crowds, the clanging band, the haughty and alien beauty of the women, the gold embroidered housings, the stark majesty of the acrobats subdued us into silent worship.

I here pay tribute to the men who brought these marvels to my eyes. To rob me of my memories of the circus would leave me as poor as those to whom life was a drab and hopeless round of toil. It was our brief season of imaginative life. In one day—in a part of one day—we gained a thousand new conceptions of the world and of human nature. It was an embodiment of all that was skillful and beautiful in manly action. It was a compendium of biologic research but more important still, it brought to our ears the latest band pieces and taught us the most popular songs. It furnished us with jokes. It relieved our dullness. It gave us something to talk about.

We always went home wearied with excitement, and dusty and fretful—but content. We had seen it. We had grasped as much of it as anybody and could remember it as well as the best. Next day as we resumed work in the field the memory of its splendors went with us like a golden cloud.

Most of the duties of the farmer's life require the lapse of years to seem beautiful in my eyes, but haying was a season of well-defined charm. In Iowa, summer was at its most exuberant stage of vitality during the last days of June, and it was not strange that the faculties of even the toiling hay-maker, dulled and deadened with never ending drudgery, caught something of the superabundant glow and throb of nature's life.

As I write I am back in that marvellous time.—The cornfield, dark-green and sweetly cool, is beginning to ripple in the wind with multitudinous stir of shining, swirling leaf. Waves of dusk and green and gold, circle across the ripening barley, and long leaves upthrust, at intervals, like spears. The trees are in heaviest foliage, insect life is at its height, and the shimmering air is filled with buzzing, dancing forms, and the clover is gay with the sheen of innumerable gauzy wings.

The west wind comes to me laden with ecstatic voices. The bobolinks sail and tinkle in the sensuous hush, now sinking, now rising, their exquisite notes filling the air as with the sound of fairy bells. The king-bird, alert, aggressive, cries out sharply as he launches from the top of a poplar tree upon some buzzing insect, and the plover makes the prairie sad with his wailing call. Vast purple-and-white clouds move like stately ships before the breeze, dark with rain, which they drop momentarily in trailing garments upon the earth, and so pass in majesty amidst a roll of thunder.

The grasshoppers move in clouds with snap and buzz, and out of the luxurious stagnant marshes comes the ever-thickening chorus of the toads, while above them the kildees and the snipe shuttle to and fro in sounding flight. The blackbirds on the cat-tails sway and swing, uttering through lifted throats their liquid gurgle, mad with delight of the sun and the season—and over all, and laving all, moves the slow wind, heavy with the breath of the far-off blooms of other lands, a wind which covers the sunset plain with a golden entrancing haze.

At such times it seemed to me that we had reached the "sunset region" of our song, and that we were indeed "lords of the soil."

I am not so sure that haying brought to our mothers anything like this rapture, for the men added to our crew made the duties of the kitchens just that much heavier. I doubt if the women—any of them—got out into the fields or meadows long enough to enjoy the birds and the breezes. Even on Sunday as they rode away to church, they were too tired and too worried to re-act to the beauties of the landscape.

I now began to dimly perceive that my mother was not well. Although large and seemingly strong, her increasing weight made her long days of housework a torture. She grew very tired and her sweet face was often knotted with physical pain.

She still made most of our garments as well as her own. She tailored father's shirts and underclothing, sewed carpet rags, pieced quilts and made butter for market,—and yet, in the midst of it all, found time to put covers on our baseball, and to do up all our burns and bruises. Being a farmer's wife in those days, meant laboring outside any regulation of the hours of toil. I recall hearing one of the tired housewives say, "Seems like I never get a day off, not even on Sunday," a protest which my mother thoroughly understood and sympathized with, notwithstanding its seeming inhospitality.

No history of this time would be complete without a reference to the doctor. We were a vigorous and on the whole a healthy tribe but accidents sometimes happened and "Go for the doctor!" was the first command when the band-cutter slashed the hand of the thresher or one of the children fell from the hay-rick.

One night as I lay buried in deep sleep close to the garret eaves I heard my mother call me—and something in her voice pierced me, roused me. A poignant note of alarm was in it.

"Hamlin," she called, "get up—at once. You must go for the doctor. Your father is very sick. *Hurry!*"

I sprang from my bed, dizzy with sleep, yet understanding her appeal. "I hear you, I'm coming," I called down to her as I started to dress.

"Call Hattie. I need her too."

The rain was pattering on the roof, and as I dressed I had a disturbing vision of the long cold ride which lay before me. I hoped the case was not so bad as mother thought. With limbs still numb and weak I stumbled down the stairs to the sitting room where a faint light shone.

Mother met me with white, strained face. "Your father is suffering terribly. Go for the doctor at once."

I could hear the sufferer groan even as I moved about the kitchen, putting on my coat and lighting the lantern. It was about one o'clock of the morning, and the wind was cold as I picked my way through the mud to the barn. The thought of the long miles to town made me shiver but as the son of a soldier I could not falter in my duty.

In their warm stalls the horses were resting in dreamful doze. Dan and Dick, the big plow team, stood near the door. Jule and Dolly came next. Wild Frank, a fleet but treacherous Morgan, stood fifth and for a moment I considered taking him. He was strong and of wonderful staying powers but so savage and unreliable that I dared not risk an accident. I passed on to bay Kittie whose bright eyes seemed to inquire, "What is the matter?"

Flinging the blanket over her and smoothing it carefully, I tossed the light saddle to her back and cinched it tight, so tight that she grunted. "I can't take any chances of a spill," I explained to her, and she accepted the bit willingly. She was always ready for action and fully dependable.

Blowing out my lantern I hung it on a peg, led Kit from her stall out into the night, and swung to the saddle. She made off with a spattering rush through the yard, out into the road. It was dark as pitch but I was fully awake now. The dash of the rain in my face had cleared my brain but I trusted to the keener senses of the mare to find the road which showed only in the strips of water which filled the wagon tracks.

We made way slowly for a few minutes until my eyes expanded to take in the faint lines of light along the lane. The road at last became a river of ink running between faint gray banks of sward, and my heart rose in confidence. I took on dignity. I was a courier riding through the night to save a city, a messenger on whose courage and skill thousands of lives depended.

"Get out o' this!" I shouted to Kit, and she leaped away like a wolf, at a tearing gallop.

She knew her rider. We had herded the cattle many days on the prairie, and in races with the wild colts I had tested her speed. Snorting with vigor at every leap she seemed to say, "My heart is brave, my limbs are strong. Call on me."

Out of the darkness John Martin's Carlo barked. A half-mile had passed. Old Marsh's fox hound clamored next. Two miles were gone. From here the road ran diagonally across the prairie, a velvet-black band on the dim sod. The ground was firmer but there were swales full of water. Through these Kittie dashed with unhesitating confidence, the water flying from her drumming hooves. Once she went to her knees and almost unseated me, but I regained my saddle and shouted, "Go on, Kit."

The fourth mile was in the mud, but the fifth brought us to the village turnpike and the mare was as glad of it as I. Her breath was labored now. She snorted no more in exultation and confident strength. She began to wonder—to doubt, and I, who knew her ways as well as I knew those of a human being, realized that she was beginning to flag. The mud had begun to tell on her.

It hurt me to urge her on, but the memory of my mother's agonized face and the sound of my father's groan of pain steeled my heart. I set lash to her side and so kept her to her highest speed.

At last a gleam of light! Someone in the village was awake. I passed another lighted window. Then the green and red lamps of the drug store cheered me with their promise of aid, for the doctor lived next door. There too a dim ray shone.

Slipping from my weary horse I tied her to the rail and hurried up the walk toward the doctor's bell. I remembered just where the knob rested. Twice I pulled sharply, strongly, putting into it some part of the anxiety and impatience I felt. I could hear its imperative jingle as it died away in the silent house.

At last the door opened and the doctor, a big blonde handsome man in a long night gown, confronted me with impassive face. "What is it, my boy?" he asked kindly.

As I told him he looked down at my water-soaked form and wild-eyed countenance with gentle patience. Then he peered out over my head into the dismal night. He was a man of resolution but he hesitated for a moment. "Your father is suffering sharply, is he?"

"Yes, sir. I could hear him groan.—Please hurry."

He mused a moment. "He is a soldier. He would not complain of a little thing—I will come."

Turning in relief, I ran down the walk and climbed upon my shivering mare. She wheeled sharply, eager to be off on her homeward way. Her spirit was not broken, but she was content to take a slower pace. She seemed to know that our errand was accomplished and that the warm shelter of the stall was to be her reward.

Holding her down to a slow trot I turned often to see if I could detect the lights of the doctor's buggy which was a familiar sight on our road. I had heard that he kept one of his teams harnessed ready for calls like this, and I confidently expected him to overtake me. "It's a terrible night to go out, but he said he would come," I repeated as I rode.

At last the lights of a carriage, crazily rocking, came into view and pulling Kit to a walk I twisted in my saddle, ready to shout with admiration of the speed of his team. "He's driving the 'Clay-Banks,'" I called in great excitement.

The Clay-Banks were famous throughout the county as the doctor's swiftest and wildest team, a span of bronchos whose savage spirits no journey could entirely subdue, a team he did not spare, a team that scorned petting and pity, bony, sinewy, big-headed. They never walked and had little care of mud or snow.

They came rushing now with splashing feet and foaming, half-open jaws, the big doctor, calm, iron-handed, masterful, sitting in the swaying top of his light buggy, his feet against the dash board, keeping his furious span in hand as easily as if they were a pair of Shetland ponies. The nigh horse was running, the off horse pacing, and the splatter of their feet, the slash of the wheels and the roaring of their heavy breathing, made my boyish heart leap. I could hardly repress a yell of delight.

As I drew aside to let him pass the doctor called out with mellow cheer, "Take your time, boy, take your time!"

Before I could even think of an answer, he was gone and I was alone with Kit and the night.

My anxiety vanished with him. I had done all that could humanly be done, I had fetched the doctor. Whatever happened I was guiltless. I knew also that in a few minutes a sweet relief would come to my tortured mother, and with full faith and loving confidence in the man of science, I jogged along homeward, wet to the bone but triumphant.

14

Wheat and the Harvest

The early seventies were years of swift change on the Middle Border. Day by day the settlement thickened. Section by section the prairie was blackened by the plow. Month by month the sweet wild meadows were fenced and pastured and so at last the colts and cows all came into captivity, and our horseback riding ceased, cut short as if by some imperial decree. Lanes of barbed wire replaced the winding wagon trails, our saddles gathered dust in the grain-sheds, and groves of Lombardy poplar and European larch replaced the tow-heads of aspen and hazel through which we had pursued the wolf and fox.

I will not say that this produced in me any keen sense of sorrow at the time, for though I missed our horse-herds and the charm of the open spaces, I turned to tamer sports with the resilient adaptability of youth. If I could not ride I could at least play baseball, and the swimming hole in the Little Cedar remained untouched. The coming in of numerous Eastern settlers brought added charm to neighborhood life. Picnics, conventions, Fourth of July celebrations—all intensified our interest, and in their increasing drama we were compensated, in some degree at least, for the delights which were passing with the prairie.

Our school-house did not change—except for the worse. No one thought of adding a tree or a vine to its ugly yard. Sun-smit, bare as a nose it stood at the cross-roads, receiving us through its drab door-way as it had done from the first. Its benches, hideously hacked and thick with grime, were as hard and uncomfortable as when I first saw them, and the windows remained unshaded and unwashed. Most of the farmhouses in the region remained equally unadorned, but Deacon Gammons had added an "ell" and established a "parlor," and Anson Burtch had painted his barn. The plain began to take on a comfortable look, for some of the trees of the windbreaks had risen above the roofs, and growing maples softened the effect of the bleak expanse.

My mother, like most of her neighbors, still cooked and served meals in our one living room during the winter but moved into a "summer kitchen" in April. This change always gave us a sense of luxury—which is pathetic, if you look at it that way. Our front room became suddenly and happily a parlor, and was so treated. Mother at once got down the rag carpet and gave orders for us to shake out and bring in some clean straw to put under it, and when we had tacked it down and rearranged the furniture, it was no longer a place for muddy boots and shirt-sleeved shiftlessness, it had an air of being in perpetual Sabbath leisure.

The Garlands were not so poor as all this would seem to imply, for we were now farming over three hundred acres of land and caring for a herd of cattle and many swine. It merely meant that my father did not feel the need of a "best room" and mother and Harriet were not yet able to change his mind. Harriet wanted an organ like Mary Abby Gammons, mother longed for a real "ingrain" carpet and we all clamored for a spring wagon. We got the wagon first.

That bleak little house is clearly defined in my mind at this moment. The low lean-to kitchen, the rag-carpeted sitting room with its two chromos of Wide Awake and Fast Asleep—its steel engraving of General Grant, and its tiny melodeon in the corner—all these come back to me. There are very few books or magazines in the scene, but there are piles of newspapers, for my father was an omnivorous reader of all things political. It was not a hovel, it was a pioneer cabin persisting into a settled community, that was all.

During these years the whole middle border was menaced by bands of horse-thieves operating under a secret well-organized system. Horses disappeared night by night and were never recovered, till at last the farmers, in despair of the local authorities, organized a Horse Thief Protective Association which undertook to pursue and punish the robbers and to pay for such animals as were not returned. Our county had an association of this sort and shortly after we opened our new farm my father became a member. My first knowledge of this fact came when he nailed on our barn-door the white cloth poster which proclaimed in bold black letters a warning and a threat signed by "the Committee."—I was always a little in doubt as to whether the horse-thieves or ourselves were to be protected, for the notice was fair warning to them as well as an assurance to us. Anyhow very few horses were stolen from barns thus protected.

. The campaign against the thieves gave rise to many stirring stories which lost nothing in my father's telling of them. Jim McCarty was agent for our association and its effectiveness was largely due to his swift and fearless action. We all had a pleasant sense of the mystery of the night riding which went on during this period and no man could pass with a led horse without being under suspicion of being either a thief or a deputy. Then, too, the thieves were supposed to have in every community a spy who gave information as to the best horses, and informed the gang as to the membership of the Protective Society.

One of our neighbors fell under suspicion at this time and never got clear of it. I hope we did him no injustice in this for never after could I bring myself to enter his house, and he was clearly ostracized by all the neighbors.

As I look back over my life on that Iowa farm the song of the reaper fills large place in my mind. We were all worshippers of wheat in those days. The men thought and talked of little else between seeding and harvest, and you will not wonder at this if you have known and bowed down before such abundance as we then enjoyed.

Deep as the breast of a man, wide as the sea, heavy-headed, supple-stocked, many-voiced, full of multitudinous, secret, whispered colloquies,—a meeting place of winds and of sunlight,—our fields ran to the world's end.

We trembled when the storm lay hard upon the wheat, we exulted as the lilac shadows of noon-day drifted over it! We went out into it at noon when all was still—so still we could hear the pulse of the transforming sap as it crept from cool root to swaying plume. We stood before it at evening when the setting sun flooded it with crimson, the bearded heads lazily swirling under the wings of the wind, the mousing hawk dipping into its green deeps like the eagle into the sea, and our hearts expanded with the beauty and the mystery of it—and back of all this was the knowledge that its abundance meant a new carriage, an addition to the house or a new suit of clothes.

Haying was over, and day by day we boys watched with deepening interest while the hot sun transformed the juices of the soil into those stately stalks. I loved to go out into the fairy forest of it, and lying there, silent in its swaying deeps, hear the wild chickens peep and the wind sing its subtle song over our heads. Day by day I studied the barley as it turned yellow, first at the root and then at the neck (while the middle joints, rank and sappy, retained their blue-green sheen), until at last the lower leaves began to wither and the stems to stiffen in order to uphold the daily increasing weight of the milky berries, and then almost in an hour—lo! the edge of the field became a banded ribbon of green and yellow, languidly waving in and out with every rush of the breeze.

Now we got out the reaper, put the sickles in order, and father laid in a store of provisions. Extra hands were hired, and at last, early on a hot July morning, the boss mounted to his seat on the self-rake "McCormick" and drove into the field. Frank rode the lead horse, four stalwart hands and myself took "stations" behind the reaper and the battle was on!

Reaping generally came about the 20th of July, the hottest and dryest part of the summer, and was the most pressing work of the year. It demanded early rising for the men, and it meant an all day broiling over the kitchen stove for the women. Stern, incessant toil went on inside and out from dawn till sunset, no matter how the thermometer sizzled. On many days the mercury mounted to ninety-five in the shade, but with wide fields all yellowing at the same moment, no one thought of laying off. A storm might sweep it flat, or if neglected too long, it might "crinkle."

Our reaper in 1874 was a new model of the McCormick self-rake,—the Marsh Harvester was not yet in general use. The Woods Dropper, the Seymour and Morgan hand-rake "contraptions" seemed a long way in the past. True the McCormick required four horses to drag it but it was effective. It was hard to believe that anything more cunning would ever come to claim the farmer's money. Weird tales of a machine on which two men rode and bound twelve acres of wheat in ten hours came to us, but we did not potently believe these reports—on the contrary we accepted the self-rake as quite the final word in harvesting machinery and cheerily bent to the binding of sheaves with their own straw in the good old time-honored way.

No task save that of "cradling" surpassed in severity "binding on a station." It was a full-grown man's job, but every boy was ambitious to try his hand, and when at fourteen years of age I was promoted from "bundle boy" to be one of the five hands to bind after the reaper, I went to my corner with joy and confidence. For two years I had been serving as binder on the corners, (to keep the grain out of the way of the horses) and I knew my job.

I was short and broad-shouldered with large strong hands admirably adapted for this work, and for the first two hours, easily held my own with the rest of the crew, but as the morning wore on and the sun grew hotter, my enthusiasm waned. A painful void developed in my chest. My breakfast had been ample, but no mere stomachful of food could carry a growing boy through five hours of desperate toil. Along about a quarter to ten, I began to scan the field with anxious eye, longing to see Harriet and the promised luncheon basket.

Just when it seemed that I could endure the strain no longer she came bearing a jug of cool milk, some cheese and some deliciously fresh fried-cakes. With keen joy I set a couple of tall sheaves together like a tent and flung myself down flat on my back in their shadow to devour my lunch.

Tired as I was, my dim eyes apprehended something of the splendor of the shining clouds which rolled like storms of snow through the deep-blue spaces of sky and so, resting silently as a clod I could hear the chirp of the crickets, the buzzing wings of flies and the faint, fairy like tread of smaller unseen insects hurrying their way just beneath my ear in the stubble. Strange green worms, grasshoppers and shining beetles crept over me as I dozed.

This delicious, dreamful respite was broken by the far-off approaching purr of the sickle, flicked by the faint snap of the driver's whip, and out of the low rustle of the everstirring lilliputian forest came the wailing cry of a baby wild chicken lost from its mother—a falling, thrilling, piteous little pipe.

Such momentary communion with nature seemed all the

sweeter for the work which had preceded it, as well as that which was to follow it. It took resolution to rise and go back to my work, but I did it, sustained by a kind of soldierly pride.

At noon we hurried to the house, surrounded the kitchen table and fell upon our boiled beef and potatoes with such ferocity that in fifteen minutes our meal was over. There was no ceremony and very little talking till the hid wolf was appeased. Then came a heavenly half-hour of rest on the cool grass in the shade of the trees, a siesta as luxurious as that of a Spanish monarch—but alas!—this "nooning," as we called it, was always cut short by father's word of sharp command, "Roll out, boys!" and again the big white jugs were filled at the well, the horses, lazy with food, led the way back to the field, and the stern contest began again.

All nature at this hour seemed to invite to repose rather than to labor, and as the heat increased I longed with wordless fervor for the green woods of the Cedar River. At times the gentle wind hardly moved the bended heads of the barley, and the hawks hung in the air like trout sleeping in deep pools. The sunlight was a golden, silent, scorching cataract—yet each of us must strain his tired muscles and bend his aching back to the harvest.

Supper came at five, another delicious interval—and then at six we all went out again for another hour or two in the cool of the sunset.—However, the pace was more leisurely now for the end of the day was near. I always enjoyed this period, for the shadows lengthening across the stubble, and the fiery sun, veiled by the gray clouds of the west, had wondrous charm. The air began to moisten and grow cool. The voices of the men pulsed powerfully and cheerfully across the narrowing field of unreaped grain, the prairie hens led forth their broods to feed, and at last, father's long-drawn and musical cry, "Turn out! All hands Turn out!" rang with restful significance through the dusk. Then, slowly, with low-hung heads the freed horses moved toward the barn, walking with lagging steps like weary warriors going into camp.

In all the toil of the harvest field, the water jug filled a large place. It was a source of anxiety as well as comfort. To keep it cool, to keep it well filled was a part of my job. No man passed it at the "home corner" of the field. It is a delightful part of my recollections of the harvest.

O cool gray jug that touched the lips
In kiss that softly closed and clung,
No Spanish wine the tippler sips,
No port the poet's praise has sung—
Such pure, untainted sweetness yields
As cool gray jug in harvest fields.

I see it now!—a clover leaf
Out-spread upon its sweating side!—
As from the sheltering sheaf
I pluck and swing it high, the wide
Field glows with noon-day heat,
The winds are tangled in the wheat.

The swarming crickets blithely cheep,
Across the stir of waving grain
I see the burnished reaper creep—
The lunch-boy comes, and once again
The jug its crystal coolness yields—
O cool gray jug in harvest fields!

My father did not believe in serving strong liquor to his men, and seldom treated them to even beer. While not a teetotaler he was strongly opposed to all that intemperance represented. He furnished the best of food, and tea and coffee, but no liquor, and the men respected him for it.

The reaping on our farm that year lasted about four weeks. Barley came first, wheat followed, the oats came last of all. No sooner was the final swath cut than the barley was ready to be put under cover, and "stacking," a new and less exacting phase of the harvest, began.

This job required less men than reaping, hence a part of our hands were paid off, only the more responsible ones were retained. The rush, the strain of the reaping gave place to a leisurely, steady, day-by-day garnering of the thoroughly seasoned shocks into great conical piles, four in a place in the midst of the stubble, which was already growing green with swiftly-springing weeds.

A full crew consisted of a stacker, a boy to pass bundles, two drivers for the heavy wagon-racks, and a pitcher in the field who lifted the sheaves from the shock with a three-tined fork and threw them to the man on the load.

At the age of ten I had been taught to "handle bundles" on the stack, but now at fourteen I took my father's place as stacker, whilst he passed the sheaves and told me how to lay them. This exalted me at the same time that it increased my responsibility. It made a man of me—not only in my own estimation, but in the eyes of my boy companions to whom I discoursed loftily on the value of "bulges" and the advantages of the stack over the rick.

No sooner was the stacking ended than the dreaded task of plowing began for Burton and John and me. Every morning while our fathers and the hired men shouldered their forks and went away to help some neighbor thrash—("changing works") we drove our teams into the field, there to plod round and round in solitary course. Here I acquired the feeling which I afterward put into verse—

> A lonely task it is to plow!
> All day the black and shining soil
> Rolls like a ribbon from the mold-board's
> Glistening curve. All day the horses toil,
> Battling with savage flies, and strain
> Their creaking single-trees. All day
> The crickets peer from wind-blown stacks of grain.

Franklin's job was almost as lonely. He was set to herd the cattle on the harvested stubble and keep them out of the corn field. A little later, in October, when I was called to take my place as corn-husker, he was promoted to the plow. Our only respite during the months of October and November was the occasional cold rain which permitted us to read or play cards in the kitchen.

Cards! I never look at a certain type of playing card without experiencing a return of the wonder and the guilty joy with which I bought of Metellus Kirby my first "deck," and slipped it into my pocket. There was an alluring oriental imaginative quality in the drawing on the face cards. They brought to me vague hints of mad monarchs, desperate stakes, and huge sudden rewards. All that I had heard or read of Mississippi gamblers came back to make those gaudy bits of pasteboard marvellous.

My father did not play cards, hence, although I had no reason to think he would forbid them to me, I took a fearsome joy in assuming his bitter opposition. For a time my brother and I played in secret, and then one day, one cold bleak day as we were seated on the floor of the granary playing on an upturned half-bushel measure, shivering with the chill, our fingers numb and blue, the door opened and father looked in.

We waited, while his round, eagle-gray eyes took in the situation and it seemed a long, terrifying interval, then at last he mildly said, "I guess you'd better go in and play by the stove. This isn't very comfortable."

Stunned by this unexpected concession, I gathered up the cards, and as I took my way to the house, I thought deeply. The meaning of that quiet voice, that friendly invitation was not lost on me. The soldier rose to grand heights by that single act, and when I showed the cards to mother and told her that father had consented to our playing, she looked grave but made no objection to our use of the kitchen table. As a matter of fact they both soon after joined our game. "If you are going to play," they said, "we'd rather you played right here with us." Thereafter rainy days were less dreary, and the evenings shorter.

Everybody played Authors at this time also, and to this day I cannot entirely rid myself of the estimations which our pack of cards fixed in my mind. *Prue and I* and *The Blithedale Romance* were on an equal footing, so far as our game went, and Howells, Bret Harte and Dickens were all of far-off romantic horizon. Writers were singular, exalted beings found only in the East—in splendid cities. They were not folks, they were demigods, men and women living aloof and looking down benignantly on toiling common creatures like us.

It never entered my mind that anyone I knew could ever by any chance meet an author, or even hear one lecture—although it was said that they did sometimes come west on altruistic educational journeys and that they sometimes reached our county town.

I am told—I do not know that it is true—that I am one of the names on a present-day deck of Author cards. If so, I wish I could call in that small plow-boy of 1874 and let him play a game with this particular pack!

The crops on our farms in those first years were enormous and prices were good, and yet the homes of the neighborhood were slow in taking on grace or comfort. I don't know why this was so, unless it was that the men were continually buying more land and more machinery. Our own stables were still straw-roofed sheds, but the trees which we had planted had grown swiftly into a grove, and a garden, tended at odd moments by all hands, brought small fruits and vegetables in season. Although a constantly improving collection of farm machinery lightened the burdens of the husbandman, the drudgery of the house-wife's dish-washing and cooking did not correspondingly lessen. I fear it increased, for with the widening of the fields came the doubling of the harvest hands, and my mother continued to do most of the housework herself—cooking, sewing, washing, churning, and nursing the sick from time to time. No one in trouble ever sent for Isabelle Garland in vain, and I have many recollections of neighbors riding up in the night and calling for her with agitated voices.

Of course I did not realize, and I am sure my father did not realize, the heavy burden, the endless grind of her toil. Harriet helped, of course, and Frank and I churned and carried wood and brought water; but even with such aid, the round of mother's duties must have been as relentless as a tread-mill. Even on Sunday, when we were free for a part of the day, she was required to furnish forth three meals, and to help Frank and Jessie dress for church.—She sang less and less, and the songs we loved were seldom referred to.—If I could only go back for one little hour and take her in my arms, and tell her how much I owe her for those grinding days!

Meanwhile we were all growing away from our life in the old Wisconsin Coulee. We heard from William but seldom, and David, who had bought a farm of his own some ten miles to the south of us, came over to see us only at long intervals. He still owned his long-barrelled rifle but it hung unused on a peg in the kitchen. Swiftly the world of the hunter was receding, never to return. Prairie chickens, rabbits, ducks, and other small game still abounded but they did not call for the bullet, and turkey shoots were events of the receding past. Almost in a year the ideals of the country-side changed. David was in truth a survival of a more heroic age, a time which he loved to lament with my father who was almost as great a lover of the wilderness as he. None of us sang "O'er the hills in legions, boys." Our share in the conquest of the west seemed complete.

Threshing time, which was becoming each year less of a "bee" and more of a job (many of the men were mere hired hands), was made distinctive by David who came over from Orchard with his machine—the last time as it turned out—and stayed to the end. As I cut bands beside him in the dust and thunder of the cylinder I regained something of my boyish worship of his strength and skill. The tireless easy swing of his great frame was wonderful to me and when, in my weariness, I failed to slash a band he smiled and tore the sheaf apart—thus deepening my love for him. I looked up at him at such times as a sailor regards his captain on the bridge. His handsome immobile bearded face, his air of command, his large gestures as he rolled the broad sheaves into the howling maw of the machine made of him a chieftain.—The touch of melancholy which even then had begun to develop, added to his manly charm.

One day in late September as I was plowing in the field at the back of the farm, I encountered a particularly troublesome thicket of weeds and vines in the stubble, and decided to burn the way before the coulter. We had been doing this ever since the frost had killed the vegetation but always on lands after they had been safeguarded by strips of plowing. On this particular land no fire had been set for the reason that four large stacks of wheat still stood waiting the thresher. In my irritation and self-confidence I decided to clear away the matted stubble on the same strip though at some distance from the stacks. This seemed safe enough at the time for the wind was blowing gently from the opposite direction.

It was a lovely golden day and as I stood watching the friendly flame clearing the ground for me, I was filled with satisfaction. Suddenly I observed that the line of red was moving steadily against the wind and toward the stacks. My satisfaction changed to alarm. The matted weeds furnished a thick bed of fuel, and against the progress of the flame I had nothing to offer. I could only hope that the thinning stubble would permit me to trample it out. I tore at the ground in desperation, hoping to make a bare spot which the flame could not leap. I trampled the fire with my bare feet. I beat at it with my hat. I screamed for help.—Too late I thought of my team and the plow with which I might have drawn a furrow around the stacks. The flame touched the high-piled sheaves. It ran lightly, beautifully up the sides—and as I stood watching it, I thought, "It is all a dream. It can't be true."

But it was. In less than twenty minutes the towering piles had melted into four glowing heaps of ashes. Four hundred dollars had gone up in that blaze.

Slowly, painfully I hobbled to the plow and drove my team to the house. Although badly burned, my mental suffering was so much greater that I felt only part of it.—Leaving the horses at the well I hobbled into the house to my mother. She, I knew, would sympathize with me and shield me from the just wrath of my father who was away, but was due to return in an hour or two.

Mother received me in silence, bandaged my feet and put me to bed where I lay in shame and terror.

At last I heard father come in. He questioned, mother's voice replied. He remained ominously silent. She went on quietly but with an eloquence unusual in her. What she said to him I never knew, but when he came up the stairs and stood looking down at me his anger had cooled. He merely asked me how I felt, uncovered my burned feet, examined them, put the sheet back, and went away, without a word either of reproof or consolation.

None of us except little Jessie, ever alluded to this tragic matter again; she was accustomed to tell my story as she remembered it,—"an 'nen the moon changed—the fire ran up the stacks and burned 'em all down—"

When I think of the myriads of opportunities for committing mistakes of this sort, I wonder that we had so few accidents. The truth is our captain taught us to think before we acted at all times, and we had little of the heedlessness which less experienced children often show. We were in effect small soldiers and carried some of the responsibilities of soldiers into all that we did.

While still I was hobbling about, suffering from my wounds my uncles William and Frank McClintock drove over from Neshonoc bringing with them a cloud of strangely-moving revived memories of the hills and woods of our old Wisconsin home. I was peculiarly delighted by this visit, for while the story of my folly was told, it was not dwelt upon. They soon forgot me and fell naturally into discussion of ancient neighbors and far-away events.

To me it was like peering back into a dim, dawn-lit world wherein all forms were distorted or wondrously aggrandized. William, big, black-bearded and smiling, had lost little of his romantic appeal. Frank, still the wag, was able to turn handsprings and somersaults almost as well as ever, and the talk which followed formed an absorbing review of early days in Wisconsin.

It brought up and defined many of the events of our life in the coulee, pictures which were becoming a little vague, a little blurred. Al Randal and Ed Green, who were already almost mythical, were spoken of as living creatures and thus the far was brought near. Comparisons between the old and the new methods of seeding and harvest also gave me a sense of change, a perception which troubled me a little, especially as a wistful note had crept into the voices of these giants of the middle border. They all loved the wilderness too well not to be a little saddened by the clearing away of bosky coverts and the drying up of rippling streams.

We sent for Uncle David who came over on Sunday to spend a night with his brothers and in the argument which followed, I began to sense in him a spirit of restlessness, a growing discontent which covered his handsome face with a deepening shadow. He disliked being tied down to the dull life of the farm, and his horsepower threshing machine no longer paid him enough to compensate for the loss of time and care on the other phases of his industry. His voice was still glorious and he played the violin when strongly urged, though with a sense of dissatisfaction.

He and mother and Aunt Deborah sang *Nellie Wildwood* and *Lily Dale* and *Minnie Minturn* just as they used to do in the coulee, and I forgot my disgrace and the pain of my blistered feet in the rapture of that exquisite hour of blended melody and memory. The world they represented was passing and though I did not fully realize this, I sensed in some degree the transitory nature of this reunion. In truth it never came again. Never again did these three brothers meet, and when they said good-bye to us next morning, I wondered why it was, we must be so widely separated from those we loved the best.

15

Harriet Goes Away

Girls on the Border came to womanhood early. At fifteen my sister Harriet considered herself a young lady and began to go out to dances with Cyrus and Albert and Frances. She was small, moody and silent, and as all her interests became feminine I lost that sense of comradeship with which we used to ride after the cattle and I turned back to my brother who was growing into a hollow-chested lanky lad—and in our little sister Jessie we took increasing interest. She was a joyous child, always singing like a canary. She was never a "trial."

Though delicate and fair and pretty, she manifested a singular indifference to the usual games of girls. Contemptuous of dolls, she never played house so far as I know. She took no interest in sewing, or cooking, but had a whole yard full of "horses," that is to say, sticks of varying sizes and shapes. Each pole had its name and its "stall" and she endlessly repeated the chores of leading them to water and feeding them hay. She loved to go with me to the field and was never so happy as when riding on old Jule.—Dear little sister, I fear I neglected you at times, turning away from your sweet face and pleading smile to lose myself in some worthless book. I am comforted to remember that I did sometimes lift you to the back of a real horse and permit you to ride "a round," chattering like a sparrow as we plodded back and forth across the field.

Frank cared little for books but he could take a hand at games although he was not strong. Burton who at sixteen was almost as tall as his father was the last to surrender his saddle to the ash-bin. He often rode his high-headed horse past our house on his way to town, and I especially recall one day, when as Frank and I were walking to town (one fourth of July) Burt came galloping along with five dollars in his pocket.—We could not see the five dollars but we did get the full force and dignity of his cavalier approach, and his word was sufficient proof of the cash he had to spend. As he rode on we, in crushed humility, resumed our silent plodding in the dust of his horse's hooves.

His round of labor, like my own, was well established. In spring he drove team and drag. In haying he served as stacker. In harvest he bound his station. In stacking he pitched bundles. After stacking he plowed or went out "changing works" and ended the season's work by husking corn—a job that increased in severity from year to year, as the fields grew larger. In '74 it lasted well into November. Beginning in the warm and golden September we kept at it (off and on) until sleety rains coated the ears with ice and the wet soil loaded our boots with huge balls of clay and grass—till the snow came whirling by on the wings of the north wind and the last flock of belated geese went sprawling side-wise down the ragged sky. Grim business this! At times our wet gloves froze on our hands.

How primitive all our notions were! Few of the boys owned overcoats and the same suit served each of us for summer and winter alike. In lieu of ulsters most of us wore long, gay-colored woolen scarfs wound about our heads and necks—scarfs which our mothers, sisters or sweethearts had knitted for us. Our footwear continued to be boots of the tall cavalry model with pointed toes and high heels. Our collars were either home-made ginghams or "boughten" ones of paper at fifteen cents per box. Some men went so far as to wear "dickies," that is to say, false shirt fronts made of paper, but this was considered a silly cheat. No one in our neighborhood ever saw a tailor-made suit, and nothing that we wore fitted,—our clothes merely enclosed us.

Harriet, like the other women, made her own dresses, assisted by my mother, and her best gowns in summer were white muslin tied at the waist with ribbons. All the girls dressed in this simple fashion, but as I write, recalling the glowing cheeks and shining eyes of Hattie and Agnes and Bess, I feel again the thrill of admiration which ran through my blood as they came down the aisle at church, or when at dancing parties they balanced or "sashayed" in *Honest John* or *Money Musk*.—To me they were perfectly clothed and divinely fair.

The contrast between the McClintocks, my hunter uncles, and Addison Garland, my father's brother who came to visit us at about this time was strikingly significant even to me. Tall, thoughtful, humorous and of frail and bloodless body, "A. Garland" as he signed himself, was of the Yankee merchant type. A general store in Wisconsin was slowly making him a citizen of substance and his quiet comment brought to me an entirely new conception of the middle west and its future. He was a philosopher. He peered into the years that were to come and paid little heed to the passing glories of the plain. He predicted astounding inventions and great cities, and advised my father to go into dairying and diversified crops. "This is a natural butter country," said he.

He was an invalid, and it was through him that we first learned of graham flour. During his stay (and for some time after) we suffered an infliction of sticky "gems" and dark soggy bread. We all resented this displacement of our usual salt-rising loaf and delicious saleratus biscuits but we ate the hot gems, liberally splashed with butter, just as we would have eaten dog-biscuit or hardtack had it been put before us.

One of the sayings of my uncle will fix his character in the mind of the reader. One day, apropos of some public event which displeased him, he said, "Men can be infinitely more foolish in their collective capacity than on their own individual account." His quiet utterance of these words and especially the phrase "collective capacity" made a deep impression on me. The underlying truth of the saying came to me only later in my life.

He was full of "*citrus-belt*" enthusiasm and told us that he was about to sell out and move to Santa Barbara. He did not urge my father to accompany him, and if he had, it would have made no difference. A winterless climate and the raising of fruit did not appeal to my Commander. He loved the prairie and the raising of wheat and cattle, and gave little heed to anything else, but to me Addison's talk of "the citrus belt" had the value of a romance, and the occasional Spanish phrases which he used afforded me an indefinable delight. It was unthinkable that I should ever see an *arroya* but I permitted myself to dream of it while he talked.

I think he must have encouraged my sister in her growing desire for an education, for in the autumn after his visit she entered the Cedar Valley Seminary at Osage and her going produced in me a desire to accompany her. I said nothing of it at the time, for my father gave but reluctant consent to Harriet's plan. A district school education seemed to him ample for any farmer's needs.

Many of our social affairs were now connected with "the Grange." During these years on the new farm while we were busied with breaking and fencing and raising wheat, there had been growing up among the farmers of the west a social organization officially known as The Patrons of Husbandry. The places of meeting were called "Granges" and very naturally the members were at once called "Grangers."

My father was an early and enthusiastic member of the order, and during the early seventies its meetings became very important dates on our calendar. In winter "oyster suppers," with debates, songs and essays, drew us all to the Burr Oak Grove school-house, and each spring, on the twelfth of June, the Grange Picnic was a grand "turn-out." It was almost as well attended as the circus.

We all looked forward to it for weeks and every young man who owned a top-buggy got it out and washed and polished it for the use of his best girl, and those who were not so fortunate as to own "a rig" paid high tribute to the livery stable of the nearest town. Others, less able or less extravagant, doubled teams with a comrade and built a "bowery wagon" out of a wagon-box, and with hampers heaped with food rode away in state, drawn by a four or six-horse team. It seemed a splendid and daring thing to do, and some day I hoped to drive a six-horse bowery wagon myself.

The central place of meeting was usually in some grove along the Big Cedar to the west and south of us, and early on the appointed day the various lodges of our region came together one by one at convenient places, each one moving in procession and led by great banners on which the women had blazoned the motto of their home lodge. Some of the columns had bands and came preceded by far faint strains of music, with marshals in red sashes galloping to and fro in fine assumption of military command.

It was grand, it was inspiring—to us, to see those long lines of carriages winding down the lanes, joining one to another at the cross roads till at last all the granges from the northern end of the county were united in one mighty column advancing on the picnic ground, where orators awaited our approach with calm dignity and high resolve. Nothing more picturesque, more delightful, more helpful has ever risen out of American rural life. Each of these assemblies was a most grateful relief from the sordid loneliness of the farm.

Our winter amusements were also in process of change. We held no more singing schools—the "Lyceum" had taken its place. Revival meetings were given up, although few of the church folk classed them among the amusements. The County Fair on the contrary was becoming each year more important as farming diversified. It was even more glorious than the Grange Picnic, was indeed second only to the fourth of July, and we looked forward to it all through the autumn.

It came late in September and always lasted three days. We all went on the second day, (which was considered the best day) and mother, by cooking all the afternoon before our outing, provided us a dinner of cold chicken and cake and pie which we ate while sitting on the grass beside our wagon just off the race-track while the horses munched hay and oats from the box. All around us other families were grouped, picnicking in the same fashion, and a cordial interchange of jellies and pies made the meal a delightful function. However, we boys never lingered over it,—we were afraid of missing something of the program.

Our interest in the races was especially keen, for one of the citizens of our town owned a fine little trotting horse called "Huckleberry" whose honest friendly striving made him a general favorite. Our survey of fat sheep, broad-backed bulls and shining colts was a duty, but to cheer Huckleberry at the home stretch was a privilege.

To us from the farm the crowds were the most absorbing show of all. We met our chums and their sisters with a curious sense of strangeness, of discovery. Our playmates seemed alien somehow—especially the girls in their best dresses walking about two and two, impersonal and haughty of glance.

Cyrus and Walter were there in their top-buggies with Harriet and Bettie but they seemed to be having a dull time, for while they sat holding their horses we were dodging about in freedom—now at the contest of draft horses, now at the sledgehammer throwing, now at the candy-booth. We were comical figures, with our long trousers, thick gray coats and faded hats, but we didn't know it and were happy.

One day as Burton and I were wandering about on the fair grounds we came upon a patent medicine cart from which a fakir, a handsome fellow with long black hair and an immense white hat, was addressing the crowd while a young and beautiful girl with a guitar in her lap sat in weary relaxation at his feet. A third member of the "troupe," a short and very plump man of commonplace type, was handing out bottles. It was "Doctor" Lightner, vending his "Magic Oil."

At first I perceived only the doctor whose splendid gray suit and spotless linen made the men in the crowd rustic and graceless, but as I studied the woman I began to read into her face a sadness, a weariness, which appealed to my imagination. Who was she? Why was she there? I had never seen a girl with such an expression. She saw no one, was interested in nothing before her—and when her master, or husband, spoke to her in a low voice, she raised her guitar and joined in the song which he had started, all with the same air of weary disgust. Her voice, a childishly sweet soprano, mingled with the robust baritone of the doctor and the shouting tenor of the fat man, like a thread of silver in a skein of brass.

I forgot my dusty clothes, my rough shoes,—I forgot that I was a boy. Absorbed and dreaming I listened to these strange new songs and studied the singular faces of these alien songsters. Even the shouting tenor had a far-away gleam in the yellow light of his cat-like eyes. The leader's skill, the woman's grace and the perfect blending of their voices made an ineffaceable impression on my sensitive, farm-bred brain.

The songs which they sang were not in themselves of a character to warrant this ecstasy in me. One of them ran as follows:

O Mary had a little lamb,
Its fleece was black as jet,
In the little old log cabin in the lane;
And everywhere that Mary went,
The lamb went too, you bet.
In the little old log cabin in the lane.

In the little old log cabin O!
The little old log cabin O!
The little old log cabin in the lane,
They're hangin' men and women now
For singing songs like this
In the little old log cabin in the lane.

Nevertheless I listened without a smile. It was art to me. It gave me something I had never known. The large, white, graceful hand of the doctor sweeping the strings, the clear ringing shout of the tenor and the chiming, bird-like voice of the girl lent to the absurd words of this ballad a singular dignity. They made all other persons and events of the day of no account.

In the intervals between the songs the doctor talked of catarrh and its cure, and offered his medicines for sale, and in this dull part of the program the tenor assisted, but the girl, sinking back in her seat, resumed her impersonal and weary air.

That was forty years ago, and I can still sing those songs and imitate the whoop of the shouting tenor, but I have never been able to put that woman into verse or fiction although I have tried. In a story called *Love or the Law* I once made a laborious attempt to account for her, but I did not succeed, and the manuscript remains in the bottom of my desk.

No doubt the doctor has gone to his long account and the girl is a gray old woman of sixty-five but in this book they shall be forever young, forever beautiful, noble with the grace of art. The medicine they peddled was of doubtful service, but the songs they sang, the story they suggested were of priceless value to us who came from the monotony of the farm, and went back to it like bees laden with the pollen of new intoxicating blooms.

Sorrowfully we left Huckleberry's unfinished race, reluctantly we climbed into the farm wagon, sticky with candy, dusty, tired, some of us suffering with sick-headache, and rolled away homeward to milk the cows, feed the pigs and bed down the horses.

As I look at a tintype of myself taken at about this time, I can hardly detect the physical relationship between that mop-headed, long-lipped lad, and the gray-haired man of today. But the coat, the tie, the little stick-pin on the lapel of my coat all unite to bring back to me with painful stir, the curious debates, the boyish delights, the dawning desires which led me to these material expressions of manly pride. There is a kind of pathos too, in the memory of the keen pleasure I took in that absurd ornament—and yet my joy was genuine, my satisfaction complete.

Harriet came home from school each Friday night but we saw little of her, for she was always engaged for dances or socials by the neighbors' sons, and had only a young lady's interest in her cub brothers. I resented this and was openly hostile to her admirers. She seldom rode with us to spelling schools or "soshybles." There was always some youth with a cutter, or some noisy group in a big bob-sleigh to carry her away, and on Monday morning father drove her back to the county town with growing pride in her improving manners.

Her course at the Seminary was cut short in early spring by a cough which came from a long ride in the keen wind. She was very ill with a wasting fever, yet for a time refused to go to bed. She could not resign herself to the loss of her school-life.

The lack of room in our house is brought painfully to my mind as I recall that she lay for a week or two in a corner of our living room with all the noise and bustle of the family going on around her. Her own attic chamber was unwarmed (like those of all her girl friends), and so she was forced to lie near the kitchen stove.

She grew rapidly worse all through the opening days of April and as we were necessarily out in the fields at work, and mother was busied with her household affairs, the lonely sufferer was glad to have her bed in the living room—and there she lay, her bright eyes following mother at her work, growing whiter and whiter until one beautiful, tragic morning in early May, my father called me in to say good-bye to her.

She was very weak, but her mind was perfectly clear, and as she kissed me farewell with a soft word about being a good boy, I turned away blinded with tears and fled to the barnyard, there to hide like a wounded animal, appalled by the weight of despair and sorrow which her transfigured face had suddenly thrust upon me. All about me the young cattle called, the spring sun shone and the gay fowls sang, but they could not mitigate my grief, my dismay, my sense of loss. My sister was passing from me—that was the agonizing fact which benumbed me. She who had been my playmate, my comrade, was about to vanish into air and earth!

This was my first close contact with death, and it filled me with awe. Human life suddenly seemed fleeting and of a part with the impermanency and change of the westward moving Border Line.—Like the wild flowers she had gathered, Harriet was now a fragrant memory. Her dust mingled with the soil of the little burial ground just beyond the village bounds.

My mother's heart was long in recovering from the pain of this loss, but at last Jessie's sweet face, which had in it the light of the sky and the color of a flower, won back her smiles. The child's acceptance of the funeral as a mere incident of her busy little life, in some way enabled us all to take up and carry forward the routine of our shadowed home.

Those years on the plain, from '71 to '75, held much that was alluring, much that was splendid. I did not live an exceptional life in any way. My duties and my pleasures were those of the boys around me. In all essentials my life was typical of the time and place. My father was counted a good and successful farmer. Our neighbors all lived in the same restricted fashion as ourselves, in barren little houses of wood or stone, owning few books, reading only weekly papers. It was a pure democracy wherein my father was a leader and my mother beloved by all who knew her. If anybody looked down upon us we didn't know it, and in all the social affairs of the township we fully shared.

Nature was our compensation. As I look back upon it, I perceive transcendent sunsets, and a mighty sweep of golden grain beneath a sea of crimson clouds. The light and song and motion of the prairie return to me. I hear again the shrill, myriad-voiced choir of leaping insects whose wings flash fire amid the glorified stubble. The wind wanders by, lifting my torn hat-rim. The locusts rise in clouds before my weary feet. The prairie hen soars out of the unreaped barley and drops into the sheltering deeps of the tangled oats, green as emerald. The lone quail pipes in the hazel thicket, and far up the road the cowbell's steady clang tells of the homecoming herd.

Even in our hours of toil, and through the sultry skies, the sacred light of beauty broke; worn and grimed as we were, we still could fall a-dream before the marvel of a golden earth beneath a crimson sky.

16

We Move to Town

One day, soon after the death of my sister Harriet, my father came home from a meeting of the Grange with a message which shook our home with the force of an earth-quake. The officers of the order had asked him to become the official grain-buyer for the county, and he had agreed to do it. "I am to take charge of the new elevator which is just being completed in Osage," he said.

The effect of this announcement was far-reaching. First of all it put an end not merely to our further pioneering but, (as the plan developed) promised to translate us from the farm to a new and shining world, a town world where circuses, baseball games and county fairs were events of almost daily occurrence. It awed while it delighted us for we felt vaguely our father's perturbation.

For the first time since leaving Boston, some thirty years before, Dick Garland began to dream of making a living at something less back-breaking than tilling the soil. It was to him a most abrupt and startling departure from the fixed plan of his life, and I dimly understood even then that he came to this decision only after long and troubled reflection. Mother as usual sat in silence. If she showed exultation, I do not recall the fashion of it.

Father assumed his new duties in June and during all that summer and autumn, drove away immediately after breakfast each morning, to the elevator some six miles away, leaving me in full charge of the farm and its tools. All his orders to the hired men were executed through me. On me fell the supervision of their action, always with an eye to his general oversight. I never forgot that fact. He possessed the eye of an eagle. His uncanny powers of observation kept me terrified. He could detect at a glance the slightest blunder or wrong doing in my day's activities. Every afternoon, about sunset he came whirling into the yard, his team flecked with foam, his big gray eyes flashing from side to side, and if any tool was out of place or broken, he discovered it at once, and his reproof was never a cause of laughter to me or my brother.

As harvest came on he took command in the field, for most of the harvest help that year were rough, hardy, wanderers from the south, nomads who had followed the line of ripening wheat from Missouri northward, and were not the most profitable companions for boys of fifteen. They reached our neighborhood in July, arriving like a flight of alien unclean birds, and vanished into the north in September as mysteriously as they had appeared. A few of them had been soldiers, others were the errant sons of the poor farmers and rough mechanics of older States, migrating for the adventure of it. One of them gave his name as "Harry Lee," others were known by such names as "Big Ed" or "Shorty." Some carried valises, others had nothing but small bundles containing a clean shirt and a few socks.

They all had the most appalling yet darkly romantic conception of women. A "girl" was the most desired thing in the world, a prize to be worked for, sought for and enjoyed without remorse. She had no soul. The maid who yielded to temptation deserved no pity, no consideration, no aid. Her sufferings were amusing, her diseases a joke, her future of no account. From these men Burton and I acquired a desolating fund of information concerning South Clark Street in Chicago, and the river front in St. Louis. Their talk did not allure, it mostly shocked and horrified us. We had not known that such cruelty, such baseness was in the world and it stood away in such violent opposition to the teaching of our fathers and uncles that it did not corrupt us. That man, the stronger animal, owed chivalry and care to woman, had been deeply grounded in our concept of life, and we shrank from these vile stories as from something disloyal to our mothers and sisters.

To those who think of the farm as a sweetly ideal place in which to bring up a boy, all this may be disturbing—but the truth is, low-minded men are low-minded everywhere, and farm hands are often creatures with enormous appetites and small remorse, men on whom the beauty of nature has very little effect.

To most of our harvest hands that year Saturday night meant a visit to town and a drunken spree, and they did not hesitate to say so in the presence of Burton and myself. Some of them did not hesitate to say anything in our presence. After a hard week's work we all felt that a trip to town was only a fair reward.

Saturday night in town! How it all comes back to me! I am a timid visitor in the little frontier village. It is sunset. A whiskey-crazed farmhand is walking bare footed up and down the middle of the road defying the world.—From a corner of the street I watch with tense interest another lithe, pock-marked bully menacing with cat-like action, a cowering young farmer in a long linen coat. The crowd jeers at him for his cowardice—a burst of shouting is heard. A trampling follows and forth from the door of a saloon bulges a throng of drunken steaming, reeling, cursing ruffians followed by brave Jim McCarty, the city marshal, with an offender under each hand.—The scene changes to the middle of the street. I am one of a throng surrounding a smoothhanded fakir who is selling prize boxes of soap and giving away dollars.— "Now, gentlemen," he says, "if you will hand me a dollar I will give you a sample package of soap to examine, afterwards if you don't want the soap, return it to me, and I'll return your dollar." He repeats this several times, returning the dollars faithfully, then slightly varies his invitation by saying, "so that I can return your dollars."

No one appears to observe this significant change, and as he has hitherto returned the dollars precisely according to promise, he now proceeds to his harvest. Having all his boxes out he abruptly closes the lid of his box and calmly remarks, "I said, 'so that I can return your dollars,' I didn't say I would.—Gentlemen, I have the dollars and you have the experience." He drops into his seat and takes up the reins to drive away. A tall man who has been standing silently beside the wheel of the carriage, snatches the whip from its socket, and lashes the swindler across the face. Red streaks appear on his cheek.—The crowd surges forward. Up from behind leaps a furious little Scotchman who snatches off his right boot and beats the stranger over the head with such fury that he falls from his carriage to the ground.—I rejoice in his punishment, and admire the tall man who led the assault.—The marshal comes, the man is led away, and the crowd smilingly scatters.—

We are on the way home. Only two of my crew are with me. The others are roaring from one drinking place to another, having a "good time." The air is soothingly clean and sweet after the tumult and the reek of the town. Appalled, yet fascinated, I listen to the oft repeated tales of just how Jim McCarty sprang into the saloon and cleaned out the brawling mob. I feel very young, very defenceless, and very sleepy as I listen.—

On Sunday, Burton usually came to visit me or I went over to his house and together we rode or walked to service at the Grove school-house. He was now the owner of a razor, and I was secretly planning to buy one. The question of dress had begun to trouble us both acutely. Our best suits were not only made from woolen cloth, they were of blizzard weight, and as on week days (in summer) our entire outfit consisted of a straw hat, a hickory shirt and a pair of brown denim overalls you may imagine what tortures we endured when fully encased in our "Sunday best," with starched shirts and paper collars.

No one, so far as I knew, at that time possessed an extra, lightweight suit for hot-weather wear, although a long, yellow, linen robe called a "duster" was in fashion among the smart dressers. John Gammons, who was somewhat of a dandy in matters of toilet, was among the first of my circle to purchase one of these very ultra garments, and Burton soon followed his lead, and then my own discontent began. I, too, desired a duster.

Unfortunately my father did not see me as I saw myself. To him I was still a boy and subject to his will in matters of dress as in other affairs, and the notion that I needed a linen coat was absurd. "If you are too warm, take your coat off," he said, and I not only went without the duster, but suffered the shame of appearing in a flat-crown black hat while Burton and all the other fellows were wearing light brown ones, of a conical shape.

I was furious. After a period of bitter brooding I rebelled, and took the matter up with the Commander-in-Chief. I argued, "As I am not only doing a man's work on a boy's pay but actually superintending the stock and tools, I am entitled to certain individual rights in the choice of a hat."

The soldier listened in silence but his glance was stern. When I had ended he said, "You'll wear the hat I provide."

For the first time in my life I defied him. "I will not," I said. "And you can't make me."

He seized me by the arm and for a moment we faced each other in silent clash of wills. I was desperate now. "Don't you strike me," I warned. "You can't do that any more."

His face changed. His eyes softened. He perceived in my attitude something new, something unconquerable. He dropped my arm and turned away. After a silent struggle with himself he took two dollars from his pocket and extended them to me. "Get your own hat," he said, and walked away.

This victory forms the most important event of my fifteenth year. Indeed the chief's recession gave me a greater shock than any punishment could have done. Having forced him to admit the claims of my growing personality as well as the value of my services, I retired in a panic. The fact that he, the inexorable old soldier, had surrendered to my furious demands awed me, making me very careful not to go too fast or too far in my assumption of the privileges of manhood.

Another of the milestones on my road to manhood was my first employment of the town barber. Up to this time my hair had been trimmed by mother or mangled by one of the hired men,—whereas both John and Burton enjoyed regular hair-cuts and came to Sunday school with the backs of their necks neatly shaved. I wanted to look like that, and so at last, shortly after my victory concerning the hat, I plucked up courage to ask my father for a quarter and got it! With my money tightly clutched in my hand I timidly entered the Tonsorial Parlor of Ed Mills and took my seat in his marvellous chair—thus touching another high point on the road to self-respecting manhood. My pleasure, however, was mixed with ignoble childish terror, for not only did the barber seem determined to force upon me a shampoo (which was ten cents extra), but I was in unremitting fear lest I should lose my quarter, the only one I possessed, and find myself accused as a swindler.

Nevertheless I came safely away, a neater, older and graver person, walking with a manlier stride, and when I confronted my class-mates at the Grove school-house on Sunday, I gave evidence of an accession of self-confidence. The fact that my back hair was now in fashionable order was of greatest comfort to me. If only my trousers had not continued their distressing habit of climbing up my boot-tops I would have been almost at ease but every time I rose from my seat it became necessary to make each instep smooth the leg of the other pantaloon, and even then they kept their shameful wrinkles, and a knowledge of my exposed ankles humbled me.

Burton, although better dressed than I, was quite as confused and wordless in the presence of girls, but John Gammons was not only confident, he was irritatingly facile. Furthermore, as son of the director of the Sunday school he had almost too much distinction. I bitterly resented his linen collars, his neat suit and his smiling assurance, for while we professed to despise everything connected with church, we were keenly aware of the bright eyes of Bettie and noted that they rested often on John's curly head. He could sing, too, and sometimes, with sublime audacity, held the hymn book with her.

The sweetness of those girlish faces held us captive through many a long sermon, but there were times when not even their beauty availed. Three or four of us occasionally slipped away into the glorious forest to pick berries or nuts, or to loaf in the odorous shade of the elms along the creek. The cool aisles of the oaks seemed more sweetly sanctifying (after a week of sun-smit soil on the open plain) than the crowded little church with its droning preacher, and there was something mystical in the melody of the little brook and in the flecking of light and shade across the silent wood-land path.

To drink of the little ice-cold spring beneath the maple tree in Frazer's pasture was almost as delight-giving as the plate of ice-cream which we sometimes permitted ourselves to buy in the village on Saturday, and often we wandered on and on, till the sinking sun warned us of duties at home and sent us hurrying to the open.

It was always hard to go back to the farm after one of these days of leisure—back to greasy overalls and milk-bespattered boots, back to the society of fly-bedevilled cows and steaming, salty horses, back to the curry-comb and swill bucket,—but it was particularly hard during this our last summer on the prairie. But we did it with a feeling that we were nearing the end of it. "Next year we'll be living in town!" I said to the boys exultantly. "No more cow-milking for me!"

I never rebelled at hard, clean work, like haying or harvest, but the slavery of being nurse to calves and scrub-boy to horses cankered my spirits more and more, and the thought of living in town filled me with an incredulous anticipatory delight. A life of leisure, of intellectual activity seemed about to open up to me, and

I met my chums in a restrained exaltation which must have been trying to their souls. "I'm sorry to leave you," I jeered, "but so it goes. Some are chosen, others are left. Some rise to glory, others remain plodders—" such was my airy attitude. I wonder that they did not roll me in the dust.

Though my own joy and that of my brother was keen and outspoken, I have no recollection that my mother uttered a single word of pleasure. She must have been as deeply excited, and as pleased as we, for it meant more to her than to us, it meant escape from the drudgery of the farm, from the pain of early rising, and yet I cannot be sure of her feeling. So far as she knew this move was final. Her life as a farmer's wife was about to end after twenty years of early rising and never ending labor, and I think she must have palpitated with joy of her approaching freedom from it all.

As we were not to move till the following March, and as winter came on we went to school as usual in the bleak little shack at the corner of our farm and took part in all the neighborhood festivals. I have beautiful memories of trotting away across the plain to spelling schools and "Lyceums" through the sparkling winter nights with Franklin by my side, while the low-hung sky blazed with stars, and great white owls went flapping silently away before us.—I am riding in a long sleigh to the north beneath a wondrous moon to witness a performance of *Lord Dundreary* at the Barker school-house.—I am a neglected onlooker at a Christmas tree at Burr Oak. I am spelled down at the Shehan school—and through all these scenes runs a belief that I am leaving the district never to return to it, a conviction which lends to every experience a peculiar poignancy of appeal.

Though but a shaggy colt in those days, I acknowledged a keen longing to join in the parties and dances of the grown-up boys and girls. I was not content to be merely the unnoticed cub in the corner. A place in the family bob-sled no longer satisfied me, and when at the "sociable" I stood in the corner with tousled hair and clumsy ill-fitting garments I was in my desire, a confident, graceful squire of dames.

The dancing was a revelation to me of the beauty and grace latent in the awkward girls and hulking men of the farms. It amazed and delighted me to see how gloriously Madeleine White swayed and tip-toed through the figures of the "Cotillion," and the sweet aloofness of Agnes Farwell's face filled me with worship. I envied Edwin Blackler his supple grace, his fine sense of rhythm, and especially the calm audacity of his manner with his partners. Bill, Joe, all the great lunking farm hands seemed somehow uplifted, carried out of their everyday selves, ennobled by some deep-seated emotion, and I was eager for a chance to show that I, too, could balance and bow and pay court to women, but—alas, I never did, I kept to my corner even though Stelle Gilbert came to drag me out.

Occasionally a half-dozen of these audacious young people would turn a church social or donation party into a dance, much to the scandal of the deacons. I recall one such performance which ended most dramatically. It was a "shower" for the minister whose salary was too small to be even an honorarium, and the place of meeting was at the Durrells', two well-to-do farmers, brothers who lived on opposite sides of the road just south of the Grove school-house.

Mother put up a basket of food, father cast a quarter of beef into the back-part of the sleigh, and we were off early of a cold winter night in order to be on hand for the supper. My brother and I were mere passengers on the straw behind, along with the slab of beef, but we gave no outward sign of discontent. It was a clear, keen, marvellous twilight, with the stars coming out over the woodlands to the east. On every road the sound of bells and the voices of happy young people came to our ears. Occasionally some fellow with a fast horse and a gay cutter came slashing up behind us and called out "Clear the track!" Father gave the road, and the youth and his best girl went whirling by with a gay word of thanks. Watch-dogs guarding the Davis farmhouse, barked in savage warning as we passed and mother said, "Everybody's gone. I hope we won't be late."

We were, indeed, a little behind the others for when we stumbled into the Ellis Durrell house we found a crowd of merry folks clustered about the kitchen stove. Mrs. Ellis flattered me by saying, "The young people are expecting you over at Joe's." Here she laughed, "I'm afraid they are going to dance."

As soon as I was sufficiently thawed out I went across the road to the other house which gave forth the sound of singing and the rhythmic tread of dancing feet. It was filled to overflowing with the youth of the neighborhood, and Agnes Farwell, Joe's niece, the queenliest of them all, was leading the dance, her dark face aglow, her deep brown eyes alight.

The dance was "The Weevilly Wheat" and Ed Blackler was her partner. Against the wall stood Marsh Belford, a tall, crude, fierce young savage with eyes fixed on Agnes. He was one of her suitors and mad with jealousy of Blackler to whom she was said to be engaged. He was a singular youth, at once bashful and baleful. He could not dance, and for that reason keenly resented Ed's supple grace and easy manners with the girls.

Crossing to where Burton stood, I heard Belford say as he replied to some remark by his companions, "I'll roll him one o' these days." He laughed in a constrained way, and that his mood was dangerous was evident. In deep excitement Burton and I awaited the outcome.

The dancing was of the harmless "donation" sort. As musical instruments were forbidden, the rhythm was furnished by a song in which we all joined with clapping hands.

Come hither, my love, and trip together
In the morning early,
Give to you the parting hand
Although I love you dearly.
I won't have none of your weevilly wheat
I won't have none of your barley,
I'll have some flour
In half an hour
To bake a cake for Charley.—
Oh, Charley, he is a fine young man,
Charley he is a dandy,
Charley he is a fine young man
For he buys the girls some candy.

The figures were like those in the old time "Money Musk" and as Agnes bowed and swung and gave hands down the line I thought her the loveliest creature in the world, and so did Marsh, only that which gladdened me, maddened him. I acknowledged Edwin's superior claim,—Marsh did not.

Burton, who understood the situation, drew me aside and said, "Marsh has been drinking. There's going to be war."

As soon as the song ceased and the dancers paused, Marsh,

white with resolution, went up to Agnes, and said something to her. She smiled, but shook her head and turned away. Marsh came back to where his brother Joe was standing and his face was tense with fury. "I'll make her wish she hadn't," he muttered.

Edwin, as floor manager, now called out a new "set" and as the dancers began to "form on," Joe Belford hunched his brother. "Go after him now," he said. With deadly slowness of action, Marsh sauntered up to Blackler and said something in a low voice.

"You're a liar!" retorted Edwin sharply.

Belford struck out with a swing of his open hand, and a moment later they were rolling on the floor in a deadly grapple. The girls screamed and fled, but the boys formed a joyous ring around the contestants and cheered them on to keener strife while Joe Belford, tearing off his coat, stood above his brother, warning others to keep out of it. "This is to be a fair fight," he said. "The best man wins!"

He was a redoubtable warrior and the ring widened. No one thought of interfering, in fact we were all delighted by this sudden outbreak of the heroic spirit.

Ed threw off his antagonist and rose, bleeding but undaunted. "You devil," he said, "I'll smash your face."

Marsh again struck him a staggering blow, and they were facing each other in watchful fury as Agnes forced her way through the crowd and, laying her hand on Belford's arm, calmly said, "Marsh Belford, what are you doing?"

Her dignity, her beauty, her air of command, awed the bully and silenced every voice in the room. She was our hostess and as such assumed the right to enforce decorum. Fixing her glance upon Joe whom she recognized as the chief disturber, she said, "You'd better go home. This is no place for either you or Marsh."

Sobered, shamed, the Belfords fell back and slipped out while Agnes turned to Edwin and wiped the blood from his face with self-contained tenderness.

This date may be taken as fairly ending my boyhood, for I was rapidly taking on the manners of men. True, I did not smoke or chew tobacco and I was not greatly given to profanity, but I was able to shoulder a two bushel sack of wheat and could hold my own with most of the harvesters. Although short and heavy, I was deft with my hands, as one or two of the neighborhood bullies had reason to know and in many ways I was counted a man.

I read during this year nearly one hundred dime novels, little paper-bound volumes filled with stories of Indians and wild horsemen and dukes and duchesses and men in iron masks, and sewing girls who turned out to be daughters of nobility, and marvellous detectives who bore charmed lives and always trapped the villains at the end of the story—

Of all these tales, those of the border naturally had most allurement. There was the *Quaker Sleuth,* for instance, and *Mad Matt the Trailer,* and *Buckskin Joe* who rode disdainfully alone (like Lochinvar), rescuing maidens from treacherous Apaches, cutting long rows of death notches on the stock of his carbine. One of these narratives contained a phantom troop of skeleton horsemen, a grisly squadron, which came like an icy wind out of the darkness, striking terror to the hearts of the renegades and savages, only to vanish with clatter of bones, and click of hoofs.

In addition to these delight-giving volumes, I traded stock with other boys of the neighborhood. From Jack Sheet I derived a bundle of *Saturday Nights* in exchange for my *New York Weeklys* and from one of our harvest hands, a near-sighted old German, I borrowed some twenty-five or thirty numbers of *The Sea Side Library.* These also cost a dime when new, but you could return them and get a nickel in credit for another,—provided your own was in good condition.

It is a question whether the reading of all this exciting fiction had an ill effect on my mind or not. Apparently it had very little effect of any sort other than to make the borderland a great deal more exciting than the farm, and yet so far as I can discover, I had no keen desire to go West and fight Indians and I showed no disposition to rob or murder in the manner of my heroes. I devoured *Jack Harkaway* and *The Quaker Sleuth* precisely as I played ball—to pass the time and because I enjoyed the game.

Deacon Garland was highly indignant with my father for permitting such reading, and argued against it furiously, but no one paid much attention to his protests—especially after we caught the old gentleman sitting with a very lurid example of "The Damnable

Lies" open in his hand. "I was only looking into it to see how bad it was," he explained.

Father was so tickled at the old man's downfall that he said, "Stick to it till you find how it turns out."

Grandsire, we all perceived, was human after all. I think we liked him rather better after this sign of weakness.

It would not be fair to say that we read nothing else but these easy-going tales. As a matter of fact, I read everything within reach, even the copy of *Paradise Lost* which my mother presented to me on my fifteenth birthday. Milton I admit was hard work, but I got considerable joy out of his cursing passages. The battle scenes also interested me and I went about spouting the extraordinary harangues of Satan with such vigor that my team one day took fright of me, and ran away with the plow, leaving an erratic furrow to be explained. However, my father was glad to see me taking on the voice of the orator.

The five years of life on this farm had brought swift changes into my world. Nearly all the open land had been fenced and plowed, and all the cattle and horses had been brought into pasture, and around most of the buildings, groves of maples were beginning to make the homesteads a little less barren and ugly. And yet with all these growing signs of prosperity I realized that something sweet and splendid was dying out of the prairie. The whistling pigeons, the wailing plover, the migrating ducks and geese, the soaring cranes, the shadowy wolves, the wary foxes, all the untamed things were passing, vanishing with the blue-joint grass, the dainty wild rose and the tiger-lily's flaming torch. Settlement was complete.

17

A Taste of Village Life

The change from farm to village life, though delightful, was not so complete as we had anticipated, for we not only carried with us several cows and a span of horses, but the house which we had rented stood at the edge of town and possessed a large plot; therefore we not only continued to milk cows and curry horses, but set to work at once planting potatoes and other vegetables almost as if still upon the farm. The soil had been poorly cultivated for several years, and the weeds sprang up like dragons' teeth. Work, it seemed, was not to be escaped even in the city.

Though a little resentful of this labor and somewhat disappointed in our dwelling, we were vastly excited by certain phases of our new surroundings. To be within a few minutes' walk of the postoffice, and to be able to go to the store at any moment, were conditions quite as satisfactory as we had any right to expect. Also we slept later, for my father was less disposed to get us out of bed at dawn and this in itself was an enormous gain, especially to my mother.

Osage, a small town, hardly more than a village, was situated on the edge of a belt of hard-wood timber through which the Cedar River ran, and was quite commonplace to most people but to me it was both mysterious and dangerous, for it was the home of an alien tribe, hostile and pitiless—"The Town Boys."

Up to this time I had both hated and feared them, knowing that they hated and despised me, and now, suddenly I was thrust among them and put on my own defenses. For a few weeks I felt like a young rooster in a strange barn-yard,—knowing that I would be called upon to prove my quality. In fact it took but a week or two to establish my place in the tribe for one of the leaders of the gang was Mitchell Scott, a powerful lad of about my own age, and to his friendship I owe a large part of my freedom from persecution.

Uncle David came to see us several times during the spring and his talk was all about "going west." He was restless under the conditions of his life on a farm. I don't know why this was so, but a growing bitterness clouded his voice. Once I heard him say, "I don't know what use I am in the world. I am a failure." This was the first note of doubt, of discouragement that I had heard from any member of my family and it made a deep impression on me. Disillusionment had begun.

During the early part of the summer my brother and I worked in the garden with frequent days off for fishing, swimming and berrying, and we were entirely content with life. No doubts assailed us. We swam in the pond at Rice's Mill and we cast our hooks in the sunny ripples below it. We saw the circus come to town and go into camp on a vacant lot, and we attended every movement of it with a delicious sense of leisure. We could go at night with no long ride to take after it was over.—The fourth of July came to seek us this year and we had but to step across the way to see a ball-game. We were at last in the center of our world.

In June my father called me to help in the elevator and this turned out to be a most informing experience. "The Street," as it was called, was merely a wagon road which ran along in front of a row of wheat ware-houses of various shapes and sizes, from which the buyers emerged to meet the farmers as they drove into town. Two or three or more of the men would clamber upon the load, open the sacks, sample the grain and bid for it. If one man wanted the load badly, or if he chanced to be in a bad temper, the farmer was the gainer. Hence very few of them, even the members of the Grange, were content to drive up to my father's elevator and take the honest market price. They were all hoping to get a little more than the market price.

This vexed and embittered my father who often spoke of it to me. "It only shows," he said, "how hard it will be to work out any reform among the farmers. They will never stand together. These other buyers will force me off the market and then there will be no one here to represent the farmers' interest."

These merchants interested me greatly. Humorous, self-contained, remorseless in trade, they were most delightful companions when off duty. They liked my father in his private capacity, but as a factor of the Grange he was an enemy. Their kind was new to me and I loved to linger about and listen to their banter when there was nothing else to do.

One of them by reason of his tailor-made suit and a large ring on his little finger, was especially attractive to me. He was a handsome man of a sinister type and I regarded his expressionless face as that of a gambler. I didn't know that he was a poker player but it amused me to think so. Another buyer was a choleric Cornishman whom the other men sometimes goaded into paying five or six cents more than the market admitted, by shrewdly playing on his hot temper. A third was a tall gaunt old man of New England type, obstinate, honest, but of sanguine temperament. He was always on the bull side of the market and a loud debater. The fourth, a quiet little man of smooth address, acted as peacemaker.

Among these men my father moved as an equal, notwithstanding the fact of his country training and prejudices, and it was through the man Morley that we got our first outlook upon the bleak world of Agnosticism, for during the summer a series of lectures by Robert Ingersoll was reported in one of the Chicago papers and the West rang with the controversy.

On Monday as soon as the paper came to town it was the habit of the grain-buyers to gather at their little central office, and while Morley, the man with the seal ring, read the lecture aloud, the others listened and commented on the heresies. Not all were sympathizers with the great iconoclast, and the arguments which followed were often heated and sometimes fiercely personal.

After they had quite finished with the paper, I sometimes secured it for myself, and hurrying back to my office in the elevator pored over it with intense zeal. Undoubtedly my father as well as I was profoundly influenced by "The Mistakes of Moses." The faith in which we had been reared had already grown dim, and under the light of Ingersoll's remorseless humor most of our superstitions vanished. I do not think my father's essential Christianity was in any degree diminished, he merely lost his respect for certain outworn traditions and empty creeds.

My work consisted in receiving the grain and keeping the elevator going and as I weighed the sacks, made out checks for the payment and kept the books—in all ways taking a man's place,—I lost all sense of being a boy.

The motive power of our hoisting machinery was a blind horse, a handsome fellow weighing some fifteen hundred pounds, and it was not long before he filled a large space in my thoughts. There was something appealing in his sightless eyes and I never watched him (as he patiently went his rounds in the dusty shed) without pity. He had a habit of kicking the wall with his right hind foot at a certain precise point as he circled, and a deep hollow in the sill attested his accuracy. He seemed to do this purposely—to keep count, as I imagined, of his dreary circling through sunless days.

A part of my duty was to watch the fanning mill (in the high cupola) in order that the sieves should not clog. Three flights of stairs led to the mill and these had to be mounted many times each day. I always ran up the steps when the mill required my attention, but in coming down I usually swung from beam to beam, dropping from footway to footway like a monkey from a tall tree. My mother in seeing me do this called out in terror, but I assured her that there was not the slightest danger—and this was true, for I was both sure-footed and sure-handed in those days.

This was a golden summer for us all. My mother found time to read. My father enjoyed companionship with the leading citizens of the town, while Franklin, as first assistant in a candy store, professed himself to be entirely content. My own holidays were spent in fishing or in roving the woods with Mitchell and George, but on Sundays the entire family dressed for church as for a solemn social function, fully alive to the dignity of Banker Brush, and the grandeur of Congressman Deering who came to service regularly—but on foot, so intense was the spirit of democracy among us.

Theoretically there were no social distinctions in Osage, but after all a large house and a two seated carriage counted, and my mother's visitors were never from the few pretentious homes of the town but from the farms. However, I do not think she worried over her social position and I know she welcomed callers from Dry Run and Burr Oak with cordial hospitality. She was never envious or bitter.

In spite of my busy life, I read more than ever before, and everything I saw or heard made a deep and lasting record on my mind. I recall with a sense of gratitude a sermon by the preacher in the Methodist Church which profoundly educated me. It was the first time I had ever heard the power of art and the value of its mission to man insisted upon. What was right and what was wrong had been pointed out to me, but things of beauty were seldom mentioned.

With most eloquent gestures, with a face glowing with enthusiasm, the young orator enumerated the beautiful phases of nature. He painted the starry sky, the sunset clouds, and the purple hills in words of prismatic hue and his rapturous eloquence held us rigid. "We have been taught," he said in effect, "that beauty is a snare of the evil one; that it is a lure to destroy, but I assert that God desires loveliness and hates ugliness. He loves the shimmering of dawn, the silver light on the lake and the purple and snow of every summer cloud. He honors bright colors, for has he not set the rainbow in the heavens and made water to reflect the moon? He prefers joy and pleasure to hate and despair. He is not a God of pain, of darkness and ugliness, he is a God of beauty, of delight, of consolation."

In some such strain he continued, and as his voice rose in fervent chant and his words throbbed with poetry, the sunlight falling through the window-pane gave out a more intense radiance, and over the faces of the girls, a more entrancing color fell. He opened my eyes to a new world, the world of art.

I recognized in this man not only a moving orator but a scholar and I went out from that little church vaguely resolved to be a student also, a student of the beautiful. My father was almost equally moved and we all went again and again to hear our young evangel speak but never again did he touch my heart. That one discourse was his contribution to my education and I am grateful to him for it. In after life I had the pleasure of telling him how much he had suggested to me in that sermon.

There was much to allure a farmer boy in the decorum of well-dressed men and the grace of daintily clad women as well as in the music and the dim interior of the church (which seemed to me of great dignity and charm) and I usually went both morning and evening to watch the regal daughters of the county aristocracy go up the aisle. I even joined a Sunday school class because charming Miss Culver was the teacher. Outwardly a stocky, ungraceful youth, I was inwardly a bold squire of romance needing only a steed and a shield to fight for my lady love. No one could be more essentially romantic than I was at this time—but fortunately no one knew it!

Mingling as I did with young people who had been students at the Seminary, I naturally developed a new ambition. I decided to enter for the autumn term, and to that end gained from my father a leave of absence during August and hired myself out to bind grain in the harvest field. I demanded full wages and when one blazing hot day I rode on a shining new Marsh harvester into a field of wheat just south of the Fair Ground, I felt myself a man, and entering upon a course which put me nearer the clothing and the education I desired.

Binding on a harvester was desperately hard work for a sixteen-year-old boy for it called for endurance of heat and hunger as well as for unusual celerity and precision of action. But as I considered myself full-grown physically, I could not allow myself a word of complaint. I kept my place beside my partner hour after hour, talking care of my half of ten acres of grain each day. My fingers, raw and bleeding with the briars and smarting with the rust on the grain, were a torture but I persisted to the end of harvest. In this way I earned enough money to buy myself a Sunday suit, some new boots and the necessary books for the seminary term which began in September.

Up to this time I had never owned an overcoat nor a suit that fitted me. My shirts had always been made by my mother and had no real cuffs. I now purchased two boxes of paper cuffs and a real necktie. My intense satisfaction in these garments made mother smile with pleasure and understanding humor.

In spite of my store suit and my high-heeled calf-skin boots I felt very humble as I left our lowly roof that first day and started for the chapel. To me the brick building standing in the center of its ample yard was as imposing as I imagine the Harper Memorial Library must be to the youngster of today as he enters the University of Chicago.

To enter the chapel meant running the gauntlet of a hundred citified young men and women, fairly entitled to laugh at a clod-jumper like myself, and I would have balked completely had not David Pointer, a neighbor's son, volunteered to lead the way. Gratefully I accepted his offer, and so passed for the first time into the little hall which came to mean so much to me in after years.

It was a large room swarming with merry young people and the Corinthian columns painted on the walls, the pipe organ, the stately professors on the platform, the self-confident choir, were all of such majesty that I was reduced to hare-like humility. What right had I to share in this splendor? Sliding hurriedly into a seat I took refuge in the obscurity which my youth and short stature guaranteed to me.

Soon Professor Bush, the principal of the school, gentle, blue-eyed, white-haired, with a sweet and mellow voice, rose to greet the old pupils and welcome the new ones, and his manner so won my confidence that at the close of the service I went to him and told him who I was. Fortunately he remembered my sister Harriet, and politely said, "I am glad to see you, Hamlin," and from that moment I considered him a friend, and an almost infallible guide.

The school was in truth a very primitive institution, hardly more than a high school, but it served its purpose. It gave farmers' boys like myself the opportunity of meeting those who were older, finer, more learned than they, and every day was to me like turning a fresh and delightful page in a story book, not merely because it brought new friends, new experiences, but because it symbolized freedom from the hay fork and the hoe. Learning was easy for me. In all but mathematics I kept among the highest of my class without much effort, but it was in the "Friday Exercises" that I earliest distinguished myself.

It was the custom at the close of every week's work to bring a section of the pupils upon the platform as essayists or orators, and these "exercises" formed the most interesting and the most passionately dreaded feature of the entire school. No pupil who took part in it ever forgot his first appearance. It was at once a pillory and a burning. It called for self-possession, memory, grace of gesture and a voice!

My case is typical. For three or four days before my first ordeal, I could not eat. A mysterious uneasiness developed in my solar plexus, a pain which never left me except possibly in the morning before I had time to think. Day by day I drilled and drilled and drilled, out in the fields at the edge of the town or at home when mother was away, in the barn while milking—at every opportunity I went through my selection with most impassioned voice and lofty gestures, sustained by the legends of Webster and Demosthenes, resolved upon a blazing victory. I did everything but mumble a smooth pebble—realizing that most of the boys in my section were going through precisely the same struggle. Each of us knew exactly how the others felt, and yet I cannot say that we displayed acute sympathy one with another; on the contrary, those in the free section considered the antics of the suffering section a very amusing spectacle and we were continually being "joshed" about our lack of appetite.

The test was, in truth, rigorous. To ask a bashful boy or shy girl fresh from the kitchen to walk out upon a platform and face that crowd of mocking students was a kind of torture. No desk was permitted. Each victim stood bleakly exposed to the pitiless gaze of three hundred eyes, and as most of us were poorly dressed, in coats that never fitted and trousers that climbed our boot-tops, we suffered the miseries of the damned. The girls wore gowns which they themselves had made, and were, of course, equally self-conscious. The knowledge that their sleeves did not fit was of more concern to them than the thought of breaking down—but the fear of forgetting their lines also contributed to their dread and terror.

While the names which preceded mine were called off that first afternoon, I grew colder and colder till at last I shook with a nervous chill, and when, in his smooth, pleasant tenor, Prof. Bush called out "Hamlin Garland" I rose in my seat with a spring like Jack from his box. My limbs were numb, so numb that I could scarcely feel the floor beneath my feet and the windows were only faint gray glares of light. My head oscillated like a toy balloon, seemed indeed to be floating in the air, and my heart was pounding like a drum.

However, I had pondered upon this scene so long and had figured my course so exactly that I made all the turns with moderate degree of grace and succeeded finally in facing my audience without falling up the steps (as several others had done) and so looked down upon my fellows like Tennyson's eagle on the sea. In that instant a singular calm fell over me, I became strangely master of myself. From somewhere above me a new and amazing power fell upon me and in that instant I perceived on the faces of my classmates a certain expression of surprise and serious respect. My subconscious oratorical self had taken charge.

I do not at present recall what my recitation was, but it was probably *Catiline's Defense* or some other of the turgid declamatory pieces of classic literature with which all our readers were filled.

It was bombastic stuff, but my blind, boyish belief in it gave it dignity. As I went on my voice cleared. The window sashes regained their outlines. I saw every form before me, and the look of surprise and pleasure on the smiling face of my principal exalted me

Closing amid hearty applause, I stepped down with a feeling that I had won a place among the orators of the school, a belief which did no harm to others and gave me a good deal of satisfaction. As I had neither money nor clothes, and was not of figure to win admiration, why should I not express the pride I felt in my power to move an audience? Besides I was only sixteen!

The principal spoke to me afterwards, both praising and criticising my method. The praise I accepted, the criticism I naturally resented. I realized some of my faults of course, but I was not ready to have even Prof. Bush tell me of them. I hated "elocution" drill in class. I relied on "inspiration." I believed that orators were born, not made.

There was one other speaker in my section, a little girl, considerably younger than myself, who had the mysterious power of the born actress, and I recognized this quality in her at once. I perceived that she spoke from a deep-seated, emotional, Celtic impulse. Hardly more than a child in years, she was easily the most dramatic reader in the school. She too, loved tragic prose and passionate, sorrowful verse and to hear her recite,

> One of them dead in the East by the sea
> And one of them dead in the West by the sea,

was to be shaken by inexplicable emotion. Her face grew pale as silver as she went on and her eyes darkened with the anguish of the poet mother.

Most of the students were the sons and daughters of farmers round about the county, but a few were from the village homes in western Iowa and southern Minnesota. Two or three boys wore real tailor-made suits, and the easy flow of their trouser legs and the set of their linen collars rendered me at once envious and discontented. "Some day," I said to myself, "I too, will have a suit that will not gape at the neck and crawl at the ankle," but I did not rise to the height of expecting a ring and watch.

Shoes were just coming into fashion and one young man wore pointed "box toes" which filled all the rest of us with despair. John

Cutler also wore collars of linen—real linen—which had to be laundered, but few of us dared fix our hopes as high as that. John also owned three neckties, and wore broad cuffs with engraved gold buttons, and on Fridays waved these splendors before our eyes with a malicious satisfaction which aroused our hatred. Of such complexion are the tragedies and triumphs of youth!

How I envied Arthur Peters his calm and haughty bearing! Most of us entered chapel like rabbits sneaking down a turnip patch, but Arthur and John and Walter loitered in with the easy and assured manner of Senators or Generals—so much depends upon leather and prunella. Gradually I lost my terror of this ordeal, but I took care to keep behind some friendly bulk like young Blakeslee, who stood six feet two in his gaiters.

With all these anxieties I loved the school and could hardly be wrested from it even for a day. I bent to my books with eagerness, I joined a debating society, and I took a hand at all the games. The days went by on golden, noiseless, ball-bearing axles—and almost before I realized it, winter was upon the land. But oh! the luxury of that winter, with no snow drifts to climb, no corn-stalks to gather and no long walk to school. It was sweet to wake each morning in the shelter of our little house and know that another day of delightful schooling was ours. Our hands softened and lightened. Our walk became each day less of a "galumping plod." The companionship of bright and interesting young people, and the study of well-dressed men and women in attendance upon lectures and socials was a part of our instruction and had their refining effect upon us, graceless colts though we were.

Sometime during this winter Wendell Phillips came to town and lectured on *The Lost Arts*. My father took us all to see and hear this orator hero of his boyhood days in Boston.

I confess to a disappointment in the event. A tall old gentleman with handsome clean-cut features, rose from behind the pulpit in the Congregational Church, and read from a manuscript—read quietly, colloquially, like a teacher addressing a group of students, with scarcely a gesture and without raising his voice. Only once toward the end of the hour did he thrill us, and then only for a moment.

Father was a little saddened. He shook his head gravely. "He isn't the orator he was in the good old anti-slavery days," he explained and passed again into a glowing account of the famous "slave speech" in Faneuil Hall when the pro-slavery men all but mobbed the speaker.

Per contra, I liked, (and the boys all liked) a certain peripatetic temperance lecturer named Beale, for *he* was an orator, one of those who rise on an impassioned chant, soaring above the snows of Chimborazo, mingling the purple and gold of sunset with the saffron and silver of the dawn. None of us could tell just what these gorgeous passages meant, but they were beautiful while they lasted, and sadly corrupted our oratorical style. It took some of us twenty years to recover from the fascination of this man's absurd and high falutin' elocutionary singsong.

I forgot the farm, I forgot the valley of my birth, I lived wholly and with joy in the present. Song, poetry, history mingled with the sports which made our life so unceasingly interesting. There was a certain girl, the daughter of the shoe merchant, who (temporarily) displaced the image of Agnes in the niche of my shrine, and to roll the platter for her at a "sociable" was a very high honor indeed, and there was another, a glorious contralto singer, much older than I—but there I must not claim to have even attracted her eyes, and my meetings with Millie were so few and so public that I cannot claim to have ever conversed with her. They were all boyish adorations.

Much as I enjoyed this winter, greatly as it instructed me, I cannot now recover from its luminious dark more than here and there an incident, a poem, a song. It was all delightful, that I know, so filled with joyous hours that I retain but a mingled impression of satisfaction and regret—satisfaction with life as I found it, regret at its inevitable ending—for my father, irritated by the failure of his renter, announced that he had decided to put us all back upon the farm!

18

Back to the Farm

Judging from the entries in a small diary of this date, I was neither an introspective youth nor one given to precocious literary subtleties.

On March 27th, 1877, I made this entry; "To-day we move back upon the farm."

This is all of it! No more, no less. Not a word to indicate whether I regretted the decision or welcomed it, and from subsequent equally bald notes, I derive the information that my father retained his position as grain buyer, and that he drove back and forth daily over the five miles which lay between the farm and the elevator. There is no mention of my mother, no hint as to how she felt, although the return to the loneliness and drudgery of the farm must have been as grievous to her as to her sons.

Our muscles were soft and our heads filled with new ambitions but there was no alternative. It was "back to the field," or "out into the cold, cold world," so forth we went upon the soil in the old familiar way, there to plod to and fro endlessly behind the seeder and the harrow. It was harder than ever to follow a team for ten hours over the soft ground, and early rising was more difficult than it had ever been before, but I discovered some compensations which helped me bear these discomforts. I saw more of the beauty of the landscape and I now had an aspiration to occupy my mind. My memories of the Seminary, the echoes of the songs we had heard, gave the morning chorus of the prairie chickens a richer meaning than before. The west wind, laden with the delicious smell of uncovered earth, the tender blue of the sky, the cheerful chirping of the ground sparrows, the jocund whistling of the gophers, the winding flight of the prairie pigeons—all these sights and sounds of spring swept back upon me, bringing something sweeter and more significant than before. I had gained in perception and also in the power to assimilate what I perceived.

This year in town had other far-reaching effects. It tended to warp us from our father's designs. It placed the rigorous, filthy drudgery of the farm-yard in sharp contrast with the care-free companionable existence led by my friends in the village, and we longed to be of their condition. We had gained our first set of comparative ideas, and with them an unrest which was to carry us very far away.

True, neither Burton nor I had actually shared the splendors of Congressman Deering's house but we had obtained revelatory glimpses of its well-kept lawn, and through the open windows we had watched the waving of its lace curtains. We had observed also how well Avery Brush's frock coat fitted and we comprehended something of the elegant leisure which the sons and daughters of Wm. Petty's general store enjoyed.

Over against these comforts, these luxurious conditions, we now set our ugly little farmhouse, with its rag carpets, its battered furniture, its barren attic, and its hard, rude beds.—All that we possessed seemed very cheap and deplorably commonplace.

My brother, who had passed a vivid and wonderful year riding race horses, clerking in an ice cream parlor, with frequent holidays of swimming and baseball, also went groaning and grumbling to the fields. He too resented the curry-comb and the dung fork. We both loathed the smell of manure and hated the greasy clothing which our tasks made necessary. Secretly we vowed that when we were twenty-one we would leave the farm, never to return to it. However, as the ground dried off, and the grass grew green in the door-yard some part of this bitterness, this resentment, faded away, and we made no further complaint.

My responsibilities were now those of a man. I was nearly full grown, quick and powerful of hand, and vain of my strength, which was, in fact, unusual and of decided advantage to me. Nothing ever really tired me out. I could perform any of my duties with ease, and none of the men under me ever presumed to question my authority. As harvest came on I took my place on our new Marsh harvester, and bound my half of over one hundred acres of heavy grain.

The crop that year was enormous. At times, as looked out over the billowing acres of wheat which must not only be reaped and bound and shocked and stacked but also threshed, before there was the slightest chance of my returning to the Seminary, my face grew long and my heart heavy.

Burton shared this feeling, for he, too, had become profoundly interested in the Seminary and was eager to return, eager to renew the friendships he had gained. We both wished to walk once more beneath the maple trees in clean well-fitting garments, and above all we hungered to escape the curry-comb and the cow.

Both of us retained our membership in the Adelphian Debating Society, and occasionally drove to town after the day's work to take part in the Monday meetings. Having decided, definitely, to be an orator, I now went about with a copy of Shakespeare in my pocket and ranted the immortal soliloquies of *Hamlet* and *Richard* as I held the plow, feeling certain that I was following in the footprints of Lincoln and Demosthenes.

Sundays brought a special sweet relief that summer, a note of finer poetry into all our lives, for often after a bath behind the barn we put on clean shirts and drove away to Osage to meet George and Mitchell, or went to church to see some of the girls we had admired at the Seminary. On other Sabbaths we returned to our places at the Burr Oak school-house, enjoying as we used to do, a few hours' forgetfulness of the farm.

My father, I am glad to say, never insisted upon any religious observance on the part of his sons, and never interfered with any reasonable pleasure even on Sunday. If he made objection to our trips it was usually on behalf of the cattle. "Go where you please," he often said, "only get back in time to do the milking." Sometimes he would ask, "Don't you think the horses ought to have a rest as well as yourselves?" He was a stern man but a just man, and I am especially grateful to him for his noninterference with my religious affairs.

All that summer and all the fall I worked like a hired man, assuming in addition the responsibilities of being boss. I bound grain until my arms were raw with briars and in stacking-time I wallowed round and round upon my knees, building great ricks of grain, taking obvious pride in the skill which this task required until my trousers, re-inforced at the knees, bagged ungracefully and my hands, swollen with the act of grappling the heavy bundles as they were thrown to me, grew horny and brown and clumsy, so that I quite despaired of ever being able to write another letter. I was very glad not to have my Seminary friends see me in this unlovely condition.

However, I took a well-defined pride in stacking, for it was a test of skill. It was clean work. Even now, as I ride a country lane, and see men at work handling oats or hay, I recall the pleasurable sides of work on the farm and long to return to it.

The radiant sky of August and September on the prairie was a never failing source of delight to me. Nature seemed resting, opulent, self-satisfied and honorable. Every phase of the landscape indicated a task fulfilled. There were still and pulseless days when slaty-blue clouds piled up in the west and came drifting eastward with thunderous accompaniment, to break the oppressive heat and leave the earth cool and fresh from having passed. There were misty, windy days when the sounding, southern breeze swept the yellow stubble like a scythe; when the sky, without a cloud, was whitened by an overspreading haze; when the crickets sang sleepily as if in dream of eternal summer; and the grasshoppers clicked and buzzed from stalk to stalk in pure delight of sunshine and the harvest.

Another humbler source of pleasure in stacking was the watermelon which, having been picked in the early morning and hidden under the edge of the stack, remained deliciously cool till midforenoon, when at a signal, the men all gathered in the shadow of the rick, and leisurely ate their fill of juicy "mountain sweets." Then there was the five o'clock supper, with its milk and doughnuts and pie which sent us back to our task—replete, content, ready for another hour of toil.

Of course, there were unpleasant days later in the month, noons when the skies were filled with ragged, swiftly moving clouds, and the winds blew the sheaves inside out and slashed against my face the flying grain as well as the leaping crickets. Such days gave prophecy of the passing of summer and the coming of fall. But there was a mitigating charm even in these conditions, for they were all welcome promises of an early return to school.

Crickets during stacking time were innumerable and voracious as rust or fire. They ate our coats or hats if we left them beside the stack. They gnawed the fork handles and devoured any straps that were left lying about, but their multitudinous song was a beautiful inwrought part of the symphony.

That year the threshing was done in the fields with a traction engine. My uncle David came no more to help us harvest. He had almost passed out of our life, and I have no recollection of him till several years later. Much of the charm, the poetry of the old-time threshing vanished with the passing of horse power and the coming of the nomadic hired hand. There was less and less of the "changing works" which used to bring the young men of the farms together. The grain was no longer stacked round the stable. Most of it we threshed in the field and the straw after being spread out upon the stubble was burned. Some farmers threshed directly from the shock, and the new "Vibrator" took the place of the old Buffalo Pitts Separator with its ringing bell-metal pinions. Wheeled plows were common and self-binding harvesters were coming in.

Although my laconic little diary does not show it, I was fiercely resolved upon returning to the Seminary. My father was not very sympathetic. In his eyes I already had a very good equipment for the battle of life, but mother, with a woman's ready understanding, divined that I had not merely set my heart on graduating at the Seminary, but that I was secretly dreaming of another and far more romantic career than that of being a farmer. Although a woman of slender schooling herself, she responded helpfully to every effort which her sons made to raise themselves above the commonplace level of neighborhood life.

All through the early fall whenever Burton and I met the other boys of a Sunday our talk was sure to fall upon the Seminary, and Burton stoutly declared that he, too, was going to begin in September. As a matter of fact the autumn term opened while we were still hard at work around a threshing machine with no definite hope of release till the plowing and corn-husking were over. Our fathers did not seem to realize that the men of the future (even the farmers of the future) must have a considerable amount of learning and experience, and so October went by and November was well started before parole was granted and we were free to return to our books.

With what sense of liberty, of exultation, we took our way down the road on that gorgeous autumn morning! No more dust, no more grime, no more mud, no more cow milking, no more horse currying! For five months we were to live the lives of scholars, of boarders.—Yes, through some mysterious channel our parents had been brought to the point of engaging lodgings for us in the home of a townsman named Leete. For two dollars a week it was arranged that we could eat and sleep from Monday night to Friday noon, but we were not expected to remain for supper on Friday; and Sunday supper, was of course, extra. I thought this a great deal of money then, but I cannot understand at this distance how our landlady was able to provide, for that sum, the raw material of her kitchen, to say nothing of bed linen and soap.

The house, which stood on the edge of the town, was small and without upstairs heat, but it seemed luxurious to me, and the family straightway absorbed my interest. Leete, the nominal head of the establishment, was a short, gray, lame and rather inefficient man of changeable temper who teamed about the streets with a span of roans almost as dour and crippled as himself. His wife, who did nearly all the housework for five boarders as well as for the members of her own family, was a soul of heroic pride and most indomitable energy. She was a tall, dark, thin woman who had once been handsome. Poor creature—how incessantly she toiled, and how much she endured!

She had three graceful and alluring daughters,—Ella, nineteen, Cora, sixteen, and Martha, a quiet little mouse of about ten years of age. Ella was a girl of unusual attainment, a teacher, self-contained and womanly, with whom we all, promptly, fell in love. Cora, a moody, dark-eyed, passionate girl who sometimes glowed with friendly smiles and sometimes glowered in anger, was less adored. Neither of them considered Burton or myself worthy of serious notice. On the contrary, we were necessary nuisances.

To me Ella was a queen, a kindly queen, ever ready to help me out with my algebra. Everything she did seemed to me instinct with womanly grace. No doubt she read the worship in my eyes, but her attitude was that of an older sister. Cora, being nearer my own age, awed me not at all. On the contrary, we were more inclined to battle than to coo. Her coolness toward me, I soon discovered, was sustained by her growing interest in a young man from Cerro Gordo County.

We were a happy, noisy gang, and undoubtedly gave poor Mrs. Leete a great deal of trouble. There was Boggs (who had lost part of one ear in some fracas with Jack Frost) who paced up and down his room declining Latin verbs with painful pertinacity, and Burton who loved a jest but never made one, and Joe Pritchard, who was interested mainly in politics and oratory, and finally that criminally well-dressed young book agent (with whom we had very little in common) and myself. In cold weather we all herded in the dining room to keep from freezing, and our weekly scrub took place after we got home to our own warm kitchens and the family wash-tubs.

Life was a pure joy to Burton as to me. Each day was a poem, each night a dreamless sleep! Each morning at half past eight we went to the Seminary and at four o'clock left it with regret. I should like to say that we studied hard every night, burning a great deal of kerosene oil, but I cannot do so.—We had a good time. The learning, (so far as I can recall) was incidental.

It happened that my closest friends, aside from Burton, were pupils of the public school and for that reason I kept my membership in the Adelphian Society which met every Monday evening. My activities there, I find, made up a large part of my life during this second winter. I not only debated furiously, disputing weighty political questions, thus advancing the forensic side of my education, but later in the winter I helped to organize a dramatic company which gave a play for the benefit of the Club Library.

Just why I should have been chosen "stage director" of our "troupe," I cannot say, but something in my ability to declaim *Regulus* probably led to this high responsibility. At any rate, I not only played the leading juvenile, I settled points of action and costume without the slightest hesitation. Cora was my *ingenue* opposite, it fell out, and so we played at lovemaking, while meeting coldly at the family dining table.

Our engagement in the town hall extended through two March evenings and was largely patronized. It would seem that I was a dominant figure on both occasions, for I declaimed a "piece" on the opening night, one of those resounding orations (addressed to the Carthaginians), which we all loved, and which permitted of thunderous, rolling periods and passionate gestures. If my recollection is not distorted, I was masterful that night—at least, Joe Pritchard agreed that I was "the best part of the show." Joe was my friend, and I hold him in especial affection for his hearty praise of my effort.

On this same night I also appeared in a little sketch representing the death of a veteran of the Revolutionary War, in which the dying man beholds in a vision his beloved Leader. Walter Blakeslee was the "Washington" and I, with heavily powdered hair, was the veteran. On the second night I played the juvenile lover in a drama called *His Brother's Keeper.* Cora as "Shellie," my sweetheart, was very lovely in pink mosquito netting, and for the first time I regretted her interest in the book agent from Cerro Gordo. Strange to say I had no fear at all as I looked out over the audience which packed the town hall to the ceiling. Father and mother were there with Frank and Jessie, all quite dazed (as I imagined) by my transcendent position behind the foot lights.

It may have been this very night that Willard Eaton, the county attorney, spoke to my father saying, "Richard, whenever that boy of yours finishes school and wants to begin to study law, you send him right to me," which was, of course, a very great compliment, for the county attorney belonged to the best known and most influential firm of lawyers in the town. At the moment his offer would have seemed very dull and commonplace to me. I would have refused it.

Our success that night was so great that it appeared a pity not to permit other towns to witness our performance, hence we boldly organized a "tour." We booked a circuit which included St. Ansgar and Mitchell, two villages, one four, the other ten miles to the north. Audacious as this may seem, it was deliberately decided upon, and one pleasant day Mitchell and George and I loaded all our scenery into a wagon and drove away across the prairie to our first "stand" very much as Moliére did in his youth, leaving the ladies to follow (in the grandeur of hired buggies) later in the day.

That night we played with "artistic success"—that is to say, we lost some eighteen dollars, which so depressed the management that it abandoned the tour, and the entire organization returned to Osage in diminished glory. This cut short my career as an actor. I never again took part in a theatrical performance.

Not long after this disaster, "Shellie," as I now called Cora, entered upon some mysterious and romantic drama of her own. The travelling man vanished, and soon after she too disappeared. Where she went, what she did, no one seemed to know, and none of us quite dared to ask. I never saw her again but last year, after nearly forty years of wandering, I was told that she is married and living in luxurious ease near London. Through what deep valleys she has travelled to reach this height, with what loss or gain, I cannot say, but I shall always remember her as she was that night in St. Ansgar, in her pink-mosquito-bar dress, her eyes shining with excitement, her voice vibrant with girlish gladness.

Our second winter at the Seminary passed all too quickly, and when the prairie chickens began to boom from the ridges our hearts sank within us. For the first time the grouse's cheery dance was unwelcome for it meant the closing of our books, the loss of our pleasant companions, the surrender of our leisure, and a return to the mud of the fields.

It was especially hard to say good-bye to Ella and Maud, for though they were in no sense sweethearts they were very pleasant companions. There were others whom it was a pleasure to meet in the halls and to emulate in the class-rooms, and when early in April, we went home to enter upon the familiar round of seeding, corn-planting, corn plowing, harvesting, stacking and threshing, we had only the promise of an occasional trip to town to cheer us.

It would seem that our interest in the girls of Burr Oak had diminished, for we were less regular in our attendance upon services in the little school-house, and whenever we could gain consent to use a horse, we hitched up and drove away to town. These trips have golden, unforgettable charm, and indicate the glamor which approaching manhood was flinging over my world.

My father's world was less jocund, was indeed filled with increasing anxiety, for just before harvest time a new and formidable enemy of the wheat appeared in the shape of a minute, ill-smelling insect called the chinch bug. It already bore an evil reputation with us for it was reported to have eaten out the crops of southern Wisconsin and northern Illinois, and, indeed, before barley cutting was well under way the county was overrun with laborers from the south who were anxious to get work in order to recoup them for the loss of their own harvest. These fugitives brought incredible tales of the ravages of the enemy and prophesied our destruction but, as a matter of fact, only certain dry ridges proclaimed the presence of the insect during this year.

The crop was rather poor for other reasons, and Mr. Babcock, like my father, objected to paying board bills. His attitude was so unpromising that Burton and I cast about to see how we could lessen the expense of upkeep during our winter term of school.

Together we decided to hire a room and board ourselves (as many of the other fellows did) and so cut our expenses to a mere trifle. It was difficult, even in those days, to live cheaper than two dollars per week, but we convinced our people that we could do it, and so at last wrung from our mothers a reluctant consent to our trying it. We got away in October, only two weeks behind our fellows.

I well remember the lovely afternoon on which we unloaded our scanty furniture into the two little rooms which we had hired for the term. It was still glorious autumn weather, and we were young and released from slavery. We had a table, three chairs, a little strip of carpet, and a melodeon, which belonged to Burton's sister, and when we had spread our carpet and put up our curtains we took seats, and cocking our feet upon the window sill surveyed our surroundings with such satisfaction as only autocrats of the earth may compass. We were absolute masters of our time—that was our chiefest joy. We could rise when we pleased and go to bed when we pleased. There were no stables to clean, no pigs to feed, nothing marred our days. We could study or sing or dance at will. We could even wrestle at times with none to molest or make us afraid.

My photograph shows the new suit which I had bought on my own responsibility this time, but no camera could possibly catch the glow of inward satisfaction which warmed my heart. It was a brown cassimere, coat, trousers and vest all alike,—and the trousers fitted me! Furthermore as I bought it without my father's help, my selection was made for esthetic reasons without regard to durability or warmth. It was mine—in the fullest sense—and when I next entered chapel I felt not merely draped, but defended. I walked to my seat with confident security, a well-dressed person. I had a "boughten" shirt also, two boxes of paper cuffs, and two new ties, a black one for every day and a white one for Sunday.

I don't know that any of the girls perceived my new suit, but I hoped one or two of them did. The boys were quite outspoken in their approval of it.

I had given up boots, also, for most of the townsmen wore shoes, thus marking the decline of the military spirit. I never again owned a pair of those man-killing top-boots—which were not only hard to get on and off but pinched my toes, and interrupted the flow of my trouser-legs. Thus one great era fades into another. The Jack-boot period was over, the shoe, commonplace and comfortable, had won.

Our housekeeping was very simple. Each of us brought from home on Monday morning a huge bag of doughnuts together with several loaves of bread, and (with a milkman near at hand) our cooking remained rudimentary. We did occasionally fry a steak and boil some potatoes, and I have a dim memory of several disastrous attempts to make flapjacks out of flour and sweet milk. However we never suffered from hunger as some of the other fellows actually did.

Pretty Ethel Beebe comes into the record of this winter, like a quaint illustration to an old-fashioned story, for she lived near us and went to school along the same sidewalk. Burton was always saying, "Some day I am going to brace up and ask Ethel to let me carry her books, and I'm going to walk beside her right down Main Street." But he never did. Ultimately I attained to that incredible boldness, but Burton only followed along behind.

Ethel was a slender, smiling, brown-eyed girl with a keen appreciation of the ridiculous, and I have no doubt she catalogued all our peculiarities, for she always seemed to be laughing at us, and I think it must have been her smiles that prevented any romantic attachment. We walked and talked without any deeper interest than good comradeship.

Mrs. Babcock was famous for her pies and cakes, and Burton always brought some delicious samples of her skill. As regularly as the clock, on every Tuesday evening he said, in precisely the same tone, "Well, now, we'll have to eat these pies right away or they'll spoil," and as I made no objection, we had pie for luncheon, pie and cake for supper, and cake and pie for breakfast until all these "goodies" which were intended to serve as dessert through the week were consumed. By Thursday morning we were usually down to dry bread and butter.

We simplified our housework in other ways in order that we might have time to study and Burton wasted a good deal of time at the fiddle, sawing away till I was obliged to fall him upon and roll him on the floor to silence him.

I still have our ledger which gives an itemized account of the cost of this experiment in self board, and its footings are incredibly small. Less than fifty cents a day for both of us! Of course our mothers, sisters and aunts were continually joking us about our housekeeping, and once or twice Mrs. Babcock called upon us unexpectedly and found the room "a sight." But we did not mind her very much. We only feared the bright eyes of Ethel and Maude and Carrie. Fortunately they could not properly call upon us, even if they had wished to do so, and we were safe. It is probable, moreover, that they fully understood our methods, for they often slyly hinted at hasty dish-washing and primitive cookery. All of this only amused us, so long as they did not actually discover the dirt and disorder of which our mothers complained.

Our school library at that time was pitifully small and ludicrously prescriptive, but its shelves held a few of the fine old classics, Scott, Dickens and Thackeray—the kind of books which can always be had in sets at very low prices—and in nosing about among these I fell, one day, upon two small red volumes called *Mosses from an Old Manse.* Of course I had read of the author, for these books were listed in my *History of American Literature,* but I had never, up to this moment, dared to open one of them. I was a discoverer.

I turned a page or two, and instantly my mental horizon widened. When I had finished the *Artist of the Beautiful,* the great Puritan romancer had laid his spell upon me everlastingly. Even as I walked homeward to my lunch, I read. I ate with the book beside my plate. I neglected my classes that afternoon, and as soon as I had absorbed this volume I secured the other and devoted myself to it with almost equal intensity. The stately diction, the rich and glowing imagery, the mystical radiance, and the aloofness of the author's personality all united to create in me a worshipful admiration which made all other interests pale and faint. It was my first profound literary passion and I was dazzled by the glory of it.

It would be a pleasant task to say that this book determined my career—it would form a delightful literary assumption, but I cannot claim it. As a realist I must remain faithful to fact. I did not then and there vow to be a romantic novelist like Hawthorne. On the contrary, I realized that this great poet (to me he was a poet) like Edgar Allan Poe, was a soul that dwelt apart from ordinary mortals.

To me he was a magician, a weaver of magic spells, a dreamer whose visions comprehended the half-lights, the borderlands, of the human soul. I loved the roll of his words in *The March of Time* and the quaint phrasing of the *Rill from the Town Pump; Rappacini's Daughter* whose breath poisoned the insects in the air, uplifted me. *Drowne and His Wooden Image,* the *Great Stone Face*—each story had its special appeal. For days I walked amid enchanted mist, my partner—(even the maidens I most admired), became less appealing, less necessary to me. Eager to know more of this necromancer I searched the town for others of his books, but found only *American Notes* and *The Scarlet Letter.*

Gradually I returned to something like my normal interests in baseball and my classmates, but never again did I fall to the low level of *Jack Harkaway.* I now possessed a literary touchstone with which I tested the quality of other books and other minds, and my intellectual arrogance, I fear, sometimes made me an unpleasant companion. The fact that Ethel did not "like" Hawthorne, sank her to a lower level in my estimation.

19

End of School Days

Though my years at the Seminary were the happiest of my life they are among the most difficult for me to recover and present to my readers. During half the year I worked on the farm fiercely, unsparing of myself, in order that I might have an uninterrupted season of study in the village. Each term was very like another so far as its broad program went but innumerable, minute but very important progressions carried me toward manhood, events which can hardly be stated to an outsider.

Burton remained my room-mate and in all our vicissitudes we had no vital disagreements but his unconquerable shyness kept him from making a good impression on his teachers and this annoyed me—it made him seem stupid when he was not. Once, as chairman of a committee it became his duty to introduce a certain lecturer who was to speak on "Elihu Burritt," and by some curious twist in my chum's mind this name became "Lu-hi Burritt" and he so stated it in his introductory remarks. This amused the lecturer and raised a titter in the audience. Burton bled in silence over this mishap for he was at heart deeply ambitious to be a public speaker. He never alluded to that speech even to me without writhing in retrospective shame.

Another incident will illustrate his painfully shy character. One of our summer vacations was made notable by the visit of an exceedingly pretty girl to the home of one of Burton's aunts who lived on the road to the Grove, and my chum's excitement over the presence of this alien bird of paradise was very amusing to me as well as to his brother Charles who was inclined, as an older brother, to "take it out" of Burt.

I listened to my chum's account of his cousin's beauty with something more than fraternal interest. She came, it appeared, from Dubuque and had the true cosmopolitan's air of tolerance. Our small community amused her. Her hats and gowns (for it soon developed that she had at least two), were the envy of all the girls, and the admiration of the boys. No disengaged or slightly obligated beau of the district neglected to hitch his horse at Mrs. Knapp's gate.

Burton's opportunity seemed better than that of any other youth, for he could visit his aunt as often as he wished without arousing comment, whereas for me, a call would have been equivalent to an offer of marriage. My only chance of seeing the radiant stranger was at church. Needless to say we all made it a point to attend every service during her stay.

One Sunday afternoon as I was riding over to the Grove, I met Burton plodding homeward along the grassy lane, walking with hanging head and sagging shoulders. He looked like a man in deep and discouraged thought, and when he glanced up at me, with a familiar defensive smile twisting his long lips, I knew something had gone wrong.

"Hello," I said. "Where have you been?"

"Over to Aunt Sallie's," he said.

His long, linen duster was sagging at the sides, and peering down at his pockets I perceived a couple of quarts of lovely Siberian crab-apples. "Where did you get all that fruit?" I demanded.

"At home."

"What are you going to do with it?"

"Take it back again."

"What do you mean by such a performance?"

With the swift flush and silent laugh which always marked his confessions of weakness, or failure, he replied, "I went over to see Nettie. I intended to give her these apples," he indicated the fruit by a touch on each pocket, "but when I got there I found old Bill Watson, dressed to kill and large as life, sitting in the parlor. I was so afraid of his finding out what I had in my pockets that I didn't go in. I came away leaving him in possession."

Of course I laughed—but there was an element of pathos in it after all. Poor Burt! He always failed to get his share of the good things in this world.

We continued to board ourselves,—now here, now there, and always to the effect of being starved out by Friday night, but we kept well and active even on doughnuts and pie, and were grateful of any camping place in town.

Once Burton left a soup-bone to simmer on the stove while we went away to morning recitations, and when we reached home, smoke was leaking from every keyhole. The room was solid with the remains of our bone. It took six months to get the horrid smell of charred beef out of our wardrobe. The girls all sniffed and wondered as we came near.

On Fridays we went home and during the winter months very generally attended the Lyceum which met in the Burr Oak schoolhouse. We often debated, and on one occasion I attained to the honor of being called upon to preside over the session. Another memorable evening is that in which I read with what seemed to me distinguished success Joaquin Miller's magnificent new poem, *Kit Carson's Ride* and in the splendid roar and trample of its lines discovered a new and powerful American poet. His spirit appealed to me. He was at once American and western. I read every line of his verse which the newspapers or magazines brought to me, and was profoundly influenced by its epic quality.

And so, term by term, in growing joy and strength, in expanding knowledge of life, we hurried toward the end of our four years' course at this modest little school, finding in it all the essential elements of an education, for we caught at every chance quotation from the scientists, every fleeting literary allusion in the magazines, attaining, at last, a dim knowledge of what was going on in the great outside world of letters and discovery. Of course there were elections and tariff reforms and other comparatively unimportant matters taking place in the state but they made only the most transient impression on our minds.

During the last winter of our stay at the Seminary, my associate in housekeeping was one Adelbert Jones, the son of a well-to-do farmer who lived directly east of town. "Del," as we called him, always alluded to himself as "Ferguson." He was tall, with a very large blond face inclined to freckle and his first care of a morning was to scrutinize himself most anxiously to see whether the troublesome brown flecks were increasing or diminishing in number. Often upon reaching the open air he would sniff the east wind and say lugubriously, "This is the kind of day that brings out the freckles on your Uncle Ferg."

He was one of the best dressed men in the school, and especially finicky about his collars and ties,—was, indeed, one of the earliest to purchase linen. He also parted his yellow hair in the middle (which was a very noticeable thing in those days) and was always talking of taking a girl to a social or to prayer meeting. But, like Burton, he never did. So far as I knew he never "went double," and most of the girls looked upon him as more or less of a rustic, notwithstanding his fine figure and careful dress.

As for me I did once hire a horse and carriage of a friend and took Alice for a drive! More than thirty-five years have passed since that adventure and yet I can see every turn in that road! I can hear the crackle of my starched shirt and the creak of my suspender buckles as I write.

Alice, being quite as bashful as myself, kept our conversation to the high plane of Hawthorne and Poe and Schiller with an occasional tired droop to the weather, hence I infer that she was as much relieved as I when we reached her boarding house some two hours later. It was my first and only attempt at this, the most common of all ways of entertaining one's best girl.

The youth who furnished the carriage betrayed me, and the outcry of my friends so intimidated me that I dared not look Alice in the face. My only comfort was that no one but ourselves could possibly know what an erratic conversationalist I had been. However, she did not seem to lay it up against me. I think she was as much astonished as I and I am persuaded that she valued the compliment of my extravagant gallantry.

It is only fair to say that I had risen by this time to the dignity of "boughten shirts," linen collars and "Congress gaiters," and my suit purchased for graduating purposes was of black diagonal with a long tail, a garment which fitted me reasonably well. It was hot, of course, and nearly parboiled me of a summer evening, but I bore my suffering like the hero that I was, in order that I might make a presentable figure in the eyes of my classmates. I longed for a white vest but did not attain to that splendor.

Life remained very simple and very democratic in our little town. Although the county seat, it was slow in taking on city ways. I don't believe a real bath-tub distinguished the place (I never heard of one) but its side-walks kept our feet out of the mud (even in March or April), and this was a marvellous fact to us. One or two fine lawns and flower gardens had come in, and year by year the maples had grown until they now made a pleasant shade in June, and in October glorified the plank walks. To us it was beautiful.

As county town, Osage published two papers and was, in addition, the home of two Judges, a state Senator and a Congressman. A new opera house was built in '79 and an occasional "actor troupe" presented military plays like *Our Boys* or farces like *Solon Shingle*. The brass band and the baseball team were the best in the district, and were loyally upheld by us all.

With all these attractions do you wonder that whenever Ed and Bill and Joe had a day of leisure they got out their buggies, washed them till they glistened like new, and called for their best girls on the way to town?

Circuses, Fourth of Julys, County Fairs, all took place in Osage, and to own a "covered rig" and to take your sweetheart to the show were the highest forms of affluence and joy—unless you were actually able to live in town, as Burton and I now did for five days in each week, in which case you saw everything that was free and denied yourself everything but the circus. Nobody went so far in economy as that.

As a conscientious historian I have gone carefully into the records of this last year, in the hope of finding something that would indicate a feeling on the part of the citizens that Dick Garland's boy was in some ways a remarkable youth, but (I regret to say) I cannot lay hands on a single item. It appears that I was just one of a hundred healthy, hearty, noisy students—but no wait! There is one incident which has slight significance. One day during my final term of school, as I stood in the postoffice waiting for the mail to be distributed, I picked up from the counter a book called *The Undiscovered Country*.

"What is this about?" I asked.

The clerk looked up at me with an expression of disgust. "I bought it for a book of travel," said he, "but it is only a novel. Want it? I'll sell it cheap."

Having no money to waste in that way, I declined, but as I had the volume in my hands, with a few minutes to spare, I began to read. It did not take me long to discover in this author a grace and precision of style which aroused both my admiration and my resentment. My resentment was vague, I could not have given a reason for it, but as a matter of fact, the English of this new author made some of my literary heroes seem either crude or stilted. I was just young enough and conservative enough to be irritated and repelled by the modernity of William Dean Howells.

I put the book down and turned away, apparently uninfluenced by it. Indeed, I remained, if anything, more loyal to the grand manner of Hawthorne, but my love of realism was growing. I recall a rebuke from my teacher in rhetoric, condemning, in my essay on Mark Twain, an over praise of *Roughing It.* It is evident, therefore that I was even then a lover of the modern when taken off my guard.

Meanwhile I had definitely decided not to be a lawyer, and it happened in this way. One Sunday morning as I was walking toward school, I met a young man named Lohr, a law student several years older than myself, who turned and walked with me for a few blocks.

"Well, Garland," said he, "what are you going to do after you graduate this June?"

"I don't know," I frankly replied. "I have a chance to go into a law office."

"Don't do it," protested he with sudden and inexplicable bitterness. "Whatever you do, don't become a lawyer's hack."

His tone and the words, "lawyer's hack" had a powerful effect upon my mind. The warning entered my ears and stayed there. I decided against the law, as I had already decided against the farm.

Yes, these were the sweetest days of my life for I was carefree and glowing with the happiness which streams from perfect health and unquestioning faith. If any shadow drifted across this sunny year it fell from a haunting sense of the impermanency of my leisure. Neither Burton nor I had an ache or a pain. We had no fear and cherished no sorrow, and we were both comparatively free from the lover's almost intolerable longing. Our loves were hardly more than admirations.

As I project myself back into those days I re-experience the keen joy I took in the downpour of vivid sunlight, in the colorful clouds of evening, and in the song of the west wind harping amid the maple leaves. The earth was new, the moonlight magical, the dawns miraculous. I shiver with the boy's solemn awe in the presence of beauty. The little recitation rooms, dusty with floating chalk, are wide halls of romance and the voices of my girl classmates (even though their words are algebraic formulas), ring sweet as bells across the years.

During the years '79 and '80, while Burton and I had been living our carefree jocund life at the Seminary, a series of crop failures had profoundly affected the county, producing a feeling of unrest and bitterness in the farmers which was to have a far-reaching effect on my fortunes as well as upon those of my fellows. For two years the crop had been almost wholly destroyed by chinch bugs.

The harvest of '80 had been a season of disgust and disappointment to us for not only had the pestiferous mites devoured the grain, they had filled our stables, granaries, and even our kitchens with their ill-smelling crawling bodies—and now they were coming again in added billions. By the middle of June they swarmed at the roots of the wheat—innumerable as the sands of the sea. They sapped the growing stalks till the leaves turned yellow. It was as if the field had been scorched, even the edges of the corn showed signs of blight. It was evident that the crop was lost unless some great change took place in the weather, and many men began to offer their land for sale.

Naturally the business of grain-buying had suffered with the decline of grain-growing, and my father, profoundly discouraged by the outlook, sold his share in the elevator and turned his face toward the free lands of the farther west. He became again the pioneer.

DAKOTA was the magic word. The "Jim River Valley" was now the "land of delight," where "herds of deer and buffalo" still "furnished the cheer." Once more the spirit of the explorer flamed up in the soldier's heart. Once more the sunset allured. Once more my mother sang the marching song of the McClintocks,

> O'er the hills in legions, boys,
>   Fair freedom's star
> Points to the sunset regions, boys,
>   Ha, ha, ha-ha!

and sometime, in May I think it was, father again set out—this time by train, to explore the Land of The Dakotas which had but recently been wrested from the control of Sitting Bull.

He was gone only two weeks, but on his return announced with triumphant smile that he had taken up a homestead in Ordway, Brown County, Dakota. His face was again alight with the hope of the borderman, and he had much to say of the region he had explored.

As graduation day came on, Burton and I became very serious. The question of our future pressed upon us. What were we to do when our schooling ended? Neither of us had any hope of going to college, and neither of us had any intention of going to Dakota, although I had taken "Going West" as the theme of my oration. We were also greatly worried about these essays. Burton fell off in appetite and grew silent and abstracted. Each of us gave much time to declaiming our speeches, and the question of dress troubled us. Should we wear white ties and white vests, or white ties and black vests?

The evening fell on a dark and rainy night, but the Garlands came down in their best attire and so did the Babcocks, the Gilchrists and many other of our neighbors. Burton was hoping that his people would not come, he especially dreaded the humorous gaze of his brother Charles who took a much less serious view of Burton's powers as an orator than Burton considered just. Other interested parents and friends filled the New Opera House to the doors, producing in us a sense of awe for this was the first time the "Exercises" had taken placc outside the chapel.

Never again shall I feel the same exultation, the same pleasure mingled with bitter sadness, the same perception of the irrevocable passing of beautiful things, and the equally inexorable coming on of care and trouble, as filled my heart that night. Whether any of the other members of my class vibrated with similar emotion or not I cannot say, but I do recall that some of the girls annoyed me by their excessive attentions to unimportant ribbons, flounces, and laces. "How do I look?" seemed their principal concern. Only Alice expressed anything of the prophetic sadness which mingled with her exultation.

The name of my theme, (which was made public for the first time in the little programme) is worthy of a moment's emphasis. *Going West* had been suggested, of course by the emigration fever, then at its height, and upon it I had lavished a great deal of anxious care. As an oration it was all very excited and very florid, but it had some stirring ideas in it and coming in the midst of the profound political discourses of my fellows and the formal essays of the girls, it seemed much more singular and revolutionary, both in form and in substance, than it really was.

As I waited my turn, I experienced that sense of nausea, that numbness which always preceded my platform trials, but as my name was called I contrived to reach the proper place behind the foot-lights, and to bow to the audience. My opening paragraph perplexed my fellows, and naturally, for it was exceedingly florid, filled with phrases like "the lure of the sunset," "the westward urge of men," and was neither prose nor verse. Nevertheless I detected a slight current of sympathy coming up to me, and in the midst of the vast expanse of faces, I began to detect here and there a friendly smile. Mother and father were near but their faces were very serious.

After a few moments the blood began to circulate through my limbs and I was able to move about a little on the stage. My courage came back, but alas!—just in proportion as I attained confidence my emotional chant mounted too high! Since the writing was extremely ornate, my manner should have been studiedly cold and simple. This I knew perfectly well, but I could not check the perfervid rush of my song. I ranted deplorably, and though I closed amid fairly generous applause, no flowers were handed up to me. The only praise I received came from Charles Lohr, the man who had warned me against becoming a lawyer's hack. He, meeting me in the wings of the stage as I came off, remarked with ironic significance, "Well, that was an original piece of business!"

This delighted me exceedingly, for I had written with special deliberate intent to go outside the conventional grind of graduating orations. Feeling dimly, but sincerely, the epic march of the American pioneer I had tried to express it in an address which was in fact a sloppy poem. I should not like to have that manuscript printed precisely as it came from my pen, and a phonographic record of my voice would serve admirably as an instrument of blackmail. However, I thought at the time that I had done moderately well, and my mother's shy smile confirmed me in the belief.

Burton was white with stage-fright as he stepped from the wings but he got through very well, better than I, for he attempted no oratorical fiights.

Now came the usual hurried and painful farewells of classmates. With fervid hand-clasp we separated, some of us never again to meet. Our beloved principal (who was even then shadowed by the illness which brought about his death) clung to us as if he hated to see us go, and some of us could not utter a word as we took his hand in parting. What I said to Alice and Maud and Ethel I do not know, but I do recall that I had an uncomfortable lump in my throat while saying it.

As a truthful historian, I must add that Burton and I, immediately after this highly emotional close of our school career, were both called upon to climb into the family carriage and drive away into the black night, back to the farm,—an experience which seemed to us at the time a sad anticlimax. When we entered our ugly attic rooms and tumbled wearily into our hard beds, we retained very little of our momentary sense of victory. Our carefree school life was ended. Our stern education in life had begun.

20

The Land of the Dakotas

The movement of settlers toward Dakota had now become an exodus, a stampede. Hardly anything else was talked about as neighbors met one another on the road or at the Burr Oak school-house on Sundays. Every man who could sell out had gone west or was going. In vain did the county papers and Farmer's Institute lecturers advise cattle raising and plead for diversified tillage, predicting wealth for those who held on; farmer after farmer joined the march to Kansas, Nebraska, and Dakota. "We are wheat raisers," they said, "and we intend to keep in the wheat belt."

Our own family group was breaking up. My uncle David of pioneer spirit had already gone to the far Missouri Valley. Rachel had moved to Georgia, and Grandad McClintock was with his daughters, Samantha and Deborah, in western Minnesota. My mother, thus widely separated from her kin, resigned herself once more to the thought of founding a new home. Once more she sang, "O'er the hills in legions, boys," with such spirit as she could command, her clear voice a little touched with the huskiness of regret.

I confess I sympathized in some degree with my father's new design. There was something large and fine in the business of wheat-growing, and to have a plague of insects arise just as our harvesting machinery was reaching such perfection that we could handle our entire crop without hired help, was a tragic, abominable injustice. I could not blame him for his resentment and dismay.

My personal plans were now confused and wavering. I had no intention of joining this westward march; on the contrary, I was looking toward employment as a teacher, therefore my last weeks at the Seminary were shadowed by a cloud of uncertainty and vague alarm. It seemed a time of change, and immense, far-reaching, portentous readjustment. Our homestead was sold, my world was broken up. "What am I to do?" was my question.

Father had settled upon Ordway, Brown County, South Dakota,

as his future home, and immediately after my graduation, he and my brother set forth into the new country to prepare the way for the family's removal, leaving me to go ahead with the harvest alone. It fell out, therefore, that immediately after my flowery oration on *Going West* I found myself more of a slave to the cattle than ever before in my life.

Help was scarce; I could not secure even so much as a boy to aid in milking the cows; I was obliged to work double time in order to set up the sheaves of barley which were in danger of mouldering on the wet ground. I worked with a kind of bitter, desperate pleasure, saying, "This is the last time I shall ever lift a bundle of this accursed stuff."

And then, to make the situation worse, in raising some heavy machinery connected with the self-binder I strained my side so seriously that I was unable to walk. This brought the harvesting to a stand, and made my father's return necessary. For several weeks I hobbled about, bent like a gnome, and so helped to reap what the chinch bugs had left, while my mother prepared to "follow the sunset" with her "Boss."

September first was the day set for saying good-bye to Dry Run, and it so happened that her wedding anniversary fell close upon the same date and our neighbors, having quietly passed the word around, came together one Sunday afternoon to combine a farewell dinner with a Silver Wedding "surprise party."

Mother saw nothing strange in the coming of the first two carriages, the Buttons often came driving in that way,—but when the Babcocks, the Coles, and the Gilchrists clattered in with smiling faces, we all stood in the yard transfixed with amazement. "What's the meaning of all this?" asked my father.

No one explained. The women calmly clambered down from their vehicles, bearing baskets and bottles and knobby parcels, and began instant and concerted bustle of preparation. The men tied their horses to the fence and hunted up saw-horses and planks, and soon a long table was spread beneath the trees on the lawn. One by one other teams came whirling into the yard. The assembly resembled a "vandoo" as Asa Walker said. "It's worse than that," laughed Mrs. Turner. "It's a silver wedding and a 'send off' combined."

They would not let either the "bride" or the "groom" do a thing.

and with smiling resignation my mother folded her hands and sank into a chair. "All right," she said. "I am perfectly willing to sit by and see you do the work. I won't have another chance right away." And there was something sad in her voice. She could not forget that this was the beginning of a new pioneering adventure.

The shadows were long on the grass when at the close of the supper old John Gammons rose to make a speech and present the silver tea set. His voice was tremulous with emotion as he spoke of the loss which the neighborhood was about to suffer, and tears were in many eyes when father made reply. The old soldier's voice failed him several times during his utterance of the few short sentences he was able to frame, and at last he was obliged to take his seat, and blow his nose very hard on his big bandanna handkerchief to conceal his emotion.

It was a very touching and beautiful moment to me, for as I looked around upon that little group of men and women, rough-handed, bent and worn with toil, silent and shadowed with the sorrow of parting, I realized as never before the high place my parents had won in the estimation of their neighbors. It affected me still more deeply to see my father stammer and flush with uncontrollable emotion. I had thought the event deeply important before, but I now perceived that our going was all of a piece with the West's elemental restlessness. I could not express what I felt then, and I can recover but little of it now, but the pain which filled my throat comes back to me mixed with a singular longing to relive it.

There, on a low mound in the midst of the prairie, in the shadow of the house we had built, beneath the slender trees we had planted, we were bidding farewell to one cycle of emigration and entering upon another. The border line had moved on, and my indomitable Dad was moving with it. I shivered with dread of the irrevocable decision thus forced upon me. I heard a clanging as of great gates behind me and the field of the future was wide and wan.

From this spot we had seen the wild prairies disappear. On every hand wheat and corn and clover had taken the place of the wild oat, the hazelbush and the rose. Our house, a commonplace frame cabin, took on grace. Here Hattie had died. Our yard was ugly, but there Jessie's small feet had worn a slender path. Each of our lives was knit into these hedges and rooted in these fields and yet, notwithstanding all this, in response to some powerful yearning call, my father was about to set out for the fifth time into the still more remote and untrodden west. Small wonder that my mother sat with bowed head and tear-blinded eyes, while these good and faithful friends crowded around her to say goodbye.

She had no enemies and no hatreds. Her rich singing voice, her smiling face, her ready sympathy with those who suffered, had endeared her to every home into which she had gone, even as a momentary visitor. No woman in childbirth, no afflicted family within a radius of five miles had ever called for her in vain. Death knew her well, for she had closed the eyes of youth and age, and yet she remained the same laughing, bounteous, whole-souled mother of men that she had been in the valley of the Neshonoc. Nothing could permanently cloud her face or embitter the sunny sweetness of her creed.

One by one the women put their worn, ungraceful arms about her, kissed her with trembling lips, and went away in silent grief. The scene became too painful for me at last, and I fled away from it—out into the fields, bitterly asking, "Why should this suffering be? Why should mother be wrenched from all her dearest friends and forced to move away to a strange land?"

I did not see the actual packing up and moving of the household goods, for I had determined to set forth in advance and independently, eager to be my own master, and at the moment I did not feel in the least like pioneering.

Some two years before, when the failure of our crop had made the matter of my continuing at school an issue between my father and myself, I had said, "If you will send me to school until I graduate, I will ask nothing further of you," and these words I now took a stern pleasure in upholding. Without a dollar of my own, I announced my intention to fare forth into the world on the strength of my two hands, but my father, who was in reality a most affectionate parent, offered me thirty dollars to pay my carfare.

This I accepted, feeling that I had abundantly earned this money, and after a sad parting with my mother and my little sister, set out one September morning for Osage. At the moment I was oppressed with the thought that this was the fork in the trail, that my family and I had started on differing roads. I had become a man. With all the ways of the world before me I suffered from a feeling of doubt. The open gate allured me, but the homely scenes I was leaving suddenly put forth a latent magic.

I knew every foot of this farm. I had traversed it scores of times in every direction, following the plow, the harrow, or the seeder. With a great lumber wagon at my side I had husked corn from every acre of it, and now I was leaving it with no intention of returning. My action, like that of my father, was final. As I looked back up the lane at the tall Lombardy poplar trees bent like sabres in the warm western wind, the landscape I was leaving seemed suddenly very beautiful, and the old home very peaceful and very desirable. Nevertheless I went on.

Try as I may, I cannot bring back out of the darkness of that night any memory of how I spent the time. I must have called upon some of my classmates, but I cannot lay hold upon a single word or look or phrase from any of them. Deeply as I felt my distinction in thus riding forth into the world, all the tender incidents of farewell are lost to me. Perhaps my boyish self-absorption prevented me from recording outside impressions, for the idea of travelling, of crossing the State line, profoundly engaged me. Up to this time, notwithstanding all my dreams of conquest in far countries, I had never ridden in a railway coach! Can you wonder therefore that I trembled with joyous excitement as I paced the platform next morning waiting for the chariot of my romance? The fact that it was a decayed little coach at the end of a "mixed accommodation train" on a stub road did not matter. I was ecstatic.

However, I was well dressed, and my inexperience appeared only in a certain tense watchfulness. I closely observed what went on around me and was careful to do nothing which could be misconstrued as ignorance. Thrilling with excitement, feeling the mighty significance of my departure, I entered quietly and took my seat, while the train roared on through Mitchell and St. Ansgar, the little towns in which I had played my part as an actor,—on into distant climes and marvellous cities. My emotion was all very boyish, but very natural as I look back upon it.

The town in which I spent my first night abroad should have been called Thebes or Athens or Palmyra; but it was not. On the contrary, it was named Ramsey, after an old pioneer, and no one but a youth of fervid imagination at the close of his first day of adventure in the world would have found it worth a second glance. To me it was both beautiful and inspiring, for the reason that it was new territory and because it was the home of Alice, my most brilliant school mate, and while I had in mind some notion of a conference with the county superintendent of schools, my real reason for stopping off was a desire to see this girl whom I greatly admired.

I smile as I recall the feeling of pride with which I stepped into the 'bus and started for the Grand Central Hotel. And yet, after all, values are relative. That boy had something which I have lost. I would give much of my present knowledge of the world for the keen savor of life which filled my nostrils at that time.

The sound of a violin is mingled with my memories of Ramsey, and the talk of a group of rough men around the bar-room stove is full of savage charm. A tall, pale man, with long hair and big black eyes, one who impressed me as being a man of refinement and culture, reduced by drink to poverty and to rebellious bitterness of soul, stands out in powerful relief—a tragic and moving figure.

Here, too, I heard my first splendid singer. A patent medicine cart was in the street and one of its troupe, a basso, sang *Rocked in the Cradle of the Deep* with such art that I listened with delight. His lion-like pose, his mighty voice, his studied phrasing, revealed to me higher qualities of musical art than I had hitherto known.

From this singer, I went directly to Alice's home. I must have appeared singularly exalted as I faced her. The entire family was in the sitting room as I entered—but after a few kindly inquiries concerning my people and some general remarks they each and all slipped away, leaving me alone with the girl—in the good old-fashioned American way.

It would seem that in this farewell call I was permitting myself an exaggeration of what had been to Alice only a pleasant association, for she greeted me composedly and waited for me to justify my presence.

After a few moments of explanation, I suggested that we go out and hear the singing of the "troupe." To this she consented, and rose quietly—she never did anything hurriedly or with girlish alertness—and put on her hat. Although so young, she had the dignity of a woman, and her face, pale as a silver moon, was calm and sweet, only her big gray eyes expressed the maiden mystery. She read my adoration and was a little afraid of it.

As we walked, I spoke of the good days at "the Sem," of our classmates, and their future, and this led me to the announcement of my own plans. "I shall teach," I said. "I hope to be able to work into a professorship in literature some day.—What do you intend to do?"

"I shall go on with my studies for a while," she replied. "I may go to some eastern college for a few years."

"You must not become too learned," I urged. "You'll forget me."

She did not protest this as a coquette might have done. On the contrary, she remained silent, and I was aware that while she liked and respected me, she was not profoundly moved by this farewell call. Nevertheless I hoped, and in that hope I repeated, "You will write to me, won't you?"

"Of course!" she replied, and again I experienced a chilling perception that her words arose from friendliness rather than from tenderness, but I was glad of even this restrained promise, and I added, "I shall write often, for I shall be lonely—for a while."

As I walked on, the girl's soft warm arm in mine, a feeling of uncertainty, of disquiet, took possession of me. "Success," seemed a long way off and the road to it long and hard. However, I said nothing further concerning my doubts.

The street that night had all the enchantment of Granada to me. The girl's voice rippled with a music like that of the fountain Lindarazza, and when I caught glimpses of her sweet, serious face beneath her hat-rim, I dreaded our parting. The nearer to her gate we drew the more tremulous my voice became, and the more uncertain my step. At last on the door-step she turned and said, "Won't you come in again?"

In her tone was friendly dismissal, but I would not have it so. "You will write to me, won't you?" I pleaded with choking utterance.

She was moved (by pity perhaps).

"Why, yes, with pleasure," she answered. "Goodbye, I hope you'll succeed. I'm sure you will."

She extended her hand and I, recalling the instructions of my most romantic fiction, raised it to my lips. "Goodbye!" I huskily said, and turned away.

My next night was spent in Fairibault. Here I touched storied ground, for near this town Edward Eggleston had laid the scene of his novel, *The Mystery of Metropolisville* and my imagination responded to the magic which lay in the influence of the man of letters. I wrote to Alice a long and impassioned account of my sensations as I stood beside the Cannonball River.

My search for a school proving futile, I pushed on to the town of Farmington, where the Dakota branch of the Milwaukee railroad crossed my line of march. Here I felt to its full the compelling power of the swift stream of immigration surging to the west. The little village had doubled in size almost in a day. It was a junction point, a place of transfer, and its thin-walled unpainted pine hotels were packed with men, women and children laden with bags and bundles (all bound for the west) and the joyous excitement of these adventurers compelled me to change my plan. I decided to try some of the newer counties in western Minnesota. Romance was still in the West for me.

I slept that night on the floor in company with four or five young Iowa farmers, and the smell of clean white shavings, the wailing of tired children, the excited muttering of fathers, the plaintive voices of mothers, came through the partitions at intervals, producing in my mind an effect which will never pass away. It seemed to me at the moment as if all America were in process of change, all hurrying to overtake the vanishing line of the middle border, and the women at least were secretly or openly doubtful of the outcome. Woman is not by nature an explorer. She is the home-lover.

Early the next morning I bought a ticket for Aberdeen, and entered the train crammed with movers who had found the "prairie schooner" all too slow. The epoch of the canvas-covered wagon had passed. The era of the locomotive, the day of the chartered car, had arrived. Free land was receding at railroad speed, the borderline could be overtaken only by steam, and every man was in haste to arrive.

All that day we rumbled and rattled into a strange country, feeding our little engine with logs of wood, which we stopped occasionally to secure from long ricks which lined the banks of the river. At Chaska, at Granite Falls, I stepped off, but did not succeed in finding employment. It is probable that being filled with the desire of exploration I only half-heartedly sought for work; at any rate, on the third day, I found myself far out upon the unbroken plain where only the hairlike buffalo grass grew—beyond trees, beyond the plow, but not beyond settlement, for here at the end of my third day's ride at Millbank, I found a hamlet six months old, and the flock of shining yellow pine shanties strewn upon the sod, gave me an illogical delight, but then I was twenty-one—and it was sunset in the Land of the Dakotas!

All around me that night the talk was all of land, land! Nearly every man I met was bound for the "Jim River valley," and each voice was aquiver with hope, each eye alight with anticipation of certain success. Even the women had begun to catch something of this enthusiasm, for the night was very beautiful and the next day promised fair.

Again I slept on a cot in a room of rough pine, slept dreamlessly, and was out early enough to witness the coming of dawn,—a wonderful moment that sunrise was to me. Again, as eleven years before, I felt myself a part of the new world, a world fresh from the hand of God. To the east nothing could be seen but a vague expanse of yellow plain, misty purple in its hollows, but to the west rose a long low wall of hills, the Eastern Coteaux, up which a red line of prairie fire was slowly creeping.

It was middle September. The air, magnificently crisp and clear, filled me with desire of exploration, with vague resolution to do and dare. The sound of horses and mules calling for their feed, the clatter of hammers and the rasping of saws gave evidence of eager builders, of alert adventurers, and I was hotly impatient to get forward.

At eight o'clock the engine drew out, pulling after it a dozen box-cars laden with stock and household goods, and on the roof of a freight caboose, together with several other young Jasons, I rode, bound for the valley of the James.

It was a marvellous adventure. All the morning we rattled and rumbled along, our engine snorting with effort, struggling, with a load almost too great for its strength. By noon we were up amid the rounded grassy hills of the Sisseton Reservation where only the coyote ranged and the Sioux made residence.

Here we caught our first glimpse of the James River valley, which seemed to us at the moment as illimitable as the ocean and as level as a floor, and then pitching and tossing over the rough track, with our cars leaping and twisting like a herd of frightened buffaloes, we charged down the western slope, down into a level land of ripened grass, where blackbirds chattered in the willows, and prairie chickens called from the tall rushes which grew beside the sluggish streams.

Aberdeen was the end of the line, and when we came into it that night it seemed a near neighbor to Sitting Bull and the bison. And so, indeed, it was, for a buffalo bull had been hunted across its site less than a year before.

It was twelve miles from here to where my father had set his stakes for his new home, hence I must have stayed all night in some small hotel, but that experience has also faded from my mind. I remember only my walk across the dead-level plain next day. For the first time I set foot upon a landscape without a tree to break its sere expanse—and I was at once intensely interested in a long flock of gulls, apparently rolling along the sod, busily gathering their morning meal of frosted locusts. The ones left behind kept flying over the ones in front so that a ceaseless change of leadership took place.

There was beauty in this plain, delicate beauty and a weird charm, despite its lack of undulation. Its lonely unplowed sweep gave me the satisfying sensation of being at last among the men who held the outposts,—sentinels for the marching millions who were approaching from the east. For two hours I walked, seeing Aberdeen fade to a series of wavering, grotesque notches on the southern horizon line, while to the north an equally irregular and insubstantial line of shadows gradually took on weight and color until it became the village in which my father was at this very moment busy in founding his new home.

My experienced eyes saw the deep, rich soil, and my youthful imagination looking into the future, supplied the trees and vines and flowers which were to make this land a garden.

I was converted. I had no doubts. It seemed at the moment that my father had acted wisely in leaving his Iowa farm in order to claim his share of Uncle Sam's rapidly-lessening unclaimed land.

21

The Grasshopper and the Ant

Without a doubt this trip, so illogical and so recklessly extravagant, was due entirely to a boy's thirst for adventure. Color it as I may, the fact of my truancy remains. I longed to explore. The valley of the James allured me, and though my ticket and my meals along the route had used up my last dollar, I felt amply repaid as I trod this new earth and confronted this new sky—for both earth and sky were to my perception subtly different from those of Iowa and Minnesota.

The endless stretches of short, dry grass, the gorgeous colors of the dawn, the marvellous, shifting, phantom lakes and headlands, the violet sunset afterglow,—all were widely different from our old home, and the far, bare hills were delightfully suggestive of the horseman, the Indian and the buffalo. The village itself was hardly more than a summer camp, and yet its hearty, boastful citizens talked almost deliriously of "corner lots" and "boulevards," and their chantings were timed to the sound of hammers. The spirit of the builder seized me and so with my return ticket in my pocket, I joined the carpenters at work on my father's claim some two miles from the village with intent to earn money for further exploration.

Grandfather Garland had also taken a claim (although he heartily disliked the country) and in order to provide for both families a double house was being built across the line between the two farms.

I helped shingle the roof, and being twenty-one now, and my own master, I accepted wages from my father without a qualm. I earned every cent of my two dollars per day, I assure you, but I carefully omitted all reference to shingling, in my letters to my classmates.

At the end of a fortnight with my pay in my pocket I started eastward on a trip which I fully intended to make very long and profoundly educational. That I was green, very green, I knew but all that could be changed by travel.

At the end of my second day's journey, I reached Hastings, a small town on the Mississippi river, and from there decided to go by water to Red Wing some thirty miles below. All my life I had longed to ride on a Mississippi steamboat, and now, as I waited on the wharf at the very instant of the fulfillment of my desire, I expanded with anticipatory satisfaction.

The arrival of the *War Eagle* from St. Paul carried a fine foreign significance, and I ascended its gang-plank with the air of a traveller embarking at Cairo for Assouan. Once aboard the vessel I mingled, aloofly, with the passengers, absorbed in study of the river winding down among its wooded hills.

This ecstasy lasted during the entire trip—indeed it almost took on poetic form as the vessel approached the landing at Red Wing, for at this point the legendary appeal made itself felt. This lovely valley had once been the home of a chieftain, and his body, together with that of his favorite warhorse, was buried on the summit of a hill which overlooks the river, "in order" (so runs the legend) "that the chief might see the first faint glow of the resurrection morn and ride to meet it."

In truth Red Wing was a quiet, excessively practical little town, quite commonplace to every other passenger, except myself. My excited imagination translated it into something very distinctive and far-off and shining.

I took lodgings that night at a very exclusive boarding house at six dollars per week, reckless of the effect on my very slender purse. For a few days I permitted myself to wander and to dream. I have disturbing recollections of writing my friends from this little town, letters wherein I rhapsodized on the beauty of the scenery in terms which I would not now use in describing the Grand Cañon, or in picturing the peaks of Wyoming. After all I was right. A landscape is precisely as great as the impression it makes upon the perceiving mind. I was a traveller at last!—that seemed to be my chiefest joy and I extracted from each day all the ecstasy it contained.

My avowed object was to obtain a school and I did not entirely neglect my plans but application to the county superintendent came to nothing. I fear I was half-hearted in my campaign.

At last, at the beginning of the week and at the end of my money, I bought passage to Wabasha and from there took train to a small town where some of my mother's cousins lived. I had been in correspondence with one of them, a Mrs. Harris, and I landed at her door (after a glorious ride up through the hills, amid the most gorgeous autumn colors) with just three cents in my pocket—a poverty which you may be sure I did not publish to my relations who treated me with high respect and manifested keen interest in all my plans.

As nothing offered in the township round about the Harris home, I started one Saturday morning to walk to a little crossroads village some twenty miles away, in which I was told a teacher was required. My cousins, not knowing that I was penniless, supposed, of course, that I would go by train, and I was too proud to tell them the truth. It was very muddy, and when I reached the home of the committeeman his midday meal was over, and his wife did not ask if I had dined—although she was quick to tell me that the teacher had just been hired.

Without a cent in my pocket, I could not ask for food—therefore, I turned back weary, hungry and disheartened. To make matters worse a cold rain was falling and the eighteen or twenty miles between me and the Harris farm looked long.

I think it must have been at this moment that I began, for the first time, to take a really serious view of my plan "to see the world." It became evident with startling abruptness, that a man might be both hungry and cold in the midst of abundance. I recalled the fable of the grasshopper who, having wasted the summer hours in singing, was mendicant to the ant. My weeks of careless gayety were over. The money I had spent in travel looked like a noble fortune to me at this hour.

The road was deep in mud, and as night drew on the rain thickened. At last I said, "I will go into some farmhouse and ask the privilege of a bed." This was apparently a simple thing to do and yet I found it exceedingly hard to carry out. To say bluntly, "Sir, I have no money, I am tired and hungry," seemed a baldly disgraceful way of beginning. On the other hand to plead relationship with Will Harris involved a relative, and besides they might not know my cousin, or they might think my statement false.

Arguing in this way I passed house after house while the water dripped from my hat and the mud clogged my feet. Though chilled and hungry to the point of weakness, my suffering was mainly mental. A sudden realization of the natural antagonism of the well-to-do toward the tramp appalled me. Once, as I turned in toward the bright light of a kitchen window, the roar of a watch dog stopped me before I had fairly passed the gate. I turned back with a savage word, hot with resentment at a house-owner who would keep a beast like that. At another cottage I was repulsed by an old woman who sharply said, "We don't feed tramps."

I now had the precise feeling of the penniless outcast. With morbidly active imagination I conceived of myself as a being forever set apart from home and friends, condemned to wander the night alone. I worked on this idea till I achieved a bitter, furtive and ferocious manner.

However, I knocked at another door and upon meeting the eyes of the woman at the threshold, began with formal politeness to explain, "I am a teacher, I have been to look for a school, and I am on my way back to Byron, where I have relatives. Can you keep me all night?"

The woman listened in silence and at length replied with ungracious curtness, "I guess so. Come in."

She gave me a seat by the fire, and when her husband returned from the barn, I explained the situation to him. He was only moderately cordial. "Make yourself at home. I'll be in as soon as I have finished my milking," he said and left me beside the kitchen fire.

The woman of the house, silent, suspicious (it seemed to me) began to spread the table for supper while I, sitting beside the stove, began to suffer with the knowledge that I had, in a certain sense, deceived them. I was fairly well dressed and my voice and manner, as well as the fact that I was seeking a school, had given them, no doubt, the impression that I was able to pay for my entertainment, and the more I thought of this the more uneasy I became. To eat of their food without making an explanation was impossible but the longer I waited the more difficult the explanation grew.

Suffering keenly, absurdly, I sat with hanging head going over and over the problem, trying to formulate an easy way of letting them know my predicament.

There was but one way of escape—and I took it. As the woman stepped out of the room for a moment, I rose, seized my hat and rushed out into the rain and darkness like a fugitive.

I have often wondered what those people thought when they found me gone. Perhaps I am the great mystery of their lives, an unexplained visitant from "the night's Plutonian shore."

I plodded on for another mile or two in the darkness, which was now so intense I could scarcely keep the road. Only by the feel of the mud under my feet could I follow the pike. Like Jean Valjean, I possessed a tempest in my brain. I experienced my first touch of despair.

Although I had never had more than thirty dollars at any one time, I had never been without money. Distinctions had not counted largely in the pioneer world to which I belonged. I was proud of my family. I came of good stock, and knew it and felt it, but now here I was, wet as a sponge and without shelter simply because I had not in my pocket a small piece of silver with which to buy a bed.

I walked on until this dark surge of rebellious rage had spent its force and reason weakly resumed her throne. I said, "What nonsense! Here I am only a few miles from relatives. All the farmers on this road must know the Harris family. If I tell them who I am, they will certainly feel that I have the claim of a neighbor upon them."—But these deductions, admirable as they were, did not lighten my sky or make begging easier.

After walking two miles further I found it almost impossible to proceed. It was black night and I did not know where I stood. The wind had risen and the rain was falling in slant cataracts. As I looked about me and caught the gleam from the windows of a small farmhouse, my stubborn pride gave way. Stumbling up the path I rapped on the door. It was opened by a middle aged farmer in his stocking feet, smoking a pipe. Having finished his supper he was taking his ease beside the fire, and fortunately for me, was in genial mood.

"Come in," he said heartily. " 'Tis a wet night."

I began, "I am a cousin of William Harris of Byron—"

"You don't say! Well, what are you doing on the road a night like this? Come in!"

I stepped inside and finished my explanation there.

This good man and his wife will forever remain the most hospitable figures in my memory. They set me close beside the stove insisting that I put my feet in the oven to dry, talking meanwhile of my cousins and the crops, and complaining of the incessant rainstorms which were succeeding one another almost without intermission, making this one of the wettest and most dismal autumns the country had ever seen. Never in all my life has a roof seemed more heavenly, or hosts more sweet and gracious.

After breakfast next morning I shook hands with the farmer saying: "I shall send you the money for my entertainment the first time my cousin comes to town," and under the clamor of his hospitable protestations against payment, set off up the road.

The sun came out warm and beautiful and all about me on every farm the teamsters were getting into the fields. The mud began to dry up and with the growing cheer of the morning my heart expanded and the experience of the night before became as unreal as a dream and yet it had happened, and it had taught me a needed lesson. Hereafter I take no narrow chances, I vowed to myself.

Upon arrival at my cousin's home I called him aside, and said, "Will, you have work to do and I have need of wages,—I am going to strip off this 'boiled shirt' and white collar, and I am going to work for you just the same as any other hand, and I shall expect the full pay of the best man on your place."

He protested, "I don't like to see you do this. Don't give up your plans. I'll hitch up and we'll start out and keep going till we find you a school."

"No," I said, "not till I earn a few dollars to put in my pocket. I've played the grasshopper for a few weeks—from this time on I'm the busy ant."

So it was settled, and the grasshopper went forth into the fields and toiled as hard as any slave. I plowed, threshed, and husked corn, and when at last December came, I had acquired money enough to carry me on my way. I decided to visit Onalaska and the old coulee where my father's sister and two of the McClintocks were still living. With swift return of confidence, I said good-bye to my friends in Zumbrota and took the train. It seemed very wonderful that after a space of thirteen years I should be returning to the scenes of my childhood, a full-grown man and paying my own way. I expanded with joy of the prospect.

Onalaska, the reader may remember, was the town in which I had gone to school when a child, and in my return to it I felt somewhat like the man in the song, *Twenty Years Ago*—indeed I sang, "I've wandered through the village, Tom, I've sat beneath the tree" for my uncle that first night. There was the river, filled as of old with logs, and the clamor of the saws still rose from the sawdust islands. Bleakly white the little church, in which we used to sit in our Sunday best, remained unchanged but the old school-house was not merely altered, it was gone! In its place stood a commonplace building of brick. The boys with whom I used to play "Mumblety Peg" were men, and some of them had developed into worthless loafers, lounging about the doors of the saloons, and although we looked at one another with eyes of sly recognition, we did not speak.

Eagerly I visited the old coulee, but the magic was gone from the hills, the glamour from the meadows. The Widow Green no longer lived at the turn of the road, and only the Randals remained. The marsh was drained, the big trees cleared away. The valley was smaller, less mysterious, less poetic than my remembrances of it, but it had charm nevertheless, and I responded to the beauty of its guarding bluffs and the deep-blue shadows which streamed across its sunset fields.

Uncle William drove down and took me home with him, over the long hill, back to the little farm where he was living much the same as I remembered him. One of his sons was dead, the other had shared in the rush for land, and was at this time owner of a homestead in western Minnesota. Grandfather McClintock, still able to walk about, was spending the autumn with William and we had a great deal of talk concerning the changes which had come to the country and especially to our family group. "Ye scatter like the leaves of autumn," he said sadly—then added, "Perhaps in the Final Day the trumpet of the Lord will bring us all together again."

We sang some of his old Adventist hymns together and then he asked me what I was planning to do. "I haven't any definite plans," I answered, "except to travel. I want to travel. I want to see the world."

"To see the world!" he exclaimed. "As for me I wait for it to pass away. I watch daily for the coming of the Chariot."

This gray old crag of a man interested me as deeply as ever and yet, in a sense, he was an alien. He was not of my time—scarcely of my country. He was a survival of the days when the only book was the Bible, when the newspaper was a luxury. Migration had been his life long adventure and now he was waiting for the last great remove. His thought now was of "the region of the Amaranth," his new land "the other side of Jordan."

He engaged my respect but I was never quite at ease with him. His valuations were too intensely religious; he could not understand my ambitions. His mind filled with singular prejudices,—notions which came down from the Colonial age, was impervious to new ideas. His character had lost something of its mellow charm—but it had gained in dramatic significance. Like my uncles he had ceased to be a part of my childish world.

I went away with a sense of sadness, of loss as though a fine picture on the walls of memory had been dimmed or displaced. I perceived that I had idealized him as I had idealized all the figures and scenes of my boyhood—"but no matter, they were beautiful to me then and beautiful they shall remain," was the vague resolution with which I dismissed criticism.

The whole region had become by contrast with Dakota, a "settled" community. The line of the middle border had moved on some three hundred miles to the west. The Dunlaps, McIldowneys, Dudleys and Elwells were the stay-at-homes. Having had their thrust at the job of pioneering before the war they were now content on their fat soil. To me they all seemed remote. Their very names had poetic value, for they brought up in my mind shadowy pictures of the Coulee country as it existed to my boyish memories.

I spent nearly two months in Onalaska, living with my Aunt Susan, a woman of the loveliest character. Richard Bailey, her husband, one of the kindliest of men, soon found employment for me, and so, for a time, I was happy and secure.

However, this was but a pause by the roadside. I was not satisfied. It was a show of weakness to settle down on one's relations. I wanted to make my way among strangers. I scorned to lean upon my aunt and uncle, though they were abundantly able to keep me. It was mid-winter, nothing offered and so I turned (as so many young men similarly placed have done), toward a very common yet difficult job. I attempted to take subscriptions for a book.

After a few days' experience in a neighboring town I decided that whatever else I might be fitted for in this world, I was not intended for a book agent. Surrendering my prospectus to the firm, I took my way down to Madison, the capital of the state, a city which seemed at this time very remote, and very important in my world. Only when travelling did I have the feeling of living up to the expectations of Alice and Burton who put into their letters to me, an envy which was very sweet. To them I was a bold adventurer!

Alas for me! In the shining capital of my state I felt again the world's rough hand. First of all I tried The State House. This was before the general use of typewriters and I had been told that copyists were in demand. I soon discovered that four men and two girls were clamoring for every job. Nobody needed me. I met with blunt refusals and at last turned to other fields.

Every morning I went among the merchants seeking an opportunity to clerk or keep books, and at last obtained a place at six dollars per week in the office of an agricultural implement firm. I was put to work in the accounting department, as general slavey, under the immediate supervision of a youth who had just graduated from my position and who considered me his legitimate victim. He was only seventeen and not handsome, and I despised him with instant bitterness. Under his direction I swept out the office, made copies of letters, got the mail, stamped envelopes and performed other duties of a manual routine kind, to which I would have made no objection, had it not been for the gloating joy with which that chinless cockerel ordered me about. I had never been under that kind of discipline, and to have a pin-headed gamin order me to clean spittoons was more than I could stomach.

At the end of the week I went to the proprietor, and said, "If you have nothing better for me to do than sweep the floor and run errands, I think I'll quit."

With some surprise my boss studied me. At last said: "Very well, sir, you can go, and from all accounts I don't think we'll miss you much," which was perfectly true. I was an absolute failure so far as any routine work of that kind was concerned.

So here again I was thrown upon a cruel world with only six dollars between myself and the wolf. Again I fell back upon my physical powers. I made the round of all the factories seeking manual labor. I went out on the Catfish, where, through great sheds erected for the manufacture of farm machinery, I passed from superintendent to foreman, from foreman to boss,—eager to wheel sand, paint woodwork, shovel coal—anything at all to keep from sending home for money—for, mind you, my father or my uncle would have helped me out had I written to them, but I could not do that. So long as I was able to keep a roof over my head, I remained silent. I was in the world and I intended to keep going without making a cent from anyone. Besides, the grandiloquent plans for travel and success which I had so confidently outlined to Burton must be carried out.

I should have been perfectly secure had it been summertime, for I knew the farmer's life and all that pertained to it, but it was winter. How to get a living in a strange town was my problem. It was a bright, clear, intensely cold February, and I was not very warmly dressed—hence I kept moving.

Meanwhile I had become acquainted with a young clergyman in one of the churches, and had showed to him certain letters and papers to prove that I was not a tramp, and no doubt his word kept my boarding mistress from turning me into the street.

Mr. Eaton was a man of books. His library contained many volumes of standard value and we met as equals over the pages of Scott and Dickens. I actually forced him to listen to a lecture which I had been writing during the winter and so wrought upon him that he agreed to arrange a date for me in a neighboring country church.—Thereafter while I glowed with absurd dreams of winning money and renown by delivering that lecture in the churches and school-houses of the state, I continued to seek for work, any work that would bring me food and shelter.

One bitter day in my desperate need I went down upon the lake to watch the men cutting ice. The wind was keen, the sky gray and filled with glittering minute flecks of frost, and my clothing (mainly cotton) seemed hardly thicker than gossamer, and yet I looked upon those working men with a distinct feeling of envy. Had I secured "a job" I should have been pulling a saw up and down through the ice, at the same time that I dreamed of touring the west as a lecturer—of such absurd contradictions are the visions of youth.

I don't know exactly what I would have done had not my brother happened along on his way to a school near Chicago. To him I confessed my perplexity. He paid my board bill (which was not very large) and in return I talked him into a scheme which promised great things for us both—I contracted to lecture under his management! He was delighted at the opportunity of advancing me, and we were both happy.

Our first engagement was at Cyene, a church which really belonged to Eaton's circuit, and according to my remembrance the lecture was a moderate success. After paying all expenses we had a little money for carfare, and Franklin was profoundly impressed. It really seemed to us both that I had at last entered upon my career. It was the kind of service I had been preparing for during all my years at school—but alas! our next date was a disaster. We attempted to do that which an older and fully established lecturer would not have ventured. We tried to secure an audience with only two days' advance work, and of course we failed.

I called a halt. I could not experiment on the small fund which my father had given Frank for his business education.

However, I borrowed a few dollars of him and bought a ticket to Rock River, a town near Chicago. I longed to enter the great western metropolis, but dared not do so—yet. I felt safe only when in sight of a plowed field.

At a junction seventy miles out of the city, we separated, he to attend a school, and I to continue my education in the grim realities of life.

From office to office in Rock River I sullenly plodded, willing to work for fifty cents a day, until at last I secured a clerkship in a small stationery jobbing house which a couple of school teachers had strangely started, but on Saturday of the second week the proprietor called me to him and said kindly, but firmly, "Garland, I'm afraid you are too literary and too musical for this job. You have a fine baritone voice and your ability to vary the text set before you to copy, is remarkable, and yet I think we must part."

The reasons for this ironical statement were (to my mind) ignoble; first of all he resented my musical ability, secondly, my literary skill shamed him, for as he had put before me a badly composed circular letter, telling me to copy it one hundred times, I quite naturally improved the English.—However, I admitted the charge of insubordination, and we parted quite amicably.

It was still winter, and I was utterly without promise of employment. In this extremity, I went to the Y. M. C. A. (which had for one of its aims the assistance of young men out of work) and confided my homelessness to the secretary, a capital young fellow who knew enough about men to recognize that I was not a "bum." He offered me the position of night-watch and gave me a room and cot at the back of his office. These were dark hours!

During the day I continued to pace the streets. Occasionally some little job like raking up a yard would present itself, and so I was able to buy a few rolls, and sometimes I indulged in milk and meat. I lived along from noon to noon in presentable condition, but I was always hungry. For four days I subsisted on five cents worth of buns.

Having left my home for the purpose of securing experience in the world, I had this satisfaction—I was getting it! Very sweet and far away seemed all that beautiful life with Alice and Burton and Hattie at the Seminary, something to dream over, to regret, to versify, something which the future (at this moment) seemed utterly incapable of reproducing. I still corresponded with several of my classmates, but was careful to conceal the struggle that I was undergoing. I told them only of my travels and my reading.

As the ironical jobber remarked, I had a good voice, and upon being invited to accompany the Band of Hope which went to sing and pray in the County Jail, I consented, at least I took part in the singing. In this way I partly paid the debt I owed the Association, and secured some vivid impressions of prison life which came into use at a later time. My three associates in this work were a tinner, a clothing salesman and a cabinet maker. More and more I longed for the spring, for with it I knew would come seeding, building and a chance for me.

At last in the midst of a grateful job of raking up yards and planting shrubs, I heard the rat-tat-tat of a hammer, and resolved upon a bold plan. I decided to become a carpenter, justifying myself by reference to my apprenticeship to my grandfather. One fine April morning I started out towards the suburbs, and at every house in process of construction approached the boss and asked for a job. Almost at once I found encouragement. "Yes, but where are your tools?"

In order to buy the tools I must work, work at anything. Therefore, at the next place I asked if there was any rough labor required around the house. The foreman replied: "Yes, there is some grading to be done." Accordingly I set to work with a wheelbarrow, grading the bank around the almost completed building. This was hard work, the crudest form of manual labor, but I grappled with it desperately, knowing that the pay (a dollar and a half a day) would soon buy a kit of tools.

Oh, that terrible first day! The heavy shovel blistered my hands and lamed my wrists. The lifting of the heavily laden wheelbarrow strained my back and shoulders. Half-starved and weak, quite unfitted for sustained effort of this kind, I struggled on, and at the end of an interminable afternoon staggered home to my cot. The next morning came soon,—too soon. I was not merely lame, I was lacerated. My muscles seemed to have been torn asunder, but I toiled (or made a show of toiling) all the second day. On the warrant of my wages I borrowed twenty-five cents of a friend and with this bought a meat dinner which helped me through another afternoon.

The third day was less painful and by the end of the week, I was able to do anything required of me. Upon receiving my pay I went immediately to the hardware store and bought a set of tools and a carpenter's apron, and early on Monday morning sallied forth in the *opposite direction* as a carpenter seeking a job. I soon came to a big frame house in course of construction. "Do you need another hand?" I asked. "Yes," replied the boss. "Take hold, right here, with this man."

"This man" turned out to be a Swede, a good-natured fellow, who made no comment on my deficiencies. We sawed and hammered together in very friendly fashion for a week, and I made rapid gains in strength and skill and took keen pleasure in my work. The days seemed short and life promising and as I was now getting two dollars per day, I moved out of my charity bed and took a room in a decayed mansion in the midst of a big lawn. My bearing became confident and easy. Money had straightened my back.

The spring advanced rapidly while I was engaged on this work and as my crew occasionally took contracts in the country I have vivid pictures of the green and pleasant farm lands, of social farmers at barn-raisings, and of tables filled with fatness. I am walking again in my stocking feet, high on the "purline plate," beetle in hand, driving home the oaken "pins." I am shingling on the broad roof of a suburban house from which I can see the sunny slopes of a meadow and sheep feeding therein. I am mending a screen door for a farmer's wife while she confides to me the tragedy of her life—and always I have the foolish boyish notion that I am out in the world and seeing life.

Into the midst of this busy peaceful season of manual labor came my first deeply romantic admiration. Edwin Booth was announced as "the opening attraction of the New Opera House" and I fairly trembled with anticipatory delight, for to me the word *Booth* meant all that was splendid and tragic and glorious in the drama. I was afraid that something might prevent me from hearing him.

At last the night came and so great was the throng, so strong the pressure on the doors that the lock gave way and I, with my dollar clutched tightly in my hand, was borne into the hall and half-way up the stairs without touching foot to the floor, and when at last, safe in my balcony seat I waited for the curtain to rise, I had a distinct realization that a shining milestone was about to be established in my youthful trail.

My father had told me of the elder Booth, and of Edwin's beautiful Prince of Denmark I had heard many stories, therefore I waited with awe as well as eagerness, and when the curtain, rising upon the court scene, discovered the pale, handsome face and graceful form of the noble Dane, and the sound of his voice,—that magic velvet voice—floated to my ear with the words, "Seems, madame, I know not seems," neither time nor space nor matter existed for me—I was in an ecstasy of attention.

I had read much of Shakespeare. I could recite many pages of the tragedies and historical plays, and I had been assured by my teachers that *Hamlet* was the greatest of all dramas, but Edwin Booth in one hour taught me more of its wonders, more of the beauty of the English language than all my instructors and all my books. He did more, he aroused in me a secret ambition to read as he read, to make the dead lines of print glow with color and throb with music. There was something magical in his interpretation of the drama's printed page. With voice and face and hand he restored for duller minds the visions of the poet, making Hamlet's sorrows as vital as our own.

From this performance, which filled me with vague ambitions

and a glorious melancholy, I returned to my association with a tinker, a tailor, and a tinner, whose careless and stupid comments on the play both pained and angered me. I went to my work next day in such absorbed silence as only love is supposed to give.

I re-read my Hamlet now with the light of Booth's face in my eyes and the music of his glorious voice in my ear. As I nailed and sawed at pine lumber, I murmured inaudibly the lofty lines of the play, in the hope of fixing forever in my mind the cadences of the great tragedian's matchless voice.

Great days! Growing days! Lonely days! Days of dream and development, needing only the girl to be perfect—but I had no one but Alice to whom I could voice my new enthusiasm and she was not only out of the reach of my voice, but serenely indifferent to my rhapsodic letters concerning *Hamlet* and the genius of Edwin Booth.

22

We Discover New England

Edwin Booth's performance of *Hamlet* had another effect. It brought to my mind the many stories of Boston which my father had so often related to his children. I recalled his enthusiastic accounts of the elder Booth and Edwin Forrest, and especially his descriptions of the wonderful scenic effects in *Old Put* and *The Gold Seekers,* wherein actors rode down mimic stone steps or debarked from theatrical ships which sailed into pictured wharves, and one day in the midst of my lathing and sawing, I evolved a daring plan—I decided to visit Boston and explore New England.

With all his feeling for the East my father had never revisited it. This was a matter of pride with him. "I never take the back trail," he said, and yet at times, as he dwelt on the old home in the state of Maine a wistful note had crept into his voice, and so now in writing to him, I told him that I intended to seek out his boyhood haunts in order that I might tell him all about the friends and relations who still lived there.

Without in any formal way intending it the old borderman had endowed both his sons with a large sense of the power and historic significance of Massachusetts. He had contrived to make us feel some part of his idolatry of Wendell Phillips, for his memory of the great days of *The Liberator* were keen and worshipful. From him I derived a belief that there were giants in those days and the thought of walking the streets where Garrison was mobbed and standing in the hall which Webster had hallowed with his voice gave me a profound anticipatory stir of delight.

As first assistant to a quaint and dirty old carpenter, I was now earning two dollars per day, and saving it. There was no occasion in those days for anyone to give me instructions concerning the care of money. I knew how every dollar came and I was equally careful to know where every nickel went. Travel cost three cents per mile, and the number of cities to be visited depended upon the number of dimes I should save.

With my plan of campaign mapped out to include a stop at Niagara Falls and fourth of July on Boston Common I wrote to my brother at Valparaiso, Indiana, inviting him to join me in my adventure. "If we run out of money and of course we shall, for I have only about thirty dollars, we'll flee to the country. One of my friends here says we can easily find work in the meadows near Concord."

The audacity of my design appealed to my brother's imagination. "I'm your huckleberry!" he replied. "School ends the last week in June. I'll meet you at the Atlantic House in Chicago on the first. Have about twenty dollars myself."

At last the day came for my start. With all my pay in my pocket and my trunk checked I took the train for Chicago. I shall never forget the feeling of dismay with which, an hour later, I perceived from the car window a huge smoke-cloud which embraced the whole eastern horizon, for this, I was told was the soaring banner of the great and gloomy inland metropolis, whose dens of vice and houses of greed had been so often reported to me by wandering hired men. It was in truth only a huge flimsy country town in those days, but to me it was august as well as terrible.

Up to this moment Rockford was the largest town I had ever seen, and the mere thought of a million people stunned my imagination. "How can so many people find a living in one place?" Naturally I believed most of them to be robbers. "If the city is miles across, how am I to get from the railway station to my hotel without being assaulted?" Had it not been for the fear of ridicule, I think I should have turned back at the next stop. The shining lands beyond seemed hardly worth a struggle against the dragon's brood with which the dreadful city was a-swarm. Nevertheless I kept my seat and was carried swiftly on.

Soon the straggling farmhouses thickened into groups, the villages merged into suburban towns, and the train began to clatter through sooty freight yards filled with box cars and switching engines; at last, after crawling through tangled, thickening webs of steel, it plunged into a huge, dark and noisy shed and came to a halt and a few moments later I faced the hackmen of Chicago, as verdant a youth as these experienced pirates had ever made common cause against.

I knew of them (by report), and was prepared for trouble, but their clanging cries, their cynical eyes, their clutching insolent hands were more terrifying than anything I had imagined. Their faces expressed something remorseless, inhuman and mocking. Their grins were like those of wolves.

In my hand I carried an imitation leather valise, and as I passed, each of the drivers made a snatch at it, almost tearing it from my hands, but being strong as well as desperate, I cleared myself of them, and so, following the crowd, not daring to look to right or left, reached the street and crossed the bridge with a sigh of relief. So much was accomplished.

Without knowing where I should go, I wandered on, shifting my bag from hand to hand, till my mind recovered its balance. My bewilderment, my depth of distrust, was augmented by the roar and tumult of the crowd. I was like some wild animal with exceedingly sensitive ears. The waves of sound smothered me.

At last, timidly approaching a policeman, I asked the way to the Atlantic Hotel.

"Keep straight down the street five blocks and turn to the left," he said, and his kind voice filled me with a glow of gratitude.

With ears benumbed and brain distraught, I threaded the rush, the clamor of Clark street and entered the door of the hotel, with such relief as a sailor must feel upon suddenly reaching safe harbor after having been buffetted on a wild and gloomy sea by a heavy northeast gale.

It was an inconspicuous hotel of the "Farmer's Home" type, but I approached the desk with meek reluctance and explained, "I am expecting to meet my brother here. I'd like permission to set my bag down and wait."

With bland impersonal courtesy the clerk replied, "Make yourself at home."

Gratefully sinking into a chair by the window, I fell into study of the people streaming by, and a chilling sense of helplessness fell upon me. I realized my ignorance, my feebleness. As a minute bubble in this torrent of human life, with no friend in whom I could put trust, and with only a handful of silver between myself and the gray wolf, I lost confidence. The Boston trip seemed a foolish tempting of Providence and yet, scared as I was, I had no real intention of giving it up.

My brother's first words as he entered the door, were gayly derisive. "Oh, see the whiskers!" he cried and his calm acceptance of my plan restored my own courage.

Together we planned our itinerary. We were to see Niagara Falls, of course, but to spend the fourth of July on Boston Common, was our true objective. "When our money is used up," I said, "we'll strike out into the country."

To all this my brother agreed. Neither of us had the slightest fear of hunger in the country. It was the city that gave us pause.

All the afternoon and evening we wandered about the streets (being very careful not to go too far from our hotel), counting the stories of the tall buildings, and absorbing the drama of the pavement. Returning now and again to our sanctuary in the hotel lobby we ruminated and rested our weary feet.

Everything interested us. The business section so sordid to others was grandly terrifying to us. The self-absorption of the men, the calm glances of the women humbled our simple souls. Nothing was commonplace, nothing was ugly to us.

We slept that night in a room at the extreme top of the hotel. It couldn't have been a first class accommodation, for the frame of the bed fell in the moment we got into it, but we made no complaint—we would not have had the clerk know of our mishap for twice our bill. We merely spread the mattress on the floor and slept till morning.

Having secured our transportation we were eager to be off, but as our tickets were second class, and good only on certain trains, we waited. We did not even think of a sleeping car. We had never known anyone rich enough to occupy one. Grant and Edwin Booth probably did, and senators were ceremonially obliged to do so, but ordinary folks never looked forward to such luxury. Neither of us would have known what to do with a berth if it had been presented to us, and the thought of spending two dollars for a night's sleep made the cold chills run over us. We knew of no easier way to earn two dollars than to save them, therefore we rode in the smoker.

Late that night as we were sitting stoically in our places, a brakeman came along and having sized us up for the innocents we were, good-naturedly said, "Boys, if you'll get up I'll fix your seats so's you can lie down and catch a little sleep."

Silently, gratefully we watched him while he took up the cushions and turned them lengthwise, thus making a couch. To be sure, it was a very short and very hard bed but with the health and strength of nineteen and twenty-two, we curled up and slept the remainder of the night like soldiers resting on their guns. Pain, we understood, was an unavoidable accompaniment of travel.

When morning dawned the train was running through Canada, and excitedly calling upon Franklin to rouse, I peered from the window, expecting to see a land entirely different from Wisconsin and Illinois. We were both somewhat disappointed to find nothing distinctive in either the land or its inhabitants. However, it was a foreign soil and we had seen it. So much of our exploration was accomplished.

It was three o'clock in the afternoon when we came in sight of the suspension bridge and Niagara Falls. I suppose it would be impossible for anyone now to feel the same profound interest in any natural phenomenon whatsoever. We believed that we were approaching the most stupendous natural wonder in all the world, and we could scarcely credit the marvel of our good fortune.

All our lives we had heard of this colossal cataract. Our school readers contained stately poems and philosophical dissertations concerning it. Gough, the great orator, had pointed out the likeness of its resistless torrent to the habit of using spirituous liquors. The news papers still printed descriptions of its splendor and no foreigner (so we understood) ever came to these shores without visiting and bowing humbly before the voice of its waters.—And to think that we, poor prairie boys, were soon to stand upon the illustrious brink of that dread chasm and listen to its mighty song was wonderful, incredible, benumbing!

Alighting at the squalid little station on the American side, we went to the cheapest hotel our keen eyes could discover, and leaving our valises, we struck out immediately toward the towering white column of mist which could be seen rising like a ghostly banner behind the trees. We were like those who first discover a continent.

As we crept nearer, the shuddering roar deepened, and our awe, our admiration, our patriotism deepened with it, and when at last we leaned against the rail and looked across the tossing spread of river swiftly sweeping to its fall, we held our breaths in wonder. It met our expectations.

Of course we went below and spent two of our hard earned dollars in order to be taken behind the falls. We were smothered with spray and forced to cling frenziedly to the hands of our guide, but it was a part of our duty, and we did it. No one could rob us of the glory of having adventured so far.

That night we resumed our seats in the smoking car, and pushed on toward Boston in patiently-endured discomfort. Early the following morning we crossed the Hudson, and as the Berkshire hills began to loom against the dawn, I asked the brakeman, with much emotion, "Have we reached the Massachusetts line?" "We have," he said, and by pressing my nose against the glass and shading my face with my hands I was able to note the passing landscape.

Little could be seen other than a tumbled, stormy sky with wooded heights dimly outlined against it, but I had all the emotions of a pilgrim entering upon some storied oriental vale. Massachusetts to me meant Whittier and Hawthorne and Wendell Phillips and Daniel Webster. It was the cradle of our liberty, the home of literature, the province of art—and it contained Boston!

As the sun rose, both of us sat with eyes fixed upon the scenery, observant of every feature. It was all so strange, yet familiar! Barns with long, sloping roofs stood with their backs against the hillsides, precisely as in the illustrations to Hawthorne's stories, and Whittier's poems. The farmhouses, old and weather-beaten and guarded by giant elms, looked as if they might have sheltered Emerson and Lowell. The little villages with narrow streets lined with queer brick-walled houses (their sides to the gutter) reminded us of the pictures in Ben Franklin's *Autobiography.*

Everything was old, delightfully old. Nothing was new.—Most of the people we saw were old. The men working in the fields were bent and gray, scarcely a child appeared, though elderly women abounded. (This was thirty-five years ago, before the Canadians and Italians had begun to swarm). Everywhere we detected signs of the historical, the traditional, the Yankee. The names of the stations rang in our ears like bells, *Lexington, Concord, Cambridge, Charlestown,* and—at last *Boston!*

What a strange, new world this ancient city was to us, as we issued from the old Hoosac Tunnel station! The intersection of every street was a bit of history. The houses standing sidewise to the gutter, the narrow, ledge-like pavements, the awkward two-wheeled drays and carts, the men selling lobsters on the corner, the newsboys with their "papahs," the faces of the women so thin and pale, the men, neat, dapper, small, many of them walking with finicky precision as though treading on eggs,—everything had a Yankee tang, a special quality, and then, the noise! We had thought Chicago noisy, and so it was, but here the clamor was high-keyed, deafening for the reason that the rain-washed streets were paved with cobble stones over which enormous carts bumped and clattered with resounding riot.

Bewildered,—with eyes and ears alert, we toiled up Haymarket Square shoulder to shoulder, seeking the Common. Of course we carried our hand-bags—(the railway had no parcel rooms in those days, or if it had we didn't know it) clinging to them like ants to their eggs and so slowly explored Tremont Street. Cornhill entranced us with its amazing curve. We passed the Granary Burying Ground and King's Chapel with awe, and so came to rest at last on the upper end of the Common! We had reached the goal of our long pilgrimage.

To tell the truth, we were a little disappointed in our first view of it. It was much smaller than we had imagined it to be and the pond was ONLY a pond, but the trees were all that father had declared them to be. We had known broad prairies and splendid primitive woodlands—but these elms dated back to the days of Washington, and were to be reverenced along with the State House and Bunker Hill.

We spent considerable time there on that friendly bench, resting in the shadows of the elms, and while sitting there, we ate our lunch, and watched the traffic of Tremont Street, in perfect content till I remembered that the night was coming on, and that we had no place to sleep.

Approaching a policeman I inquired the way to a boarding house.

The officer who chanced to be a good-natured Irishman, with a courtesy almost oppressive, minutely pointed the way to a house on Essex Street. Think of it—Essex Street! It sounded like Shakespeare and Merrie England!

Following his direction, we found ourselves in the door of a small house on a narrow alley at the left of the Common. The landlady, a kindly soul, took our measure at once and gave us a room just off her little parlor, and as we had not slept, normally, for three nights, we decided to go at once to bed. It was about five o'clock, one of the noisiest hours of a noisy street, but we fell almost instantly into the kind of slumber in which time and tumult do not count.

When I awoke, startled and bewildered, the sounds of screaming children, roaring, jarring drays, and the clatter of falling iron filled the room. At first I imagined this to be the business of the morning, but as I looked out of the window I perceived that it was sunset! "Wake up!" I called to Franklin. *"It's the next day!"* "We've slept twenty-four hours!—What will the landlady think of us"

Frank did not reply. He was still very sleepy, but he dressed, and with valise in hand dazedly followed me into the sitting room. The woman of the house was serving supper to her little family. To her I said, "You've been very kind to let us sleep all this time. We were very tired."

"All this time?" she exclaimed.

"Isn't it the next day?" I asked.

Then she laughed, and her husband laughed, doubling himself into a knot of merriment. "Oh, but that's rich!" said he. "You've been asleep exactly an hour and a quarter," he added. "How long did you think you'd slept—two days?"

Sheepishly confessing that I thought we had, I turned back to bed, and claimed ten hours more of delicious rest.

All "the next day" we spent in seeing Bunker Hill, Faneuil Hall, the old North Church, King's Chapel, Longfellow's home, the Washington Elm, and the Navy Yard.—It was all glorious but a panic seized us as we found our money slipping away from us, and late in the afternoon we purchased tickets for Concord, and fled the roaring and turbulent capital.

We had seen the best of it anyway. We had tasted the ocean and found it really salt, and listened to "the sailors with bearded lips" on the wharves where the ships rocked idly on the tide,—The tide! Yes, that most inexplicable wonder of all we had proved. We had watched it come in at the Charles River Bridge, mysterious as the winds. We knew it was so.

Why Concord, do you ask? Well, because Hawthorne had lived there, and because the region was redolent of Emerson and

Thoreau, and I am glad to record that upon reaching it of a perfect summer evening, we found the lovely old village all that it had been pictured by the poets. The wide and beautiful meadows, the stone walls, the slow stream, the bridge and the statue of the "Minute Man" guarding the famous battlefield, the gray old Manse where Hawthorne lived, the cemetery of Sleepy Hollow, the grave of Emerson—all these historic and charming places enriched and inspired us. This land, so mellowed, so harmonious, so significant, seemed hardly real. It was a vision.

We rounded out our day by getting lodgings in the quaint old Wright's tavern which stood (and still stands) at the forks of the road, a building whose date painted on its chimney showed that it was nearly two hundred years old! I have since walked Carnarvon's famous walls, and sat in the circus at Nismes—but I have never had a deeper thrill of historic emotion than when I studied the beamed ceiling of that little dining room. Our pure joy in its age amused our landlord greatly.

Being down to our last dollar, we struck out into the country next morning, for the purpose of finding work upon a farm but met with very little encouragement. Most of the fields were harvested and those that were not were well supplied with "hands." Once we entered a beautiful country place where the proprietor himself (a man of leisure, a type we had never before seen) interrogated us with quizzical humor, and at last sent us to his foreman with honest desire to make use of us. But the foreman had nothing to give, and so we went on.

All day we loitered along beautiful wood roads, passing wonderful old homesteads gray and mossy, sheltered by trees that were almost human in the clasp of their protecting arms. We paused beside bright streams, and drank at mossy wells operated by rude and ancient sweeps, contrivances which we had seen only in pictures. It was all beautiful, but we got no work. The next day, having spent our last cent in railway tickets, we rode to Ayer Junction, where we left our trunks in care of the baggage man and resumed our tramping.

23

Coasting down Mt. Washington

In spite of all our anxiety, we enjoyed this search for work. The farmers were all so comically inquisitive. A few of them took us for what we were, students out on a vacation. Others though kind enough, seemed lacking in hospitality, from the western point of view and some were openly suspicious—but the roads, the roads! In the west thoroughfares ran on section lines and were defined by wire fences. Here they curved like Indian trails following bright streams, and the stone walls which bordered them were festooned with vines as in a garden.

That night we lodged in the home of an old farmer, an octogenarian who had never in all his life been twenty miles from his farm. He had never seen Boston, or Portland, but he had been twice to Nashua, returning, however, in time for supper. He, as well as his wife (dear simple soul), looked upon us as next door to educated Indians and entertained us in a flutter of excited hospitality.

We told them of Dakota, of the prairies, describing the wonderful farm machinery, and boasting of the marvellous crops our father had raised in Iowa, and the old people listened in delighted amaze.

They put us to bed at last in a queer high-posted, corded bedstead and I had a feeling that we were taking part in a Colonial play. It was like living a story book. We stared at each other in a stupor of satisfaction. We had never hoped for such luck. To be thrust back abruptly into the very life of our forebears was magical, and the excitement and delight of it kept us whispering together long after we should have been asleep.

This was thirty years ago, and those kindly old souls have long since returned to dust, but their big four-posted bed is doing service, no doubt, in the home of some rich collector. I have forgotten their names but they shall live here in my book as long as its print shall endure.

They seemed sorry to have us go next morning, but as they had nothing for us to do, they could only say, "Good-bye, give our love to Jane, if you see her, she lives in Illinois." Illinois and Dakota were all the same to them!

Again we started forth along the graceful, irregular, elm-shaded roads, which intersected the land in every direction, perfectly happy except when we remembered our empty pockets. We could not get accustomed to the trees and the beauty of the vineclad stone walls. The lanes made *pictures* all the time. So did the apple trees and the elms and the bending streams.

About noon of this day we came to a farm of very considerable size and fairly level, on which the hay remained uncut. "Here's our chance," I said to my brother, and going in, boldly accosted the farmer, a youngish man with a bright and pleasant face. "Do you want some skilled help?" I called out.

The farmer admitted that he did, but eyed us as if jokers. Evidently we did not look precisely like workmen to him, but I jolted him by saying, "We are Iowa schoolboys out for a vacation. We were raised on a farm, and know all about haying. If you'll give us a chance we'll make you think you don't know much about harvesting hay."

This amused him. "Come in." he said, "and after dinner we'll see about it."

At dinner we laid ourselves out to impress our host. We told him of the mile-wide fields of the west, and enlarged upon the stoneless prairies of Dakota. We described the broad-cast seeders they used in Minnesota and bragged of the amount of hay we could put up, and both of us professed a contempt for two-wheeled carts. In the end we reduced our prospective employer to humbleness. He consulted his wife a moment and then said, "All right, boys, you may take hold."

We stayed with him two weeks and enjoyed every moment of our stay.

"Our expedition is successful," I wrote to my parents.

On Sundays we picked berries or went fishing or tumbled about the lawn. It was all very beautiful and delightfully secure, so that when the time came to part with our pleasant young boss and his bright and cheery wife, we were as sorry as they.

"We must move on," I insisted. "There are other things to see."

After a short stay in Portland we took the train for Bethel, eager to visit the town-which our father had described so many times. We had resolved to climb the hills on which he had gathered berries and sit on the "Overset" from which he had gazed upon the landscape. We felt indeed, a certain keen regret that he could not be with us.

At Locks Mills, we met his old playmates, Dennis and Abner Herrick, men bent of form and dim of eye, gnarled and knotted by their battle with the rocks and barren hillsides, and to them we, confident lads, with our tales of smooth and level plow-lands, must have seemed like denizens from some farmers' paradise,—or perhaps they thought us fictionists. I certainly put a powerful emphasis on the pleasant side of western life at that time.

Dennis especially looked upon us with amazement, almost with awe. To think that we, unaided and alone, had wandered so far and dared so much, while he, in all his life, had not been able to visit Boston, was bewildering. This static condition of the population was a constant source of wonder to us. How could people stay all their lives in one place? Must be something the matter with them.—Their ox-teams and tipcarts amused us, their stony fields appalled us, their restricted, parsimonious lives saddened us, and so, not wishing to be a burden, we decided to cut our stay short.

On the afternoon of our last day, Abner took us on a tramp over the country, pointing out the paths "where Dick and I played," tracing the lines of the old farm, which had long since been given over to pasture, and so to the trout brook and home. In return for our "keep" we sang that night, and told stories of the west, and our hosts seemed pleased with the exchange. Shouldering our faithful "grips" next morning, we started for the railway and took the train for Gorham.

Each mile brought us nearer the climax of our trip. We of the plains had longed and dreamed of the peaks. To us the White Mountains were at once the crowning wonder and chief peril of our expedition. They were to be in a very real sense the test of our courage. The iron crest of Mount Washington allured us as a lighthouse lures sea-birds.

Leaving Gorham on foot, and carrying our inseparable valises, we started westward along the road leading to the peaks, expecting to get lodging at some farmhouse, but as we stood aside to let gay coaches pass laden with glittering women and haughty men, we began to feel abused.

We were indeed, quaint objects. Each of us wore a long yellow linen "duster" and each bore a valise on a stick, as an Irishman carries a bundle. We feared neither wind nor rain, but wealth and coaches oppressed us.

Nevertheless we trudged cheerily along, drinking at the beautiful springs beside the road, plucking blackberries for refreshment, lifting our eyes often to the snow-flecked peaks to the west. At noon we stopped at a small cottage to get some milk, and there again met a pathetic lonely old couple. The woman was at least eighty, and very crusty with her visitors, till I began to pet the enormous maltese cat which came purring to our feet. "What a magnificent animal!" I said to Frank.

This softened the old woman's heart. She not only gave us bread and milk but sat down to gossip with us while we ate. She, too, had relatives "out there, somewhere in Iowa" and would hardly let us go, so eager was she to know all about her people. "Surely you must have met them."

As we neared the foot of the great peak we came upon hotels of all sizes but I had not the slightest notion of staying even at the smallest. Having walked twelve miles to the foot of the mountain we now decided to set out for the top, still carrying those precious bags upon our shoulders.

What we expected to do after we got to the summit, I cannot say, for we knew nothing of conditions there and were too tired to imagine—we just kept climbing, sturdily, doggedly, breathing heavily, more with excitement than with labor, for it seemed that we were approaching the moon,—so bleak and high the roadway ran. I had miscalculated sadly. It had looked only a couple of hours' brisk walk from the hotel, but the way lengthened out toward the last in a most disheartening fashion.

"Where will we stay?" queried Frank.

"Oh, we'll find a place somewhere," I answered, but I was far from being as confident as I sounded.

We had been told that it cost five dollars for a night's lodging at the hotel, but I entertained some vague notion that other and cheaper places offered. Perhaps I thought that a little village on the summit presented boarding houses.

"No matter, we're in for it now," I stoutly said. "We'll find a place—we've got to find a place."

It grew cold as we rose, surprisingly, dishearteningly cold and we both realized that to sleep in the open would be to freeze. As the night fell, our clothing, wet with perspiration, became almost as clammy as sheet iron, and we shivered with weakness as well as with frost. The world became each moment more barren, more windswept and Frank was almost at his last gasp.

It was long after dark, and we were both trembling with fatigue and hollow with hunger as we came opposite a big barn just at the top of the trail. The door of this shelter stood invitingly open, and creeping into an empty stall we went to sleep on the straw like a couple of homeless dogs. We did not for a moment think of going to the hotel which loomed like a palace a few rods further on.

A couple of hours later I was awakened by the crunch of a boot upon my ankle, followed by an oath of surprise. The stage-driver, coming in from his last trip, was looking down upon me. I could not see his face, but I did note the bright eyes and pricking ears of a noble gray horse standing just behind his master and champing his bit with impatience.

Sleepy, scared and bewildered, I presented my plea with such eloquence that the man put his team in another stall and left us to our straw. "But you get out o' here before the boss sees you," said he, "or there'll be trouble."

"We'll get out before daybreak," I replied heartily.

When I next awoke it was dawn, and my body was so stiff I could hardly move. We had slept cold and our muscles resented it. However, we hurried from the barn. Once safely out of reach of the "boss" we began to leap and dance and shout to the sun as it rose out of the mist, for this was precisely what we had come two thousand miles to see—sunrise on Mount Washington! It chanced, gloriously, that the valleys were filled with a misty sea, breaking soundlessly at our feet and we forgot cold, hunger, poverty, in the wonder of being "above the clouds!"

In course of time our stomachs moderated our transports over the view and I persuaded my brother (who was younger and more delicate in appearance) to approach the kitchen and purchase a handout. Frank being harshly persuaded by his own need, ventured forth and soon came back with several slices of bread and butter and part of a cold chicken, which made the day perfectly satisfactory, and in high spirits we started to descend the western slope of the mountain.

Here we performed the incredible. Our muscles were so sore and weak that as we attempted to walk down the railway track, our knees refused to bear our weight, and while creeping over the ties, groaning and sighing with pain, a bright idea suddenly irradiated my mind. As I studied the iron groove which contained the cogs in the middle of the track, I perceived that its edges were raised a little above the level of the rails and covered with oil. It occurred to me that it might be possible to slide down this track on a plank—if only I had a plank!

I looked to the right. A miracle! There in the ditch lay a plank of exactly the right dimensions. I seized it, I placed it cross-wise of the rails. "All aboard," I called. Frank obeyed. I took my place at the other end, and so with our valises between us, we began to slip slowly, smoothly, and with joyous ease down the shining track! Hoopla! We had taken wing!

We had solved our problem. The experiment was successful. Laughing and shouting with exultation, we swept on. We had but to touch every other tie with our heels in order to control our speed, so we coasted, smoothly, genially.

On we went, mile after mile, slipping down the valley into the vivid sunlight, our eyes on the glorious scenery about us, down, down like a swooping bird. Once we passed above some workmen, who looked up in open-mouthed amazement, and cursed us in voices which seemed far and faint and futile. A little later the superintendent of the water tank warningly shouted, *"Stop that! Get Off!"* but we only laughed at him and swept on, out over a high trestle, where none could follow.

At times our heads grew dizzy with the flicker and glitter of the rocks beneath us and as we rounded dangerous curves of the track, or descended swift slides with almost uncontrollable rapidity, I had some doubts, but we kept our wits, remained upon the rails, and at last spun round the final bend and came to a halt upon a level stretch of track, just above the little station.

There, kicking aside our faithful plank, we took up our valises and with trembling knees and a sense of triumph set off down the valley of the wild Amonoosuc.

24

Tramping, New York, Washington, and Chicago

For two days we followed the Amonoosuc (which is a lovely stream), tramping along exquisite winding roads, loitering by sunny ripples or dreaming in the shadow of magnificent elms. It was all very, very beautiful to us of the level lands of Iowa and Dakota. These brooks rushing over their rocky beds, these stately trees and these bleak mountain-tops looming behind us, all glowed with the high splendor of which we had dreamed.

At noon we called at a farmhouse to get something to eat and at night we paid for lodging in a rude tavern beside the way, and so at last reached the railway and the Connecticut River. Here we gained our trunks (which had been sent round by express) and as the country seemed poor and the farms barren, we spent nearly all our money in riding down the railway fifty or sixty miles. At some small town (I forget the name), we again took to the winding roads, looking for a job.

Jobs, it turned out, were exceedingly hard to get. The haying was over, the oats mainly in shock, and the people on the highway suspicious and inhospitable. As we plodded along, our dimes melting away, hunger came, at last, to be a grim reality. We looked less and less like college boys and more and more like tramps, and the house-holders began to treat us with hostile contempt.

No doubt these farmers, much beset with tramps, had reasonable excuse for their inhospitable ways, but to us it was all bitter and uncalled for. I knew that cities were filled with robbers, brigands, burglars and pirates, but I had held (up to this time), the belief that the country, though rude and barren of luxury was nevertheless a place of plenty where no man need suffer hunger.

Frank, being younger and less hardy than I, became clean disheartened, and upon me fell the responsibility and burden of the campaign. I certainly was to blame for our predicament.

We came finally to the point of calling at every house where any crops lay ungathered, desperately in hope of securing something to do. At last there came a time when we no longer had money for a bed, and were forced to sleep wherever we could find covert. One night we couched on the floor of an old school-house, the next we crawled into an oat-shock and covered ourselves with straw. Let those who have never slept out on the ground through an August night say that it is impossible that one should be cold! During all the early warm part of the night a family of skunks rustled about us, and toward morning we both woke because of the chill.

On the third night we secured the blessed opportunity of nesting in a farmer's granary. All humor had gone out of our expedition. Each day the world grew blacker, and the men of the Connecticut Valley more cruel and relentless. We both came to understand (not to the full, but in a large measure) the bitter rebellion of the tramp. To plod on and on into the dusk, rejected of comfortable folk, to couch at last with pole-cats in a shock of grain is a liberal education in sociology.

On the fourth day we came upon an old farmer who had a few acres of badly tangled oats which he wished gathered and bound. He was a large, loose-jointed, good natured sloven who looked at me with stinging, penetrating stare, while I explained that we were students on a vacation tramping and in need of money. He seemed not particularly interested till Frank said with tragic bitterness, "If we ever get back to Dakota we'll never even look this way again." This interested the man. He said, "Turn in and cut them oats," and we gladly buckled to our job.

Our spirits rose with the instant resiliency of youth, but what a task that reaping proved to be! The grain, tangled and flattened close to the ground, had to be caught up in one hand and cut with the old-fashioned reaping-hook, the kind they used in Egypt five thousand years ago—a thin crescent of steel with a straight handle, and as we bowed ourselves to the ground to clutch and clip the grain, we nearly broke in two pieces. It was hot at mid-day and the sun fell upon our bended shoulders with amazing power, but we toiled on, glad of the opportunity to earn a dollar. "Every cent means escape from this sad country," I repeated.

We stayed some days with this reticent gardener, sleeping in the attic above his kitchen like two scullions, uttering no complaint till we had earned seven dollars apiece; then we said, "Good luck," and bought tickets for Greenfield, Massachusetts. We chose this spot for the reason that a great railway alluringly crossed the river at that place. We seemed in better situation to get west from such a point.

Greenfield was so like Rockford (the western town in which I had worked as a carpenter), that I at once purchased a few tools and within a few hours secured work shingling a house on the edge of the town, while my brother took a hand at harvesting worms from a field of tobacco near by.

The builder, a tall man, bent and grizzled, complimented me warmly at the close of my second day, and said, "You may consider yourself hired for as long as you please to stay. You're a rattler." No compliment since has given me more pleasure than this. A few days later he invited both of us to live at his home. We accepted and were at once established in most comfortable quarters.

Tranquil days followed. The country was very attractive, and on Sundays we walked the neighboring lanes, or climbed the high hills, or visited the quaint and lonely farmhouses round about, feeling more akin each week to the life of the valley, but we had no intention of remaining beyond a certain time. Great rivers called and cities allured. New York was still to be explored and to return to the west before winter set in was our plan.

At last the time came when we thought it safe to start toward Albany and with grateful words of thanks to the carpenter and his wife, we set forth upon our travels. Our courage was again at topmost gauge. My success with the saw had given me confidence. I was no longer afraid of towns, and in a glow of high resolution and with thirty dollars in my pocket, I planned to invade New York which was to me the wickedest and the most sorrowful as well as the most splendid city in the world.

Doubtless the true story of how I entered Manhattan will endanger my social position, but as an unflinching realist, I must begin by acknowledging that I left the Hudson River boat carrying my own luggage. I shudder to think what we two boys must have looked like as we set off, side by side, prospecting for Union Square and the Bowery. Broadway, we knew, was the main street and Union Square the center of the island, therefore we turned north and paced along the pavement, still clamped to our everlasting bags.

Broadway was not then the deep cañon that it is today. It was walled by low shops of red brick—in fact, the whole city seemed low as compared with the high buildings of Chicago, nevertheless I was keenly worried over the question of housing.

Food was easy. We could purchase a doughnut and a cup of coffee almost anywhere, or we could eat a sandwich in the park, but the matter of a bed, the business of sleeping in a maelstrom like New York was something more than serious—it was dangerous. Frank, naturally of a more prodigal nature, was all for going to the Broadway Hotel. "It's only for one night," said he. He always was rather careless of the future!

I reminded him that we still had Philadelphia, Baltimore and Washington to "do" and every cent must be husbanded—so we moved along toward Union Square with the question of a hotel still undecided, our arms aching with fatigue. "If only we could get rid of these awful bags," moaned Frank.

To us Broadway was a storm, a cyclone, an abnormal unholy congestion of human souls. The friction of feet on the pavement was like the hissing of waves on the beach. The passing of trucks jarred upon our ears like the sevenfold thunders of Patmos, but we kept on, shoulder to shoulder, watchful, alert, till we reached Union Square, where with sighs of deep relief we sank upon the benches along with the other "rubes" and "jay-hawkers" lolling in sweet repose with weary soles laxly turned to the kindly indiscriminating breeze.

The evening was mild, the scene enthralling, and we would have been perfectly happy but for the deeply disturbing question of a bed. Franklin, resting upon my resourceful management, made no motion even when the sun sank just about where that Venetian fronted building now stands, but whilst the insolent, teeming populace in clattering carts and drays charged round our peaceful sylvan haven (each driver plying the lash with the fierce aspect of a Roman charioteer) I rose to a desperate mission.

With a courage born of need I led the way straight toward the basement portal of a small brown hotel on Fourth Avenue, and was startled almost into flight to find myself in a barroom. Not knowing precisely how to retreat, I faltered out, "Have you a bed for us?"

It is probable that the landlord, a huge foreign-looking man understood our timidity—at any rate, he smiled beneath his black mustache and directed a clerk to show us a room.

In charge of this man, a slim youth, with a very bad complexion, we climbed a narrow stairway (which grew geometrically shabbier as we rose) until, at last, we came into a room so near the roof that it could afford only half-windows—but as we were getting the chamber at half-price we could not complain.

No sooner had the porter left us than we both stretched out on the bed, in such relief and ecstasy of returning confidence as only weary youth and honest poverty can know.—It was heavenly sweet, this sense of safety in the heart of a tempest of human passion but as we rested, our hunger to explore returned. "Time is passing. We shall probably never see New York again," I argued, "and besides our bags are now safely *cached.* Let's go out and see how the city looks by night."

To this Franklin agreed, and forth we went into the Square, rejoicing in our freedom from those accursed bags.

Here for the first time, I observed the electric light shadows, so clear-cut, so marvellous. The park was lighted by several sputtering, sizzling arc-lamps, and their rays striking down through the trees, flung upon the pavement a wavering, exquisite tracery of sharply defined, purple-black leaves and branches. This was, indeed, an entirely new effect in our old world and to my mind its wonder surpassed nature. It was as if I had suddenly been translated to some realm of magic art.

Where we dined I cannot say, probably we ate a doughnut at some lunch counter but I am glad to remember that we got as far as Madison Square—which was like discovering another and still more enchanting island of romance. To us the Fifth Avenue Hotel was a great and historic building, for in it Grant and Sherman and Lincoln and Greeley had often registered.

Ah, what a night that was! I did not expend a dollar, not even a quarter, but I would give half of all I now own for the sensitive heart, the absorbent brain I then possessed. Each form, each shadow was a miracle. Romance and terror and delight peopled every dusky side street.

Submerged in the wondrous, drenched with the spray of this measureless ocean of human life, we wandered on and on till overborne nature called a halt. It was ten o'clock and prudence as well as weariness advised retreat. Decisively, yet with a feeling that we would never again glow beneath the lights of this radiant city, I led the way back to our half-rate bed in the Union Square Hungarian hotel.

It is worth recording that on reaching our room, we opened our small window and leaning out, gazed away over the park, what time the tumult and the thunder and the shouting died into a low, continuous roar. The poetry and the majesty of the city lost nothing of its power under the moon.

Although I did not shake my fist over the town and vow to return and conquer it (as penniless writers in fiction generally do) I bowed down before its power. "It's too much for us," I told my brother. "Two millions of people—think of it—of course London is larger, but then London is so far off."

Sleep for us both was but a moment's forgetfulness. At one moment it was night and at another it was morning. We were awakened by the voice of the pavement, that sound which Whitman calls "the loud, proud, restive bass of the streets," and again I leaned forth to listen to the wide-spread crescendo roar of the deepening traffic. The air being cool and clear, the pedestrians stepped out with brisker, braver movement, and we, too, rose eager to meet the day at the gate of the town.

All day we tramped, absorbing everything that went on in the open. Having explored the park, viewed the obelisk and visited the zoo, we wandered up and down Broadway, mooning upon the life of the streets. Curb-stone fights, police maneuvres, shop-window comedies, building operations—everything we saw instructed us. We soaked ourselves in the turbulent rivers of the town with a feeling that we should never see them again.

We had intended to stay two days but a tragic encounter with a restaurant bandit so embittered and alarmed us that we fled New York (as we supposed), forever. At one o'clock, being hungry, very hungry, we began to look for a cheap eating house, and somewhere in University Place we came upon a restaurant which looked humble enough to afford a twenty-five cent dinner (which was our limit of extravagance), and so, timidly, we ventured in.

A foreign-looking waiter greeted us, and led us to one of a number of very small tables covered with linen which impressed even Frank's uncritical eyes with its mussiness. With a feeling of having inadvertently entered a den of thieves, I wished myself out of it but lacked the courage to rise and when the man returned and placed upon the table two glasses and a strange looking bottle with a metal stopper which had a kind of lever at the side, Frank said, "Hi! Good thing!—I'm thirsty." Quite against my judgment he fooled around with the lever till he succeeded in helping himself to some of the liquid with which the bottle was filled. It was soda water and he drank heartily, although I was sure it would be extra on the bill.

The food came on slowly, by fits and starts, and the dishes were all so cold and queer of taste that even Frank complained. But we ate with a terrifying premonition of trouble. "This meal will cost us at least thirty-five cents each!" I said.

"No matter, it's an experience," my spendthrift brother retorted.

At last when the limp lettuce, the amazing cheese and the bitter coffee were all consumed, I asked the soiled, outlandish waiter the price.

In reply he pencilled on a slip as though we were deaf, and finally laid the completed bill face down beside my plate. I turned it over and grew pale.

It totalled *one dollar and twenty cents!*

I felt weak and cold as if I had been suddenly poisoned. I trembled, then grew hot with indignation. "Sixty cents apiece!" I gasped. "Didn't I warn you?"

Frank was still in reckless mood. "Well, this is the only time we have to do it. They won't catch us here again."

I paid the bill and hurried out, bitterly exclaiming, "No more New York for me. I will not stay in such a robbers' den another night."

And I didn't. At sunset we crossed the ferry and took the train for New Brunswick, New Jersey. Why we selected this town I cannot say, but I think it must have been because it was half-way to Philadelphia—and that we were just about as scared of Philadelphia as we were resentful of New York.

After a night battle with New Jersey mosquitoes and certain plantigrade bed-fellows native to cheap hotels, we passed on to

Philadelphia and to Baltimore, and at sunset of the same day reached Washington, the storied capital of the nation.

Everything we saw here was deeply significant, national, rousing our patriotism. We were at once and profoundly interested by the negro life which flowered here in the free air of the District as under an African sun; the newsboys, the bootblacks, the mule-drivers, all amused us. We spent that first night in Washington in a little lodging house just at the corner of the Capitol grounds where beds were offered for twenty-five cents. It was a dreadful place, but we slept without waking. It took a large odor, a sharp lance to keep either of us awake in those days.

Tramping busily all the next day, we climbed everything that could be climbed. We visited the Capitol, the war building, the Treasury and the White House grounds. We toiled through all the museums, working harder than we had ever worked upon the farm, till Frank cried out for mercy. I was inexorable. "Our money is getting low. We must be very saving of carfare," I insisted. "We must see all we can. We'll never be here again."

Once more we slept (among the negroes in a bare little lodging house), and on the third day, brimming with impressions, boarded the Chicago express and began our glorious, our exultant return over the Alleghanies, toward the west.

It was with a feeling of joy, of distinct relief that we set our faces toward the sunset. Every mile brought us nearer home. I knew the West. I knew the people, and I had no fear of making a living beyond the Alleghanies. Every mile added courage and hope to our hearts, and increased the value of the splendid, if sometimes severe experiences through which we had passed. Frank was especially gay for he was definitely on his way home, back to Dakota.

And when next day on the heights of the Alleghany mountains, the train dipped to the west, and swinging around a curve, disclosed to us the tumbled spread of mountain-land descending to the valley of the Ohio, we sang "O'er the hills in legions, boys" as our forefathers did of old. We were about to re-enter the land of the teeming furrow.

Late that night as we were riding through the darkness in the smoking car, I rose and, placing in my brother's hands all the money I had, said good-bye, and at Mansfield, Ohio, swung off the train, leaving him to proceed on his homeward way alone.

It was about one o'clock of an autumn night, sharp and clear, and I spent the remainder of the morning on a bench in the railway station, waiting for the dawn. I could not sleep, and so spent the time in pondering on my former experiences in seeking work. "Have I been wrong?" I asked myself. "Is the workman in America, as in the old world, coming to be a man despised?"

Having been raised in the splendid patriotism, perhaps one might say flamboyant patriotism, of the West during and following our Civil War, I had been brought up to believe that labor was honorable, that idlers were to be despised, but now as I sat with bowed head, cold, hungry and penniless, knowing that I must go forth at daylight—seeking work, the world seemed a very hostile place to me. Of course I did not consider myself a workman in the ordinary hopeless sense. My need of a job was merely temporary, for it was my intention to return to the Middle West in time to secure a position as teacher in some country school. Nevertheless a lively imagination gave me all the sensations of the homeless man.

The sun rose warm and golden, and with a return of my courage I started forth, confident of my ability to make a place for myself. With a wisdom which I had not hitherto shown I first sought a home, and luckily, I say luckily because I never could account for it, I knocked at the door of a modest little boarding house, whose mistress, a small blonde lady, invited me in and gave me a room without a moment's hesitation. Her dinner—a delicious mid-day meal, so heartened me that before the end of the day, I had secured a place as one of a crew of carpenters. My spirits rose. I was secure.

My evenings were spent in reading Abbott's *Life of Napoleon* which I found buried in an immense pile of old magazines. I had never before read a full history of the great Corsican, and this chronicle moved me almost as profoundly as Hugo's *Les Misérables* had done the year before.

On Sundays I walked about the country under the splendid oaks and beeches which covered the ridges, dreaming of the West, and of the future which was very vague and not very cheerful in coloring. My plan so far as I had a plan, was not ambitious. I had decided to return to some small town in Illinois and secure employment as a teacher, but as I lingered on at my carpenter trade till October nothing was left for me but a country school, and when Orrin Carter, county superintendent of Grundy County, (he is Judge Carter now) informed me that a district school some miles out would pay fifty dollars a month for a teacher, I gladly accepted the offer.

On the following afternoon I started forth a passenger with Hank Ring on his way homeward in an empty corn wagon. The box had no seat, therefore he and I both rode standing during a drive of six miles. The wind was raw, and the ground, frozen hard as iron, made the ride a kind of torture, but our supper of buckwheat pancakes and pork sausages at Deacon Ring's was partial compensation. On the following Monday I started my school.

The winter which followed appalled the oldest inhabitant. Snow fell almost daily, and the winds were razor-bladed. In order to save every dollar of my wages, I built my own fires in the school-house. This means that on every week-day morning, I was obliged to push out into the stinging dawn, walk a mile to the icy building, split kindling, start a flame in the rude stove, and have the room comfortable at half-past eight. The thermometer often went to a point twenty degrees below zero, and my ears were never quite free from peeling skin and fevered tissues.

My pupils were boys and girls of all sizes and qualities, and while it would be too much to say that I made the best teacher of mathematics in the county, I think I helped them in their reading, writing, and spelling, which after all are more important than algebra. On Saturday I usually went to town, for I had in some way become acquainted with the principal of a little normal school which was being carried on in Morris by a young Quaker from Philadelphia. Prof. Forsythe soon recognized in me something more than the ordinary "elocutionist" and readily aided me in securing a class in oratory among his students.

This work and Forsythe's comradeship helped me to bear the tedium of my work in the country. No Saturday was too stormy, and the roads were never too deep with snow to keep me from my weekly visit to Morris where I came in contact with people nearer to my ways of thinking and living.

But after all this was but the final section of my eastern excursion—for as the spring winds set in, the call of "the sunset regions" again overcame my love of cities. The rush to Dakota in March was greater than ever before and a power stronger than my will drew me back to the line of the middle border which had moved on into the Missouri Valley, carrying my people with it. As the spring odors filled my nostrils, my wish to emigrate was like that of the birds. "Out there is my share of the government land—and, if I am to carry out my plan of fitting myself for a professorship," I argued—"these claims are worth securing. My rights to the public domain are as good as any other man's."

My recollections of the James River Valley were all pleasant. My brother and father both wrote urging me to come and secure a claim, and so at last I replied, "I'll come as soon as my school is out," thus committing all my future to the hazard of the homestead.

And so it came about that in the second spring after setting my face to the east I planned a return to the Border. I had had my glimpse of Boston, New York and Washington. I was twenty-three years of age, and eager to revisit the plain whereon my father with the faith of a pioneer, was again upturning the sod and building a fourth home. And yet, Son of the Middle Border—I had discovered that I was also a Grandson of New England.

25

The Land of the Straddle-Bug

At night in Chicago (where I saw Salvini play Othello), a day in Neshonoc to visit my Uncle Richard, and I was again in the midst of a jocund rush of land-seekers.

The movement which had begun three years before was now at its height. Thousands of cars, for lack of engines to move them, were lying idle on the switches all over the west. Trains swarming with immigrants from every country of the world were haltingly creeping out upon the level lands. Norwegians, Swedes, Danes, Scotchmen, Englishmen, and Russians all mingled in this flood of land-seekers rolling toward the sundown plain, where a fat-soiled valley had been set aside by good Uncle Sam for the enrichment of every man. Such elation, such hopefulness could not fail to involve an excitable youth like myself.

My companion, Forsythe, dropped off at Milbank, but I kept on, on into the James Valley, arriving at Ordway on the evening of the second day—a clear cloudless evening in early April, with the sun going down red in the west, the prairie chickens calling from the knolls and hammers still sounding in the village, their tattoo denoting the urgent need of roofs to shelter the incoming throng.

The street swarmed with boomers. All talk was of lots, of land. Hour by hour as the sun sank, prospectors returned to the hotel from their trips into the unclaimed territory, hungry and tired but jubilant, and as they assembled in my father's store after supper, their boastful talk of "claims secured" made me forget all my other ambitions. I was as eager to clutch my share of Uncle Sam's bounty as any of them. The world seemed beginning anew for me as well as for these aliens from the crowded eastern world. "I am ready to stake a claim," I said to my father.

Early the very next day, with a party of four (among them Charles Babcock, a brother of Burton), I started for the unsurveyed country where, some thirty miles to the west, my father had already located a pre-emption claim and built a rough shed, the only shelter for miles around.

"We'll camp there," said Charles.

It was an inspiring ride! The plain freshly uncovered from the snow was swept by a keen wind which held in spite of that an acrid prophecy of sudden spring. Ducks and geese rose from every icy pond and resumed their flight into the mystic north, and as we advanced the world broadened before us. The treelessness of the wide swells, the crispness of the air and the feeling that to the westward lay the land of the Sioux, all combined to make our trip a kind of epic in miniature. Charles also seemed to feel the essential poetry of the expedition, although he said little except to remark, "I wish Burton were here."

It was one o'clock before we reached the cabin and two before we finished luncheon. The afternoon was spent in wandering over the near-by obtainable claims and at sundown we all returned to the shed to camp.

As dusk fell, and while the geese flew low gabbling confidentially, and the ducks whistled by overhead in swift unerring flight, Charles and I lay down on the hay beside the horses, feeling ourselves to be, in some way, partners with God in this new world. I went to sleep hearing the horses munching their grain in the neighboring stalls, entirely contented with my day and confident of the morrow. All questions were answered, all doubts stilled.

We arose with the sun and having eaten our rude breakfast set forth, some six miles to the west, to mark the location of our claims with the "straddle-bugs."

The straddle-bug, I should explain, was composed of three boards set together in tripod form and was used as a monument, a sign of occupancy. Its presence defended a claim against the next comer. Lumber being very scarce at the moment, the building of a shanty was impossible, and so for several weeks these signs took the place of "improvements" and were fully respected. No one could honorably jump these claims within thirty days and no one did.

At last, when far beyond the last claimant, we turned and looked back upon a score of these glittering guidons of progress, banners of the army of settlement, I realized that I was a vedette in the van of civilization, and when I turned to the west where nothing was to be seen save the mysterious plain and a long low line of still more mysterious hills, I thrilled with joy at all I had won.

It seemed a true invasion, this taking possession of the virgin sod, but as I considered, there was a haunting sadness in it, for these shining pine pennons represented the inexorable plow. They prophesied the death of all wild creatures and assured the devastation of the beautiful, the destruction of all the signs and seasons of the sod.

Apparently none of my companions shared this feeling, for they all leaped from the wagon and planted their stakes, each upon his chosen quarter-section with whoops of joy, cries which sounded faint and far, like the futile voices of insects, diminished to shrillness by the echoless abysses of the unclouded sky.

As we had measured the distance from the township lines by counting the revolutions of our wagon-wheels, so now with pocket compass and a couple of laths, Charles and I laid out inner boundaries and claimed three quarter-sections, one for Frank and one each for ourselves. Level as a floor these acres were, and dotted with the bones of bison.

We ate our dinner on the bare sod while all around us the birds of spring-time moved in myriads, and over the swells to the east other wagons laden with other land-seekers crept like wingless beetles—stragglers from the main skirmish line.

Having erected our pine-board straddle-bugs with our names written thereon, we jubilantly started back toward the railway. Tired but peaceful, we reached Ordway at dark and Mrs. Wynn's supper of ham and eggs and potatoes completed our day most satisfactorily.

My father, who had planned to establish a little store on his claim, now engaged me as his representative, his clerk, and I spent the next week in hauling lumber and in helping to build the shanty and ware-room on the section line. As soon as the place was habitable, my mother and sister Jessie came out to stay with me, for in order to hold his pre-emption my father was obliged to make it his "home."

Before we were fairly settled, my mother was forced to feed and house a great many land-seekers who had no other place to stay. This brought upon her once again all the drudgery of a pioneer house-wife, and filled her with longing for the old home in Iowa. It must have seemed to her as if she were never again to find rest except beneath the sod.

Nothing that I have ever been called upon to do caused me more worry than the act of charging those land-seekers for their meals and bunks, and yet it was perfectly right that they should pay. Our buildings had been established with great trouble and at considerable expense, and my father said, "We cannot afford to feed so many people without return," and yet it seemed to me like taking an unfair advantage of poor and homeless men. It was with the greatest difficulty that I brought myself to charge them anything at all. Fortunately the prices had been fixed by my father.

Night by night it became necessary to lift a lantern on a high pole in front of the shack, in order that those who were traversing the plain after dark might find their way, and often I was aroused from my bed by the arrival of a worn and bewildered party of pilgrims rescued from a sleepless couch upon the wet sod.

For several weeks mother was burdened with these wayfarers, but at last they began to thin out. The skirmish line moved on, the ranks halted, and all about the Moggeson ranch hundreds of yellow shanties sparkled at dawn like flecks of gold on a carpet of green velvet. Before the end of May every claim was taken and "improved"—more or less.

Meanwhile I had taken charge of the store and Frank was the stage driver. He was a very bad salesman, but I was worse—that must be confessed. If a man wanted to purchase an article and had the money to pay for it, we exchanged commodities right there, but as far as my selling anything—father used to say, "Hamlin couldn't sell gold dollars for ninety cents a piece," and he was right—entirely right.

I found little to interest me in the people who came to the store for they were "just ordinary folk" from Illinois, and Iowa, and I had never been a youth who made acquaintances easily, so with nothing of the politician in me, I seldom inquired after the babies or gossiped with the old women about their health and housekeeping. I regretted this attitude afterward. A closer relationship with the settlers would have furnished me with a greater variety of fictional characters, but at the time I had no suspicion that I was missing anything.

As the land dried off and the breaking plow began its course, a most idyllic and significant period of life came on. The plain became very beautiful as the soil sent forth its grasses. On the shadowed sides of the ridges exquisite shades of pink and purple bloomed, while the most radiant yellow-green flamed from slopes on which the sunlight fell. The days of May and June succeeded one another in perfect harmony like the notes in a song, broken only once or twice by thunderstorms.

An opalescent mist was in the air, and everywhere, on every swell, the settlers could be seen moving silently to and fro with their teams, while the women sang at their work about the small shanties, and in their new gardens. On every side was the most cheerful acceptance of hard work and monotonous fare. No one acknowledged the transient quality of this life, although it was only a novel sort of picnic on the prairie, soon to end.

Many young people and several groups of girls (teachers from the east) were among those who had taken claims, and some of these made life pleasant for themselves and helpful to others by bringing to their cabins, books and magazines and pictures. The store was not only the social center of the township but the post-office, and Frank, who carried the mail (and who was much more gallant than I) seemed to draw out all the school ma'ams of the neighborhood. The raising of a flag on a high pole before the door was the signal for the post which brought the women pouring in from every direction eager for news of the eastern world.

In accordance with my plan to become a teacher, I determined to go to the bottom of the laws which govern literary development, and so with an unexpurgated volume of Taine, a set of Chambers' *Encyclopoedia of English Literature,* and a volume of Greene's *History of the English People,* I set to work to base myself profoundly in the principles which govern a nation's self-expression. I still believed that in order to properly teach an appreciation of poetry, a man should have the power of dramatic expression, that he should be able to read so as to make the printed page live in the ears of his pupils. In short I had decided to unite the orator and the critic.

As a result, I spent more time over my desk than beside the counter. I did not absolutely refuse to wait on a purchaser but no sooner was his package tied up than I turned away to my work of digesting and transcribing in long hand Taine's monumental book.

Day after day I bent to this task, pondering all the great Frenchman had to say of *race, environment,* and *momentum* and on the walls of the cabin I mapped out in chalk the various periods of English society as he had indicated them. These charts were the wonder and astonishment of my neighbors whenever they chanced to enter the living room, and they appeared especially interested in the names written on the ceiling over my bed. I had put my favorites there so that when I opened my eyes of a morning, I could not help absorbing a knowledge of their dates and works.

However, on Saturday afternoon when the young men came in from their claims, I was not above pitching quoits or "putting the shot" with them—in truth I took a mild satisfaction in being able to set a big boulder some ten inches beyond my strongest competitor. Occasionally I practiced with the rifle but was not a crack shot. I could still pitch a ball as well as any of them and I served as pitcher in the games which the men occasionally organized.

As harvest came on, mother and sister returned to Ordway, and cooking became a part of my daily routine. Charles occasionally helped out and we both learned to make biscuits and even pies. Frank loyally declared my apple-pies to be as good as any man could make.

Meanwhile an ominous change had crept over the plain. The winds were hot and dry and the grass, baked on the stem, had became as inflammable as hay. The birds were silent. The sky, absolutely cloudless, began to scare us with its light. The sun rose through the dusty air, sinister with flare of horizontal heat. The little gardens on the breaking withered, and many of the women began to complain bitterly of the loneliness, and lack of shade. The tiny cabins were like ovens at midday.

Smiling faces were less frequent. Timid souls began to inquire, "Are all Dakota summers like this?" and those with greatest penetration reasoned, from the quality of the grass which was curly and fine as hair, that they had unwittingly settled upon an arid soil.

And so, week by week the holiday spirit faded from the colony and men in feverish unrest uttered words of bitterness. Eyes ached with light and hearts sickened with loneliness. Defeat seemed facing every man.

By the first of September many of those who were in greatest need of land were ready to abandon their advanced position on the border and fall back into the ranks behind. We were all nothing but squatters. The section lines had not been run and every pre-emptor looked and longed for the coming of the surveying crew, because once our filings were made we could all return to the east, at least for six months, or we could prove up and buy our land. In other words, the survey offered a chance to escape from the tedious monotony of the burning plain into which we had so confidently thrust ourselves.

But the surveyors failed to appear though they were reported from day to day to be at work in the next township and so, one by one, these of us who were too poor to buy ourselves food, dropped away. Hundreds of shanties were battened up and deserted. The young women returned to their schools, and men who had counted upon getting work to support their families during the summer, and who had failed to do so, abandoned their claims and went east where settlement had produced a crop. Our song of emigration seemed but bitter mockery now.

Moved by the same desire to escape, I began writing to various small towns in Minnesota and Iowa in the hope of obtaining a school, but with little result. My letters written from the border line did not inspire confidence in the School Boards of "the East." Then winter came.

Winter! No man knows what winter means until he has lived through one in a pine-board shanty on a Dakota plain with only buffalo bones for fuel. There were those who had settled upon this land, not as I had done with intent to prove up and sell, but with plans to make a home, and many of these, having toiled all the early spring in hope of a crop, now at the beginning of winter found themselves with little money and no coal. Many of them would have starved and frozen had it not been for the buffalo skeletons which lay scattered over the sod and for which a sudden market developed. Upon the proceeds of this singular harvest they almost literally lived. Thus "the herds of deer and buffalo" did indeed strangely "furnish the cheer."

As for Charles and myself, we also returned to Ordway and there spent a part of each month, brooding darkly over the problem of our future. I already perceived the futility of my return to the frontier. The mysterious urgings of a vague yet deep-seated longing to go east rendered me restless, sour and difficult. I saw nothing before me, and yet my hard experiences in Wisconsin and in New England made me hesitate about going far. Teaching a country school seemed the only thing I was fitted for, and there shone no promise of that.

Furthermore, like other pre-emptors I was forced to hold my claim by visiting it once every thirty days, and these trips became each time more painful, more menacing. February and March were of pitiless severity. One blizzard followed another with ever-increasing fury. No sooner was the snow laid by a north wind than it took wing above a southern blast and returned upon us sifting to and fro until at last its crystals were as fine as flour, so triturated that it seemed to drive through an inch board. Often it filled the air for hundreds of feet above the earth like a mist, and lay in long ridges behind every bush or weed. Nothing lived on these desolate uplands but the white owl and the wolf.

One cold, bright day I started for my claim accompanied by a young Englishman, a fair-faced delicate young clerk from London, and before we had covered half our journey the west wind met us with such fury that the little cockney would certainly have frozen had I not forced him out of the sleigh to run by its side.

Poor little man! This was not the romantic home he had expected to gain when he left his office on the Strand.

Luckily, his wretched shanty was some six miles nearer than mine or he would have died. Leaving him safe in his den, I pushed on toward my own claim, in the teeth of a terrific gale, the cold growing each moment more intense. "The sunset regions" at that moment did not provoke me to song.

In order to reach my cabin before darkness fell, I urged my team desperately, and it was well that I did, for I could scarcely see my horses during the last mile, and the wind was appalling even to me—an experienced plainsman. Arriving at the barn I was disheartened to find the doors heavily banked with snow, but I fell to in desperate haste, and soon shoveled a passageway.

This warmed me, but in the delay one of my horses became so chilled that he could scarcely enter his stall. He refused to eat also, and this troubled me very much. However, I loaded him with blankets and fell to work rubbing his legs with wisps of hay, to start the circulation, and did not desist until the old fellow began nibbling his forage.

By this time the wind was blowing seventy miles an hour, and black darkness was upon the land. With a rush I reached my shanty only to find that somebody had taken all my coal and nearly all my kindling, save a few pieces of pine. This was serious, but I kindled a fire with the blocks, a blaze which was especially grateful by reason of its quick response.

Hardly was the stove in action, when a rap at the door startled me. "Come," I shouted. In answer to my call, a young man, a neighbor, entered, carrying a sack filled with coal. He explained with some embarrassment, that in his extremity during the preceding blizzard, he had borrowed from my store, and that (upon seeing my light) he had hurried to restore the fuel, enough, at any rate, to last out the night. His heroism appeased my wrath and I watched him setting out on his return journey with genuine anxiety.

That night is still vivid in my memory. The frail shanty, cowering close, quivered in the wind like a frightened hare. The powdery snow appeared to drive directly through the solid boards, and each hour the mercury slowly sank. Drawing my bed close to the fire, I covered myself with a buffalo robe and so slept for an hour or two.

When I woke it was still dark and the wind, though terrifying, was intermittent in its attack. The timbers of the house creaked as the blast lay hard upon it, and now and again the faint fine crystals came sifting down upon my face,—driven beneath the shingles by the tempest. At last I lit my oil lamp and shivered in my robe till dawn. I felt none of the exultation of a "king in fairyland" nor that of a "lord of the soil."

The morning came, bright with sun but with the thermometer forty degrees below zero. It was so cold that the horses refused to face the northwest wind. I could not hitch them to the sleigh until I had blanketed them both beneath their harness; even then they snorted and pawed in terror. At last, having succeeded in hooking the traces I sprang in and, wrapping the robe about me, pushed eastward with all speed, seeking food and fire.

This may be taken as a turning point in my career, for this experience (followed by two others almost as severe) permanently chilled my enthusiasm for pioneering the plain. Never again did I sing "Sunset Regions" with the same exultant spirit. "O'er the hills in legions, boys," no longer meant sunlit savannahs, flower meadows and deer-filled glades. The mingled "wood and prairie land" of the song was gone and Uncle Sam's domain, bleak, semi-arid, and wind-swept, offered little charm to my imagination. From that little cabin on the ridge I turned my face toward settlement, eager to escape the terror and the loneliness of the treeless sod. I began to plan for other work in other airs.

Furthermore, I resented the conditions under which my mother lived and worked. Our home was in a small building next to the shop, and had all the short-comings of a cabin and none of its charm. It is true nearly all our friends lived in equal discomfort, but it seemed to me that mother had earned something better. Was it for this she had left her home in Iowa? Was she never to enjoy a roomy and comfortable dwelling?

She did not complain and she seldom showed her sense of discomfort. I knew that she longed for the friends and neighbors she had left behind, and yet so far from being able to help her I was even then planning to leave her.

In a sullen rage I endured the winter and when at last the sun began to ride the sky with fervor and the prairie cock announced the spring, hope of an abundant crop, the promise of a new railroad, the incoming of jocund settlers created in each of us a confidence which expressed itself in a return to the land. With that marvellous faith which marks the husbandmen, we went forth once more with the drill and the harrow, planting seed against another harvest.

Sometime during these winter days, I chanced upon a book which effected a profound change in my outlook on the world and led to far-reaching complications in my life. This volume was the Lovell edition of *Progress and Poverty* which was at that time engaging the attention of the political economists of the world.

Up to this moment I had never read any book or essay in which our land system had been questioned. I had been raised in the belief that this was the best of all nations in the best of all possible worlds, in the happiest of all ages. I believed (of course) that the wisdom of those who formulated our constitution was but little less than that of archangels, and that all contingencies of our progress in government had been provided for or anticipated in that inspired and deathless instrument.

Now as I read this book, my mind following step by step the author's advance upon the citadel of privilege, I was forced to admit that his main thesis was right. Unrestricted individual ownership of the earth I acknowledged to be wrong and I caught some glimpse of the radiant plenty of George's ideal Commonwealth. The trumpet call of the closing pages filled me with a desire to battle for the right. Here was a theme for the great orator. Here was opportunity for the most devoted evangel.

Raw as I was, inconspicuous as a grasshopper by the roadside, I still had something in me which responded to the call of "the prophet of San Francisco," and yet I had no definite intention of becoming a missionary. How could I?

Penniless, dependent upon the labor of my hands for a livelihood, discontented yet unable to decide upon a plan of action, I came and went all through that long summer with laggard feet and sorrowful countenance.

My brother Franklin having sold his claim had boldly advanced upon Chicago. His ability as a book-keeper secured him against want, and his letters were confident and cheerful.

At last in the hour when my perplexity was greatest—the decisive impetus came, brought by a chance visitor, a young clergyman from Portland, Maine, who arrived in the town to buy some farms for himself and a friend. Though a native of Madison Mr. Bashford had won a place in the east and had decided to put some part of his salary into Dakota's alluring soil. Upon hearing that we were also from Wisconsin he came to call and stayed to dinner, and being of a jovial and candid nature soon drew from me a fairly coherent statement of my desire to do something in the world.

At the end of a long talk he said, "Why don't you come to Boston and take a special course at the University? I know the Professor of Literature, and I can also give you a letter to the principal of a school of Oratory."

This offer threw me into such excitement that I was unable to properly thank my adviser, but I fell into depths of dejection as soon as he left town. "How can I go east? How can I carry out such a plan?" I asked myself with bitter emphasis.

All I had in the world was a small trunk, a couple of dozen books, a valise and a few acres of barren unplowed land. My previous visit to Boston was just the sort to tempt me to return, but my experiences as a laborer in New England had lessened my confidence in its resources—and yet the thought of being able to cross the Common every day opened a dazzling vista. The very fact that Mr. Bashford had gone there from the west as a student, a poor student, made the prodigiously daring step seem possible to me. "If only I had a couple of hundred dollars," I said to my mother who listened to my delirious words in silence. She divined what was surging in my heart and feared it.

Thereafter I walked the floor of my room or wandered the prairie roads in continual debate. "What is there for me to do out here?" I demanded. "I can farm on these windy dusty acres—that's all. I am a failure as a merchant and I am sick of the country."

There were moments of a morning or at sunset when the plain was splendid as a tranquil sea, and in such moments I bowed down before its mysterious beauty—but for the most part it seemed an empty, desolate, mocking world. The harvest was again light and the earth shrunk and seamed for lack of moisture.

A hint of winter in the autumn air made me remember the remorseless winds and the iron earth over which the snows swept as if across an icy polar sea. I shuddered as I thought of again fighting my way to that desolate little cabin in McPherson County. I recalled but dimly the exultation with which I had made my claim. Boston, by contrast, glowed with beauty, with romance, with history, with glory like the vision of some turretted town built in the eastern sky at sunset.

"I'll do it," I said at last. "I'll sell my claim. I'll go east. I'll find some little hole to creep into. I'll study night and day and so fit myself for teaching, then I'll come back west to Illinois or Wisconsin. Never will I return to this bleak world."

I offered my claim for sale and while I continued my daily labor on the farm, my mind was faraway amid the imagined splendors of the east.

My father was puzzled and a good deal irritated by his son's dark moods. My failure to fit into the store was unaccountable and unreasonable. "To my thinking," said he, "you have all the school you need. You ought to find it easy to make a living in a new, progressive community like this."

To him, a son who wanted to go east was temporarily demented. It was an absurd plan. "Why, it's against the drift of things. You can't make a living back east. Hang onto your land and you'll come out all right. The place for a young man is in the west."

Bitter and rebellious of mood, uneasy and uncertain of purpose my talks with him resulted only in irritation and discord, but my mother, with an abiding faith in my powers, offered no objection. She could not advise, it was all so far above and beyond her, but she patted my hand and said, "Cheer up! I'm sure it will come out all right. I hate to have you go, but I guess Mr. Bashford is right. You need more schooling."

I could see that she was saddened by the thought of the separation which was to follow—with a vague knowledge of the experience of all the mothers of pioneer sons she feared that the days of our close companionship were ended. The detachment was not for a few months, it was final. Her face was very wistful and her voice tremulous as she told me to go.

"It is hard for me to leave you and sister," I replied, "but I must. I'm only rotting here. I'll come back—at least to visit you."

In tremendous excitement I mortgaged my claim for two hundred dollars and with that in my hand, started for the land of Emerson, Longfellow, and Hawthorne, believing that I was in truth reversing all the laws of development, breasting the current of progress, stemming the tide of emigration. All about me other young men were streaming toward the sunset, pushing westward to escape the pressure of the earth-lords behind, whilst I alone and poor, was daring all the dangers, all the difficulties from which they were so eagerly escaping.

There was in my heart an illogical exaltation as though I too were about to escape something—and yet when the actual moment of parting came, I embraced my sorrowing mother, and kissed my quaint little sister good-bye without feeling in the least heroic or self-confident. At the moment sadness weakened me, reducing me to boyish timidity.

26

On to Boston

With plenty of time to think, I thought, crouched low in my seat silent as an owl. True, I dozed off now and again but even when shortened by these periods of forgetfulness, the journey seemed interminable and when I reached the grimy old shed of a station which was the Chicago terminal of the Northwestern in those days, I was glad of a chance to taste outside air, no matter how smoky it reported itself to be.

My brother, who was working in the office of a weekly farm journal, met me with an air of calm superiority. He had become a true Chicagoan. Under his confident leadership I soon found a boarding place and a measure of repose. I must have stayed with him for several days for I recall being hypnotized into ordering a twenty-dollar tailor-made suit from a South Clark street merchant—you know the kind. It was a "Prince Albert Soot"—my first made-to-order outfit, but the extravagance seemed justified in face of the known elegance of man's apparel in Boston.

It took me thirty-six hours more to get to Boston, and as I was ill all the way (I again rode in the smoking car) a less triumphant Jason never entered the City of Light and Learning. The day was a true November day, dark and rainy and cold, and when I confronted my cloud-built city of domes and towers I was concerned only with a place to sleep—I had little desire of battle and no remembrance of the Golden Fleece.

Up from the Hoosac Station and over the slimy, greasy pavement I trod with humped back, carrying my heavy valise (it was the same imitation-leather concern with which I had toured the city two years before), while gay little street cars tinkled by, so close to my shoulder that I could have touched them with my hand.

Again I found my way through Haymarket Square to Tremont street and so at last to the Common, which presented a cold and dismal face at this time. The glory of my dream had fled. The trees, bare and brown and dripping with rain, offered no shelter. The benches were sodden, the paths muddy, and the sky, lost in a desolate mist shut down over my head with oppressive weight. I crawled along the muddy walk feeling about as important as a belated beetle in a July thunderstorm. Half of me was ready to surrender and go home on the next train but the other half, the obstinate half, sullenly forged ahead, busy with the problem of a roof and bed.

My experience in Rock River now stood me in good hand. Stopping a policeman I asked the way to the Young Men's Christian Association. The officer pointed out a small tower not far away, and down the Tremont street walk I plodded as wretched a youth as one would care to see.

Humbled, apologetic, I climbed the stairway, approached the desk, and in a weak voice requested the address of a cheap lodging place.

From the cards which the clerk carelessly handed to me I selected the nearest address, which chanced to be on Boylston Place, a short narrow street just beyond the Public Library. It was a deplorably wet and gloomy alley, but I ventured down its narrow walk and desperately knocked on the door of No. 12.

A handsome elderly woman with snow-white hair met me at the threshold. She looked entirely respectable, and as she named a price which I could afford to pay I accepted her invitation to enter. The house swarmed with life. Somebody was strumming a banjo, a girl was singing, and as I mounted the stair to the first floor, a slim little maid of about fourteen met us. "This is my daughter Fay," said the landlady with manifest pride.

Left to myself I sank into a chair with such relief as only the poor homeless country boy knows when at the end of a long tramp from the station, he lets slip his handbag and looks around upon a room for which he has paid. It was a plain little chamber, but it meant shelter and sleep and I was grateful. I went to bed early.

I slept soundly and the world to which I awoke was new and resplendent. My headache was gone, and as I left the house in search of breakfast I found the sun shining.

Just around the corner on Tremont street I discovered a little old man who from a side-walk booth, sold delicious coffee in cups of two sizes,—one at three cents and a larger one at five cents. He also offered doughnuts at a penny each.

Having breakfasted at an outlay of exactly eight cents I returned to my chamber, which was a hall-room, eight feet by ten, and faced the north. It was heated (theoretically) from a register in the floor, and there was just space enough for my trunk, a cot and a small table at the window but as it cost only six dollars per month I was content. I figured that I could live on five dollars per week which would enable me to stay till spring. I had about one hundred and thirty dollars in my purse.

From this sunless nook, this narrow niche, I began my study of Boston, whose historic significance quite overpowered me. I was alone. Mr. Bashford, in Portland, Maine, was the only person in all the east on whom I could call for aid or advice in case of sickness. My father wrote me that he had relatives living in the city but I did not know how to find them. No one could have been more absolutely alone than I during that first month. I made no acquaintances, I spoke to no one.

A part of each day was spent in studying the historical monuments of the city, and the remaining time was given to reading at the Young Men's Union or in the Public Library, which stood next door to my lodging house.

At night I made detailed studies of the habits of the cockroaches with which my room was peopled. There was something uncanny in the action of these beasts. They were new to me and apparently my like had never before been observed by them. They belonged to the shadow, to the cold and to the damp of the city, whereas I was fresh from the sunlight of the plain, and as I watched them peering out from behind my wash-basin, they appeared to marvel at me and to confer on my case with almost elfish intelligence.

Tantalized by an occasional feeble and vacillating current of warm air from the register, I was forced at times to wear my overcoat as I read, and at night I spread it over my cot. I did not see the sun for a month. The wind was always filled with rain or sleet, and as the lights in Bates' Hall were almost always blazing, I could hardly tell when day left off and night began. It seemed as if I had been plunged into another and darker world, a world of storm, of gray clouds, of endless cold.

Having resolved to keep all my expenses within five dollars per week, I laid down a scientific plan for cheap living. I first nosed out every low-priced eating place within ten minutes walk of my lodging and soon knew which of these "joints" were wholesome, and which were not. Just around the corner was a place where a filling dinner could be procured for fifteen cents, including pudding, and the little lunch counter on Tremont street supplied my breakfast. Not one nickel did I spend in carfare, and yet I saw almost every celebrated building in the city. However, I tenderly regarded my shoe soles each night, for the cost of tapping was enormous.

My notion of studying at some school was never carried out. The Boston University classes did not attract me. The Harvard lectures were inaccessible, and my call upon the teacher of "Expression" to whom Mr. Bashford had given me a letter led to nothing. The professor was a nervous person and made the mistake of assuming that I was as timid as I was silent. His manner irritated me and the outburst of my resentment was astonishing to him. I was hungry at the moment and to be patronized was too much!

This encounter plunged me into deep discouragement and I went back to my reading in the library with a despairing resolution to improve every moment, for my stay in the east could not last many weeks. At the rate my money was going May would see me bankrupt.

I read both day and night, grappling with Darwin, Spencer, Fiske, Helmholtz, Haeckel,—all the mighty masters of evolution whose books I had not hitherto been able to open. For diversion I dived into early English poetry and weltered in that sea of song which marks the beginnings of every literature, conning the ballads of Ireland and Wales, the epics of Ireland, the early German and the songs of the troubadours, a course of reading which started me on a series of lectures to be written directly from a study of the authors themselves. This dimly took shape as a volume to be called *The Development of English Ideals,* a sufficiently ambitious project.

Among other proscribed books I read Whitman's *Leaves of Grass* and without doubt that volume changed the world for me as it did for many others. Its rhythmic chants, its wonderful music filled me with a keen sense of the mystery of the near at hand. I rose from that first reading with a sense of having been taken up into high places. The spiritual significance of America was let loose upon me.

Herbert Spencer remained my philosopher and master. With eager haste I sought to compass the "Synthetic Philosophy." The universe took on order and harmony as, from my five cent breakfast, I went directly to the consideration of Spencer's theory of the evolution of music or painting or sculpture. It was thrilling, it was joyful to perceive that everything moved from the simple to the complex—how the bow-string became the harp, and the egg the chicken. My mental diaphragm creaked with the pressure of inrushing ideas. My brain young, sensitive to every touch, took hold of facts and theories like a phonographic cylinder, and while my body softened and my muscles wasted from disuse, I skittered from pole to pole of the intellectual universe like an impatient bat. I learned a little of everything and nothing very thoroughly. With so many peaks in sight, I had no time to spend on digging up the valley soil.

My only exercise was an occasional slow walk. I could not afford to waste my food in physical effort, and besides I was thinly dressed and could not go out except when the sun shone. My overcoat was considerably more than half cotton and a poor shield against the bitter wind which drove straight from the arctic sea into my bones. Even when the weather was mild, the crossings were nearly always ankle deep in slush, and walking was anything but a pleasure, therefore it happened that for days I took no outing whatsoever. From my meals I returned to my table in the library and read until closing time, conserving in every way my thirty cents' worth of "food units."

In this way I covered a wide literary and scientific territory. Humped over my fitful register I discussed the Nebular Hypothesis. My poets and scientists not merely told me of things I had never known, they confirmed me in certain conceptions which had come to me without effort in the past. I became an evolutionist in the fullest sense, accepting Spencer as the greatest living thinker. Fiske and Galton and Allen were merely assistants to the

Master Mind whose generalizations included in their circles all modern discovery.

It was a sad change when, leaving the brilliant reading room where my mind had been in contact with these masters of scientific world, I crept back to my minute den, there to sit humped and shivering (my overcoat thrown over my shoulders) confronting with scared resentment the sure wasting of my little store of dollars. In spite of all my care, the pennies departed from my pockets like grains of sand from an hour-glass and most disheartening of all I was making no apparent gain toward fitting myself for employment in the west.

Furthermore, the greatness, the significance, the beauty of Boston was growing upon me. I felt the neighboring presence of its autocrats more definitely and powerfully each day. Their names filled the daily papers, their comings and goings were carefully noted. William Dean Howells, Oliver Wendell Holmes, John G. Whittier, Edwin Booth, James Russell Lowell, all these towering personalities seemed very near to me now, and their presence, even if I never saw their faces, was an inspiration to one who had definitely decided to compose essays and poems, and to write possibly a history of American Literature. Symphony concerts, the Lowell Institute Lectures, the *Atlantic Monthly*—(all the distinctive institutions of the Hub) had become very precious to me notwithstanding the fact that I had little actual share in them. Their nearness while making my poverty more bitter, aroused in me a vague ambition to succeed—in something. "I won't be beaten, I will not surrender," I said.

Being neither a resident of the city nor a pupil of any school I could not take books from the library and this inhibition wore upon me till at last I determined to seek the aid of Edward Everett Hale who had long been a great and gracious figure in my mind. His name had been among the "Authors" of our rainy-day game on the farm. I had read his books, and I had heard him preach and as his "Lend-a-hand" helpfulness was proverbial, I resolved to call upon him at his study in the church, and ask his advice. I was not very definite as to what I expected him to do, probably I hoped for sympathy in some form.

The old man received me with kindness, but with a look of

weariness which I quickly understood. Accustomed to helping people he considered me just another "Case." With hesitation I explained my difficulty about taking out books.

With a bluff roar he exclaimed, "Well, well! That is strange! Have you spoken to the Librarian about it?"

"I have, Dr. Hale, but he told me there were twenty thousand young students in the city in precisely my condition. People not residents and with no one to vouch for them cannot take books home."

"I don't like that," he said. "I will look into that. You shall be provided for. Present my card to Judge Chamberlain; I am one of the trustees, and he will see that you have all the books you want." I thanked him and withdrew, feeling that I had gained a point. I presented the card to the librarian whose manner softened at once. As a protégé of Dr. Hale I was distinguished. "I will see what can be done for you," said Judge Chamberlain. Thereafter I was able to take books to my room, a habit which still further imperilled my health, for I read fourteen hours a day instead of ten.

Naturally I grew white and weak. My Dakota tan and my cornfed muscle melted away. The only part of me which flourished was my hair. I begrudged every quarter which went to the barbers and I was cold most of the time (except when I infested the library) and I was hungry *all* the time.

I knew that I was physically on the down-grade, but what could I do? Nothing except to cut down my expenses. I was living on less than five dollars a week, but even at that the end of my *stay* in the city was not far off. Hence I walked gingerly and read fiercely.

Bates' Hall was deliciously comfortable, and every day at nine o'clock I was at the door eager to enter. I spent most of my day at a desk in the big central reading room, but at night I haunted the Young Men's Union, thus adding myself to a dubious collection of half-demented, ill-clothed derelicts, who suffered the contempt of the attendants by reason of their filling all the chairs and monopolizing all the newspaper racks. We never conversed one with another and no one knew my name, but there came to be a certain diplomatic understanding amongst us somewhat as snakes, rabbits, hyenas, and turtles sometimes form "happy families."

There was one old ruffian who always sniffled and snuffled like a fat hog as he read, monopolizing my favorite newspaper. Another member of the circle perused the same page of the same book day after day, laughing vacuously over its contents. Never by any mistake did he call for a different book, and I never saw him turn a leaf. No doubt I was counted as one of this group of irresponsibles.

All this hurt me. I saw no humor in it then, for I was even at this time an intellectual aristocrat. I despised brainless folk. I hated these loafers. I loathed the clerk at the desk who dismissed me with a contemptuous smirk, and I resented the formal smile and impersonal politeness of Mr. Baldwin, the President. Of course I understood that the attendants knew nothing of my dreams and my ambitions, and that they were treating me quite as well as my looks warranted, but I blamed them just the same, furious at my own helplessness to demonstrate my claims for higher honors.

During all this time the only woman I knew was my landlady, Mrs. Davis, and her daughter Fay. Once a week I curtly said, "Here is your rent, Mrs. Davis," and yet, several times she asked with concern, "How are you feeling?—You don't look well. Why don't you board with me? I can feed you quite as cheaply as you can board yourself."

It is probable that she read slow starvation in my face, but I haughtily answered, "Thank you, I prefer to take my meals out." As a matter of fact, I dreaded contact with the other boarders.

As a member of the Union a certain number of lectures were open to me and so night by night, in company with my fellow "nuts," I called for my ticket and took my place in line at the door, like a charity patient at a hospital. However, as I seldom occupied a seat to the exclusion of anyone else and as my presence usually helped to keep the speaker in countenance, I had no qualms.

The Union audience was notoriously the worst audience in Boston, being in truth a group of intellectual mendicants waiting for oratorical hand-me-outs. If we didn't happen to like the sandwiches or the dry doughnuts given us, we threw them down and walked away.

Nevertheless in this hall I heard nearly all the great preachers of the city, and though some of their cant phrases worried me, I was benefited by the literary allusions of others. Carpenter retained nothing of the old-fashioned theology, and Hale was always a delight—so was Minot Savage. Dr. Bartol, a quaint absorbing survival of the Concord School of Philosophy, came once, and I often went to his Sunday service. It was always joy to enter the old West Meeting House for it remained almost precisely as it was in Revolutionary days. Its pews, its curtains, its footstools, its pulpit, were all deliciously suggestive of the time when stately elms looked in at the window, and when the minister, tall, white-haired, black-cravatted arose in the high pulpit and began to read with curious, sing-song cadences a chant from *Job* I easily imagined myself listening to Ralph Waldo Emerson.

His sermons held no cheap phrases and his sentences delighted me by their neat literary grace. Once in an address on Grant he said, "He was an atmospheric man. He developed from the war-cloud like a bolt of lightning."

Perhaps Minot Savage pleased me best of all for he too was a disciple of Spencer, a logical, consistent, and fearless evolutionist. He often quoted from the poets in his sermon. Once he read Whitman's "Song of Myself" with such power, such sense of rhythm that his congregation broke into applause at the end. I heard also (at Tremont temple and elsewhere) men like George William Curtis, Henry Ward Beecher, and Frederick Douglas, but greatest of all in a certain sense was the influence of Edwin Booth who taught me the greatness of Shakespeare and the glory of English speech.

Poor as I was, I visited the old Museum night after night, paying thirty-five cents which admitted me to a standing place in the first balcony, and there on my feet and in complete absorption, I saw in wondrous procession *Hamlet, Lear, Othello, Petruchio, Sir Giles Overreach, Macbeth, Iago,* and *Richelieu* emerge from the shadow and re-enact their tragic lives before my eyes. These were my purple, splendid hours. From the light of this glorious mimic world I stumbled down the stairs out into the night, careless of wind or snow, my brain in a tumult of revolt, my soul surging with high resolves.

The stimulation of these performances was very great The art of this "Prince of Tragedy" was a powerful educational influence along the lines of oratory, poetry and the drama. He expressed to me the soul of English Literature. He exemplified the music of English speech. His acting was at once painting and sculpture and music and I became still more economical of food in order that I might the more often bask in the golden atmosphere of his world. I said, "I, too, will help to make the dead lines of the great poets speak to the living people of today," and with new fervor bent to the study of oratory as the handmaid of poetry.

The boys who acted as ushers in the balcony came at length to know me, and sometimes when it happened that some unlucky suburbanite was forced to leave his seat near the railing, one of the lads would nod at me and allow me to slip down and take the empty place.

In this way I got closer to the marvellous lines of the actor's face, and was enabled to read and record the subtler, fleeter shadows of his expression. I have never looked upon a face with such transcendent power of externalizing and differentiating emotions, and I have never heard a voice of equal beauty and majesty.

Booth taught millions of Americans the dignity, the power and the music of the English tongue. He set a high mark in grace and precision of gesture, and the mysterious force of his essentially tragic spirit made so deep an impression upon those who heard him that they confused him with the characters he portrayed. As for me—I could not sleep for hours after leaving the theater.

Line by line I made mental note of the actor's gestures, accents, and cadences and afterward wrote them carefully down. As I closed my eyes for sleep I could hear that solemn chant *"Duncan is in his grave. After life's fitful fever he sleeps well."* With horror and admiration I recalled him, when as *Sir Giles,* with palsied hand helpless by his side, his face distorted, he muttered as if to himself, "Some undone widow sits upon my sword," or when as *Petruchio* in making a playful snatch at Kate's hand with the blaze of a lion's anger in his eye his voice rang out, "Were it the paw of an angry bear, I'd smite it off—but as it's Kate's I kiss it."

To the boy from the cabin on the Dakota plain these stage pictures were of almost incommunicable beauty and significance. They justified me in all my daring. They made any suffering past, present, or future, worth while, and the knowledge that these glories were evanescent and that I must soon return to the Dakota plain only deepened their power and added to the grandeur of every scene.

Booth's home at this time was on Beacon Hill, and I used to walk reverently by just to see where the great man housed. Once, the door being open, I caught a momentary glimpse of a curiously ornate umbrella stand, and the soft glow of a distant lamp, and the vision greatly enriched me. This singularly endowed artist presented to me the radiant summit of human happiness and glory, and to see him walk in or out of his door was my silent hope, but alas, this felicity was denied me!

Under the spell of these performers, I wrote a series of studies of the tragedian in his greatest roles. "Edwin Booth as Lear," "Edwin Booth as Hamlet," and so on, recording with minutest fidelity every gesture, every accent, till four of these impersonations were preserved on the page as if in amber. I re-read my Shakespeare in the light of Booth's eyes, in the sound of his magic voice, and when the season ended, the city grew dark, doubly dark for me. Thereafter I lived in the fading glory of that month.

These were growing days! I had moments of tremendous expansion, hours when my mind went out over the earth like a freed eagle, but these flights were always succeeded by fits of depression as I realized my weakness and my poverty. Nevertheless I persisted in my studies.

Under the influence of Spencer I traced a parallel development of the Arts and found a measure of scientific peace. Under the inspiration of Whitman I pondered the significance of democracy and caught some part of its spiritual import. With Henry George as guide, I discovered the main cause of poverty and suffering in the world, and so in my little room, living on forty cents a day, I was in a sense profoundly happy. So long as I had a dollar and a half with which to pay my rent and two dollars for the keepers of the various dives in which I secured my food, I was imaginatively the equal of Booth and brother to the kings of song.

And yet one stern persistent fact remained, my money was passing and I was growing weaker and paler every day. The cockroaches no longer amused me. Coming as I did from a land where the sky made up half the world I resented being thus condemned to a nook from which I could see only a gray rag of mist hanging above a neighboring chimney.

In the moments when I closely confronted my situation the glory of the western sky came back to me, and it must have been during one of these dreary storms that I began to write a poor faltering little story which told of the adventures of a cattleman in the city. No doubt it was the expression of the homesickness at my own heart but only one or two of the chapters ever took shape, for

I was tortured by the feeling that no matter how great the intellectual advancement caused by hearing Edwin Booth in *Hamlet* might be, it would avail me nothing when confronted by the school committee of Blankville, Illinois.

I had moments of being troubled and uneasy and at times experienced a feeling that was almost despair.

27

Enter a Friend

One night seeing that the principal of a well known School of Oratory was bulletined to lecture at the Young Men's Union upon "The Philosophy of Expression" I went to hear him, more by way of routine than with any expectation of being enlightened or even interested, but his very first words surprised and delighted me. His tone was positive, his phrases epigrammatic, and I applauded heartily. "Here is a man of thought," I said.

At the close of the address I ventured to the platform and expressed to him my interest in what he had said. He was a large man with a broad and smiling face, framed in a brown beard. He appeared pleased with my compliments and asked if I were a resident of Boston. "No, I am a western man," I replied. "I am here to study and I was especially interested in your quotations from Darwin's book on *Expression in Man and Animals.*"

His eyes expressed surprise and after a few minutes' conversation, he gave me his card saying, "Come and see me to-morrow morning at my office."

I went home pleasantly excited by this encounter. After months of unbroken solitude in the midst of throngs of strangers, this man's cordial invitation meant much to me.

On the following morning, at the hour set, I called at the door of his office on the top floor of No. 7 Beacon Street, which was an old-fashioned one-story building without an elevator.

Brown asked me where I came from, what my plans were, and I replied with eager confidence. Then we grew harmoniously enthusiastic over Herbert Spencer and Darwin and Mantegazza and I talked a stream! My long silence found vent. Words poured from me in a torrent but he listened smilingly, his big head cocked on one side, waiting patiently for me to blow off steam. Later, when given a chance, he showed me the manuscript of a book upon which he was at work and together we discussed its main thesis.

He asked me my opinion of this passage and that—and I replied, not as a pupil but as an equal, and the author seemed pleased at my candor.

Two hours passed swiftly in this way and as the interview was about to end he asked, "Where do you live?"

I told him and explained that I was trying to fit myself for teaching and that I was living as cheaply as possible. "I haven't any money for tuition," I confessed.

He mused a moment, then said, "If you wish to come into my school I shall be glad to have you do so. Never mind about tuition,—pay me when you can."

This generous offer sent me away filled with gratitude and an illogical hope. Not only had I gained a friend, I had found an intellectual comrade, one who was far more widely read, at least in science, than I. I went to my ten-cent lunch with a feeling that a door had unexpectedly opened and that it led into broader, sunnier fields of toil.

The school, which consisted of several plain offices and a large class-room, was attended by some seventy or eighty pupils, mostly girls from New England and Canada with a few from Indiana and Ohio. It was a simple little work-shop but to me it was the most important institution in Boston. It gave me welcome, and as I came into it on Monday morning at nine o'clock and was introduced to the pretty teacher of Delsarte, Miss Maida Craigen, whose smiling lips and big Irish-gray eyes made her beloved of all her pupils, I felt that my lonely life in Boston was ended.

The teachers met me with formal kindliness, finding in me only another crude lump to be moulded into form, and while I did not blame them for it, I instantly drew inside my shell and remained there—thus robbing myself of much that would have done me good. Some of the girls went out of their way to be nice to me, but I kept aloof, filled with a savage resentment of my poverty and my threadbare clothing.

Before the week was over, Professor Brown asked me to assist in reading the proof-sheets of his new book and this I did, going over it with him line by line. His deference to my judgment was a sincere compliment to my reading and warmed my heart like some elixir. It was my first authoritative appreciation and when at the end of the third session he said, "I shall consider your criticism more than equal to the sum of your tuition," I began to faintly forecast the time when my brain would make me self-supporting.

My days were now cheerful. My life had direction. For two hours each afternoon (when work in the school was over) I sat with Brown discussing the laws of dramatic art, and to make myself still more valuable in this work, I read every listed book or article upon expression, and translated several French authorities, transcribing them in longhand for his use.

In this work the weeks went by and spring approached. In a certain sense I felt that I was gaining an education which would be of value to me but I was not earning one cent of money, and my out-go was more than five dollars per week, for I occasionally went to the theater, and I had also begun attendance at the Boston Symphony concerts in Music Hall.

By paying twenty-five cents students were allowed to fill the gallery and to stand on the ground floor, and Friday afternoons generally found me leaning against the wall listening to Brahms and Wagner. At such times I often thought of my mother, and my uncle David and wished that they too might hear these wondrous harmonies. I tried to imagine what the effect of this tumult of sound would be, as it beat in upon their inherited deeply musical brain-cells!

One by one I caught up the threads of certain other peculiar Boston interests, and by careful reading of the *Transcript* was enabled to vibrate in full harmony with the local hymn of gratitude. New York became a mere emporium, a town without a library, a city without a first class orchestra, the home of a few commercial painters and several journalistic poets! Chicago was a huge dirty town on the middle border. Washington a vulgar political camp—only Philadelphia was admitted to have the quality of a real city and her literary and artistic resources were pitiably slender and failing!

But all the time that I was feasting on these insubstantial glories, my meat was being cut down and my coat hung ever more loosely over my ribs. Pale and languid I longed for spring, for sunshine, with all the passion of a prisoner, and when at last the grass began to show green in the sheltered places on the Common and the sparrows began to utter their love notes, I went often of an afternoon to a bench in lee of a clump of trees and there sprawled out like a debilitated fox, basking in the tepid rays of a diminished sun.

For all his expressed admiration of my literary and scientific acumen, Brown did not see fit to invite me to dinner, probably because of my rusty suit and frayed cuffs. I did not blame him. I was in truth a shabby figure, and the dark-brown beard which had come upon me added to the unhealthy pallor of my skin, so that Mrs. Brown, a rather smart and socially ambitious lady, must have regarded me as something of an anarchist, a person to avoid. She always smiled as we met, but her smile was defensive.

However, a blessed break in the monotony of my fare came during April when my friend Bashford invited me to visit him in Portland. I accepted his invitation with naive precipitation and furbished up my wardrobe as best I could, feeling that even the wife of a clergyman might not welcome a visitor with fringed cuffs and celluloid collars.

This was my first sea voyage and I greatly enjoyed the trip—after I got there!

Mrs. Bashford received me kindly, but (I imagined) with a trace of official hospitality in her greeting. It was plain that she (like Mrs. Brown) considered me a "Charity Patient." Well, no matter, Bashford and I got on smoothly.

Their house was large and its grandeur was almost oppressive to me, but I spent nearly a week in it. As I was leaving, Bashford gave me a card to Dr. Cross, a former parishioner in Jamaica Plain, saying, "Call upon the Doctor as soon as you return. He'll be glad to hear of Dakota."

My little den in Boylston Place was almost intolerable to me now. Spring sunshine, real sunshine flooded the land and my heart was full of longing for the country. Therefore—though I dreaded meeting another stranger,—I decided to risk a dime and make the trip to Jamaica Plains, to call upon Dr. Cross.

This ride was a further revelation of the beauty of New England. For half an hour the little horse-car ran along winding lanes under great overarching elm trees, past apple-orchards in bursting bloom. On every hand luscious lawns spread, filled with crocuses and dandelions just beginning to spangle the green. The effect upon me was somewhat like that which would be produced in the mind of a convict who should suddenly find his prison doors opening into a June meadow. Standing with the driver on the front platform, I drank deep of the flower-scented air. I had never seen anything more beautiful.

Dr. Cross, a sweet and gentle man of about sixty years of age (not unlike in manner and habit Professor Bush, my principal at the Cedar Valley Seminary) received his seedy visitor with a kindly smile. I liked him and trusted him at once. He was tall and very thin, with dark eyes and a long gray beard. His face was absolutely without suspicion or guile. It was impossible to conceive of his doing an unkind or hasty act, and he afterward said that I had the pallor of a man who had been living in a cellar. "I was genuinely alarmed about you," he said.

His small frame house was simple, but it stood in the midst of a clump of pear trees, and when I broke out in lyrical praise of the beauty of the grass and glory of the flowers, the doctor smiled and became even more distinctly friendly. It appeared that through Mr. Bashford he had purchased a farm in Dakota, and the fact that I knew all about it and all about wheat farming gave me distinction.

He introduced me to his wife, a wholesome hearty soul who invited me to dinner. I stayed. It was my first chance at a real meal since my visit to Portland, and I left the house with a full stomach, as well as a full heart, feeling that the world was not quite so unfriendly after all. "Come again on Sunday," the doctor almost commanded. "We shall expect you."

My money had now retired to the lower corner of my left-hand pocket and it was evident that unless I called upon my father for help I must go back to the West; and much as I loved to talk of the broad fields and pleasant streams of Dakota, I dreaded the approach of the hour when I must leave Boston, which was coming to mean more and more to me every day.

In a blind vague way I felt that to leave Boston was to leave all hope of a literary career and yet I saw no way of earning money in the city. In the stress of my need I thought of an old friend, a carpenter in Greenfield. "I'm sure he will give me a job," I said.

With this in mind I went into Professor Brown's office one morning and I said, "Well, Professor, I must leave you."

"What's that? What's the matter?" queried the principal shrilly.

"My money's gone. I've got to get out and earn more," I answered sadly.

He eyed me gravely. "What are you going to do?" he inquired.

"I am going back to shingling," I said with tragic accent.

"Shingling!" the old man exclaimed, and then began to laugh, his big paunch shaking up and down with the force of his mirth. "Shingling!" he shouted finally. "Can *you* shingle?"

"You bet I can," I replied with comical access of pride, "but I don't like to. That is to say I don't like to give up my work here in Boston just when I am beginning to feel at home."

Brown continued to chuckle. To hear that a man who knew Mantegazza and Darwin and Whitman and Browning could even *think* of shingling, was highly humorous, but as he studied my forlorn face he sensed the despairing quiver in my voice and his kind heart softened. He ceased to smile. "Oh, you mustn't do that," he said earnestly. "You mustn't surrender now. We'll fix up some way for you to earn your keep. Can't you borrow a little?"

"Yes, I could get a few dollars from home, but I don't feel justified in doing so,—times are hard out there and besides I see no way of repaying a loan."

He pondered a moment, "Well, now I'll tell you what we'll do. I'll make you our Instructor in Literature for the summer term and I'll put your Booth lecture on the programme. That will give you a start, and perhaps something else will develop for the autumn."

This noble offer so emboldened me that I sent west for twenty-five dollars to pay my board, and to have my suit dyed.—It was the very same suit I had bought of the Clark Street tailor, and the aniline purple had turned pink along the seams—or if not pink it was some other color equally noticeable in the raiment of a lecturer, and not to be endured. I also purchased a new pair of shoes and a necktie of the Windsor pattern. This cravat and my long Prince Albert frock, while not strictly in fashion, made me feel at least presentable.

Another piece of good fortune came to me soon after. Dr. Cross again invited me to dine and after dinner as we were driving together along one of the country lanes, the good doctor said, "Mrs. Cross is going up into New Hampshire for the summer and I shall be alone in the house. Why don't you come and stay with me? You need the open air, and I need company."

This generous offer nearly shipwrecked my dignity. Several moments passed before I could control my voice to thank him. At last

I said, "That's very kind of you, Doctor. I'll come if you will let me pay at least the cost of my board."

The Doctor understood this feeling and asked, "How much are you paying now? "

With slight evasion I replied, "Well, I try to keep within five dollars a week."

He smiled. "I don't see how you do it, but I can give you an attic room and you can pay me at your convenience."

This noble invitation translated me from my dark, cold, cramped den (with its night-guard of redoubtable cockroaches) into the light and air of a comfortable suburban home. It took me back to the sky and the birds and the grass—and Irish Mary, the cook, put red blood into my veins. In my sabbath walks along the beautiful country roads, I heard again the song of the cat-bird and the trill of the bobolink. For the first time in months I slept in freedom from hunger, in security of the morrow. Oh, good Hiram Cross, your golden crown should be studded with jewels, for your life was filled with kindnesses like this!

Meanwhile, in preparation for the summer term I gladly helped stamp and mail Brown's circulars. The lecture "Edwin Booth as Iago" I carefully re-wrote—for Brown had placed it on his printed programme and had also announced me as "Instructor in Literature." I took care to send this circular to all my friends and relatives in the west.

Decidedly that summer of Taine in a Dakota cabin was bearing fruit, and yet just in proportion as Brown came to believe in my ability so did he proceed to "hector" me. He never failed to ask of a morning, "Well, when are you going back to shingling?"

The Summer School opened in July. It was well attended, and the membership being made up of teachers of English and Oratory from several states was very impressive to me. Professors of elocution and of literature from well-known colleges and universities gave dignity and distinction to every session.

My class was very small and paid me very little but it brought me to know Mrs. Payne, a studious, kindly woman (a resident of Hyde Park), who for some reason which will forever remain obscure, considered me not merely a youth of promise, but a lecturer of value. Having heard from Brown how sadly I needed money—perhaps she even detected poverty in my dyed coat, she not only invited me to deliver an immediate course of lectures at her house in Hyde Park but proceeded to force tickets upon all her friends.

The importance of this engagement will appear when the reader is informed that I was owing the Doctor for a month's board, and saw no way of paying it, and that my one suit was distressingly threadbare. There are other and more interesting ways of getting famous but alas! I rose only by inches and incredible effort. My reader must be patient with me.

My subjects were ambitious enough, "The Art of Edwin Booth," was ready for delivery, but "Victor Hugo and his Prose Masterpieces," was only partly composed and "The Modern German Novel" and "The American Novel" were in notes merely, therefore with puckered brow and sturdy pen I set to work in my little attic room, and there I toiled day and night to put on paper the notions I had acquired concerning these grandiose subjects.

In after years I was appalled at the audacity of that schedule, and I think I had the grace to be scared at the time, but I swung into it recklessly. Tickets had been taken by some of the best known men among the teachers, and I was assured by Mrs. Payne that we would have the most distinguished audience that ever graced Hyde Park. "Among your listeners will be the literary editors of several Boston papers, two celebrated painters, and several well-known professors of oratory," she said, and like Lieutenant Napoleon called upon to demonstrate his powers, I graved with large and ruthless fist, and approached my opening date with palpitating but determined heart.

It was a tense moment for me as (while awaiting my introduction) I looked into the faces of the men and women seated in that crowded parlor. Just before the dais, shading his eyes with his hand, was a small man with a pale face and brown beard. This was Charles E. Hurd, literary editor of the *Transcript*. Near him sat Theodore Weld, as venerable in appearance as Socrates (with long white hair and rosy cheeks), well known as one of the anti-slavery guard, a close friend of Wendell Phillips and William Lloyd Garrison. Beside him was Professor Raymond of Princeton, the author of several books, while Churchill of Andover and half a dozen other representatives of great colleges loomed behind him. I faced them all with a gambler's composure but behind my mask I was jellied with fear.

However, when I rose to speak, the tremor passed out of my limbs, the blood came back to my brain, and I began without stammering. This first paper, fortunately for us all, dealt with Edwin Booth, whom I revered. To my mind he not only expressed the highest reach of dramatic art in his day, he was the best living interpreter of Shakespeare, and no doubt it was the sincerity of my utterance which held my hearers, for they all listened intently while I analyzed the character of *Iago,* and disclosed what seemed to me to be the sources of the great tragedian's power, and when I finished they applauded with unmistakable approval, and Mrs. Payne glowed with a sense of proprietorship in her protégé who had seized the opportunity and made it his. I was absurd but triumphant.

Many of the guests (kindly of spirit) came up to shake hands and congratulate me. Mr. Hurd gave me a close grip and said, "Come up to the *Transcript* office and see me." John J. Enneking, a big, awkward red-bearded painter, elbowed up and in his queer German way spoke in approval. Churchill, Raymond, both said, "You'll do," and Brown finally came along with a mocking smile on his big face, eyed me with an air of quizzical comradeship, nudged me slyly with his elbow as he went by, and said, "Going back to shingling, are you?"

On the homeward drive, Dr. Cross said very solemnly, "You have no need to fear the future."

It was a very small event in the history of Hyde Park, but it was a veritable bridge of Lodi for me. I never afterward felt lonely or disheartened in Boston. I had been tested both as teacher and orator and I must be pardoned for a sudden growth of boyish self-confidence.

The three lectures which followed were not so successful as the first, but my audience remained. Indeed I think it would have increased night by night had the room permitted it, and Mrs. Payne was still perfectly sure that her protégé had in him all the elements of success, but I fear Prof. Church expressed the sad truth when he said in writing, "Your man Garland is a diamond in the rough!" Of course I must have appeared very seedy and uncouth to these people and I am filled with wonder at their kindness to me. My accent was western. My coat sleeves shone at the elbows, my trousers bagged at the knees. Considering the anarch I must have been, I marvel at their toleration. No western audience could have been more hospitable, more cordial.

The ninety dollars which I gained from this series of lectures was, let me say, the less important part of my victory, and yet it was wondrous opportune. They enabled me to cancel my indebtedness to the Doctor, and still have a little something to keep me going until my classes began in October, and as my landlord did not actually evict me, I stayed on shamelessly, fattening visibly on the puddings and roasts which Mrs. Cross provided and dear old Mary cooked with joy. She was the true artist. She loved to see her work appreciated.

My class in English literature that term numbered twenty and the money which this brought carried me through till the midwinter vacation, and permitted another glorious season of Booth and the Symphony Orchestra. In the month of January I organized a class in American Literature, and so at last became self-supporting in the city of Boston! No one who has not been through it can realize the greatness of this victory.

I permitted myself a few improvements in hose and linen. I bought a leather hand-bag with a shoulder strap, and every day joined the stream of clerks and students crossing the Common. I began to feel a proprietary interest in the Hub. My sleeping room (also my study), continued to be in the attic (a true attic with a sloping roof and one window) but the window faced the south, and in it I did all my reading and writing. It was hot on sunny days and dark on cloudy days, but it was a refuge.

As a citizen with a known habitation I was permitted to carry away books from the library, and each morning from eight until half-past twelve I sat at my desk writing, tearing away at some lecture, or historical essay, and once in a while I composed a few lines of verse. Five afternoons in each week I went to my classes and to the library, returning at six o'clock to my dinner and to my reading. This was my routine, and I was happy in it.

My letters to my people in the west were confident, more confident than I ofttimes felt.

During my second summer Burton Babcock, who had decided to study for the Unitarian ministry, came east with intent to enter the Divinity School at Harvard. He was the same old Burton, painfully shy, thoughtful, quaintly abrupt in manner, and together we visited the authorities at Cambridge and presented his case as best we could.

For some reason not clear to either of us, the school refused to aid and after a week's stay with me Burton, a little disheartened but not resentful, went to Meadville, Pennsylvania. Boston seemed very wonderful to him and I enjoyed his visit keenly. We talked inevitably of old friends and old days in the manner of middle-aged men, and he told me that John Gammons had entered the Methodist ministry and was stationed in Decorah, that Charles, my former partner in Dakota, had returned to the old home very ill with some obscure disease. Mitchell Morrison was a watchmaker and jeweler in Winona and Lee Moss had gone to Superior. The scattering process had begun. The diverging wind-currents of destiny had already parted our little group and every year would see its members farther apart. How remote it all seems to me now,—like something experienced on another planet!

Each month saw me more and more the Bostonian by adoption. My teaching paid my board, leaving me free to study and to write. I never did any hack-work for the newspapers. Hawthorne's influence over me was still powerful, and in my first attempts at writing fiction I kept to the essay form and sought for a certain distinction in tone. In poetry, however, Bret Harte, Joaquin Miller, and Walt Whitman were more to my way of thinking than either Poe or Emerson. In brief I was sadly "mixed." Perhaps the enforced confinement of my city life gave all poems of the open air, of the prairies, their great and growing power over me for I had resolved to remain in Boston until such time as I could return to the West in the guise of a conqueror. Just what I was about to conquer and in what way I was to secure eminence was not very clear to me, but I was resolved none the less, and had no immediate intention of returning.

In the summer of 1886 Brown held another Summer School and again I taught a class. Autumn brought a larger success. Mrs. Lee started a Browning Class in Chelsea, and another loyal pupil organized a Shakespeare class in Waltham. I enjoyed my trips to these classes very much and one of the first stories I ever wrote was suggested by some characters I saw in an old grocery store in Waltham. As I recall my method of teaching, it consisted chiefly of readings. My critical comment could not have been profound.

I was earning now twelve dollars per week, part of this went for railway fare, but I still had a margin of profit. True I still wore reversible cuffs and carried my laundry bundles in order to secure the discount, but I dressed in better style and looked a little less like a starving Russian artist, and I was becoming an author!

My entrance into print came about through my good friend, Mr. Hurd, the book reviewer of the *Transcript.* For him I began to write an occasional critical article or poem just to try my hand. One of my regular "beats" was up the three long flights of stairs which led to Hurd's little den above Washington Street, for there I felt myself a little more of the literary man, a little nearer the current of American fiction.

Let me repeat my appreciation of the fact that I met with the quickest response and the most generous aid among the people of Boston. There was nothing cold or critical in their treatment of me. My success, admittedly, came from some sympathy in them rather than from any real deserving on my part. I cannot understand at this distance why those charming people should have consented to receive from me, opinions concerning anything whatsoever,—least of all notions of literature,—but they did, and they seemed delighted at "discovering" me. Perhaps they were surprised at finding so much intelligence in a man from the plains.

It was well that I was earning my own living at last, for things were not going especially well at home. A couple of dry seasons had made a great change in the fortunes of my people. Frank, with his usual careless good nature as clerk in the store had given credit to almost every comer, and as the hard times came on, many of those indebted failed to pay, and father was forced to give up his business and go back to the farm which he understood and could manage without the aid of an accountant.

"The Junior" as I called my brother, being footloose and discontented, wrote to say that he was planning to go farther west—to Montana, I think it was. His letter threw me into dismay. I acknowledged once again that my education had in a sense been bought at his expense. I recalled the many weeks when the little chap had plowed in my stead whilst I was enjoying the inspiration of Osage. It gave me distress to think of him separating himself from the family as David had done, and yet my own position was too insecure to warrant me promising much in his aid. Nevertheless, realizing that mother would suffer less if she knew her two sons were together, I wrote, saying, "If you have definitely decided on leaving home, don't go west. Come to Boston, and I will see if I cannot get you something to do."

It ended in his coming to Boston, and my mother was profoundly relieved. Father gave no sign either of pleasure or regret. He set to work once more increasing his acreage, vigorous and unsubdued.

Frank's coming added to my burden of responsibility and care, but increased my pleasure in the city, for I now had someone to show it to. He secured a position as an accountant in a railway office and though we seldom met during the week, on Sundays we roamed the parks, or took excursions down the bay, and in a short time he too became an enthusiastic Bostonian with no thought of returning to Dakota. Little Jessie was now the sole stay and comfort of our mother.

As I look back now upon the busy, happy days of 1885 and 1886, I can grasp only a few salient experiences.... A terrific storm is on the sea. We are at Nantasket to study it. The enormous waves are charging in from the illimitable sky like an army of horses, only to fall and waste themselves in wrath upon the sand. I feel the stinging blast against my face.... I am riding on a train over the marshes on my way to my class in Chelsea. I look across the level bay and behold a soaring banner of sunshot mist, spun by a passing engine, rising, floating, vanishing in the air.... I am sitting in an old grocery shop in Waltham listening to the quaint aphorism of a group of loafers around the stove.... I am lecturing before a summer school in Pepperel, New Hampshire.... I am at the theater, I hear Salvini thunderously clamoring on the stage. I see Modjeska's beautiful hands. I thrill to Sarah Bernhardt's velvet somber voice....

It is summer, Frank and I are walking the lovely lanes of Milton under gigantic elms, or lying on the grass of the park in West Roxbury, watching the wild birds come and go, hearing the sound of the scythestone in the meadow. Day by day, week by week, Boston, New England, comes to fuse that part of me which is eastern. I grow at last into thinking myself a fixture. Boston is the center of music, of art, of literature. My only wish now is to earn money enough to visit my people in the West.

And yet, notwithstanding all this, neither of us ever really became a Bostonian. We never got beyond a feeling for the beauty, the picturesqueness and the charm of our surroundings. The East caused me to cry out in admiration, but it did not inspire me to write. It did not appeal to me as my material. It was rather as a story already told, a song already sung.

When I walked a lane, or saw the sloping roof of a house set against a hillside I thought of Whittier or Hawthorne and was silent. The sea reminded me of Celia Thaxter or Lucy Larcom. The marshes brought up the *Wayside Inn* of Longfellow; all, all was of the past. New England, rich with its memories of great men and noble women, had no direct inspiration for me, a son of the West. It did not lay hold upon my creative imagination, neither did it inspire me to sing of its glory. I remained immutably of the Middle Border and strange to say, my desire to celebrate the West was growing.

Each season dropped a thickening veil of mist between me and the scenes of my youth, adding a poetic glamour to every rememberable form and fact. Each spring when the smell of fresh, uncovered earth returned to fret my nostrils I thought of the wide fields of Iowa, of the level plains of Dakota, and a desire to hear once more the prairie chicken calling from the ridges filled my heart. In the autumn when the wind swept through the bare branches of the elm, I thought of the lonely days of plowing on the prairie, and the poetry and significance of those wild gray days came over me with such power that I instinctively seized my pen to write of them.

One day, a man shoveling coal in the alley below my window reminded me of that peculiar ringing *scrape* which the farm shovel used to make when (on the Iowa farm) at dusk I scooped my load of corn from the wagon box to the crib, and straightway I fell a-dreaming, and from dreaming I came to composition, and so it happened that my first writing of any significance was an article depicting an Iowa corn-husking scene.

It was not merely a picture of the life my brother and I had lived,—it was an attempt to set forth a typical scene of the Middle Border. "The Farm Life of New England has been fully celebrated by means of innumerable stories and poems," I began, "its husking bees, its dances, its winter scenes are all on record; is it not time that we of the west should depict our own distinctive life? The middle border has its poetry, its beauty, if we can only see it."

To emphasize these differences I called this first article "The Western Corn Husking," and put into it the grim report of the man who had "been there," an insistence on the painful as well as the pleasant truth, a quality which was discovered afterwards to be characteristic of my work. The bitter truth was strongly developed in this first article.

Up to this time I had composed nothing except several more or less high-falutin' essays, a few poems and one or two stories somewhat in imitation of Hawthorne, but in this my first real shot at the delineation of prairie life, I had no models. Perhaps this clear field helped me to be true. It was not fiction, as I had no intention at that time of becoming a fictionist, but it was fact, for it included the mud and cold of the landscape as well as its bloom and charm.

I sent "The Corn Husking" to the *New American Magazine,* and almost by return mail the editor, William Wyckoff, wrote an inspiring letter to the effect that the life I had described was familiar to him, and that it had never been treated in this way. "I shall be very glad to read anything you have written or may write, and I suggest that you follow up this article by others of the same nature."

It was just the encouragement I needed. I fell to work at once upon other articles, taking up the seasons one by one. Wyckoff accepted them gladly, but paid for them slowly and meagerly—but I did not blame him for that. His magazine was even then struggling for life.

It must have been about this time that I sold to *Harper's Weekly* a long poem of the prairie, for which I was paid the enormous sum of twenty-five dollars. With this, the first money I ever had received for magazine writing, I hastened to purchase some silk for my mother, and the *Memoirs of General Grant* for my father, with intent to suitably record and celebrate my entrance into literature. For the first time in her life, my mother was able to wear a silk dress, and she wrote, soon after, a proud and grateful letter saying things which blurred my eyes and put a lump into my throat. If only I could have laid the silk in her lap, and caught the light of her happy smile!

28

A Visit to the West

At twenty-seven years of age, and after having been six years absent from Osage, the little town in which I went to school, I found myself able to re-visit it. My earnings were still humiliatingly less than those of a hod-carrier, but by shameless economy I had saved a little over one hundred dollars and with this as a travelling fund, I set forth at the close of school, on a vacation tour which was planned to include the old home in the Coulee, the Iowa farm, and my father's house in Dakota. I took passage in a first class coach this time, but was still a long way from buying a berth in a sleeping car.

To find myself actually on the train and speeding westward was deeply and pleasurably exciting, but I did not realize how keen my hunger for familiar things had grown, till the next day when I reached the level lands of Indiana. Every field of wheat, every broad hat, every honest treatment of the letter "r" gave me assurance that I was approaching my native place. The reapers at work in the fields filled my mind with visions of the past. The very weeds at the roadside had a magical appeal and yet, eager as I was to reach old friends, I found in Chicago a new friend whose sympathy was so stimulating, so helpful that I delayed my journey for two days in order that I might profit by his critical comment.

This meeting came about in a literary way. Some months earlier, in May, to be exact, Hurd of the *Transcript* had placed in my hands a novel called *Zury* and my review of it had drawn from its author, a western man, a letter of thanks and a cordial invitation to visit him as I passed through Chicago, on my way to my old home. This I had gladly accepted, and now with keen interest, I was on my way to his home.

Joseph Kirkland was at this time nearly sixty years of age, a small, alert, dark-eyed man, a lawyer, who lived in what seemed to me at the time, plutocratic grandeur, but in spite of all this, and notwithstanding the difference in our ages, I liked him and we formed an immediate friendship. "Mrs. Kirkland and my daughters are in Michigan for the summer," he explained, "and I am camping in my study." I was rather glad of this arrangement for, having the house entirely to ourselves, we could discuss realism, Howells and the land-question with full vigor and all night if we felt like it.

Kirkland had read some of my western sketches and in the midst of his praise of them suddenly asked, "Why don't you write fiction?"

To this I replied, "I can't manage the dialogue."

"Nonsense!" said he. "You're lazy, that's all. You use the narrative form because it's easier. Buckle to it—you can write stories as well as I can—but you must sweat!"

This so surprised me that I was unable to make any denial of his charge. The fact is he was right. To compose a page of conversation, wherein each actor uses his own accent and speaks from his own point of view, was not easy. I had dodged the hard spots.

The older man's bluntness and humor, and his almost wistful appreciation of my youth and capacity for being moved, troubled me, absorbed my mind even during our talk. Some of his words stuck like burrs, because they seemed so absurd. "When your name is known all over the West," he said in parting, "remember what I say. You can go far if you'll only work. I began too late. I can't emotionalize present day western life—you can, but you must bend to your desk like a man. You must grind!"

I didn't feel in the least like a successful fictionist and being a household word seemed very remote,—but I went away resolved to "grind" if grinding would do any good.

Once out of the city, I absorbed "atmosphere" like a sponge. It was with me no longer (as in New England) a question of warmed-over themes and appropriated characters. Whittier, Hawthorne, Holmes, had no connection with the rude life of these prairies. Each weedy field, each wire fence, the flat stretches of grass, the leaning Lombardy trees,—everything was significant rather than beautiful, familiar rather than picturesque.

Something deep and resonant vibrated within my brain as I looked out upon this monotonous commonplace landscape. I realized for the first time that the east had surfeited me with picturesqueness. It appeared that I had been living for six years amidst painted, neatly arranged pasteboard scenery. Now suddenly I dropped to the level of nature unadorned, down to the ugly unkempt lanes I knew so well, back to the pungent realities of the streamless plain.

Furthermore I acknowledged a certain responsibility for the conditions of the settlers. I felt related to them, an intolerant part of them. Once fairly out among the fields of northern Illinois everything became so homely, uttered itself so piercingly to me that nothing less than song could express my sense of joy, of power. This was my country—these my people.

It was the third of July, a beautiful day with a radiant sky, darkened now and again with sudden showers. Great clouds, trailing veils of rain, enveloped the engine as it roared straight into the west—for an instant all was dark, then forth we burst into the brilliant sunshine careening over the green ridges as if drawn by runaway dragons with breath of flame.

It was sundown when I crossed the Mississippi river (at Dubuque) and the scene which I looked out upon will forever remain a splendid page in my memory. The coaches lay under the western bluffs, but away to the south the valley ran, walled with royal purple, and directly across the flood, a beach of sand flamed under the sunset light as if it were a bed of pure untarnished gold. Behind this an island rose, covered with noble trees which suggested all the romance of the immemorial river. The redman's canoe, the explorer's batteau, the hunter's lodge, the emigrant's cabin, all stood related to that inspiring vista. For the first time in my life I longed to put this noble stream into verse.

All that day I had studied the land, musing upon its distinctive qualities, and while I acknowledged the natural beauty of it, I revolted from the gracelessness of its human habitations. The lonely box-like farmhouses on the ridges suddenly appeared to me like the dens of wild animals. The lack of color, of charm in the lives of the people anguished me. I wondered why I had never before perceived the futility of woman's life on a farm.

I asked myself, "Why have these stern facts never been put into our literature as they have been used in Russia and in England? Why has this land no storytellers like those who have made Massachusetts and New Hampshire illustrious?"

These and many other speculations buzzed in my brain. Each moment was a revelation of new uglinesses as well as of remembered beauties.

At four o'clock of a wet morning I arrived at Charles City, from which I was to take "the spur" for Osage. Stiffened and depressed by my night's ride, I stepped out upon the platform and watched the train as it passed on, leaving me, with two or three other silent and sleepy passengers, to wait until seven o'clock in the morning for the "accommodation train." I was still busy with my problem, but the salient angles of my interpretation were economic rather than literary.

Walking to and fro upon the platform, I continued to ponder my situation. In a few hours I would be among my old friends and companions, to measure and be measured. Six years before I had left them to seek my fortune in the eastern world. I had promised little,—fortunately—and I was returning, without the pot of gold and with only a tinge of glory.

Exteriorly I had nothing but a crop of sturdy whiskers to show for my years of exile but mentally I was much enriched. Twenty years of development lay between my thought at the moment and those of my simpler days. My study of Spencer, Whitman and other of the great leaders of the world, my years of absorbed reading in the library, my days of loneliness and hunger in the city had swept me into a far bleak land of philosophic doubt where even the most daring of my classmates would hesitate to follow me.

A violent perception of the mysterious, the irrevocable march of human life swept over me and I shivered before a sudden realization of the ceaseless change and shift of western life and landscape. How few of those I knew were there to greet me! Walter and Charles were dead, Maud and Lena were both married, and Burton was preaching somewhere in the West.

Six short years had made many changes in the little town and it was in thinking upon these changes that I reached a full realization of the fact that I was no longer a "promising boy" of the prairie but a man, with a notion of human life and duty and responsibility which was neither cheerful nor resigned. I was returning as from deep valleys, from the most alien climate.

Looking at the sky above me, feeling the rush of the earth beneath my feet I saw how much I had dared and how little, how pitifully little I had won. Over me the ragged rainclouds swept, obscuring the stars and in their movement and in the feeling of the dawn lay something illimitable and prophetic. Such moments do not come to men often—but to me for an hour, life was painfully purposeless. "What does it all mean?" I asked myself.

At last the train came, and as it rattled away to the north and I drew closer to the scenes of my boyhood, my memory quickened. The Cedar rippling over its limestone ledges, the gray old mill and the pond where I used to swim, the farmhouses with their weedy lawns, all seemed not only familiar but friendly, and when at last I reached the station (the same grimy little den from which I had started forth six years before), I rose from my seat with the air of a world-traveller and descended upon the warped and splintered platform, among my one time friends and neighbors, with quickened pulse and seeking eye.

It was the fourth of July and a crowd was at the station, but though I recognized half the faces, not one of them lightened at sight of me. The 'bus driver, the ragged old dray-man (scandalously profane), the common loafers shuffling about, chewing and spitting, seemed absolutely unchanged. One or two elderly citizens eyed me closely as I slung my little Boston valise with a long strap over my shoulder and started up the billowing board sidewalk toward the center of the town, but I gave out no word of recognition. Indeed I took a boyish pride in the disguising effect of my beard.

How small and flat and leisurely the village seemed! The buildings which had once been so imposing in my eyes were now of very moderate elevation indeed, and the opera house was almost indistinguishable from the two-story structures which flanked it; but the trees had increased in dignity, and some of the lawns were lovely.

With eyes singling out each familiar object I loitered along the walk. There stood the grimy wagon shop from which a hammer was ringing cheerily, like the chirp of a cricket,—just as aforetime. Orrin Blakey stood at the door of his lumber yard surveying me with curious eyes but I passed him in silence. I wished to spend an hour or two in going about in guise of a stranger. There was something instructive as well as deliciously exciting in thus seeing old acquaintances as from behind a mask. They were at once familiar and mysterious—mysterious with my new question, "Is this life worth living?"

The Merchants' Hotel which once appeared so luxurious (within the reach only of great lecturers like Joseph Cook and Wendell Phillips) had declined to a shabby frame tavern, but entering the dining room I selected a seat near an open window, from which I could look out upon the streets and survey the throng of thickening sightseers as they moved up and down before me like the figures in a vitascope.

I was waited upon by a slatternly girl and the breakfast she brought to me was so bad (after Mary's cooking) that I could only make a pretense of eating it, but I kept my seat, absorbed by the forms coming and going, almost within the reach of my hand. Among the first to pace slowly by was Lawyer Ricker, stately, solemn and bibulous as ever, his red beard flowing over a vest unbuttoned in the manner of the old-fashioned southern gentleman, his spotless linen and neat tie showing that his careful, faithful wife was still on guard.

Him I remembered for his astounding ability to recite poetry by the hour and also because of a florid speech which I once heard him make in the court room. For six mortal hours he spoke on a case involving the stealing of a horse-blanket worth about four dollars and a half. In the course of his argument he ranged with leisurely self-absorption, from ancient Egypt and the sacred Crocodile down through the dark ages, touching at Athens and Mount Olympus, reviewing Rome and the court of Charlemagne, winding at up four P.M. with an impassioned appeal to the jury to remember the power of environment upon his client. I could not remember how the suit came out, but I did recall the look of stupefaction which rested on the face of the accused as he found himself likened to Gurth the swine-herd and a peasant of Carcassone.

Ricker seemed quite unchanged save for the few gray hairs which had come into his beard and, as he stood in conversation with one of the merchants of the town, his nasal voice, his formal speech and the grandiloquent gesture of his right hand brought back to me all the stories I had heard of his drinking and of his wife's heroic rescuing expeditions to neighboring saloons. A strange, unsatisfactory end to a man of great natural ability.

Following him came a young girl leading a child of ten. I knew them at once. Ella McKee had been of the size of the little one, her sister, when I went away, and nothing gave me a keener realization of the years which had passed than the flowering of the child I had known into this charming maiden of eighteen. Her resemblance to her sister Flora was too marked to be mistaken, and the little one by her side had the same flashing eyes and radiant smile with which both of her grown up sisters were endowed. Their beauty fairly glorified the dingy street as they walked past my window.

Then an old farmer, bent and worn of frame, halted before me to talk with a merchant. This was David Babcock, Burton's father, one of our old time neighbors, a little more bent, a little thinner, a little grayer—that was all, and as I listened to his words I asked, "What purpose does a man serve by toiling like that for sixty years with no increase of leisure, with no growth in mental grace?"

There was a wistful note in his voice which went straight to my heart. He said: "No, our wheat crop ain't a-going to amount to much this year. Of course we don't try to raise much grain—it's mostly stock, but I thought I'd try wheat again. I wisht we could get back to the good old days of wheat raising—it w'ant so confining as stock-raisin'." His good days were also in the past!

As I walked the street I met several neighbors from Dry Run as well as acquaintances from the Grove. Nearly all, even the young men, looked worn and weather-beaten and some appeared both silent and sad. Laughter was curiously infrequent and I wondered whether in my days on the farm they had all been as rude of dress, as misshapen of form and as wistful of voice as they now seemed to me to be. "Have times changed? Has a spirit of unrest and complaining developed in the American farmer?"

I perceived the town from the triple viewpoint of a former resident, a man from the city, and a reformer, and every minutest detail of dress, tone and gesture revealed new meaning to me. Fancher and Gammons were feebler certainly, and a little more querulous with age, and their faded beards and rough hands gave pathetic evidence of the hard wear of wind and toil. At the moment nothing glozed the essential tragic futility of their existence.

Then down the street came "The Ragamuffins," the little Fourth of July procession, which in the old days had seemed so funny, so exciting to me. I laughed no more. It filled me with bitterness to think that such a makeshift spectacle could amuse anyone. "How dull and eventless life must be to enable such a pitiful travesty to attract and hold the attention of girls like Ella and Flora," I thought as I saw them standing with their little sister to watch "the parade."

From the window of a law office, Emma and Matilda Leete were leaning and I decided to make myself known to them. Emma, who had been one of my high admirations, had developed into a handsome and interesting woman with very little of the village in her dress or expression, and when I stepped up to her and asked, "Do you know me?" her calm gray eyes and smiling lips denoted humor. "Of course I know you—in spite of the beard. Come in and sit with us and tell all us about yourself."

As we talked, I found that they, at least, had kept in touch with the thought of the east, and Ella understood in some degree the dark mood which I voiced. She, too, occasionally doubted whether the life they were all living was worth while. "We make the best of it," she said, "but none of us are living up to our dreams."

Her musical voice, thoughtful eyes and quick intelligence, reasserted their charm, and I spent an hour or more in her company talking of old friends. It was not necessary to talk down to her. She was essentially urban in tone while other of the girls who had once impressed me with their beauty had taken on the airs of village matrons and did not interest me. If they retained aspirations they concealed the fact. Their husbands and children entirely occupied their minds.

Returning to the street, I introduced myself to Uncle Billy Fraser and Osmund Button and other Sun Prairie neighbors and when it became known that "Dick Garland's boy" was in town, many friends gathered about to shake my hand and inquire concerning "Belle" and "Dick."

The hard, crooked fingers, which they laid in my palm completed the sorrowful impression which their faces had made upon me. A twinge of pain went through my heart as I looked into their dim eyes and studied their heavy knuckles. I thought of the hand of Edwin Booth, of the flower-like palm of Helena Modjeska, of the subtle touch of Inness, and I said, "Is it not time that the human hand ceased to be primarily a bludgeon for hammering a bare living out of the earth? Nature all bountiful, undiscriminating, would, under justice, make such toil unnecessary." My heart burned with indignation. With William Morris and Henry George I exclaimed, "Nature is not to blame. Man's laws are to blame,"—but of this I said nothing at the time—at least not to men like Babcock and Fraser.

Next day I rode forth among the farms of Dry Run, retracing familiar lanes, standing under the spreading branches of the maple trees I had planted fifteen years before. I entered the low stone cabin wherein Neighbor Button had lived for twenty years (always intending sometime to build a house and make a granary of this), and at the table with the family and the hired men, I ate again of Ann's "riz" biscuit and sweet melon pickles. It was not a pleasant meal, on the contrary it was depressing to me. The days of the border were over, and yet Arvilla his wife was ill and aging, still living in pioneer discomfort toiling like a slave.

At neighbor Gardner's home, I watched his bent complaining old wife housekeeping from dawn to dark, literally dying on her feet. William Knapp's home was somewhat improved but the men still came to the table in their shirt sleeves smelling of sweat and stinking of the stable, just as they used to do, and Mrs. Knapp grown more gouty, more unwieldly than ever (she spent twelve or fourteen hours each day on her swollen and aching feet), moved with a waddling motion because, as she explained, "I can't limp—I'm just as lame in one laig as I am in t'other. But 'tain't no use to complain, I've just so much work to do and I might as well go ahead and do it."

I slept that night in her "best room," yes, at last, after thirty years of pioneer life, she had a guest chamber and a new "bedroom soot." With open pride and joy she led Belle Garland's boy in to view this precious acquisition, pointing out the soap and towels, and carefully removing the counterpane! I understood her pride, for my mother had not yet acquired anything so luxurious as this. She was still on the border!

Next day, I called upon Andrew Ainsley and while the women cooked in a red-hot kitchen, Andy stubbed about the barnyard in his bare feet, showing me his hogs and horses. Notwithstanding his town-visitor and the fact that it was Sunday, he came to dinner in a dirty, sweaty, collarless shirt, and I, sitting at his oil-cloth covered table, slipped back, deeper, ever deeper among the stern realities of the life from which I had emerged. I recalled that while my father had never allowed his sons or the hired men to come to the table unwashed or uncombed, we usually ate while clothed in our sweaty garments, glad to get food into our mouths in any decent fashion, while the smell of the horse and the cow mingled with the savor of the soup. There is no escape even on a modern "model farm" from the odor of the barn.

Every house I visited had its individual message of sordid struggle and half-hidden despair. Agnes had married and moved away to Dakota, and Bess had taken upon her girlish shoulders the burdens of wifehood and motherhood almost before her girlhood had reached its first period of bloom. In addition to the work of being cook and scrub-woman, she was now a mother and nurse. As I looked around upon her worn chairs, faded rag carpets, and sagging sofas,—the bare walls of her pitiful little house seemed a prison. I thought of her as she was in the days of her radiant girlhood and my throat filled with rebellious pain.

All the gilding of farm life melted away. The hard and bitter realities came back upon me in a flood. Nature was as beautiful as ever. The soaring sky was filled with shining clouds, the tinkle of the bobolink's fairy bells rose from the meadow, a mystical sheen was on the odorous grass and waving grain, but no splendor of cloud, no grace of sunset could conceal the poverty of these people, on the contrary they brought out, with a more intolerable poignancy, the gracelessness of these homes, and the sordid quality of the mechanical daily routine of these lives.

I perceived beautiful youth becoming bowed and bent. I saw lovely girlhood wasting away into thin and hopeless age. Some of the women I had known had withered into querulous and complaining spinsterhood, and I heard ambitious youth cursing the bondage of the farm. "Of such pain and futility are the lives of the average man and woman of both city and country composed," I acknowledged to myself with savage candor, "Why lie about it?"

Some of my playmates opened their acrid hearts to me. My presence stimulated their discontent. I was one of them, one who having escaped had returned as from some far-off glorious land of achievement. My improved dress, my changed manner of speech, every thing I said, roused in them a kind of rebellious rage and gave them unwonted power of expression. Their mood was no doubt transitory, but it was as real as my own.

Men who were growing bent in digging into the soil spoke to me of their desire to see something of the great eastern world before they died. Women whose eyes were faded and dim with tears, listened to me with almost breathless interest whilst I told them of the great cities I had seen, of wonderful buildings, of theaters, of the music of the sea. Young girls expressed to me their longing for a life which was better worth while, and lads, eager for adventure and excitement, confided to me their secret intention to leave the farm at the earliest moment. "I don't intend to wear out my life drudging on this old place," said Wesley Fancher with a bitter oath.

In those few days, I perceived life without its glamor. I no longer looked upon these toiling women with the thoughtless eyes of youth. I saw no humor in the bent forms and graying hair of the men. I began to understand that my own mother had trod a similar slavish round with never a full day of leisure, with scarcely an hour of escape from the tugging hands of children, and the need of mending and washing clothes. I recalled her as she passed from the churn to the stove, from the stove to the bedchamber, and from the bedchamber back to the kitchen, day after day, year after year, rising at daylight or before, and going to her bed only after the evening dishes were washed and the stockings and clothing mended for the night.

The essential tragedy and hopelessness of most human life under the conditions into which our society was swiftly hardening embittered me, called for expression, but even then I did not know that I had found my theme. I had no intention at the moment of putting it into fiction.

The reader may interrupt at this point to declare that all life, even the life of the city is futile, if you look at it in that way, and I reply by saying that I still have moments when I look at it that way. What is it all about, anyhow, this life of ours? Certainly to be forever weary and worried, to be endlessly soiled with thankless labor and to grow old before one's time soured and disappointed, is not the whole destiny of man!

Some of these things I said to Emma and Matilda but their optimism was too ingrained to yield to my gray mood. "We can't afford to grant too much," said Emma. "We are in it, you see."

Leaving the village of Osage, with my mind still in a tumult of revolt, I took the train for the Northwest, eager to see my mother and my little sister, yet beginning to dread the changes which I must surely find in them. Not only were my senses exceedingly alert and impressionable, my eyes saw nothing but the loneliness and the lack of beauty in the landscape, and the farther west I went, the lonelier became the box-like habitations of the plain. Here were the lands over which we had hurried in 1881, lured by the "Government Land" of the farther west. Here, now, a kind of pioneering behind the lines was going on. The free lands were gone and so, at last, the price demanded by these speculators must be paid.

This wasteful method of pioneering, this desolate business of lonely settlement took on a new and tragic significance as I studied it. Instructed by my new philosophy I now perceived that these plowmen, these wives and daughters had been pushed out into these lonely ugly shacks by the force of landlordism behind. These plodding Swedes and Danes, these thrifty Germans, these hairy Russians had all fled from the feudalism of their native lands and were here because they had no share in the soil from which they sprung, and because in the settled communities of the eastern states, the speculative demand for land had hindered them from acquiring even a leasing right to the surface of the earth.

I clearly perceived that our Song of Emigration had been, in effect, the hymn of fugitives!

And yet all this did not prevent me from acknowledging the beauty of the earth. On the contrary, social injustice intensified nature's prodigality. I said, "Yes, the landscape is beautiful, but how much of its beauty penetrates to the heart of the men who are in the midst of it and battling with it? How much of consolation does the worn and weary renter find in the beauty of cloud and tree or in the splendor of the sunset?—Grace of flower does not feed or clothe the body, and when the toiler is both badly clothed and badly fed, bird-song and leaf-shine cannot bring content." Like Millet, I asked, "Why should all of a man's waking hours be spent in an effort to feed and clothe his family? Is there not something wrong in our social scheme when the unremitting toiler remains poor?"

With such thoughts filling my mind, I passed through this belt of recent settlement and came at last into the valley of the James. One by one the familiar flimsy little wooden towns were left behind (strung like beads upon a string), and at last the elevator at Ordway appeared on the edge of the horizon, a minute, wavering projection against the skyline, and half an hour later we entered the village, a sparse collection of weatherbeaten wooden houses, without shade of trees or grass of lawns, a desolate, drab little town.

Father met me at the train, grayer of beard and hair, but looking hale and cheerful, and his voice, his peculiar expressions swept away all my city experience. In an instant I was back precisely where I had been when I left the farm. He was Captain, I was a corporal in the rear ranks.

And yet he was distinctly less harsh, less keen. He had mellowed. He had gained in sentiment, in philosophy, that was evident, and as we rode away toward the farm we fell into intimate, almost tender talk.

I was glad to note that he had lost nothing either in dignity or manliness in my eyes. His speech though sometimes ungrammatical was vigorous and precise and his stories gave evidence of his native constructive skill. "Your mother is crazy to see you," he said, "but I have only this one-seated buggy, and she couldn't come down to meet you."

When nearly a mile away I saw her standing outside the door of the house waiting for us, so eager that she could not remain seated, and as I sprang from the carriage she came hurrying out to meet me, uttering a curious little murmuring sound which touched me to the heart.

The changes in her shocked me, filled me with a sense of guilt. Hesitation was in her speech. Her voice once so glowing and so jocund, was tremulous, and her brown hair, once so abundant, was thin and gray. I realized at once that in the three years of my absence she had topped the high altitude of her life and was now descending swiftly toward defenseless age, and in bitter sadness I entered the house to meet my sister Jessie who was almost a stranger to me.

She had remained small and was quaintly stooped in neck and shoulders but retained something of her childish charm. To her I was quite alien, in no sense a brother. She was very reticent, but it did not take me long to discover that in her quiet fashion she commanded the camp. For all his military bluster, the old soldier was entirely subject to her. She was never wilful concerning anything really important, but she assumed all the rights of an individual and being the only child left in the family, went about her affairs without remark or question, serene, sweet but determined.

The furniture and pictures of the house were quite as humble as I had remembered them to be, but mother wore with pride the silk dress I had sent to her and was so happy to have me at home that she sat in silent content, while I told her of my life in Boston (boasting of my success of course, I had to do that to justify myself), and explaining that I must return, in time to resume my teaching in September.

Harvest was just beginning, and I said, "Father, if you'll pay me full wages, I'll take a hand."

This pleased him greatly, but he asked, "Do you think you can stand it? "

"I can try," I responded. Next day I laid off my city clothes and took my place as of old on the stack.

On the broad acres of the arid plains the header and not the binder was then in use for cutting the wheat, and as stacker I had to take care of the grain brought to me by the three header boxes.

It was very hard work that first day. It seemed that I could not last out the afternoon, but I did, and when at night I went to the house for supper, I could hardly sit at the table with the men, so weary were my bones. I sought my bed early and rose next day so sore that movement was torture. This wore away at last and on the third day I had no difficulty in keeping up my end of the whiffletree.

The part of labor that I hated was the dirt. Night after night as I came in covered with dust, too tired to bathe, almost too weary to change my shirt, I declared against any further harvesting. However, I generally managed to slosh myself with cold water from the well, and so went to my bed with a measure of self-respect, but even the "spare room" was hot and small, and the conditions of my mother's life saddened me. It was so hot and drear for her!

Every detail of the daily life of the farm now assumed literary significance in my mind. The quick callousing of my hands, the swelling of my muscles, the sweating of my scalp, all the unpleasant results of severe physical labor I noted down, but with no intention of exalting toil into a wholesome and regenerative thing as Tolstoi, an aristocrat, had attempted to do. Labor when so prolonged and severe as at this time my toil had to be, is warfare. I was not working as a visitor but as a hired hand, and doing my full day's work and more.

At the end of the week I wrote to my friend Kirkland, enclosing some of my detailed notes and his reply set me thinking. "You're the first actual farmer in American fiction,—now tell the truth about it," he wrote.

Thereafter I studied the glory of the sky and the splendor of the wheat with a deepening sense of the generosity of nature and monstrous injustice of social creeds. In the few moments of leisure which came to me as I lay in the shade of a grain-rick, I pencilled rough outlines of poems. My mind was in a condition of tantalizing productivity and I felt vaguely that I ought to be writing books instead of pitching grain. Conceptions for stories began to rise from the subconscious deeps of my thought like bubbles, noiseless and swift—and still I did not realize that I had entered upon a new career.

At night or on Sunday I continued my conferences with father and mother. Together we went over the past, talking of old neighbors and from one of these conversations came the theme of my first story. It was a very simple tale (told by my mother) of an old woman, who made a trip back to her York state home after an absence in the West of nearly thirty years. I was able to remember some of the details of her experience and when my mother had finished speaking I said to her, "That is too good to lose. I'm going to write it out." Then to amuse her, I added, "Why, that's worth seventy-five dollars to me. I'll go halves with you."

Smilingly she held out her hand. "Very well, you may give me my share now."

"Wait till I write it," I replied, a little taken aback.

Going to my room I set to work and wrote nearly two thousand words of the sketch. This I brought out later in the day and read to her with considerable excitement. I really felt that I had struck out a character which, while it did not conform to the actual woman in the case, was almost as vivid in my mind.

Mother listened very quietly until I had finished, then remarked with sententious approval. "That's good. Go on." She had no doubt of my ability to go on—indefinitely!

I explained to her that it wasn't so easy as all that, but that I could probably finish it in a day or two. (As a matter of fact, I completed the story in Boston but mother got her share of the "loot" just the same.)

Soon afterward, while sitting in the door looking out over the fields, I pencilled the first draft of a little poem called *Color in the Wheat* which I also read to her.

She received this in the same manner as before, from which it appeared that nothing I wrote could surprise her. Her belief in my powers was quite boundless. Father was inclined to ask, "What's the good of it?"

Of course all of my visit was not entirely made up of hard labor in the field. There were Sundays when we could rest or entertain the neighbors, and sometimes a shower gave us a few hours' respite, but for the most part the weeks which I spent at home were weeks of stern service in the ranks of the toilers.

There was a very good reason for my close application to the fork-handle. Father paid me an extra price as "boss stacker," and I could not afford to let a day pass without taking the fullest advantage of it. At the same time I was careful not to convey to my pupils and friends in Boston the disgraceful fact that I was still dependent upon my skill with a pitch-fork to earn a living. I was not quite sure of their approval of the case.

At last there came the time when I must set my face toward the east.

It seemed a treachery to say good-bye to my aging parents, leaving them and my untrained sister to this barren, empty, laborious life on the plain, whilst I returned to the music, the drama, the inspiration, the glory of Boston. Opposite poles of the world could not be farther apart. Acute self-accusation took out of my return all of the exaltation and much of the pleasure which I had expected to experience as I dropped my harvester's fork and gloves and put on the garments of civilization once more.

With heart sore with grief and rebellion at "the inexorable trend of things," I entered the car, and when from its window I looked back upon my grieving mother, my throat filled with a suffocating sense of guilt. I was deserting her, recreant to my blood!— That I was reenacting the most characteristic of all American dramas in thus pursuing an ambitious career in a far-off city I most poignantly realized and yet—I went! It seemed to me at the time that my duty lay in the way of giving up all my selfish plans in order that I might comfort my mother in her growing infirmity, and counsel and defend my sister—but I did not. I went away borne on a stream of purpose so strong that I seemed but a leaf in its resistless flood.

This feeling of bitterness, of rebellion, of dissatisfaction with myself, wore gradually away, and by the time I reached Chicago I had resolved to climb high. "I will carry mother and Jessie to comfort and to some small share, at least, in the world of art," was my resolve. In this way I sought to palliate my selfish plan.

Obscurely forming in my mind were two great literary concepts—that truth was a higher quality than beauty, and that to spread the reign of justice should everywhere be the design and intent of the artist. The merely beautiful in art seemed petty, and success at the cost of the happiness of others a monstrous egotism.

In the spirit of these ideals I returned to my small attic room in Jamaica Plain and set to work to put my new conceptions into some sort of literary form.

29

I Join the Anti-Poverty Brigade

In the slow procession of my struggling fortunes this visit to the West seems important, for it was the beginning of my career as a fictionist. My talk with Kirkland and my perception of the sordid monotony of farm life had given me a new and very definite emotional relationship to my native state. I perceived now the tragic value of scenes which had hither to appeared merely dull or petty. My eyes were opened to the enforced misery of the pioneer. As a reformer my blood was stirred to protest. As a writer I was beset with a desire to record in some form this newly-born conception of the border.

No sooner did I reach my little desk in Jamaica Plain than I began to write, composing in the glow of a flaming conviction. With a delightful (and deceptive) sense of power, I graved with heavy hand, as if with pen of steel on brazen tablets, picture after picture of the plain. I had no doubts, no hesitations about the kind of effect I wished to produce. I perceived little that was poetic, little that was idyllic, and nothing that was humorous in the man, who, with hands like claws, was scratching a scanty living from the soil of a rented farm, while his wife walked her ceaseless round from tub to churn and from churn to tub. On the contrary, the life of such a family appealed to me as an almost unrelievedly tragic futility.

In the few weeks between my return and the beginning of my teaching, I wrote several short stories, and outlined a propagandist play. With very little thought as to whether such stories would sell rapidly or not at all I began to send them away, to the *Century*, to *Harpers*, and other first class magazines without permitting myself any deep disappointment when they came back—as they all did!

However, having resolved upon being printed by the best periodicals I persisted. Notwithstanding rejection after rejection I maintained an elevated aim and continued to fire away.

There was a certain arrogance in all this, I will admit, but there was also sound logic, for I was seeking the ablest editorial judgment and in this way I got it. My manuscripts were badly put together (I used cheap paper and could not afford a typist), hence I could not blame the readers who hurried my stories back at me. No doubt my illegible writing as well as the blunt, unrelenting truth of my pictures repelled them. One or two friendly souls wrote personal notes protesting against my "false interpretation of western life."

The fact that I, a working farmer, was presenting for the first time in fiction the actualities of western country life did not impress them as favorably as I had expected it to do. My own pleasure in being true was not shared, it would seem, by others. "Give us charming love stories!" pleaded the editors.

"No, we've had enough of lies," I replied. "Other writers are telling the truth about the city,—the artisan's narrow, grimy, dangerous job is being pictured, and it appears to me that the time has come to tell the truth about the barn-yard's daily grind. I have lived the life and I know that farming is not entirely made up of berrying, tossing the new-mown hay and singing *The Old Oaken Bucket* on the porch by moonlight.

"The working farmer," I went on to argue, "has to live in February as well as June. He must pitch manure as well as clover. Milking as depicted on a blue china plate where a maid in a flounced petticoat is caressing a gentle Jersey cow in a field of daisies, is quite unlike sitting down to the steaming flank of a stinking brindle heifer in flytime. Pitching odorous timothy in a poem and actually putting it into a mow with the temperature at ninety-eight in the shade are widely separated in fact as they should be in fiction. For me," I concluded, "the grime and the mud and the sweat and the dust exist. They still form a large part of life on the farm, and I intend that they shall go into my stories in their proper proportions."

Alas! Each day made me more and more the dissenter from accepted economic as well as literary conventions. I became less and less of the booming, indiscriminating patriot. Precisely as successful politicians, popular preachers and vast traders diminished in importance in my mind, so the significance of Whitman, and Tolstoi and George increased, for they all represented qualities which make for saner, happier and more equitable conditions in the future. Perhaps I despised idlers and time-savers unduly, but I was of an age to be extreme.

During the autumn Henry George was announced to speak in Faneuil Hall, sacred ark of liberty, and with eager feet my brother and I hastened to the spot to hear this reformer whose fame already resounded throughout the English-speaking world. Beginning his campaign in California he had carried it to Ireland, where he had been twice imprisoned for speaking his mind, and now after having set Bernard Shaw and other English Fabians aflame with indignant protest, was about to run for mayor of New York City.

I have an impression that the meeting was a noon-day meeting for men, at any rate the historical old hall, which had echoed to the voices of Garrison and Phillips and Webster was filled with an eager expectant throng. The sanded floor was packed with auditors standing shoulder to shoulder and the galleries were crowded with these who, like ourselves, had gone early in order to ensure seats. From our places in the front row we looked down upon an almost solid mosaic of derby hats, the majority of which were rusty by exposure to wind and rain.

As I waited I recalled my father's stories of the stern passions of anti-slavery days. In this hall Wendell Phillips in the pride and power of his early manhood, had risen to reply to the cowardly apologies of entrenched conservatism, and here now another voice was about to be raised in behalf of those whom the law oppressed. My brother had also read *Progress and Poverty* and both of us felt that we were taking part in a distinctly historical event, the beginning of a new abolition movement.

At last, a stir at the back of the platform announced the approach of the speaker. Three or four men suddenly appeared from some concealed door and entered upon the stage. One of them, a short man with a full red beard, we recognized at once,—"The prophet of San Francisco" as he was then called (in fine derision) was not a noticeable man till he removed his hat. Then the fine line of his face from the crown of his head to the tip of his chin printed itself ineffaceably upon our minds. The dome-like brow was that of one highly specialized on lines of logic and sympathy.

There was also something in the tense poise of his body which foretold the orator.

Impatiently the audience endured the speakers who prepared the way and then, finally, George stepped forward, but prolonged waves of cheering again and again prevented his beginning. Thereupon he started pacing to and fro along the edge of the platform, his big head thrown back, his small hands clenched as if in anticipation of coming battle. He no longer appeared small. His was the master mind of that assembly.

His first words cut across the air with singular calmness. Coming after the applause, following the nervous movement of a moment before, his utterance was surprisingly cold, masterful, and direct. Action had condensed into speech. Heat was transformed into light.

His words were orderly and well chosen. They had precision and grace as well as power. He spoke as other men write, with style and arrangement. His address could have been printed word for word as it fell from his lips. This self-mastery, this graceful lucidity of utterance combined with a personal presence distinctive and dignified, reduced even his enemies to respectful silence. His altruism, his sincere pity and his hatred of injustice sent me away in the mood of a disciple.

Meanwhile a few of his followers had organized an "Anti-Poverty Society" similar to those which had already sprung up in New York, and my brother and I used to go of a Sunday evening to the old Horticultural Hall on Tremont Street, contributing our presence and our dimes in aid of the meeting. Speakers were few and as the weeks went by the audiences grew smaller and smaller till one night Chairman Roche announced with sad intonation that the meetings could not go on. "You've all got tired of hearing us repeat ourselves and we have no new speaker, none at all for next week. I am afraid we'll have to quit."

My brother turned to me—"Here's your 'call,'" he said. "Volunteer to speak for them."

Recognizing my duty I rose just as the audience was leaving and sought the chairman. With a tremor of excitement in my voice I said, "If you can use me as a speaker for next Sunday I will do my best for you."

Roche glanced at me for an instant, and then without a word of question, shouted to the audience, "Wait a moment! We *have* a speaker for next Sunday." Then, bending down, he asked of me, "What is your name and occupation?"

I told him, and again he lifted his voice, this time in triumphant shout, "Professor Hamlin Garland will speak for us next Sunday at eight o'clock. Come and bring all your friends."

"You are in for it now," laughed my brother gleefully. "You'll be lined up with the anarchists sure!"

That evening was in a very real sense a parting of the ways for me. To refuse this call was to go selfishly and comfortably along the lines of literary activity I had chosen. To accept was to enter the arena where problems of economic justice were being sternly fought out. I understood already something of the disadvantage which attached to being called a reformer, but my sense of duty and the influence of Herbert Spencer and Walt Whitman rose above my doubts. I decided to do my part.

All the week I agonized over my address, and on Sunday spoke to a crowded house with a kind of partisan success. On Monday my good friend Chamberlin, *The Listener of The Transcript* filled his column with a long review of my heretical harangue.—With one leap I had reached the lime-light of conservative Boston's disapproval!

Chamberlin, himself a "philosophical anarchist," was pleased with the individualistic note which ran through my harangue. The Single Taxers were of course, delighted for I admitted my discipleship to George, and my socialistic friends urged that the general effect of my argument was on their side. Altogether, for a penniless student and struggling story writer, I created something of a sensation. All my speeches thereafter helped to dye me deeper than ever with the color of reform.

However, in the midst of my Anti-Poverty Campaign, I did not entirely forget my fiction and my teaching. I was becoming more and more a companion of artists and poets, and my devotion to things literary deepened from day to day. A dreadful theorist in some ways, I was, after all, more concerned with literary than with social problems. Writing was my life, land reform one of my convictions.

High in my attic room I bent above my manuscript with a fierce resolve. From eight o'clock in the morning until half past twelve, I dug and polished. In the afternoon, I met my classes. In the evening I revised what I had written and in case I did not go to the theater or to a lecture (I had no social engagements) I wrote until ten o'clock. For recreation I sometimes drove with Dr. Cross on his calls or walked the lanes and climbed the hills with my brother.

In this way most of my stories of the west were written. Happy in my own work, I bitterly resented the laws which created millionaires at the expense of the poor.

These were days of security and tranquillity, and good friends thickened. Each week I felt myself in less danger of being obliged to shingle, though I still had difficulty in clothing myself properly.

Again I saw Booth play his wondrous round of parts and was able to complete my monograph which I called *The Art of Edwin Booth*. I even went so far as to send to the great actor the chapter on his *Macbeth* and received from him grateful acknowledgments, in a charming letter.

A little later I had the great honor of meeting him for a moment and it happened in this way. The veteran reader, James E. Murdock, was giving a recital in a small hall on Park Street, and it was privately announced that Edwin Booth and Lawrence Barrett would be present. This was enough to justify me in giving up one of my precious dollars on the chance of seeing the great tragedian enter the room.

He came in a little late, flushing, timid, apologetic! It seemed to me a very curious and wonderful thing that this man who had spoken to millions of people from behind the footlights should be timid as a maid when confronted by less than two hundred of his worshipful fellow citizens in a small hall. So gentle and kindly did he seem.

My courage grew, and after the lecture I approached the spot where he stood, and Mr. Barrett introduced me to him as "the author of the lecture on *Macbeth*."—Never had I looked into such eyes—deep and dark and sad—and my tongue failed me miserably. I could not say a word. Booth smiled with kindly interest and murmured his thanks for my critique, and I went away, down across the Common in a glow of delight and admiration.

In the midst of all my other duties I was preparing my brother Franklin for the stage. Yes, through some mischance, this son of the prairie had obtained the privilege of studying with a retired "leading lady" who still occasionally made tours of the "Kerosene Circuit" and who had agreed to take him out with her, provided he made sufficient progress to warrant it. It was to prepare him for this trip that I met him three nights in the week at his office (he was bookkeeper in a cutlery firm) and there rehearsed *East Lynne, Leah the Forsaken,* and *The Lady of Lyons.*

From seven o'clock until nine I held the book whilst he pranced and shouted and gesticulated through his lines.

At last, emboldened by his star's praise, he cut loose from his ledger and went out on a tour which was extremely diverting but not at all remunerative. The company ran on a reef and Frank sent for carfare which I cheerfully remitted, crediting it to his educational account.

The most vital literary man in all America at this time was Wm. Dean Howells who was in the full tide of his powers and an issue. All through the early eighties, reading Boston was divided into two parts,—those who liked Howells and those who fought him, and the most fiercely debated question at the clubs was whether his heroines were true to life or whether they were caricatures. In many homes he was read aloud with keen enjoyment of his delicate humor, and his graceful, incisive English; in other circles he was condemned because of his "injustice to the finer sex."

As for me, having begun my literary career (as the reader may recall) by assaulting this leader of the realistic school I had ended, naturally, by becoming his public advocate. How could I help it?

It is true a large part of one of my lectures consisted of a gratuitious slam at "Mr. Howells and the so-called realists," but further reading and deeper thought along the lines indicated by Whitman, had changed my view. One of Walt's immortal invitations which had appealed to me with special power was this:

> Stop this day and night with me
> And you shall possess the origin of all poems;
> You shall no longer take things at second or third hand
> Nor look through the eyes of the dead,
> Nor through my eyes either,
> But through your own eyes....
> You shall listen to all sides,
> And filter them from yourself.

Thus by a circuitous route I had arrived at a position where I found myself inevitably a supporter not only of Howells but of Henry James whose work assumed ever larger significance in my mind. I was ready to concede with the realist that the poet might go round the earth and come back to find the things nearest at hand the sweetest and best after all, but that certain injustices, certain cruel facts must not be blinked at, and so, while admiring the grace, the humor, the satire of Howells' books, I was saved from anything like imitation by the sterner and darker material in which I worked.

My wall of prejudice against the author of *A Modern Instance* really began to sag when during the second year of my stay in Boston, I took up and finished *The Undiscovered Country* (which I had begun five or six years before), but it was *The Minister's Charge* which gave the final push to my defenses and fetched them tumbling about my ears in a cloud of dust. In fact, it was a review of this book, written for the *Transcript* which brought about a meeting with the great novelist.

My friend Hurd liked the review and had it set up. The editor, Mr. Clement, upon reading it in proof said to Hurd, "This is an able review. Put it in as an editorial. Who is the writer of it?" Hurd told him about me and Clement was interested. "Send him to me," he said.

On Saturday I was not only surprised and delighted by the sight of my article in large type at the head of the literary page, I was fluttered by the word which Mr. Clement had sent to me.

Humbly as a minstrel might enter the court of his king, I went before the editor, and stood expectantly while he said: "That was an excellent article. I have sent it to Mr. Howells. You should know him and sometime I will give you a letter to him, but not now. Wait awhile. War is being made upon him just now, and if you were to meet him your criticism would have less weight. His enemies would say that you had come under his personal influence. Go ahead with the work you have in hand, and after you have put yourself on record concerning him and his books I will see that you meet him."

Like a knight enlisted in a holy war I descended the long narrow stairway to the street, and went to my home without knowing what passed me.

I ruminated for hours on Mr. Clement's praise. I read and reread my "able article" till I knew it by heart and then I started in, seriously, to understand and estimate the school of fiction to which Mr. Howells belonged. I read every one of his books as soon as I could obtain them. I read James, too, and many of the European realists, but it must have been two years before I called upon Mr. Clement to redeem his promise.

Deeply excited, with my note of introduction carefully stowed in my inside pocket, I took the train one summer afternoon bound for Lee's Hotel in Auburndale, where Mr. Howells was at this time living.

I fervently hoped that the building would not be too magnificent for I felt very small and very poor on alighting at the station, and every rod of my advance sensibly decreased my self-esteem. Starting with faltering feet I came to the entrance of the grounds in a state of panic, and as I looked up the path toward the towering portico of the hotel, it seemed to me the palace of an emperor and my resolution entirely left me. Actually I walked up the street for some distance before I was able to secure sufficient grip on myself to return and enter.

"It is entirely unwarranted and very presumptuous in me to be thus intruding on a great author's time," I admitted, but it was too late to retreat, and so I kept on. Entering the wide central hall I crept warily across its polished, hardwood floor to the desk where a highly ornate clerk presided. In a meek, husky voice I asked, "Is Mr. Howells in?"

"He is, but he's at dinner," the despot on the other side of the counter coldly replied, and his tone implied that he didn't think the great author would relish being disturbed by an individual who didn't even know the proper time to call. However, I produced my letter of introduction and with some access of spirit requested His Highness to have it sent in.

A colored porter soon returned, showed me to a reception room off the hall, and told me that Mr. Howells would be out in a few minutes. During these minutes I sat with eyes on the portieres and a frog in my throat. "How will he receive me? How will he look? What shall I say to him?" I asked myself, and behold I hadn't an idea left!

Suddenly the curtains parted and a short man with a large head stood framed in the opening. His face was impassive but his glance was one of the most piercing I had ever encountered. In the single instant before he smiled he discovered my character and my thought as though his eyes had been the lenses of some singular and powerful x-ray instrument. It was the glance of a novelist.

Of course all this took but a moment's time. Then his face softened, became winning and his glance was gracious. "I'm glad to see you," he said, and his tone was cordial. "Won't you be seated?"

We took seats at the opposite ends of a long sofa, and Mr. Howells began at once to inquire concerning the work and the purposes of his visitor. He soon drew forth the story of my coming to Boston and developed my theory of literature, listening intently while I told him of my history of American Ideals and my attempt at fiction.

My conception of the local novel and of its great importance in American literature, especially interested the master who listened intently while I enlarged upon my reasons for believing that the local novel would continue to grow in power and insight. At the end I said, "In my judgment the men and women of the south, the west and the east, are working (without knowing it) in accordance with a great principle, which is this: American literature, in order to be great, must be national, and in order to be national, must deal with conditions peculiar to our own land and climate. Every genuinely American writer must deal with the life he knows best and for which he cares the most. Thus Joel Chandler Harris, George W. Cable, Joseph Kirkland, Sarah Orne Jewett, and Mary Wilkins, like Bret Harte, are but varying phases of the same movement, a movement which is to give us at last a really vital and original literature!"

Once set going I fear I went on like the political orator who doesn't know how to sit down. I don't think I did quit. Howells stopped me with a compliment. "You're doing a fine and valuable work," he said, and I thought he meant it—and he did mean it. "Each of us has had some perception of this movement but no one has correlated it as you have done. I hope you will go on and finish and publish your essays."

These words uttered, perhaps, out of momentary conviction brought the blood to my face and filled me with conscious satisfaction. Words of praise by this keen thinker were like golden medals. I had good reason to know how discriminating he was in his use of adjectives for he was even then the undisputed leader in the naturalistic school of fiction and to gain even a moment's interview with him would have been a rich reward for a youth who had only just escaped from spreading manure on an Iowa farm. Emboldened by his gracious manner, I went on. I confessed that I too was determined to do a little at recording by way of fiction the manners and customs of my native West. "I don't know that I can write a novel, but I intend to try," I added.

He was kind enough then to say that he would like to see some of my stories of Iowa. "You have almost a clear field out there—no one but Howe seems to be tilling it."

How long he talked or how long I talked, I do not know, but at last (probably in self-defense), he suggested that we take a walk. We strolled about the garden a few minutes and each moment my spirits rose, for he treated me, not merely as an aspiring student, but as a fellow author in whom he could freely confide. At last, in his gentle way, he turned me toward my train.

It was then as we were walking slowly down the street, that he faced me with the trust of a comrade and asked, "What would you think of a story dealing with the effect of a dream on the life of a man?—I have in mind a tale to be called *The Shadow of a Dream,* or something like that, wherein a man is to be influenced in some decided way by the memory of a vision, a ghostly figure which is to pursue him and have some share in the final catastrophe, whatever it may turn out to be. What would you think of such a plot?"

Filled with surprise at his trust and confidence, I managed to stammer a judgment. "It would depend entirely upon the treatment," I answered. "The theme is a little like Hawthorne, but I can understand how, under your hand, it would not be in the least like Hawthorne."

His assent was instant. "You think it not quite like me? You are right. It does sound a little lurid. I may never write it, but if I do, you may be sure it will be treated in my own way and not in Hawthorne's way."

Stubbornly I persisted. "There are plenty who can do the weird kind of thing, Mr. Howells, but there is only one man who can write books like *The Modern Instance* and *Silas Lapham.*"

All that the novelist said, as well as his manner of saying it was wonderfully enriching to me. To have such a man, one whose fame was even at this time international, desire an expression of my opinion as to the fitness of his chosen theme, was like feeling on my shoulder the touch of a kingly accolade.

I went away, exalted. My apprenticeship seemed over! To America's chief literary man I was a fellow-writer, a critic, and with this recognition the current of my ambition shifted course. I began to hope that I, too, might some day become a social historian as well as a teacher of literature. The reformer was still present, but the literary man had been reinforced, and yet, even here, I had chosen the unpopular, unprofitable side!

Thereafter the gentle courtesy, the tact, the exquisite, yet simple English of this man was my education. Every hour of his delicious humor, his wise advice, his ready sympathy sent me away in mingled exaltation and despair—despair of my own blunt and common diction, exaltation over his continued interest and friendship.

How I must have bored that sweet and gracious soul! He could not escape me. If he moved to Belmont I pursued him. If he went to Nahant or Magnolia or Kittery I spent my money like water in order to follow him up and bother him about my work, or worry him into a public acceptance of the single tax, and yet every word he spoke, every letter he wrote was a benediction and an inspiration.

He was a constant revelation to me of the swift transitions of mood to which a Celtic man of letters is liable. His humor was like a low, sweet bubbling geyser spring. It rose with a chuckle close upon some very somber mood and broke into exquisite phrases which lingered in my mind for weeks. Side by side with every jest was a bitter sigh, for he, too, had been deeply moved by new social ideals, and we talked much of the growing contrasts of rich and poor, of the suffering and loneliness of the farmer, the despair of the proletariat, and though I could never quite get him to perceive the difference between his program and ours (he was always for some vague socialistic reform), he readily admitted that land monopoly was the chief cause of poverty, and the first injustice to be destroyed. "But you must go farther, much farther," he would sadly say.

Of all of my literary friends at this time, Edgar Chamberlin of the *Transcript* was the most congenial. He, too, was from Wisconsin, and loved the woods and fields with passionate fervor. At his house I met many of the young writers of Boston—at least they were young then—Sylvester Baxter, Imogene Guiney, Minna Smith, Alice Brown, Mary E. Wilkins, and Bradford Torrey were often there. No events in my life except my occasional calls on Mr. Howells were more stimulating to me than my visits to the circle about Chamberlin's hearth—(he was the kind of man who could not live without an open fire and Mrs. Chamberlin's boundlessly hospitable table was an equally appealing joy.

How they regarded me at that time I cannot surely define—perhaps they tolerated me out of love for the West. But I here acknowledge my obligation to "The Listener." He taught me to recognize literary themes in the city, for he brought the same keen insight, the same tender sympathy to bear upon the crowds of the streets that he used in describing the songs of the thrush or the whir of the partridge.

He was especially interested in the Italians who were just beginning to pour into The North End, displacing the Irish as workmen in the streets, and often in his column made gracious and charming references to them, softening without doubt the suspicion and dislike with which many citizens regarded them.

Hurd, on the contrary, was a very bookish man. He sat amidst mountains of "books for review" and yet he was always ready to welcome the slender volume of the new poet. To him I owe much. From him I secured my first knowledge of James Whitcomb Riley, and it was Hurd who first called my attention to Kirkland's *Zury*. Through him I came to an enthusiasm for the study of Ibsen and Bjornsen, for he was widely read in the literature of the north.

On the desk of this hard-working, ill-paid man of letters (who never failed to utter words of encouragement to me) I wish to lay a tardy wreath of grateful praise. He deserves the best of the world beyond, for he got little but hard work from this. He loved poetry of all kinds and enjoyed a wide correspondence with those "who could not choose but sing." His desk was crammed with letters from struggling youths whose names are familiar now, and in whom he took an almost paternal interest.

One day as I was leaving Hurd's office he said, "By the way, Garland, you ought to know Jim Herne. He's doing much the same sort of work on the stage that you and Miss Wilkins are putting into the short story. Here are a couple of tickets to his play. Go and see it and come back and tell what you think of it."

Herne's name was new to me but Hurd's commendation was enough to take me down to the obscure theater in the South End where *Drifting Apart* was playing. The play was advertised as "a story of the Gloucester fishermen" and Katharine Herne was the "Mary Miller" of the piece. Herne's part was that of a stalwart fisherman, married to a delicate young girl, and when the curtain went up on his first scene I was delighted with the setting. It was a veritable cottage interior—not an English cottage but an American working man's home. The worn chairs, the rag rugs, the sewing machine doing duty as a flowerstand, all were in keeping.

The dialogue was homely, intimate, almost trivial and yet contained a sweet and touching quality. It was, indeed, of a piece with the work of Miss Jewett only more humorous, and the action of Katharine and James Herne was in key with the text. The business of "Jack's" shaving and getting ready to go down the street was most delightful in spirit and the act closed with a touch of true pathos.

The second act, a "dream act" was not so good, but the play came back to realities in the last act and sent us all away in joyous mood. It was for me the beginning of the local color American drama, and before I went to sleep that night I wrote a letter to Herne telling him how significant I found his play and wishing him the success he deserved.

Almost by return mail came his reply thanking me for my good wishes and expressing a desire to meet me. "We are almost always at home on Sunday and shall be very glad to see you whenever you can find time to come."

A couple of weeks later—as soon as I thought it seemly—I went out to Ashmont to see them, for my interest was keen. I knew no one connected with the stage at this time and I was curious to know—I was almost frenziedly eager to know the kind of folk the Hernes were.

My first view of their house was a disappointment. It was quite like any other two-story suburban cottage. It had a small garden but it faced directly on the walk and was a most uninspiring color.

But if the house disappointed me the home did not. Herne, who looked older than when on the stage, met me with a curiously impassive face but I felt his friendship through this mask. Katharine who was even more charming than "Mary Miller" wore no mask. She was radiantly cordial and we were friends at once. Both persisted in calling me "professor" although I explained that I had no right to any such title. In the end they compromised by calling me "the Dean," and "the Dean" I remained in all the happy years of our friendship.

Not the least of the charms of this home was the companionship of Herne's three lovely little daughters Julie, Chrystal and Dorothy, who liked "the Dean"—I don't know why—and were always at the door to greet me when I came. No other household meant as much to me. No one understood more clearly than the Hernes the principles I stood for, and no one was more interested in my plans for uniting the scattered members of my family. Before I knew it I had told them all about my mother and her pitiful condition, and Katharine's expressive face clouded with sympathetic pain. "You'll work it out," she said, "I am sure of it," and her confident words were a comfort to me.

They were true Celts, swift to laughter and quick with tears; they inspired me to bolder flights. They met me on every plane of my intellectual interests, and our discussions of Herbert Spencer, Henry George, and William Dean Howells often lasted deep into the night. In all matters concerning the American Drama we were in accord.

Having found these rare and inspiring souls I was not content until I had introduced them to all my literary friends. I became their publicity agent without authority and without pay, for I felt the injustice of a situation where such artists could be shunted into a theater in The South End where no one ever saw them—at least no one of the world of art and letters. Their cause was my cause, their success my chief concern.

Drifting Apart, I soon discovered, was only the beginning of Herne's ambitious design to write plays which should be as true in their local color as Howells' stories. He was at this time working on two plays which were to bring lasting fame and a considerable fortune. One of these was a picture of New England coast life and the other was a study of factory life. One became *Shore Acres* and the other *Margaret Fleming.*

From time to time as we met he read me these plays, scene by scene, as he wrote them, and when *Margaret Fleming* was finished I helped him put it on at Chickering Hall. My brother was in the cast and I served as "Man in Front" for six weeks—again without pay of course—and did my best to let Boston know what was going on there in that little theater—the first of all the "Little Theaters" in America. Then came the success of *Shore Acres* at the Boston Museum and my sense of satisfaction was complete.

How all this puts me back into that other shining Boston! I am climbing again those three long flights of stairs to the *Transcript* office. Chamberlin extends a cordial hand, Clement nods as I pass his door. It is raining, and in the wet street the vivid reds, greens, and yellows of the horse-cars, splash the pavement with gaudy color. Round the tower of the Old South Church the doves are whirling.

It is Saturday. I am striding across the Common to Park Square, hurrying to catch the 5:02 train. The trees of the Mall are shaking their heavy tears upon me. Drays thunder afar off. Bells tinkle.—How simple, quiet, almost village-like this city of my vision seems in contrast with the Boston of today with its diabolic subways, its roaring overhead trains, its electric cars and its streaming automobiles!

Over and over again I have tried to re-discover that Boston, but it is gone, never to return. Herne is dead, Hurd is dead, Clement no longer edits the *Transcript,* Howells and Mary Wilkins live in New York. Louise Chandler Moulton lies deep in that grave of whose restful quiet she so often sang, and Edward Everett Hale, type of a New England that was old when I was young, has also passed into silence. His name like that of Higginson and Holmes is only a faint memory in the marble splendors of the New Public Library. The ravening years—how they destroy!

30

My Mother Is Stricken

In the summer of 1889, notwithstanding a widening opportunity for lectures in the East, I decided to make another trip to the West. In all my mother's letters I detected a tremulous undertone of sadness, of longing, and this filled me with unrest even in the midst of the personal security I had won. I could not forget the duty I owed to her who had toiled so uncomplainingly that I might be clothed and fed and educated, and so I wrote to her announcing the date of my arrival.

My friend, Dr. Cross, eager to see The Short-Grass Country which was a far-off and romantic territory to him, arranged to go with me. It was in July, and very hot the day we started, but we were both quite disposed to make the most of every good thing and to ignore all discomforts. I'm not entirely certain, but I think I occupied a sleeping car berth on this trip; if I did so it was for the first time in my life. Anyhow, I must have treated myself to regular meals, for I cannot recall being ill on the train. This, in itself, was remarkable.

Strange to say, most of the incidents of the journey between Boston and Wisconsin are blended like the faded figures on a strip of sun-smit cloth, nothing remains definitely distinguishable except the memory of our visit to my Uncle William's farm in Neshonoc, and the recollection of the pleasure we took in the vivid bands of wild flowers which spun, like twin ribbons of satin, from beneath the wheels of the rear coach as we rushed across the state. All else has vanished as though it had never been.

These primitive blossoms along the railroad's right-of way deeply delighted my friend, but to me they were more than flowers, they were cups of sorcery, torches of magic incense. Each nodding pink brought back to me the sights and sounds and smells of the glorious meadows of my boyhood's vanished world. Every weed had its mystic tale. The slopes of the hills, the cattle grouped under the trees, all wrought upon me like old half-forgotten poems.

My uncle, big, shaggy, gentle and reticent, met us at the faded little station and drove us away toward the sun-topped "sleeping camel" whose lines and shadows were so lovely and so familiar. In an hour we were at the farmhouse where quaint Aunt Maria made us welcome in true pioneer fashion, and cooked a mess of hot biscuit to go with the honey from the bees in the garden. They both seemed very remote, very primitive even to me, to my friend Cross they were exactly like characters in a story. He could only look and listen and smile from his seat in the corner.

William, a skilled bee-man, described to us his methods of tracking wild swarms, and told us how he handled those in his hives. "I can scoop 'em up as if they were so many kernels of corn," he said. After supper as we all sat on the porch watching the sunset, he reverted to the brave days of fifty-five when deer and bear came down over the hills, when a rifle was almost as necessary as a hoe, and as he talked I revived in him the black-haired smiling young giant of my boyhood days, untouched of age or care.

He was a poet, in his dreamy reticent way, for when next morning I called attention to the beauty of the view down the valley, his face took on a kind of wistful sweetness and a certain shyness as he answered with a visible effort to conceal his feeling—"I like it—No place better. I wish your father and mother had never left the valley." And in this wish I joined.

On the third day we resumed our journey toward Dakota, and the Doctor, though outwardly undismayed by the long hard ride and the increasing barrenness of the level lands, sighed with relief when at last I pointed out against the level sky-line the wavering bulk of the grain elevator which alone marked the wind-swept deserted site of Ordway, the end of our journey. He was tired.

Business, I soon learned, had not been going well on the border during the two years of my absence. None of the towns had improved. On the contrary, all had lost ground.

Another dry year was upon the land and the settlers were deeply disheartened. The holiday spirit of eight years before had entirely vanished. In its place was a sullen rebellion against government and against God. The stress of misfortune had not only destroyed hope, it had brought out the evil side of many men. Dissensions had grown common. Two of my father's neighbors had gone insane over the failure of their crops. Several had slipped away "between two days" to escape their debts, and even little Jessie, who met us at the train, brave as a meadow lark, admitted that something gray had settled down over the plain.

Graveyards, jails, asylums, all the accompaniments of civilization, were now quite firmly established. On the west lay the lands of the Sioux and beyond them the still more arid foot-hills. The westward movement of the Middle Border for the time seemed at an end.

My father, Jessie told me, was now cultivating more than five hundred acres of land, and deeply worried, for his wheat was thin and light and the price less than sixty cents per bushel.

It was nearly sunset as we approached the farm, and a gorgeous sky was overarching it, but the bare little house in which my people lived seemed a million miles distant from Boston. The trees which my father had planted, the flowers which my mother had so faithfully watered, had withered in the heat. The lawn was burned brown. No green thing was in sight, and no shade offered save that made by the little cabin. On every side stretched scanty yellowing fields of grain, and from every worn road, dust rose like smoke from crevices, giving upon deep-hidden subterranean fires. It was not a good time to bring a visitor to the homestead, but it was too late to retreat.

Mother, grayer, older, much less vigorous than she had been two years before, met us, silently, shyly, and I bled, inwardly, every time I looked at her. A hesitation had come into her speech, and the indecision of her movements scared me, but she was too excited and too happy to admit of any illness. Her smile was as sweet as ever.

Dr. Cross quietly accepted the hot narrow bedroom which was the best we could offer him, and at supper took his place among the harvest help without any noticeable sign of repugnance. It was all so remote, so characteristic of the border that interest dominated disgust.

He was much touched, as indeed was I, by the handful of wild roses which father brought in to decorate the little sitting room.

"There's nothing I like better," he said, "than a wild rose." The old trailer had noticeably softened. While retaining his clarion voice and much of his sleepless energy, he was plainly less imperious of manner, less harsh of speech.

Jessie's case trouble me. As I watched her, studied her, I perceived that she possessed uncommon powers, but that she must be taken out of this sterile environment. "She must be rescued at once or she will live and die the wife of some Dakota farmer," I said to mother.

Again I was disturbed by the feeling that in some way my own career was disloyal, something built upon the privations of my sister as well as upon those of my mother. I began definitely to plan their rescue. "They must not spend the rest of their days on this barren farm," I said to Dr. Cross, and my self-accusation spurred me to sterner resolve.

It was not a pleasant time for my good friend, but, as it turned out, there was a special providence in his being there, for a few days later, while Jessie and I were seated in the little sitting-room busily discussing plans for her schooling we heard a short, piercing cry, followed by low sobbing.

Hurrying out into the yard, I saw my mother standing a few yards from the door, her sweet face distorted, the tears streaming down her cheeks. "What is it, mother?" I called out.

"I can't lift my feet," she stammered, putting her arms about my neck. "I can't move!" and in her voice was such terror and despair that my blood chilled.

It was true! She was helpless. From the waist downward all power of locomotion had departed. Her feet were like lead, drawn to the earth by some terrible magnetic power.

In a frenzy of alarm, Jessie and I carried her into the house and laid her on her bed. My heart burned with bitter indignation. "This is the end," I said. "Here is the result of long years of ceaseless toil. She has gone as her mother went, in the midst of the battle."

At the moment I cursed the laws of man, I cursed myself. I accused my father. Each moment my remorse and horror deepened, and yet I could do nothing, nothing but kneel beside the bed and hold her hand while Jessie ran to call the doctor. She returned soon to say she could not find him.

Slowly the stricken one grew calmer and at last, hearing a

wagon drive into the yard, I hurried out to tell my father what had happened. He read in my face something wrong. "What's the matter?" he asked as I drew near.

"Mother is stricken," I said. "She cannot walk."

He stared at me in silence, his gray eyes expanding like those of an eagle, then calmly, mechanically he got down and began to unhitch the team. He performed each habitual act with most minute care, till I, impatient of his silence, his seeming indifference, repeated, "Don't you understand? Mother has had a stroke! She is absolutely helpless."

Then he asked, "Where is your friend Dr. Cross?"

"I don't know, I thought he was with you."

Even as I was calling for him, Dr. Cross came into the cabin, his arms laden with roses. He had been strolling about on the prairie.

With his coming hope returned. Calmly yet skillfully he went to the aid of the sufferer, while father, Jessie and I sat in agonized suspense awaiting his report.

At last he came back to us with gentle reassuring smile.

"There is no immediate danger," he said, and the tone in which he spoke was even more comforting than his words. "As soon as she recovers from her terror she will not suffer"—then he added gravely, "A minute blood vessel has ruptured in her brain, and a small clot has formed there. If this is absorbed, as I think it will be, she will recover. Nothing can be done for her. No medicine can reach her. It is just a question of rest and quiet." Then to me he added something which stung like a poisoned dart. "She should have been relieved from severe household labor years ago."

My heart filled with bitterness and rebellion, bitterness against the pioneering madness which had scattered our family, and rebellion toward my father who had kept my mother always on the border, working like a slave long after the time when she should have been taking her ease. Above all, I resented my own failure, my own inability to help in the case. Here was I, established in a distant city, with success just opening her doors to me, and yet still so much the struggler that my will to aid was futile for lack of means.

Sleep was difficult that night, and for days thereafter my mind was rent with a continual and ineffectual attempt to reach a solution of my problem, which was indeed typical of ambitious young America everywhere. "Shall I give up my career at this point? How can I best serve my mother?" These were my questions and I could not answer either of them.

At the end of a week the sufferer was able to sit up, and soon recovered a large part of her native cheerfulness although it was evident to me that she would never again be the woman of the ready hand. Her days of labor were over.

Her magnificent voice was now weak and uncertain. Her speech painfully hesitant. She who had been so strong, so brave, was now both easily frightened and readily confused. She who had once walked with the grace and power of an athlete was now in terror of an up-rolled rug upon the floor. Every time I looked at her my throat ached with remorseful pain. Every plan I made included a vow to make her happy if I could. My success now meant only service to her. In no other way could I justify my career.

Dr. Cross though naturally eager to return to the comfort of his own home stayed on until his patient had regained her poise. "The clot seems in process of being taken up," he said to me, one morning, "and I think it safe to leave her. But you had better stay on for a few weeks."

"I shall stay until September, at least," I replied. "I will not go back at all if I am needed here."

"Don't fail to return," he earnestly advised. "The field is just opening for you in Boston, and your earning capacity is greater there than it is here. Success is almost won. Your mother knows this and tells me that she will insist on your going on with your work."

Heroic soul! She was always ready to sacrifice herself for others.

The Doctor's parting words comforted me as I returned to the shadeless farmstead to share in the work of harvesting the grain which was already calling for the reaper, and could not wait either upon sickness or age. Again I filled the place of stacker while my father drove the four-horse header, and when at noon, covered with sweat and dust, I looked at myself, I had very little sense of being a "rising literary man."

I got back once again to the solid realities of farm life, and the majesty of the colorful sunsets which ended many of our days could not conceal from me the starved lives and lonely days of my little sister and my aging mother.

"Think of it!" I wrote to my brother. "After eight years of cultivation, father's farm possesses neither tree nor vine. Mother's head has no protection from the burning rays of the sun, except the shadow which the house casts on the dry, hard door-yard. Where are the 'woods and prairie lands' of our song? Is this the 'fairy land' in which we were all to 'reign like kings'? Doesn't the whole migration of the Garlands and McClintocks seem a madness?"

Thereafter when alone, my mother and I often talked of the good old days in Wisconsin, of David and Deborah and William and Frank. I told her of Aunt Loretta's peaceful life, of the green hills and trees.

"Oh, I wish we had never left Green's Coulee!" she said.

But this was as far as her complaint ever went, for father was still resolute and undismayed. "We'll try again," he declared. "Next year will surely bring a crop."

In a couple of weeks our patient, though unable to lift her feet, was able to shuffle across the floor into the kitchen, and thereafter insisted on helping Jessie at her tasks. From a seat in a convenient corner she picked over berries, stirred cake dough, ground coffee and wiped dishes, almost as cheerfully as ever, but to me it was a pitiful picture of bravery, and I burned ceaselessly with desire to do something to repay her for this almost hopeless disaster.

The worst of the whole situation lay in the fact that my earnings both as teacher and as story writer were as yet hardly more than enough to pay my own carefully estimated expenses, and I saw no way of immediately increasing my income. On the face of it, my plain duty was to remain on the farm, and yet I could not bring myself to sacrifice my Boston life. In spite of my pitiful gains thus far, I held a vital hope of soon,—very soon—being in condition to bring my mother and my sister east. I argued, selfishly of course, "It must be that Dr. Cross is right. My only chance of success lies in the east."

Mother did her best to comfort me. "Don't worry about us," she said. "Go back to your work. I am gaining. I'll be all right in a little while." Her brave heart was still unsubdued.

While I was still debating my problem, a letter came which

greatly influenced me, absurdly influenced all of us. It contained an invitation from the Secretary of the Cedar Valley Agriculture Society to be "the Speaker of the Day" at the County Fair on the twenty-fifth of September. This honor not only flattered me, it greatly pleased my mother. It was the kind of honor she could fully understand. In imagination she saw her son standing up before a throng of old-time friends and neighbors introduced by Judge Daly and applauded by all the bankers and merchants of the town. "You must do it," she said, and her voice was decisive.

Father, though less open in his expression, was equally delighted. "You can go round that way just as well as not," he said. "I'd like to visit the old town myself."

This letter relieved the situation in the most unexpected way. We all became cheerful. I began to say, "Of course you are going to get well," and I turned again to my plan of taking my sister back to the seminary. "We'll hire a woman to stay with you," I said, "and Jessie can run up during vacation, or you and father can go down and spend Christmas with old friends."

Yes, I confess it, I was not only planning to leave my mother again—I was intriguing to take her only child away from her. There is no excuse for this, none whatever except the fact that I had her co-operation in the plan. She wanted her daughter to be educated quite as strongly as I could wish, and was willing to put up with a little more loneliness and toil if only her children were on the road to somewhere.

Jessie was the obstructionist. She was both scared and resentful. She had no desire to go to school in Osage. She wanted to stay where she was. Mother needed her,—and besides she didn't have any decent clothes to wear.

Ultimately I overcame all her scruples, and by promising her a visit to the great city of Minneapolis (with the privilege of returning if she didn't like the school) I finally got her to start with me. Poor, little scared sister, I only half realized the agony of mind through which you passed as we rode away into the Minnesota prairies!

The farther she got from home the shabbier her gown seemed and the more impossible her coat and hat. At last, as we were leaving Minneapolis on our way to Osage she leaned her tired head against me and sobbed out a wild wish to go home.

Her grief almost wrecked my own self-control but I soothed her as best I could by telling her that she would soon be among old friends and that she couldn't turn back now. "Go on and make a little visit anyway," I added. "It's only a few hours from Ordway and you can go home at any time."

She grew more cheerful as we entered familiar scenes, and one of the girls she had known when a child took charge of her, leaving me free to play the part of distinguished citizen.

The last day of the races was in action when I, with a certain amount of justifiable pride, rode through the gate (the old familiar sagging gate) seated beside the President of the Association. I wish I could believe that as "Speaker of the Day," I filled the sons of my neighbors with some small part of the awe with which the speakers of other days filled me, and if I assumed something of the polite condescension with which all public personages carry off such an entrance, I trust it will be forgiven me.

The event, even to me, was more inspiring in anticipation than in fulfillment, for when I rose to speak in the band-stand the wind was blowing hard, and other and less intellectual attractions were in full tide. My audience remained distressingly small—and calm. I have a dim recollection of howling into the face of the equatorical current certain disconnected sentences concerning my reform theory, and of seeing on the familiar faces of David Babcock, John Gammons and others of my bronzed and bent old neighbors a mild wonder as to what I was talking about.

On the whole I considered it a defeat. In the evening I spoke in the Opera House appearing on the same platform whence, eight years before, I had delivered my impassioned graduating oration on "Going West." True, I had gone east but then, advice is for others, not for oneself. Lee Moss, one of my class-mates, and in those Seminary days a rival orator, was in my audience, and so was Burton, wordless as ever, and a little sad, for his attempt at preaching had not been successful—his ineradicable shyness had been against him. Hattie was there looking thin and old, and Ella and Matilda with others of the girls I had known eight years before. Some were accompanied by their children.

I suspect I aroused their wonder rather than their admiration. My radicalism was only an astonishment to them. However, a few of the men, the more progressive of them, came to me at the close of my talk and shook hands and said, "Go on! The country needs just such talks." One of these was Uncle Billy Frazer and his allegiance surprised me, for he had never shown radical tendencies before.

Summing it all up on my way to Chicago I must admit that as a great man returning to his native village I had not been a success.

After a few hours of talk with Kirkland I started east by way of Washington in order that I might stop at Camden and call upon old Walt Whitman whose work I had been lecturing about, and who had expressed a willingness to receive me.

It was hot and dry in the drab little city in which he lived, and the street on which the house stood was as cheerless as an ash-barrel, even to one accustomed to poverty, like myself, and when I reached the door of his small, decaying wooden tenement, I was dismayed. It was all so unlike the home of a world-famous poet.

It was indeed very like that in which a very destitute mechanic might be living, and as I mounted the steps to Walt's room on the second story my resentment increased. Not a line of beauty or distinction or grace rewarded my glance. It was all of the same unesthetic barrenness, and not overly clean at that.

The old man, majestic as a stranded sea-God, was sitting in an arm chair, his broad Quaker hat on his head, waiting to receive me. He was spotlessly clean. His white hair, his light gray suit, his fine linen all gave the effect of exquisite neatness and wholesome living. His clear tenor voice, his quiet smile, his friendly handclasp charmed me and calmed me. He was so much gentler and sweeter than I had expected him to be.

He sat beside a heap of half-read books, marked newspapers, clippings and letters, a welter of concerns which he refused to have removed by the broom of the caretaker, and now and again as he wished to show me something he rose and hobbled a step or two to fish a book or a letter out of the pile. He was quite lame but could move without a crutch. He talked mainly of his good friends in Boston and elsewhere, and alluded to his enemies without a particle of rancor. The lines on his noble face were as placid as those on the brow of an ox—not one showed petulance or discouragement. He was the optimist in every word.

He spoke of one of my stories to which Traubel had called his attention, and reproved me gently for not "letting in the light."

It was a memorable meeting for me and I went away back to my work in Boston with a feeling that I had seen one of the very greatest literary personalities of the century, a notion I have had no cause to change in the twenty-seven years which have intervened.

31

Main Travelled Roads

My second visit to the West confirmed me in all my sorrowful notions of life on the plain, and I resumed my writing in a mood of bitter resentment, with full intention of telling the truth about western farm life, irrespective of the land-boomer or the politicians. I do not defend this mood, I merely report it.

In this spirit I finished a story which I called *A Prairie Heroine* (in order that no one should mistake my meaning, for it was the study of a crisis in the life of a despairing farmer's wife), and while even here, I did not tell the whole truth, I succeeded in suggesting to the sympathetic observer a tragic and hopeless common case.

It was a tract, that must be admitted, and realizing this, knowing that it was entirely too grim to find a place in the pages of the *Century* or *Harpers* I decided to send it to the *Arena,* a new Boston review whose spirit, so I had been told, was frankly radical.

A few days later I was amazed to receive from the editor a letter of acceptance enclosing a check, but a paragraph in the letter astonished me more than the check which was for one hundred dollars.

"I herewith enclose a check" wrote the editor, "which I hope you will accept in payment of your story. . . . I note that you have cut out certain paragraphs of description with the fear, no doubt, that the editor would object to them. I hope you will restore the manuscript to its original form and return it. When I ask a man to write for me, I want him to utter his mind with perfect freedom. My magazine is not one that is afraid of strong opinions."

This statement backed up by the writer's signature on a blue slip produced in me a moment of stupefaction. Entertaining no real hope of acceptance, I had sent the manuscript in accordance with my principle of trying every avenue, and to get such an answer—an immediate answer—with a check!

As soon as I recovered the use of my head and hand, I replied in eager acknowledgment. I do not recall the precise words of my letter, but it brought about an early meeting between B. O. Flower, the editor, and myself.

Flower's personality pleased me. Hardly more than a boy at this time, he met me with the friendliest smile, and in our talk we discovered many common lines of thought.

"Your story," he said, "is the kind of fiction I need. If you have any more of that sort let me see it. My magazine is primarily for discussion but I want to include at least one story in each issue. I cannot match the prices of magazines like the *Century* of course, but I will do the best I can for you."

It would be difficult to exaggerate the value of this meeting to me, for no matter what anyone may now say of the *Arena*'s logic or literary style, its editor's life was nobly altruistic. I have never known a man who strove more single-heartedly for social progress, than B. O. Flower. He was the embodiment of unselfish public service, and his ready sympathy for every genuine reform made his editorial office a center of civic zeal. As champions of various causes we all met in his open lists.

In the months which followed he accepted for his magazine several of my short stories and bought and printed *Under the Wheel,* an entire play, not to mention an essay or two on *The New Declaration of Rights.* He named me among his "regular contributors," and became not merely my comforter and active supporter but my banker, for the regularity of his payments raised me to comparative security. I was able to write home the most encouraging reports of my progress.

At about the same time (or a little later) the *Century* accepted a short story which I called *A Spring Romance,* and a three-part tale of Wisconsin. For these I received nearly five hundred dollars! Accompanying the note of acceptance was a personal letter from Richard Watson Gilder, so hearty in its words of appreciation that I was assured of another and more distinctive avenue of expression.

It meant something to get into the *Century* in those days. The praise of its editor was equivalent to a diploma. I regarded Gilder as second only to Howells in all that had to do with the judgment of fiction. Flower's interests were ethical, Gilder's esthetic, and after all my ideals were essentially literary. My reform notions were subordinate to my desire to take honors as a novelist.

I cannot be quite sure of the precise date of this good fortune, but I think it must have been in the winter of 1890 for I remember writing a lofty letter to my father, in which I said, "If you want any money, let me know."

As it happened he had need of seed wheat, and it was with deep satisfaction that I repaid the money I had borrowed of him, together with three hundred dollars more and so faced the new year clear of debt.

Like the miner who, having suddenly uncovered a hidden vein of gold, bends to his pick in a confident belief in his "find" so I humped above my desk without doubts, without hesitations. I had found my work in the world. If I had any thought of investment at this time, which I am sure I had not, it was concerned with the west. I had no notion of settling permanently in the east.

My success in entering both the *Century* and the *Arena* emboldened me to say to Dr. Cross, "I shall be glad to come down out of the attic and take a full-sized chamber at regular rates."

Alas! he had no such room, and so after much perturbation, my brother and I hired a little apartment on Moreland street in Roxbury and moved into it joyously. With a few dollars in my pocket, I went so far as to buy a couple of pictures and a new book rack, the first property I had ever owned, and when, on that first night, with everything in place we looked around upon our "suite," we glowed with such exultant pride as only struggling youth can feel. After years of privation, I had, at last, secured a niche in the frowning escarpment of Boston's social palisade.

Frank was twenty-seven, I was thirty, and had it not been for a haunting sense of our father's defeat and a growing fear of mother's decline, we would have been entirely content. "How can we share our good fortune with her and with sister Jessie?" was the question which troubled us most. Jessie's fate seemed especially dreary by contrast with our busy and colorful life.

"We can't bring them here," I argued. "They would never be happy here. Father is a borderman. He would enjoy coming east on a visit, but to shut him up in Boston would be like caging an eagle. The case seems hopeless."

The more we discussed it the more insoluble the problem became. The best we could do was to write often and to plan for frequent visits to them.

One day, late in March, Flower, who had been using my stories in almost every issue of his magazine, said to me: "Why don't you put together some of your tales of the west, and let us bring them out in book form? I believe they would have instant success."

His words delighted me for I had not yet begun to hope for an appearance as the author of a book. Setting to work at once to prepare such a volume I put into it two unpublished novelettes called *Up the Cooley* and *The Branch Road,* for the very good reason that none of the magazines, not even *The Arena,* found them "available." This reduced the number of sketches to six so that the title page read:

MAIN TRAVELLED ROADS
Six Mississippi Valley Stories
BY HAMLIN GARLAND

The phrase "main travelled road" is common in the west. Ask a man to direct you to a farmhouse and he will say, "Keep the main travelled road till you come to the second crossing and turn to the left." It seemed to me not only a picturesque title, significant of my native country, but one which permitted the use of a grimly sardonic foreword. This I supplied.

"The main travelled road in the west (as everywhere) is hot and dusty in summer and desolate and drear with mud in fall and spring, and in winter the winds sweep the snows across it, but it does sometimes cross a rich meadow where the songs of the larks and blackbirds and bobolinks are tangled. Follow it far enough, it may lead past a bend in the river where the water laughs eternally over its shallows. Mainly it is long and wearyful and has a dull little town at one end, and a home of toil at the other. Like the main travelled road of life it is traversed by many classes of people, but the poor and the weary predominate."

This, my first book, was put together during a time of deep personal sorrow. My little sister died suddenly, leaving my father and mother alone on the bleak plain, seventeen hundred miles from both their sons. Hopelessly crippled, my mother now mourned the loss of her "baby" and the soldier's keen eyes grew dim, for he loved this little daughter above anything else in the world. The flag of his sunset march was drooping on its staff. Nothing but poverty and a lonely old age seemed before him, and yet, in his letters to me, he gave out only the briefest hints of his despair.

All this will explain, if the reader is interested to know, why the dedication of my little book was bitter with revolt: "To my father and mother, whose half-century of pilgrimage on the main travelled road of life has brought them only pain and weariness, these stories are dedicated by a son to whom every day brings a deepening sense of his parents' silent heroism." It will explain also why the comfortable, the conservative, those who farmed the farmer, resented my thin gray volume and its message of acrid accusation.

It was published in 1891 and the outcry against it was instant and astonishing—to me. I had a foolish notion that the literary folk of the west would take a local pride in the color of my work, and to find myself execrated by nearly every critic as "a bird willing to foul his own nest" was an amazement. Editorials and criticisms poured into the office, all written to prove that my pictures of the middle border were utterly false.

Statistics were employed to show that pianos and Brussels carpets adorned almost every Iowa farmhouse. Tilling the prairie soil was declared to be "the noblest vocation in the world, not in the least like the pictures this eastern author has drawn of it."

True, corn was only eleven cents per bushel at that time, and the number of alien farm-renters was increasing. True, all the bright boys and girls were leaving the farm, following the example of my critics, but these I was told were all signs of prosperity and not of decay. The American farmer was getting rich, and moving to town, only the renters and the hired man were uneasy and clamorous.

My answer to all this criticism was a blunt statement of facts. "Butter is not always golden nor biscuits invariably light and flaky in my farm scenes, because they're not so in real life," I explained. "I grew up on a farm and I am determined once for all to put the essential ugliness of its life into print. I will not lie, even to be a patriot. A proper proportion of the sweat, flies, heat, dirt and drudgery of it all shall go in. I am a competent witness and I intend to tell the whole truth."

But I didn't! Even my youthful zeal faltered in the midst of a revelation of the lives led by the women on the farms of the middle border. Before the tragic futility of their suffering, my pen refused to shed its ink. Over the hidden chamber of their maternal agonies I drew the veil.

The old soldier had nothing to say but mother wrote to me, "It scares me to read some of your stories—they are so true. You might have said more," she added, "but I'm glad you didn't. Farmers' wives have enough to bear as it is."

"My stories were not written for farmers' wives," I replied. "They were written to convict the selfish monopolistic liars of the towns."

"I hope the liars read 'em," was her laconic retort.

Nevertheless, in spite of all the outcry against my book, words of encouragement came in from a few men and women who had lived out the precise experiences which I had put into print. "You have delineated my life," one man said. "Every detail of your description is true. The sound of the prairie chickens, the hum of the threshing machine, the work of seeding, corn husking, everything is familiar to me and new in literature."

A woman wrote, "You are entirely right about the loneliness, the stagnation, the hardship. We are sick of lies. Give the world the truth."

Another critic writing from the heart of a great university said, "I value your stories highly as literature, but I suspect that in the social war which is coming you and I will be at each other's throats."

This controversy naturally carried me farther and farther from the traditional, the respectable. As a rebel in art I was prone to arouse hate. Every letter I wrote was a challenge, and one of my conservative friends frankly urged the folly of my course. "It is a mistake for you to be associated with cranks like Henry George and writers like Whitman," he said. "It is a mistake to be published by the *Arena*. Your book should have been brought out by one of the old established firms. If you will fling away your radical notions and consent to amuse the governing classes, you will succeed."

Fling away my convictions! It were as easy to do that as to cast out my bones. I was not wearing my indignation as a cloak. My rebellious tendencies came from something deep down. They formed an element in my blood. My patriotism resented the failure of our government. Therefore such advice had very little influence upon me. The criticism that really touched and influenced me was that which said, "Don't preach,—exemplify. Don't let your stories degenerate into tracts." Howells said, "Be fine, be fine—but not too fine!" and Gilder warned me not to leave Beauty out of the picture.

In the light of this friendly council I perceived my danger, and set about to avoid the fault of mixing my fiction with my polemics.

The editor of the *Arena* remained my most loyal supporter. He filled the editorial section of his magazine with praise of my fiction and loudly proclaimed my non-conformist character. No editor ever worked harder to give his author a national reputation and the book sold, not as books sell now, but moderately, steadily, and being more widely read than sold, went far. This proved of course, that my readers were poor and could not afford to pay a dollar for a book, at least they didn't, and I got very little royalty from the sale. If I had any illusions about that they were soon dispelled. On the paper bound book I got five cents, on the cloth bound, ten. The sale was mainly in the fifty-cent edition.

It was not for me to criticise the methods by which my publisher was trying to make me known, and I do not at this moment regret Flower's insistence upon the reforming side of me,—but for the reason that he was essentially ethical rather than esthetic, some part of the literary significance of my work escaped him. It was from the praise of Howells, Matthews and Stedman, that I received my enlightenment. I began to perceive that in order to make my work carry its message, I must be careful to keep a certain balance between Significance and Beauty. The artist began to check the preacher.

Howells gave the book large space in "The Study" in *Harpers* and what he said of it profoundly instructed me. Edward Everett Hale, Mary E. Wilkins, Thomas Wentworth Higginson, Charles Dudley Warner, Edmund Clarence Stedman, and many other were most generous of applause. In truth I was welcomed into the circle of American realists with an instant and generous greeting which astonished, at the same time that it delighted me.

I marvel at this appreciation as I look back upon it, and surely in view of its reception, no one can blame me for considering my drab little volume a much more important contribution to American fiction than it really was.

It was my first book, and so, perhaps, the reader will excuse me for being a good deal uplifted by the noise it made. Then too, it is only fair to call attention to the fact that aside from Edward Eggleston's *Hoosier Schoolmaster,* Howe's *Story of a Country Town,* and *Zury,* by Joseph Kirkland, I had the middle west almost entirely to myself. Not one of the group of western writers who have since won far greater fame, and twenty times more dollars than I, had at that time published a single volume. William Allen White, Albert Bigelow Payne, Stewart Edward White, Jack London, Emerson Hough, George Ade, Meredith Nicholson, Booth Tarkington, and Rex Beach were all to come. "Octave Thanet" was writing her stories of Arkansas life for *Scribners* but had published only one book.

Among all my letters of encouragement of this time, not one, except perhaps that from Mr. Howells, meant more to me than a word which came from Walt Whitman, who hailed me as one of the literary pioneers of the west for whom he had been waiting. His judgment, so impersonal, so grandly phrased, gave me the feeling of having been "praised by posterity."

In short, I was assured that my face was set in the right direction and that the future was mine, for I was not yet thirty-one years of age, and thirty-one is a most excellent period of life!

And yet, by a singular fatality, at this moment came another sorrow, the death of Alice, my boyhood's adoration. I had known for years that she was not for me, but I loved to think of her as out there walking the lanes among the roses and the wheat as of old. My regard for her was no longer that of the lover desiring and hoping, and though I acknowledged defeat I had been too broadly engaged in my ambitious literary plans to permit her deflection to permanently cloud my life. She had been a radiant and charming figure in my prairie world, and when I read the letter telling of her passing, my mind was irradiated with the picture she had made when last she said good-bye to me. Her gentle friendship had been very helpful through all my years of struggle and now, in the day of my security, her place was empty.

32

The Spirit of Revolt

During all this time while I had been living so busily and happily in Boston, writing stories, discussing Ibsen and arguing the cause of Impressionism, a portentous and widespread change of sentiment was taking place among the farmers of the Middle Border. The discouragement which I had discovered in old friends and neighbors in Dakota was finding collective expression. A vast and non-sectional union of the corn-growers, wheat-raisers, and cotton-growers had been effected and the old time politicians were uneasy.

As ten cent corn and ten per cent interest were troubling Kansas so six-cent cotton was inflaming Georgia—and both were frankly sympathetic with Montana and Colorado whose miners were suffering from a drop in the price of silver. To express the meaning of this revolt a flying squadron of radical orators had been commissioned and were in the field. Mary Ellen Lease with Cassandra voice, and Jerry Simpson with shrewd humor were voicing the demands of the plainsman, while "Coin" Harvey as champion of the Free Silver theory had stirred the Mountaineer almost to a frenzy. It was an era of fervent meetings and fulminating resolutions. The Grange had been social, or at most commercially cooperative in its activities, but The Farmers' Alliance came as a revolt.

The People's Party which was the natural outcome of this unrest involved my father. He wrote me that he had joined "the Populists," and was one of their County officers. I was not surprised at this action on his part, for I had known how high in honor he held General Weaver who was the chief advocate of a third party.

Naturally Flower sympathized with this movement, and kept the pages of his magazine filled with impassioned defenses of it. One day, early in '91, as I was calling upon him in his office, he suddenly said, "Garland, why can't you write a serial story for us?

One that shall deal with this revolt of the farmers? It's perfectly legitimate material for a novel, as picturesque in its way as *The Rise of the Vendee*—Can't you make use of it?"

To this I replied, with some excitement—"Why yes, I think I can. I have in my desk at this moment, several chapters of an unfinished story which uses the early phases of the Grange movement as a background. If it pleases you I can easily bring it down to date. It might be necessary for me to go into the field, and make some fresh studies, but I believe I can treat the two movements in the same story. Anyhow I should like to try."

"Bring the manuscript in at once," replied Flower. "It may be just what we are looking for. If it is we will print it as a serial this summer, and bring it out in book form next winter."

In high excitement I hurried home to dig up and re-read the fragment which I called at this time *Bradley Talcott*. It contained about thirty thousand words and its hero was a hired man on an Iowa farm. Of course I saw possibilities in this manuscript—I was in the mood to do that—and sent it in.

Flower read it and reported almost by return mail.

"We'll take it," he said. "And as soon as you can get away, I think that you'd better go out to Kansas and Nebraska and make the studies necessary to complete the story. We'll pay all your expenses and pay you for the serial besides."

The price agreed upon would seem very small in these days of millionaire authors, but to me the terms of Flower's commission were nobly generous. They set me free. They gave me wings!—For the first time in my life I was able to travel in comfort. I could not only eat in the dining car, and sleep in the sleeping car, but I could go to a hotel at the end of my journey with a delightful sense of freedom from worry about the bills. Do you wonder that when I left Boston a week or two later, I did so with elation—with a sense of conquest?

Eager to explore—eager to know every state of the Union and especially eager to study the far plains and the Rocky Mountains, I started westward and kept going until I reached Colorado. My stay in the mountain country was short, but my glimpses of Ouray and Telluride started me on a long series of stories of "the high trails."

On the way out as well as on the way back, I took part in meetings of rebellious farmers in bare-walled Kansas school-houses, and watched protesting processions of weather-worn Nebraska Populists as they filed through the shadeless cities of their sun-baked plain. I attended barbecues on drab and dusty fair grounds, meeting many of the best known leaders in the field.

Everywhere I came in contact with the discontented. I saw only those whose lives seemed about to end in failure, and my grim notions of farm life were in no wise softened by these experiences.

How far away all this seems in these days of three-dollar wheat and twenty-six cent cotton—these days of automobiles, tractor plows, and silos!

As I kept no diary in those days, I am a little uncertain about dates and places—and no wonder, for I was doing something every moment (I travelled almost incessantly for nearly two years) but one event of that summer does stand clearly out—that of a meeting with my father at Omaha in July.

It seems that some sort of convention was being held there and that my father was a delegate from Brown County, Dakota. At any rate I distinctly recall meeting him at the train and taking him to my hotel and introducing him to General Weaver. As a representative of the *Arena* I had come to know many of the most prominent men in the movement, and my father was deeply impressed with their recognition of me. For the first time in his life, he deferred to me. He not only let me take charge of him, he let me pay the bills.

He said nothing to me of his pride in my position, but my good friends Robert and Elia Peattie told me that to them he expressed the keenest satisfaction. "I never thought Hamlin would make a success of writing," he said, "although he was always given to books. I couldn't believe that he would ever earn a living that way, but it seems that he is doing it." My commission from Flower and the fact that the *Arena* was willing to pay my way about the country, were to him indubitable signs of prosperity. They could not be misinterpreted by his neighbors.

Elia Peattie sat beside him at a meeting when I spoke, and she heard him say to an old soldier on the right, "I never knew just what that boy of mine was fitted for, but I guess he has struck his gait at last."

It may seem illogical to the reader, but this deference on the part of the old soldier did not amuse me. On the contrary it hurt me. A little pang went through me every time he yielded his leadership. I hated to see him display the slightest evidence of age, of weakness. I would rather have had him storm than sigh. Part of his irresolution, his timidity, was due, as I could see, to the unwonted noise, and to the crowds of excited men, but more of it came from the vague alarm of self-distrust which are signs of advancing years.

For two days we went about together, attending all the sessions and meeting many of the delegates, but we found time to discuss the problems which confronted us both. "I am farming nearly a thousand acres this year," he said, "and I'm getting the work systematized so that I can raise wheat at sixty cents a bushel—if I can only get fifteen bushels to the acre. But there's no money in the country. We seem to be at the bottom of our resources. I never expected to see this country in such a state. I can't get money enough to pay my taxes. Look at my clothes! I haven't had a new suit in three years. Your mother is in the same fix. I wanted to bring her down, but she had no clothes to wear—and then, besides, it's hard for her to travel. The heat takes hold of her terribly."

This statement of the Border's poverty and drought was the more moving to me for the reason that the old pioneer had always been so patriotic, so confident, so sanguine of his country's future. He had come a long way from the buoyant faith of '66, and the change in him was typical of the change in the West—in America—and it produced in me a sense of dismay, of rebellious bitterness. Why should our great new land fall into this slough of discouragement?

My sympathy with the Alliance took on a personal tinge. My pride in my own "success" sank away. How pitiful it all seemed in the midst of the almost universal disappointment and suffering of the West! In the face of my mother's need my resources were pitifully inadequate.

"I can't go up to see mother this time," I explained to my father, "but I am coming out again this fall to speak in the campaign and I shall surely run up and visit her then."

"I'll arrange for you to speak in Aberdeen," he said. "I'm on the County Committee."

All the way back to Boston, and during the weeks of my work on my novel, I pondered the significance of the spiritual change which had swept over the whole nation—but above all others the problem of my father's desperate attempt to retrieve his fortunes engaged my sympathy. "Unless he gets a crop this year," I reported to my brother—"he is going to need help. It fills me with horror to think of those old people spending another winter out there on the plain."

My brother who was again engaged by Herne to play one of the leading parts in *Shore Acres* was beginning to see light ahead. His pay was not large but he was saving a little of it and was willing to use his savings to help me out in my plan of rescue. It was to be a rescue although we were careful never to put it in that form in our letters to the old pioneer.

Up to this month I had retained my position in the Boston School of Oratory, but I now notified Brown that I should teach no more in his school or any other school.

His big shoulders began to shake and a chuckle preceded his irritating joke—"Going back to shingling?" he demanded.

"No," I replied, "I'm not going to shingle anymore—except for exercise after I get my homestead in the west—but I *think*—I'm not sure—I think I can make a living with my pen."

He became serious at this and said, "I'm sorry to have you go—but you are entirely right. You have found your work and I give you my blessing on it. But you must always count yourself one of my teachers and come and speak for us whenever you can." This I promised to do and so we parted.

Early in September I went west and having put myself in the hands of the State Central Committee of Iowa, entered the field, campaigning in the interests of the People's Party. For six weeks I travelled, speaking nearly every day—getting back to the farms of the west and harvesting a rich fund of experiences.

It was delightful autumn weather, and in central Iowa the crops were fairly abundant. On every hand fields of corn covered the gentle hills like wide rugs of lavender velvet, and the odor of melons and ripening leaves filled the air. Nature's songs of cheer and abundance (uttered by innumerable insects) set forth the monstrous injustice of man's law by way of contrast. Why should children cry for food in our cities whilst fruits rotted on the vines and wheat had no value to the harvester?

With other eager young reformers, I rode across the odorous prairie swells, journeying from one meeting place to another, feeling as my companions did that something grandly beneficial was about to be enacted into law. In this spirit I spoke at Populist picnics, standing beneath great oaks, surrounded by men and women, work-worn like my own father and mother, shadowed by the same cloud of dismay. I smothered in small halls situated over saloons and livery stables, travelling by freight-train at night in order to ride in triumph as "Orator of the Day" at some county fair, until at last I lost all sense of being the writer and recluse.

As I went north my indignation burned brighter, for the discontent of the people had been sharpened by the drought which had again cut short the crop. At Millbank, Cyrus, one of my old Dry Run neighbors, met me. He was now a grave, stooping middle-aged man also in the midst of disillusionment. "Going west" had been a mistake for him as for my father—"But here we are," he said, "and I see nothing for it but to stick to the job."

Mother and father came to Aberdeen to hear me speak, and as I looked down on them from the platform of the opera house, I detected on their faces an expression which was not so much attention, as preoccupation. They were not listening to my words, they were thinking of my relationship to them, of the mystery involved in my being there on the platform surrounded by the men of the county whom they most respected. They could not take my theories seriously, but they did value and to the full, the honor which their neighbors paid me—their son! Their presence so affected me that I made, I fear, but an indifferent address.

We did not have much time to talk over family affairs but it was good to see them even for a few moments and to know that mother was slowly regaining the use of her limbs.

Another engagement made it necessary for me to take the night train for St. Paul and so they both went down to the station with me, and as the time came to part I went out to the little covered buggy (which was all the carriage my father owned) to start them off on their lonely twelve-mile trip back to the farm. "I don't know how it is all coming about, mother, but sometime, somewhere you and I are going to live together,—not here, back in Osage, or perhaps in Boston. It won't be long now."

She smiled, but her voice was tremulous. "Don't worry about me. I'm all right again—at least I am better. I shall be happy if only you are successful."

This meeting did me good. My mother's smile lessened my bitterness, and her joy in me, her faith in me, sent me away in renewed determination to rescue her from the destitution and loneliness of this arid land.

My return to Boston in November discovered a startling change in my relationship to it. The shining city in which I had lived for seven years, and which had become so familiar to me (and so necessary to my progress), had begun to dwindle, to recede. The warm, broad, unkempt and tumultuous west, with its clamorous movement, its freedom from tradition, its vitality of political thought, reasserted its power over me. New England again became remote. It was evident that I had not really taken root in Massachusetts after all. I perceived that Boston was merely the capital of New England while New York was fast coming to be the all-conquering capital of The Nation.

My realization of this shift of values was sharpened by the announcement that Howells had definitely decided to move to the Metropolis, and that Herne had broken up his little home in Ashmont and was to make his future home on Convent Avenue in Harlem. The process of stripping Boston to build up Manhattan had begun.

My brother who was still one of Herne's company of players in *Shore Acres,* had no home to break up, but he said, "I'm going to get some sort of headquarters in New York. If you'll come on we'll hire a little apartment up town and 'bach' it. I'm sick of theatrical boarding houses."

With suddenly acquired conviction that New York was about to become the Literary Center of America, I replied, "Very well. Get your flat. I'd like to spend a winter in the old town anyway."

My brother took a small furnished apartment on 105th Street, and together we camped above the tumult. It was only twelve-and-a-half feet wide and about forty-eight long, and its furnishings were ugly, frayed and meager, but its sitting room opened upon the sun, and there, of a morning, I continued to write in growing content. At about noon the actor commonly cooked a steak or a chop and boiled a pot of coffee, and after the dishes were washed, we both merrily descended upon Broadway by means of a Ninth Avenue elevated train. Sometimes we dined down town in reckless luxury at one of the French restaurants, "where the tip was but a nickel and the dinner thirty cents," but usually even our evening meal was eaten at home.

Herne was playing an unlimited engagement at the Broadway theater and I spent a good deal of time behind the scenes with him. His house on Convent Avenue was a handsome mansion and on a Sunday, I often dined there, and when we all got going the walls resounded with argument. Jim was a great wag and a delightful story teller, but he was in deadly earnest as a reformer, and always ready to speak on The Single Tax. He took his art very seriously also, and was one of the best stage directors of his day. Some of his dramatic methods were so far in advance of his time that they puzzled or disgusted many of his patrons, but without doubt he profoundly influenced the art of the American stage. Men like William Gillette and Clyde Fitch quite frankly acknowledged their indebtedness to him.

Jim and Katharine both had an exaggerated notion of my importance in the world of art and letters, and listened to me with a respect, a fellowship and an appreciation which increased my sense of responsibility and inspired me to greater effort as a novelist. Together we hammered out questions of art and economics, and planned new plays. Those were inspiring hours to us all and we still refer to them as "the good old Convent Avenue days!"

New York City itself was incredibly simpler and quieter than it is now, but to me it was a veritable hell because of the appalling inequality which lay between the palaces of the landlords and the tenements of the proletariat. The monstrous injustice of permitting a few men to own the land on which millions toiled for the barest living tore at my heart strings then, as it does now, and the worst of it rested in the fact that the landless seemed willing to be robbed for the pleasure of those who could not even dissipate the wealth which rolled in upon them in waves of unearned rent.

And yet, much as I felt this injustice and much as the city affected me, I could not put it into fiction. "It is not my material," I said. "My dominion is the West."

Though at ease, I had no feeling of being at home in this tumult. I was only stopping in it in order to be near the Hernes, my brother, and Howells. The Georges, whom I had come to know very well, interested me greatly and often of an evening I went over to the East Side, to the unpretentious brick house in which The Prophet and his delightful family lived. Of course this home was doctrinaire, but then I liked that flavor, and so did the Hernes, although Katharine's keen sense of humor sometimes made us all seem rather like thorough-going cranks—which we were.

In the midst of our growing security and expanding acquaintanceship, my brother and I often returned, to the problem of our aging parents.

My brother was all for bringing them east but to this I replied, "No, that is out of the question. The old pioneer would never be happy in a city."

"We could buy a farm over in Jersey."

"What would he do there? He would be among strangers and in strange conditions.—No, the only solution is to get him to go back either to Iowa or to Wisconsin. He will find even that very hard to do for it will seem like failure but he must do it. For mother's sake I'd rather see him go back to the LaCrosse valley. It would be a pleasure to visit them there."

"That is the thing to do," my brother agreed. "I'll never get out to Dakota again."

The more I thought about this the lovelier it seemed. The hills, the farmhouses, the roads, the meadows all had delightful associations in my mind, as I knew they must have in my mother's mind and the idea of a regained homestead in the place of my birth began to engage my thought whenever I had leisure to ponder my problem and especially whenever I received a letter from my mother.

There was a certain poetic justice in the return of my father and mother to the land from which they had been lured a quarter of a century before, and I was willing to make any sacrifice to bring it about. I take no credit for this, it was a purely selfish plan, for so long as they were alone out there on the plain my own life must continue to be troubled and uneasy.

33

The End of the Sunset Trail

In February while attending a conference of reformers in St. Louis I received a letter from my mother which greatly disturbed me. "I wish I could see you," she wrote. "I am not very well this winter, I can't go out very often and I get very lonesome for my boys. If only you did not live so far away!"

There was something in this letter which made all that I was doing in the convention of no account, and on the following evening I took the train for Columbia, the little village in which my parents were spending the winter, filled with remorseful forebodings. My pain and self-accusation would not let me rest. Something clutched my heart every time I thought of my crippled mother prisoned in a Dakota shanty and no express train was swift enough to satisfy my desire to reach her. The letter had been forwarded to me and I was afraid that she might be actually ill.

That ride next day from Sioux City to Aberdeen was one of the gloomiest I had ever experienced. Not only was my conscience uneasy, it seemed that I was being hurled into a region of arctic storms. A terrific blizzard possessed the plain, and the engine appeared to fight its way like a brave animal. All day it labored forward while the coaches behind it swayed in the ever-increasing power of the tempest, their wheels emitting squeals of pain as they ground through the drifts, and I sitting in my overcoat with collar turned high above my ears, my hands thrust deep in my pockets, sullenly counted the hours of my discomfort. The windows, furred deep with frost, let in but a pallid half-light, thus adding a mental dusk to the actual menace of the storm.

After each station the brakemen re-entered as if blown in by the blast, and a vapor, white as a shower of flour, filled the doorway, behind them. Occasionally as I cleared a space for a peephole through the rimy panes, I caught momentary glimpses of a level, treeless earth, desolate as the polar ocean swept by ferocious elemental warfare.

No life was to be seen save here and there a suffering steer or colt, humped under the lee of a straw-stack. The streets of the small wooden towns were deserted. No citizen was abroad, only the faint smoke of chimneys testified to the presence of life beneath the roof-trees.

Occasionally a local passenger came in, puffing and whistling with loud explosions of excited comment over the storm which he seemed to treat as an agreeable diversion, but the conductor, who followed, threshing his hands and nursing his ears, swore in emphatic dislike of the country and climate, but even this controversy offered no relief to the through passengers who sat in frozen stoical silence. There was very little humor in a Dakota blizzard for them—or for me.

At six o'clock that night I reached the desolate end of my journey. My father met me at the station and led the way to the low square bleak cottage which he had rented for the winter. Mother, still unable to lift her feet from the floor, opened the door to us, and reaching her, as I did, through that terrifying tempest, made her seem as lonely as a castaway on some gelid Greenland coast.

Father was in unwonted depression. His crop had again failed to mature. With nearly a thousand acres of wheat, he had harvested barely enough for the next year's seed. He was not entirely at the end of his faith, however; on the contrary, he was filled with desire of the farther west. "The irrigated country is the next field for development. I'm going to sell out here and try irrigation in Montana. I want to get where I can regulate the water for my crops."

"You'll do nothing of the kind," I retorted. "You'll go no further west. I have a better plan than that."

The wind roared on, all that night and all the next day, and during this time we did little but feed the stove and argue our widely separated plans. I told them of Franklin's success on the stage with Herne, and I described my own busy, though unremunerative life as a writer, and as I talked the world from which I came shone with increasing splendor.

Little by little the story of the country's decay came out. The village of Ordway had been moved away, nothing remained but the grain elevator. Many of our old neighbors had gone "to the irrigation country" and more were planning to go as soon as they could sell their farms. Columbia was also in desolate decline. Its hotel stood empty, its windows broken, its doors sagging.

Nothing could have been more depressing, more hopeless, and my throat burned with bitter rage every time my mother shuffled across the floor, and when she shyly sat beside me and took my hand in hers as if to hold me fast, my voice almost failed me. I began to plead. "Father, let's get a home together, somewhere. Suppose we compromise on old Neshonoc where you were married and where I was born. Let's buy a house and lot there and put the deed in mother's name so that it can never be alienated, and make it the Garland Homestead. Come! Mother's brothers are there, your sister is there, all your old pioneer comrades are there. It's in a rich and sheltered valley and is filled with associations of your youth.—Haven't you had enough of pioneering? Why not go back and be sheltered by the hills and trees for the rest of your lives? If you'll join us in this plan, Frank and I will spend our summers with you and perhaps we can all eat our Thanksgiving dinners together in the good old New England custom and be happy."

Mother yielded at once to the earnestness of my appeal. "I'm ready to go back," she said. "There's only one thing to keep me here, and that is Jessie's grave," (Poor little girl! It did seem a bleak place in which to leave her lying alone) but the old soldier was still too proud, too much the pioneer, to bring himself at once to a surrender of his hopes. He shook his head and said, "I can't do it, Hamlin. I've got to fight it out right here or farther west."

To this I darkly responded, "If you go farther west, you go alone. Mother's pioneering is done. She is coming with me, back to comfort, back to a real home, beside her brothers."

As I grew calmer, we talked of the past, of the early days in Iowa, of the dimmer, yet still more beautiful valleys of Wisconsin, till mother sighed, and said, "I'd like to see the folks and the old coulee once more, but I never shall."

"Yes, you shall," I asserted.

We spoke of David whose feet were still marching to the guidons of the sunset, of Burton far away on an Island in Puget Sound, and together we decided that placid old William, sitting among his bees in Gill's Coulee, was after all the wiser man. Of what avail this constant quest of gold, beneath the far horizon's rim?

"Father," I bluntly said, "you've been chasing a will-o'-the-wisp. For fifty years you've been moving westward, and always you have gone from certainty to uncertainty, from a comfortable home to a shanty. For thirty years you've carried mother on a ceaseless journey—to what end? Here you are,—snowbound on a treeless plain with mother old and crippled. It's a hard thing to say but the time has come for a 'bout face. *You must take the back trail.* It will hurt, but it must be done."

"I can't do it!" he exclaimed. "I've never 'backed water' in my life, and I won't do it now. I'm not beaten yet. We've had three bad years in succession—we'll surely have a crop next year. I won't surrender so long as I can run a team."

"Then, let me tell you something else," I resumed. "I will never visit you on this accursed plain again. You can live here if you want to, but I'm going to take mother out of it. She shall not grow old and die in such surroundings as these. I won't have it—it isn't right."

At last the stern old Captain gave in, at least to the point of saying, "Well, we'll see. I'll come down next summer, and we'll visit William and look the ground over.—But I won't consider going back to stay till I've had a crop. I won't go back to the old valley dead-broke. I can't stand being called a failure. If I have a crop and can sell out I'll talk with you."

"Very well. I'm going to stop off at Salem on my way East and tell the folks that you are about to sell out and come back to the old valley."

This victory over my pioneer father gave me such relief from my gnawing conscience that my whole sky lightened. The thought of establishing a family hearth at the point where my life began, had a fine appeal. All my schooling had been to migrate, to keep moving. "If your crop fails, go west and try a new soil. If disagreeable neighbors surround you, sell out and move—always toward the open country. To remain quietly in your native place is a sign of weakness, of irresolution. Happiness dwells afar. Wealth and fame are to be found by journeying toward the sunset star!" Such had been the spirit, the message of all the songs and stories of my youth.

Now suddenly I perceived the futility of our quest. I felt the value, I acknowledged the peace of the old, the settled. The valley of my birth even in the midst of winter had a quiet beauty. The bluffs were draped with purple and silver. Steel-blue shadows filled the hollows of the sunlit snow. The farmhouses all put forth a comfortable, settled, homey look. The farmers themselves, shaggy, fur-clad and well-fed, came into town driving fat horses whose bells uttered a song of plenty. On the plain we had feared the wind with a mortal terror, here the hills as well as the sheltering elms (which defended almost every roof) stood against the blast like friendly warders.

The village life, though rude and slow-moving, was hearty and cheerful. As I went about the streets with my uncle William—gray-haired old pioneers whose names were startlingly familiar, called out, "Hello, Bill"—adding some homely jest precisely as they had been doing for forty years. As young men they had threshed or cradled or husked corn with my father, whom they still called by his first name. "So you are Dick's boy? How is Dick getting along?"

"He has a big farm," I replied, "nearly a thousand acres, but he's going to sell out next year and come back here."

They were all frankly pleased. "Is that so! Made his pile, I s'pose?"

"Enough to live on, I guess," I answered evasively.

"I'm glad to hear of it. I always liked Dick. We were in the woods together. I hated to see him leave the valley. How's Belle?"

This question always brought the shadow back to my face. "Not very well,—but we hope she'll be better when she gets back here among her own folks."

"Well, we'll all be glad to see them both," was the hearty reply.

In this hope, with this plan in mind, I took my way back to New York, well pleased with my plan.

After nearly a third of a century of migration, the Garlands were about to double on their trail, and their decision was deeply significant. It meant that a certain phase of American pioneering had ended, that "the woods and prairie lands" having all been taken up, nothing remained but the semi-arid valleys of the Rocky Mountains. "Irrigation" was a new word and a vague word in the ears of my father's generation, and had little of the charm which lay in the "flowery savannahs" of the Mississippi valley. In the years between 1865 and 1892 the nation had swiftly passed through the buoyant era of free land settlement, and now the day of reckoning had come.

34

We Go to California

The idea of a homestead now became an obsession with me. As a proletariat I knew the power of the landlord and the value of land. My love of the wilderness was increasing year by year, but all desire to plow the wild land was gone. My desire for a home did not involve a lonely cabin in a far-off valley, on the contrary I wanted roads and bridges and neighbors. My hope now was to possess a minute isle of safety in the midst of the streaming currents of western life—a little solid ground in my native valley on which the surviving members of my family could catch and cling.

All about me as I travelled, I now perceived the mournful side of American "enterprise." Sons were deserting their work-worn fathers, daughters were forgetting their tired mothers. Families were everywhere breaking up. Ambitious young men and unsuccessful old men were in restless motion, spreading, swarming, dragging their reluctant women and their helpless and wondering children into unfamiliar hardships—At times I visioned the Middle Border as a colony of ants—which was an injustice to the ants, for ants have a reason for their apparently futile and aimless striving.

My brother and I discussed my notion in detail as we sat in our six-by-nine dining room, high in our Harlem flat. "The house must be in a village. It must be New England in type and stand beneath tall elm trees," I said. "It must be broad-based and low—you know the kind, we saw dozens of them on our tramp-trip down the Connecticut Valley and we'll have a big garden and a tennis court. We'll need a barn, too, for father will want to keep a driving team. Mother shall have a girl to do the housework so that we can visit her often,"—and so on and on!

Things were not coming our way very fast but they were coming, and it really looked as though my dream might become a reality. My brother was drawing a small but regular salary as a member of Herne's company, my stories were selling moderately well and as neither of us was given to drink or cards, whatever we earned we saved. To some minds our lives seemed stupidly regular, but we were happy in our quiet way.

It was in my brother's little flat on One Hundred and Fifth Street that Stephen Crane renewed a friendship which had begun a couple of years before, while I was lecturing in Avon, New Jersey. He was a slim, pale, hungry looking boy at this time and had just written *The Red Badge of Courage,* in fact he brought the first half of it in his pocket on his second visit, and I loaned him fifteen dollars to redeem the other half from the keep of a cruel typist.

He came again and again to see me, always with a new roll of manuscript in his ulster. Now it was *The Men in the Storm,* now a bunch of *The Black Riders,* curious poems, which he afterwards dedicated to me, and while my brother browned a steak, Steve and I usually sat in council over his dark future.

"You will laugh over these lean years," I said to him, but he found small comfort in that prospect.

To him I was a man established, and I took an absurd pleasure in playing the part of Successful Author. It was all very comical—for my study was the ratty little parlor of a furnished flat for which we paid thirty dollars per month. Still to the man at the bottom of a pit the fellow on top, in the sunlight, is a king, and to Crane my brother and I were at least dukes.

An expression used by Suderman in his preface to *Dame Care* had made a great impression on my mind and in discussing my future with the Hernes I quoted these lines and said, "I am resolved that *my* mother shall not 'rise from the feast of life empty.' Think of it! She has never seen a real play in a real theater in all her life. She has never seen a painting or heard a piece of fine music. She knows nothing of the splendors of our civilization except what comes to her in the newspapers, while here am I in the midst of every intellectual delight. I take no credit for my desire to comfort her—it's just my way of having fun. It's a purely selfish enterprise on my part."

Katharine who was familiar with the theory of Egoistic Altruism would not let my statement go uncontradicted. She tried to make a virtue of my devotion to my parents.

"No," I insisted,—"if batting around town gave me more real pleasure I would do it. It don't, in fact I shall never be quite happy till I have shown mother *Shore Acres* and given her an opportunity to hear a symphony concert."

Meanwhile, having no business adviser, I was doing honorable things in a foolish way. With no knowledge of how to publish my work I was bringing out a problem novel here, a realistic novelette there and a book of short stories in a third place, all to the effect of confusing my public and disgusting the book-seller. But then, no one in those days had any very clear notion of how to launch a young writer, and so (as I had entered the literary field by way of a side-gate) I was doing as well as could have been expected of me. My idea, it appears, was to get as many books into the same market at the same time as possible. As a matter of fact none of them paid me any royalty, my subsistence came from the sale of such short stories as I was able to lodge with *The Century,* and *Harpers, The Youth's Companion* and *The Arena.*

The "Bacheller Syndicate" took a kindly interest in me, and I came to like the big, blonde, dreaming youth from The North Country who was the nominal head of the firm. Irving Bacheller, even at that time struck me as more of a poet than a business man, though I was always glad to get his check, for it brought the Garland Homestead just that much nearer. On the whole it was a prosperous and busy winter for both my brother and myself.

Chicago was in the early stages of building a World's Fair, and as spring came on I spent a couple of weeks in the city putting *Prairie Folks* into shape for the printer. Kirkland introduced me to the Chicago Literary Club, and my publisher, Frances Schulte, took me to the Press Club and I began to understand and like the city.

As May deepened I went on up to Wisconsin, full of my plan for a homestead, and the green and luscious slopes of the old valley gave me a new delight, a kind of proprietary delight. I began to think of it as home. It seemed not only a natural deed but a dutiful deed, this return to the land of my birth, it was the beginning of a more settled order of life.

My aunt, Susan Bailey, who was living alone in the old house in Onalaska made me welcome, and showed grateful interest when I spoke to her of my ambition. "I'll be glad to help you pay for such a place," she said, "provided you will set aside a room in it for me. I am lonely now. Your father is all I have and I'd like to spend my old age with him. But don't buy a farm. Buy a house and lot here or in LaCrosse."

"Mother wants to be in West Salem," I replied. "All our talk has been of West Salem, and if you can content yourself to live with us there, I shall be very glad of your co-operation. Father is still skittish. He will not come back till he can sell to advantage. However, the season has started well and I am hoping that he will at least come down with mother and talk the matter over with us."

To my delight, almost to my surprise, mother came, alone. "Father will follow in a few days," she said—"if he can find someone to look after his stock and tools while he is gone."

She was able to walk a little now and together we went about the village, and visited relatives and neighbors in the country. We ate "company dinners" of fried chicken and short-cake, and sat out on the grass beneath the shelter of noble trees during the heat of the day. There was something profoundly restful and satisfying in this atmosphere. No one seemed in a hurry and no one seemed to fear either the wind or the sun.

The talk was largely of the past, of the fine free life of the "early days" and my mother's eyes often filled with happy tears as she met friends who remembered her as a girl. There was no doubt in her mind. "I'd like to live here," she said. "It's more like home than any other place. But I don't see how your father could stand it on a little piece of land. He likes his big fields."

One night as we were sitting on William's porch, talking of war times and of Hugh and Jane and Walter, a sweet and solemn mood came over us. It seemed as if the spirits of the pioneers, the McClintocks and Dudleys had been called back and were all about us. It seemed to me (as to my mother) as if Luke or Leonard might at any moment emerge from the odorous June dusk and speak to us. We spoke of David, and my mother's love for him vibrated in her voice as she said, "I don't suppose I'll ever see him again. He's too poor and too proud to come back here, and I'm too old and lame and poor to visit him."

This produced in me a sudden and most audacious change of plan. "I'm not so certain about that," I retorted. "Frank's company is going to play in California this winter, and I am arranging a lecture tour—I've just decided that you and father shall go along."

The boldness of my plan startled her. "Oh, we can't do a crazy thing like that," she declared.

"It's not so crazy. Father has been talking for years of a visit to his brother in Santa Barbara. Aunt Susan tells me she wants to spend one more winter in California, and so I see no reason in the world why you and father should not go. I'll pay for your tickets and Addison will be glad to house you. We're going!" I asserted firmly. "We'll put off buying our homestead till next year and make this the grandest trip of your life."

Aunt Maria here put in a word, "You do just what Hamlin tells you to do. If he wants to spend his money giving you a good time, you let him."

Mother smiled wistfully but incredulously. To her it all seemed as remote, as improbable as a trip to Egypt, but I continued to talk of it as settled and so did William and Maria.

I wrote at once to my father outlining my trip and pleading strongly for his consent and co-operation. "All your life long you and mother have toiled with hardly a day off. Your travelling has been mainly in a covered wagon. You have seen nothing of cities for thirty years. Addison wants you to spend the winter with him, and mother wants to see David once more—why not go? Begin to plan right now and as soon as your crops are harvested, meet me at Omaha or Kansas City and we'll all go along together."

He replied with unexpected half-promise. "The crops look pretty well. Unless something very destructive turns up I shall have a few dollars to spend. I'd like to make that trip. I'd like to see Addison once more."

I replied, "The more I think about it, the more wonderful it all seems. It will enable you to see the mountains, and the great plains. You can visit Los Angeles and San Francisco. You can see the ocean. Frank is to play for a month in Frisco, and we can all meet at Uncle David's for Christmas."

The remainder of the summer was taken up with the preparations for this gorgeous excursion. Mother went back to help father through the harvest, whilst I returned to Boston and completed arrangements for my lecture tour which was to carry me as far north as Puget Sound.

At last in November, when the grain was all safely marketed, the old people met me in Kansas City, and from there as if in a dream, started westward with me in such holiday spirits as mother's health permitted. Father was like a boy. Having cut loose from the farm—at least for the winter, he declared his intention to have a good time, "as good as the law allows," he added with a smile.

Of course they both expected to suffer on the journey, that's what travel had always meant to them, but I surprised them. I not only took separate lower berths in the sleeping car, I insisted on regular meals at the eating houses along the way, and they were amazed to find travel almost comfortable. The cost of all this disturbed my mother a good deal till I explained to her that my own expenses were paid by the lecture committees and that she need not worry about the price of her fare. Perhaps I even boasted about a recent sale of a story! If I did I hope it will be forgiven me for I was determined that this should be the greatest event in her life.

My father's interest in all that came to view was as keen as my own. During all his years of manhood he had longed to cross the plains and to see Pike's Peak, and now while his approach was not as he had dreamed it, he was actually on his way into Colorado. "By the great Horn Spoons," he exclaimed as we neared the foot hills, "I'd like to have been here before the railroad."

Here spoke the born explorer. His eyes sparkled, his face flushed. The farther we got into the houseless cattle range, the better he liked it. "The best times I've ever had in my life," he remarked as we were looking away across the plain at the faint shapes of the Spanish Peaks, "was when I was cruising the prairie in a covered-wagon."

Then he told me once again of his long trip into Minnesota before the war, and of the cavalry lieutenant who rounded the settlers up and sent them back to St. Paul to escape the Sioux who were on the warpath. "I never saw such a country for game as Northern Minnesota was in those days. It swarmed with waterfowl and chicken and deer. If the soldiers hadn't driven me out I would have had a farm up there. I was just starting to break a garden when the troops came."

It was all glorious to me as to them. The Spanish life of Las Vegas where we rested for a day, the Indians of Laguna, the lava beds and painted buttes of the desert, the beautiful slopes of the San

Francisco Mountains, the herds of cattle, the careering cowboys, the mines and miners—all came in for study and comment. We resented the nights which shut us out from so much that was interesting. Then came the hot sand of the Colorado valley, the swift climb to the bleak heights of the coast range—and, at last, the swift descent to the orange groves and singing birds of Riverside. A dozen times father cried out, "This alone is worth the cost of the trip."

Mother was weary, how weary I did not know till we reached our room in the hotel. She did not complain but her face was more dejected than I had ever seen it, and I was greatly disturbed by it. Our grand excursion had come too late for her.

A good night's sleep and a hearty breakfast restored her to something like her smiling self and when we took the train for Santa Barbara she betrayed more excitement that at any time on our trip. "Do we really see the ocean?" she asked.

"Yes," I explained, "we run close along the shore. You'll see waves and ships and sharks—may be a whale or two."

Father was even more excited. He spent most of his time on the platform or hanging from the window. "Well, I never really expected to see the Pacific," he said as we were nearing the end of our journey. "Now I'm determined to see Frisco and the Golden Gate."

"Of course—that is a part of our itinerary. You can see Frisco when you come up to visit David."

My uncle Addison who was living in a plain but roomy house, was genuinely glad to see us, and his wife made us welcome in the spirit of the Middle Border for she was one of the early settlers of Green County, Wisconsin. In an hour we were at home.

Our host was, as I remembered him, a tall thin man of quiet dignity and notable power of expression. His words were well chosen and his manner urbane. "I want you people to settle right down here with me for the winter," he said. "In fact I shall try to persuade Richard to buy a place here."

This brought out my own plan for a home in West Salem and he agreed with me that the old people should never again spend a winter in Dakota.

There was no question in my mind about the hospitality of this home and so with a very comfortable, a delightful sense of peace, of satisfaction, of security, I set out on my way to San Francisco, Portland and Olympia, eager to see California—all of it. Its mountains, its cities and above all its poets had long called to me. It meant the *Argonauts* and *The Songs of the Sierras* to me, and one of my main objects of destination was Joaquin Miller's home in Oakland Heights.

No one else, so far as I knew, was transmitting this Coast life into literature. Edwin Markham was an Oakland school teacher, Frank Norris, a college student, and Jack London a boy in short trousers. Miller dominated the coast landscape. The mountains, the streams, the pines were his. A dozen times as I passed some splendid peak I quoted his lines. "Sierras! Eternal tents of snow that flash o'er battlements of mountains."

Nevertheless, in all my journeying, throughout all my other interests, I kept in mind our design for a reunion at my uncle David's home in San Jose, and I wrote him to tell him when to expect us. Franklin, who was playing in San Francisco, arranged to meet me, and father and mother were to come up from Santa Barbara.

It all fell out quite miraculously as we had planned it. On the 24th of December we all met at my uncle's door.

This reunion, so American in its unexpectedness, deserves closer analysis. My brother had come from New York City. Father and mother were from central Dakota. My own home was still in Boston. David and his family had reached this little tenement by way of a long trail through Iowa, Dakota, Montana, Oregon and Northern California. We who had all started from the same little Wisconsin Valley were here drawn together, as if by the magic of a conjuror's wand, in a city strange to us all. Can any other country on earth surpass the united States in the ruthless broadcast dispersion of its families? Could any other land furnish a more incredible momentary re-assembling of scattered units?

The reader of this tale will remember that David was my boyish hero, and as I had not seen him for fifteen years, I had looked forward, with disquieting question concerning our meeting. Alas! My fears were justified. There was more of pain than pleasure in the visit, for us all. Although my brother and I did our best to make it joyous, the conditions of the reunion were sorrowful, for David, who like my father, had been following the lure of the sunset all his life, was in deep discouragement.

From his fruitful farm in Iowa he had sought the free soil of Dakota. From Dakota he had been lured to Montana. In the forests of Montana he had been robbed by his partner, reduced in a single day to the rank of a day laborer, and so in the attempt to retrieve his fortunes, had again moved westward—ever westward, and here now at last in San José, at the end of his means and almost at the end of his courage, he was working at whatever he could find to do.

Nevertheless, he was still the borderer, still the man of the open. Something in his face and voice, something in his glance set him apart from the ordinary workman. He still carried with him something of the hunter, something which came from the broad spaces of the Middle Border, and though his bushy hair and beard were streaked with white, and his eyes sad and dim, I could still discern in him some part of the physical strength and beauty which had made his young manhood so glorious to me—and deeper yet, I perceived in him the dreamer, the Celtic minstrel, the poet.

His limbs, mighty as of old, were heavy, and his towering frame was beginning to stoop. His brave heart was beating slow. Fortune had been harshly inimical to him and his outlook on life was bitter. With all his tremendous physical power he had not been able to regain his former footing among men.

In talking of his misfortunes, I asked him why he had not returned to Wisconsin after his loss in Montana, and he replied, as my father had done. "How could I do that? How could I sneak back with empty pockets?"

Inevitably, almost at once, father spoke of the violin. "Have you got it yet?" he asked.

"Yes," David replied. "But I seldom play on it now. In fact, I don't think there are any strings on it."

I could tell from the tone of his voice that he had no will to play, but he dug the almost forgotten instrument out of a closet, strung it and tuned it, and that evening after dinner, when my father called out in familiar imperious fashion, "Come, come! now for a tune," David was prepared, reluctantly, to comply.

"My hands are so stiff and clumsy now," he said by way of apology to me.

It was a sad pleasure to me, as to him, this revival of youthful memories, and I would have spared him if I could, but my father insisted upon having all of the jocund dances and sweet old songs. Although a man of deep feeling in many ways, he could not understand the tragedy of my uncle's failing skill.

But mother did! Her ear was too acute not to detect the difference in tone between his playing at this time and the power of expression he had once possessed, and in her shadowy corner she suffered sympathetically when beneath his work-worn fingers the strings cried out discordantly. The wrist, once so strong and sure, the hands so supple and swift were now hooks of horn and bronze. The magic touch of youth had vanished, and yet as he went on, some little part of his wizardry came back.

At father's request he played once more *Maggie, Air Ye Sleepin'*, and while the strings wailed beneath his bow I shivered as of old, stirred by the winds of the past, "roaring o'er Moorland craggy." Deep in my brain the sob of the song sank, filling my inner vision with flitting shadows of vanished faces, brows untouched of care, and sweet kind eyes lit by the firelight of a secure abundant hearth. I was lying once more before the fire in David's little cabin in the deep Wisconsin valley and Grandfather McClintock, a dreaming giant, was drumming on his chair, his face flame-lit, his hair a halo of snow and gold.

Tune after tune the old Borderman played, in answer to my father's insistent demands, until at last the pain of it all became unendurable and he ended abruptly. "I can't play any more.—I'll never play again," he added harshly as he laid the violin away in its box like a child in its coffin.

We sat in silence, for we all realized that never again would we hear those wistful, meaningful melodies. Wordless, with aching throats, resentful of the present, my mother and my aunt dreamed of the bright and beautiful Neshonoc days when they were young and David was young and all the west was a land of hope.

My father now joined in urging David to go back to the middle border. "I'll put you on my farm," he said. "Or if you want to go back to Neshonoc, we'll help you do that. We are thinking of going back there ourselves."

David sadly shook his grizzled head. "No, I can't do that," he repeated. "I haven't money enough to pay my carfare, and besides, Becky and the children would never consent to it."

I understood. His proud heart rebelled at the thought of the pitying or contemptuous eyes of his stay-at home neighbors. He who had gone forth so triumphantly thirty years before could not endure the notion of going back on borrowed money. Better to die among strangers like a soldier.

Father, stern old pioneer though he was, could not think of leaving his wife's brother here, working like a Chinaman. "Dave has acted the fool," he privately said to me, "but we will help him. If you can spare a little, we'll lend him enough to buy one of these fruit farms he's talking about."

To this I agreed. Together we loaned him enough to make the first payment on a small farm. He was deeply grateful for this and hope again sprang up in his heart. "You won't regret it," he said brokenly. "This will put me on my feet, and by and by perhaps we'll meet in the old valley."—But we never did. I never saw him again.

I shall always insist that a true musician, a superb violinist was lost to the world in David McClintock—but as he was born on the border and always remained on the border, how could he find himself? His hungry heart, his need of change, his search for the pot of gold beyond the sunset, had carried him from one adventure to another and always farther and farther from the things he most deeply craved. He might have been a great singer, for he had a beautiful voice and a keen appreciation of the finer elements of song.

It was hard for me to adjust myself to his sorrowful decline into old age. I thought of him as he appeared to me when riding his threshing machine up the coulee road. I recalled the long rifle with which he used to carry off the prizes at the turkey shoots, and especially I remembered him as he looked while playing the violin on that far off Thanksgiving night in Lewis Valley.

I left California with the feeling that his life was almost ended, and my heart was heavy with indignant pity for I must now remember him only as a broken and discouraged man. The David of my idolatry, the laughing giant of my boyhood world, could be found now, only in the mist which hung above the hills and valleys of Neshonoc.

35

The Homestead in the Valley

To my father the Golden Gate of San Francisco was grandly romantic. It was associated in his mind with Bret Harte and the Goldseekers of Forty Nine, as well as with Fremont and the Mexican War, hence one of his expressed desires for many years had been to stand on the hills above the bay and look out on the ocean. "I know Boston," he said, "and I want to know Frisco."

My mother's interest in the city was more personal. She was eager to see her son Franklin play his part in a real play on a real stage. For that reward she was willing to undertake considerable extra fatigue and so to please her, to satisfy my father and to gratify myself, I accompanied them to San Francisco and for several days with a delightful sense of accomplishment, my brother and I led them about the town. We visited the Seal Rocks and climbed Nob Hill, explored Chinatown and walked through the Old Spanish Quarter, and as each of these pleasures was tasted my father said, "Well now, that's done!" precisely as if he were getting through a list of tedious duties.

There was no hint of obligation, however, in the hours which they spent in seeing my brother's performance as one of the "Three Twins" in *Incog.* The piece was in truth very funny and Franklin hardly to be distinguished from his "Star," a fact which astonished and delighted my mother. She didn't know he could look so unlike Himself. She laughed herself quite breathless over the absurd situations of the farce but father was not so easily satisfied. "This foolery is all well enough," said he, "but I'd rather see you and your friend Herne in *Shore Acres.*"

At last the day came when they both expressed a desire to return to Santa Barbara. "We've had about all we can stand this trip," they confessed, whereupon, leaving Franklin at his job, we started down the valley on our way to Addison Garland's home which had come to have something of the quality of home to us all.

We were tired but triumphant. One by one the things we had promised ourselves to see we had seen. The Plains, the Mountains, the Desert, the Orange Groves, the Ocean, all had been added to the list of our achievements. We had visited David and watched Franklin play in his "troupe'" and now with a sense of fullness, of victory, we were on our way back to a safe harbor among the fruits and flowers of Southern California.

This was the pleasantest thought of all to me and in private I said to my uncle, "I hope you can keep these people till spring. They must not go back to Dakota now."

"Give yourself no concern about that!" replied Addison. "I have a program laid out which will keep them busy until May. We're going out to Catalina and up into the Ojai valley and down to Los Angeles. We are to play for the rest of the winter like a couple of boys."

With mind entirely at ease I left them on the rose-embowered porch of my uncle's home, and started east by way of Denver and Chicago, eager to resume work on a book which I had promised for the autumn.

Chicago was now full in the spot-light of the National Stage. In spite of the business depression which still engulfed the west, the promoters of the Columbian Exposition were going steadily forward with their plans, and when I arrived in the city about the middle of January, the bustle of preparation was at a very high point.

The newly-acquired studios were swarming with eager and aspiring young artists, and I believed, (as many others believed) that the city was entering upon an era of swift and shining development. All the near-by states were stirred and heartened by this esthetic awakening of a metropolis which up to this time had given but little thought to the value of art in the life of a community. From being a huge, muddy windy market-place, it seemed about to take its place among the literary capitals of the world.

Colonies of painters, sculptors, decorators and other art experts now colored its life in gratifying degree. Beauty was a work to advertise with, and writers like Harriet Monroe, Henry B. Fuller, George Ade, Peter Finley Dunne, and Eugene Field were at work celebrating, each in his kind, the changes in the thought and aspect of the town. Ambitious publishing houses were springing up and "dummies" of new magazines were being thumbed by reckless young editors. The talk was all of Art, and the Exposition. It did, indeed seem as if culture were about to hum.

Naturally this flare of esthetic enthusiasm lit the tow of my imagination. I predicted a publishing center and a literary marketplace second only to New York, a publishing center which by reason of its geographical position would be more progressive than Boston, and more American than Manhattan. "Here flames the spirit of youth. Here throbs the heart of America," I declared in *Crumbling Idols,* an essay which I was at this time writing for the *Forum.*

In the heat of this conviction, I decided to give up my residence in Boston and establish headquarters in Chicago. I belonged here. My writing was of the Middle Border, and must continue to be so. Its spirit was mine. All of my immediate relations were dwellers in the west, and as I had also definitely set myself the task of depicting certain phases of mountain life, it was inevitable that I should ultimately bring my workshop to Chicago which was my natural pivot, the hinge on which my varied activities would revolve. And, finally, to live here would enable me to keep in closer personal touch with my father and mother in the Wisconsin homestead which I had fully determined to acquire.

Following this decision, I returned to Boston, and at once announced my plan to Howells, Flower and other of my good friends who had meant so much to me in the past. Each was kind enough to express regret and all agreed that my scheme was logical. "It should bring you happiness and success," they added.

Alas! The longer I stayed, the deeper I settled into my groove and the more difficult my removal became. It was not easy to surrender the busy and cheerful life I had been leading for nearly ten years. It was hard to say good-bye to the artists and writers and musicians with whom I had so long been associated. To leave the Common, the parks, the Library and the lovely walks and drives of Roxbury, was sorrowful business—but I did it! I packed my books ready for shipment and returned to Chicago in May just as the Exposition was about to open its doors.

Like everyone else who saw it at this time I was amazed at the grandeur of "The White City," and impatiently anxious to have all my friends and relations share in my enjoyment of it. My father was back on the farm in Dakota and I wrote to him at once urging him to come down. "Frank will be here in June and we will take charge of you. Sell the cook stove if necessary and come. You must see this fair. On the way back I will go as far as West Salem and we'll buy that homestead I've been talking about."

My brother whose season closed about the twenty-fifth of May, joined me in urging them not to miss the fair and a few days later we were both delighted and a little surprised to get a letter from mother telling us when to expect them. "I can't walk very well," she explained, "but I'm coming. I am so hungry to see my boys that I don't mind the long journey."

Having secured rooms for them at a small hotel near the west gate of the exposition grounds, we were at the station to receive them as they came from the train surrounded by other tired and dusty pilgrims of the plains. Father was in high spirits and mother was looking very well considering the tiresome ride of nearly seven hundred miles. "Give us a chance to wash up and we'll be ready for anything," she said with brave intonation.

We took her at her word. With merciless enthusiasm we hurried them to their hotel and as soon as they had bathed and eaten a hasty lunch, we started out with intent to astonish and delight them. Here was another table at "the feast of life" from which we did not intend they should rise unsatisfied. "This shall be the richest experience of their lives," we said.

With a wheeled chair to save mother from the fatigue of walking we started down the line and so rapidly did we pass from one stupendous vista to another that we saw in a few hours many of the inside exhibits and all of the finest exteriors—not to mention a glimpse of the polyglot amazements of the Midway.

In pursuance of our plan to watch the lights come on, we ate our supper in one of the big restaurants on the grounds and at eight o'clock entered the Court of Honor. It chanced to be a moonlit night, and as lamps were lit and the waters of the lagoon began to reflect the gleaming walls of the great palaces with their sculptured ornaments, and boats of quaint shape filled with singers came and went beneath the arching bridges, the wonder and the beauty of it all moved these dwellers of the level lands to tears of joy which was almost as poignant as pain. In addition to its grandeur the scene had for them the transitory quality of an autumn sunset, a splendor which they would never see again.

Stunned by the majesty of the vision, my mother sat in her chair, visioning it all yet comprehending little of its meaning. Her life had been spent among homely small things, and these gorgeous scenes dazzled her, overwhelmed her, letting in upon her in one mighty flood a thousand stupefying suggestions of the art and history and poetry of the world. She was old and she was ill, and her brain ached with the weight of its new conceptions. Her face grew troubled and wistful, and her eyes as big and dark as those of a child.

At last utterly overcome she leaned her head against my arm, closed her eyes and said, "Take me home. I can't stand any more of it."

Sadly I took her away, back to her room, realizing that we had been too eager. We had oppressed her with the exotic, the magnificent. She was too old and too feeble to enjoy as we had hoped she would enjoy, the color and music and thronging streets of The Magic City.

At the end of the third day father said, "Well, I've had enough." He too, began to long for the repose of the country, the solace of familiar scenes. In truth they were both surfeited with the alien, sick of the picturesque. Their ears suffered from the clamor of strange sounds as their eyes ached with the clash of unaccustomed color. My insistent haste, my desire to make up in a few hours for all their past deprivations seemed at the moment to have been a mistake.

Seeing this, knowing that all the splendors of the Orient could not compensate them for another sleepless night, I decided to cut their visit short and hurry them back to quietude. Early on the fourth morning we started for the LaCrosse Valley by way of Madison—they with a sense of relief, I with a feeling of disappointment. "The feast was too rich, too highly-spiced for their simple tastes," I now admitted.

However, a certain amount of comfort came to me as I observed that the farther they got from the Fair the keener their enjoyment of it became!—With bodies at ease and minds untroubled, they now relived in pleasant retrospect all the excitement and bustle of the crowds, all the bewildering sights and sounds of the Midway. Scenes which had worried as well as amazed them were now recalled with growing enthusiasm, as our train, filled with other returning sight-seers of like condition, rushed steadily northward into the green abundance of the land they knew so well, and when at six o'clock of a lovely afternoon, they stepped down upon the platform of the weatherbeaten little station at West Salem, both were restored to their serene and buoyant selves. The leafy village, so green, so muddy, so lush with grass, seemed the perfection of restful security. The chuckle of robins on the lawns, the songs of catbirds in the plum trees and the whistle of larks in the pasture appealed to them as parts of a familiar sweet and homely hymn.

Just in the edge of the village, on a four-acre plot of rich level ground, stood an old two-story frame cottage on which I had fixed my interest. It was not beautiful, not in the least like the ideal New England homestead my brother and I had so long discussed, but it was sheltered on the south by three enormous maples and its gate fronted upon a double row of New England elms whose branches almost arched the wide street. Its gardens, rich in grape vines, asparagus beds, plums, raspberries and other fruiting shrubs, appealed with especial power to my mother who had lived so long on the sun-baked plains that the sight of green things growing was very precious in her eyes. Clumps of lilacs, syringa and snow-ball, and beds of old-fashioned flowers gave further evidence of the love and care which the former owners of the place had lavished upon it.

As for myself, the desire to see my aging parents safely sheltered beneath the benignant branches of those sturdy trees would have made me content even with a log cabin. In imagination I perceived this angular cottage growing into something fine and sweet and—our own!

There was charm also in the fact that its western windows looked out upon the wooded hills over which I had wandered as a boy, and whose sky-line had printed itself deep into the lowest stratum of my subconscious memory; and so it happened that on the following night, as we stood before the gate looking out upon that sunset wall of purple bluffs from beneath the double row of elms stretching like a peristyle to the west, my decision came.

"This is my choice," I declared. "Right here we take root. This shall be the Garland Homestead." I turned to my father. "When can you move?"

"Not till after my grain is threshed and marketed," he replied.

"Very well, let's call it the first of November, and we'll all meet here for our Thanksgiving dinner."

Thanksgiving with us, as with most New Englanders, had always been a date-mark, something to count upon and to count from, and no sooner were we in possession of a deed, than my mother and I began to plan for a dinner which should be at once a reunion of the Garlands and McClintocks, a homecoming and a housewarming. With this understanding I let them go back for a final harvest in Dakota.

The purchase of this small lot and commonplace house may seem very unimportant to the reader but to me and to my father it was in very truth epoch-marking. To me it was the ending of one life and the beginning of another. To him it was decisive and not altogether joyous. To accept this as his home meant a surrender of his faith in the Golden West, a tacit admission that all his explorations of the open lands with whatsoever they had meant of opportunity, had ended in a sense of failure on a barren soil. It was not easy for him to enter into the spirit of our Thanksgiving plans although he had given his consent to them. He was still the tiller of broad acres, the speculator hoping for a boom.

Early in October, as soon as I could displace the renter of the house, I started in rebuilding and redecorating it as if for the entrance of a bride. I widened the dining room, refitted the kitchen and ordered new rugs, curtains and furniture from Chicago. I engaged a cook and maid, and bought a horse so that on November first, the date of my mother's arrival, I was able to meet her at the station and drive her in a carriage of her own to an almost completely outfitted home.

It was by no means what I intended it to be, but it seemed luxurious to her. Tears dimmed her eyes as she stepped across the threshold, but when I said, "Mother, hereafter my headquarters are to be in Chicago, and my home here with you," she put her arms around my neck and wept. Her wanderings were over, her heart at peace.

My father arrived a couple of weeks later, and with his coming, mother sent out the invitations for our dinner. So far as we could, we intended to bring together the scattered units of our family group.

At last the great day came! My brother was unable to be present and there were other empty chairs, but the McClintocks were well represented. William, white-haired, gigantic, looking almost exactly like Grandad at the same age, came early, bringing his wife, his two sons, and his daughter-in-law. Frank and Lorette drove over from Lewis Valley, with both of their sons and a daughter-in-law. Samantha and Dan could not come, but Deborah and Susan were present and completed the family roll. Several of my father's old friends promised to come in after dinner.

The table, reflecting the abundance of the valley in those peaceful times, was stretched to its full length and as we gathered about it William congratulated my father on getting back where cranberries and turkeys and fat squashes grew.

My mother smiled at this jest, but my father, still loyal to Dakota, was quick to defend it. "I like it out there," he insisted. "I like wheat raising on a big scale. I don't know how I'm going to come down from operating a six-horse header to scraping with a hoe in a garden patch."

Mother, wearing her black silk dress and lace collar, sat at one end of the table, while I, to relieve my father of the task of carving the twenty-pound turkey, sat opposite her. For the first time in my life I took position as head of the family and the significance of this fact did not escape the company. The pen had proved itself to be mightier than the plow. Going east had proved more profitable than going west!

It was a noble dinner! As I regard it from the standpoint of today, with potatoes six dollars per bushel and turkeys forty cents per pound, it all seems part of a kindlier world, a vanished world—as it is! There were squashes and turnips and cranberry sauce and pumpkin pie and mince pie, (made under mother's supervision) and coffee with real cream,—all the things which are so precious now, and the talk was in praise of the delicious food and the Exposition which was just closing, and reports of the crops which were abundant and safely garnered. The wars of the world were all behind us and the nation on its way back to prosperity—and we were unafraid.

The gay talk lasted well through the meal, but as mother's pies came on, Aunt Maria regretfully remarked, "It's a pity Frank can't help eat this dinner."

"I wish Dave and Mantie were here," put in Deborah.

"And Rachel," added mother.

This brought the note of sadness which is inevitable in such a gathering, and the shadow deepened as we gathered about the fire a little later. The dead claimed their places.

Since leaving the valley thirty years before our group had suffered many losses. All my grandparents were gone. My sisters Harriet and Jessie and my uncle Richard had fallen on the march. David and Rebecca were stranded in the foot hills of the Cascade mountains. Rachel, a widow, was in Georgia. The pioneers of '48 were old and their bright world a memory.

My father called on mother for some of the old songs. "You and Deb sing *Nellie Wildwood,*" he urged, and to me it was a call to all the absent ones, an invitation to gather about us in order that the gaps in our hearthfire's broken circle might be filled.

Sweet and clear though in diminished volume, my mother's voice rose on the tender refrain:

> Never more to part, Nellie Wildwood,
> Never more to long for the spring.

and I thought of Hattie and Jessie and tried to believe that they too were sharing in the comfort and contentment of our fire.

George, who resembled his uncle David, and had much of his skill with the fiddle bow, had brought his violin with him, but when father asked Frank to play *Maggie, air ye sleepin',* he shook his head, saying, "That's Dave's tune," and his loyalty touched us all.

Quick tears sprang to mother's eyes. She knew all too well that never again would she hear her best-beloved brother touch the strings or join his voice to hers.

It was a moment of sorrow for us all but only for a moment, for Deborah struck up one of the lively "darky pieces" which my father loved so well, and with its jubilant patter young and old returned to smiling.

> It must be now in the Kingdom a-comin'
> In the year of Jubilo!

we shouted, and so translated the words of the song into an expression of our own rejoicing present.

Song after song followed, war chants which renewed my father's military youth, ballads which deepened the shadows in my mother's eyes, and then at last, at my request, she sang *The Rolling Stone,* and with a smile at father, we all joined the chorus.

> We'll stay on the farm and we'll suffer no loss
> For the stone that keeps rolling will gather no moss.

My father was not entirely convinced, but I, surrounded by these farmer folk, hearing from their lips these quaint melodies, responded like some tensely-strung instrument, whose chords are being played upon by searching winds. I acknowledged myself at home and for all time. Beneath my feet lay the rugged country rock of my nativity. It pleased me to discover my mental characteristics striking so deep into this typically American soil.

One by one our guests rose and went away, jocularly saying to my father, "Well, Dick, you've done the right thing at last. It's a comfort to have you so handy. We'll come to dinner often!" To me they said, "We'll expect to see more of you, now that the old folks are here."

"This is my home," I repeated.

When we were alone I turned to mother in the spirit of the builder. "Give me another year and I'll make this a homestead worth talking about. My head is full of plans for its improvement."

"It's good enough for me as it is," she protested.

"No, it isn't," I retorted quickly. "Nothing that I can do is good enough for you, but I intend to make you entirely happy if I can."

Here I make an end of this story, here at the close of an epoch of western settlement, here with my father and mother sitting beside me in the light of a tender Thanksgiving, in our new old home and facing a peaceful future. I was thirty-three years of age, and in a certain very real sense this plot of ground, this protecting roof may be taken as the symbols of my hard-earned first success as well as the defiant gages of other necessary battles which I must fight and win.

As I was leaving next day for Chicago, I said, "Mother, what shall I bring you from the city?"

With a shy smile she answered, "There is only one thing more you can bring me,—one thing more that I want."

"What is that?"

"A daughter. I need a daughter—and some grandchildren."

A Son of the Middle Border
was designed and set in type at the
Minnesota Historical Society Press
by Will Powers and Mike Hanson.
The text type is Clifford,
designed by Akira Kobayashi.
This book was printed by Thomson-Shore,
Dexter, Michigan.